THE DETERMINED HEART

OTHER BOOKS BY ANTOINETTE MAY

Pilate's Wife

The Sacred Well

*The Yucatan: A Guide to the Land of Maya Mysteries
Plus Sacred Sites at Belize, Tikal, and Copan*

*Haunted Houses of California: A Ghostly Guide to
Haunted Houses and Wandering Spirits*

Passionate Pilgrim

Witness to War

My Guide, Myself

Adventures of a Psychic

THE
TALE OF MARY SHELLEY AND HER
FRANKENSTEIN

The Determined Heart

ANTOINETTE MAY

LAKE UNION
PUBLISHING

Published by Lake Union Publishing, Seattle
www.apub.com

Amazon, the Amazon logo, and Lake Union Publishing are trademarks of Amazon.com, Inc., or its affiliates.

ISBN-10: 1503945189
ISBN-13: 9781503945180

Cover design by Patrick Barry

Once again, to Charles

PROLOGUE

June 1816

That dark spring, Lake Geneva tossed like an angry beast. Astronomers, citing mysterious patches on the sun, predicted the end of the world.

Mary laughed at such a notion. She was eighteen, her world just beginning. Beside her sat the handsomest, brightest, most talented man in the universe—her lover, Percy Bysshe Shelley. She and Bysshe had run off for a summer holiday. As usual Mary's stepsister, Claire, tagged along, this time her sights set on the darkly beguiling Lord Byron.

Storms swept the countryside, an atmosphere of violence accompanying the gloom. Night after night, the party fled to Byron's Villa Diodati. Their fancies heightened by laudanum, Mary, Bysshe, and Claire sought refuge before Lord Byron's great marble fireplace. As thunder crashed around them, they recited poetry and told ghost stories.

One evening, Byron, their dark, brooding host, had a surprise. After an elegant repast in his dining hall, Lord Byron led his guests to a distant chamber, a tower room. Its only occupant was a fashionably dressed woman who stood like a slim column of gray before the embers of a dying fire.

"This is Persephone," he introduced her. "She reads palms."

"Fortune-telling is frowned upon in this sober land," Bysshe reminded him.

"It's against the law in Geneva," Byron agreed, taking a pinch of snuff from an ornate silver box. "But when have petty rules troubled *me*?" He gestured for the party to be seated. Persephone's wide eyes, smoke-hued like her gown, passed over them one by one. Mary took a chair against the back wall. When no one spoke, Byron shrugged impatiently. "Here, read mine," he said, extending a well-manicured hand.

Persephone's rings flashed as she cupped his palm in hers. "Your name will live forever, but you know that."

"Indeed," he responded coolly. "Do you know anything that I do not?"

Persephone shrugged; her brightened lips curved in a smile. "Nothing that you would care to hear."

Scowling, Byron withdrew his hand. Mary suppressed a smile.

Face flushed, Claire thrust herself forward, extending her hand. Persephone looked up from the small white palm, her eyes moving over Claire's lithe form. "You carry a child. It will be a girl. You will travel far and wide, but always . . . always alone."

"Alone?" Claire's voice quavered.

Mary looked across the room at Byron, his broad form burnished by firelight, and saw his eyes widen in surprise. *So, he was unaware of the pregnancy.* Byron glowered at Claire, who looked down at the marble floor.

Bysshe broke the silence. "Have a look at my hand."

Persephone's fingers moved over his palm. "Your star has only begun to rise."

Byron patted Bysshe's shoulder. "Even the heavens concur. Fame is the thirst of youth and Shelley will be famous indeed."

"There will be much acclaim, yes," Persephone agreed. A sapphire gleamed as she pointed her finger. "But I see dark pools of water."

Bysshe's smile froze. "What are you saying?"

Persephone studied Bysshe's face. "The poems you carry in your head, write them down. Write them now. You had best not tarry."

Mary's breath caught; she leaned forward. "What sort of warning is this?"

Byron rose abruptly from his chair. "Enough gloom." His hand pressed Mary's shoulder. "You with your illustrious parentage, your turn has come. Let us hear what the future has in store for the daughter of the immortal Mary Wollstonecraft and the brilliant William Godwin."

She sought to elude his grasp. Persephone's messages were dark. Mary wanted no part of them.

Thunder rumbled closer, one long echoing crash after another. The rain slammed hard against the windowpanes, drops loud as snare drums. Mary could not return to the Maison Chapuis in this weather. "I would rather not . . ." She looked at Bysshe, pleading with her eyes.

He lightly caressed her arm. "Are you not even a little curious?"

Smiling brightly, Persephone took Mary's hand. The seer's manner was practiced, her black-edged eyes knew much of the world, but Mary read no menace in her face. *I'll humor her,* she decided, *humor them all, and play along with the entertainment that Byron has devised.*

Mary took a deep breath and slipped into the small chair opposite Persephone. "Yes, yes of course, I, too, am curious. What do you see for me?"

The seer looked down, her smile slowly fading as she studied first one hand and then the other. Raising her head quizzically, Persephone met Mary's eyes. "Your mind is like a crystal, sharp and clear." She looked again at Mary's palms, brows furrowed. "But there is something dark here. You"—she hesitated for a moment, her gray eyes wide as they stared into Mary's—"you will create a fearsome thing."

There was another crash of thunder, followed by a brilliant shaft of lightning that illuminated the crystal chandelier and inlaid mother-of-pearl tabletops.

Mary pulled her hand away. "A child?" she asked, her voice a whisper. Thunder crashed again, drowning out everything. Mary wanted to hear no more, but Persephone would not be silenced.

"Like a birth, but not of your body. There is a secret—black and malevolent. A creature cursed."

Persephone looked deep into Mary's eyes. "I do not understand the monstrous things I see. It is you who must search. Go back—back to the beginning. You must seek the truth yourself. I know only that your monster must be loosed. Only then will you yourself be free."

PART I

Everything must have a beginning . . . and that beginning must be linked to something that went before.
—Mary Shelley, *Frankenstein*

ONE

October 1801

Mary knew something terrible was about to happen. Standing on tiptoes before the windowsill, she looked out over the garden and shuddered.

"Fan, come," she called to her sister. "That awful woman is back. She's talking to Papa." Yesterday Mary had seen her father take the woman's hand. Papa's smile had frightened Mary as she watched him open the gate and lead the woman through the rose garden. *Her* garden.

Now he walked eagerly down the path, an arm raised in greeting. Mary thought the intruder looked like a strutting goose stuffed into a red silk dress. Geese were big and sometimes mean. They could turn and chase you in an instant. Mary's heart thumped.

"Close the window," Fan said, placing a protective arm about Mary's shoulders. "It's beginning to rain."

The sun, brilliant only moments before, was clouding over. A strong wind blew. Trees swayed, fluttering nervous leaves.

Papa's booming voice called from downstairs as the tea bell tinkled. Mary longed to ignore his summons but dared not.

Pausing outside the drawing room, the two girls watched from the doorway as the woman settled into a wing-back chair. Her gaze lingered on the mahogany shelves lining the far wall, the scarlet velvet drapes framing the windows. Her dark eyes darted from the brick fireplace to the grandfather clock, and then to the French paintings on the walls. Had she never seen furniture? Mary thought it curious, but her father's lips curved in a smile. Mary stared at him, wondering. Papa hardly ever smiled.

"Oh," the ugly goose sighed. "And to think that here I am in the home of the celebrated philosopher William Godwin." She leaned back, smoothing the folds of her dress, expanding into the chair.

Papa beamed and for once said nothing. His eyes lit on the girls and he strode forward, taking Mary and Fan each by the hand and leading them into the drawing room. "Mrs. Clairmont, these are my daughters," he introduced them. "Fanny is seven and Mary four."

The woman picked up her quizzing glass and examined Fan. "What a nice, tall girl you are. A misfortune that you've had the pox, but your features are pleasant enough."

Then her plump fingers pressed beneath Mary's chin, forcing her to look up. "What a shy little one Mary is." When Mary backed away, the lady frowned, but only for an instant. "No need to fear me, sweetheart. My own daughter, Clara, is about your age." She leaned closer, her pasty visage inches from Mary's. "Forgive me for not introducing myself. I am Jane Clairmont—but you can call me 'Auntie.' I and my little darlings, Clara and Charlie, have rooms in the brick house right next door." She gestured with her head, plumed bonnet quivering over elaborate black curls.

She turned to Papa. "You have a very pretty little girl here, Mr. Godwin. Such beautiful gray eyes. Does she resemble her mother?"

"Yes," Papa sighed. His eyes turned sad.

"All the world knows of your famous wife . . . a tragic loss." The woman arranged her round face into a sympathetic expression.

Her narrow eyes locked on Papa. "I can tell that you are a brave man, struggling to bring up these very young girls. It must be difficult without a loving woman at your side."

"At times," he agreed.

She leaned closer. "Oh, to be the mother of such a pair! Two little princesses!"

"We have a mother, madam," Fanny told Mrs. Clairmont. "She watches over us."

The woman looked quizzically at Papa, who shrugged. Mary lifted her head to see their faces better. Grown-ups were so awfully tall. It was hard to talk to them and, even when she found the words, there was little certainty that they would listen and less that they would understand. "Our mother lives here with us," Mary explained.

Fan moved forward shyly and took Mrs. Clairmont's hand. Reluctantly, Mary took the other one. Together they pulled her to their papa's book-lined study. Mary breathed a sigh. There, as always, smiling down at her from the wall, was the mother she knew so well. How gentle she looked, how full of kindness and beauty with her soft auburn hair and smiling eyes. "*This* is our mother," she informed Mrs. Clairmont.

The awful woman's forehead wrinkled as she studied the painting. Mary's legs trembled; she looked up at Papa, who had followed them.

"John Opie painted her portrait some years ago," Papa explained. "It is quite a good likeness."

"Indeed." The goose lady's lips tightened in a smile. "How very nice."

———

A fortnight later Mrs. Clairmont appeared on the Godwin doorstep, holding the hand of a girl about Mary's size. "This is my daughter, Clara," she announced to Mary. "I feel certain that you and she will be friends. More than friends—sisters."

Clara and Mary stood looking straight into each other's eyes. Mary doubted that they would ever be friends. As for sisters! Clara's black curly hair and dark eyes looked too much like her goose mother's.

"A little gypsy," Papa said upon greeting her. He smiled broadly at the girl. "Invite Clara in, Mary," Papa instructed, placing his hand firmly on Mary's shoulder. "Show her your room. Yours, too," he told Fan, who stood quietly by the door. "Be off now. Mrs. Clairmont and I have things to talk about."

Fan turned obediently, leading the way. Clara followed, flouncing up the narrow circular stairs to the second floor. Reluctantly, Mary trailed after them. "This is my room," Fan said at the top of the stairs. "I have a dollhouse."

Fan's room was large, with an armoire for her dresses and shelves for playthings. "What a lot of toys you have," Clara said, studying the dollhouse. She reached inside and plucked out a tiny rocking horse. Still holding the horse, turning it over and over, Clara strolled about the room, touching first a puppet, then a top, as though she owned them. She shoved the horse back into the house with a sweep of her hand that knocked the roof to one side and left the tiny furniture tumbled in all directions. "A lot more."

Mary's room was smaller than Fanny's, but she liked it better. Mornings were bright with sunlight. She had a view of the front garden and the road, and lots of bookshelves. Flora, a favorite china doll with real hair, rested on the bed. Mary hastily picked up the doll, holding Flora protectively against her chest.

Clara walked about, staring up at the bookshelves lining the walls. "Have you really read these books?" she asked, her voice rising in disbelief.

"Some of them. Fanny helps me. Papa explains the big words. We look them up in the dictionary. I know some books by heart.

Papa's friend Mr. Southey has been telling me a new story about a little girl and three bears. It's scary, but I like it. He's promised to write the words down for me so I can learn them."

"Mary makes up her own stories," Fan said. "Papa thinks that she will write books like our mama did."

Clara turned to Mary, her small brows raised. She looked just like Mrs. Clairmont. "I want this room for my own—once Mama, Charlie, and I move in."

Mary was horrified. "No! You are not moving in here! This is *my* room. You will never have it. It was my mother's room."

Clara glared at her. "You think you're smart because your mother was famous. *My* mama says she was a bad lady."

Mary stamped her foot. "Everyone loved my mother. She was a grand lady."

Clara leaned forward, her dark eyes staring straight into Mary's. "Grand, was she? Don't go acting stuck up. *You* are the one who killed her."

TWO

William Godwin pushed open the heavy oak door to his cluttered study. As Jane preceded him inside, he once again found himself comparing her to his deceased wife.

Mary Wollstonecraft Godwin had been bold and brilliant. William's friends adored her, quoted her constantly. Jane Clairmont, on the other hand, was . . . cozy. Clearly she thought *he* was wonderful. And was that not his due? There were other qualities that he liked about Jane as well. She was practical, quick and clever about the house, and splendid with his children.

Hastily he brushed the papers off the worn velvet settee, then took Jane's hand in his as they sat down. Just then the door flew open and little Mary hurtled into the room. Godwin frowned; this was so unlike her. She was crying, too, great gasping sobs. Mary never cried. He sighed impatiently. Marguerite was supposed to care for the children, keep them not only safe but out of his way. *Confound it!* Where was she?

William rose reluctantly as Mary ran to him. She clung to him tightly. Such a little girl, he observed, almost in surprise. Mary barely reached to his belt buckle. *What could be the matter?* "Tell me . . . sweetheart." He stumbled over the unaccustomed endearment. "What troubles you?"

Mary could only gulp. "Clara—Clara—"

"What about Clara?" Jane, too, rose to her feet. "Is she all right?"

William held Mary at arm's length, searching her face. "Is anyone hurt? What has happened?"

The child stiffened; her sobs slowed. "There is nothing wrong with her, Papa. Clara is in my bedroom. She says that she is going to *live* there, in the room that was *Mother's*. Will you not send her home? I—I don't like her."

"Mary!" William exclaimed. A squabble between the girls was all he needed.

"It is merely a childish misunderstanding," Jane intervened, leaning down to stroke Mary's shoulder.

Mary backed away, her gray eyes wide and pleading. "I need to talk to you, Papa"—her voice trembled—"alone."

This was not his shy little Mary at all. Moments such as these caused William to grieve all the more for his dead wife. For all her advocacy of women's rights, the late Mrs. Godwin was a devoted mother and had written a book about rearing children. She would have known exactly what to do.

He looked at Jane and shrugged apologetically. "If you will excuse us, my dear."

She frowned, her cheeks flaming red. Then quickly her expression changed, and she smiled sweetly. William thought he must have imagined her impatience. Jane's even temper, her understanding of children, were among her greatest charms. "Whatever you think best, William," she said. The door closed behind her, perhaps a little louder than necessary.

In an instant Mary was crying again, almost unable to frame the words. "Papa—Papa—Clara said—I killed—Mama." Her voice dropped to a whisper. "Did I?"

For a moment William felt ill. "That was a dreadful thing to say!" His legs trembled as he took Mary into his arms. Where were the words; how was he to explain to her? Carefully he lowered himself onto the tufted couch, settling the child onto his lap.

William's heart beat so rapidly that he wondered if Mary could feel it beneath his starched cravat.

"Your mother died of a fever," he answered at last. Surely that was enough information for a little girl.

Clearly it was not. Mary met his eyes. "Then it was I—I who made her sick?"

"Confound it, you did not make her sick." How was William to explain childbed fever to a small girl? "Clara must have heard something and misunderstood." Mary's large gray eyes watched him intently. "After you were born—a few days later—your mother became ill. We tried . . . we tried everything."

"*After* I was born," Mary repeated.

He could imagine that bright little mind of hers turning his words over and over, analyzing each of them. Tentatively he stroked her hair and shoulders. William rarely held his children. "It was not your fault, Mary. Your mother adored you. You were a most desired child."

"But she died," the little girl persisted. "She left me. Why? I must have done something awful to her." Mary was crying again.

William held his child tighter as he struggled with the awful recollection of his wife's death. Little Mary had been there. What might she have known or felt? Could she remember any of it? William ran his fingers through thinning hair. Of course not! Such fanciful thoughts were rubbish. His rational mind strove against their absurdity . . . Still, the human brain remained a mystery. When did memory begin? What dark thoughts lay hidden within Mary's consciousness?

He turned the child's face to meet her eyes squarely. "Childbirth is always a risk, you might as well know that. Many mothers do not survive, but they are brave, yours the bravest. She loved you. She would never have left you—left this life—had she a choice. In the end, death always prevails."

"But Papa," Mary began.

This was all too much to deal with. It made William uneasy. He took the silver bell from the table beside him and rang it. Marguerite came almost immediately, wiping the flour from her hands on her white apron. She smelled of apples and cinnamon.

"Take Mary," he said, rising. "She needs to nap. Read her a story until she falls asleep."

"And Mrs. Clairmont and her daughter?"

William hesitated, then shook his head impatiently. "It is time for them to leave. I have work to go over, an essay to write. Explain that to them."

Marguerite bobbed her head. Taking Mary gently by the hand, she led the little girl from the room. When the door closed behind her, William seated himself at his large walnut desk and picked up a quill to write, but words eluded him. Rising to his feet, he moved to the console table by the window, where decanters of liqueurs and a few tumblers waited. His hand trembled slightly as he poured himself a glass of brandy.

William's mind filled with images as he stared up at the portrait of Mary Wollstonecraft, *his* Mary, the woman who had melted his heart. He remembered their first meeting at a literary salon, she so warm and unaffected despite her celebrity. A purple gown fanning the flames of her auburn hair, its deep décolletage accenting her full breasts.

Mary had been thirty-eight, a woman of the world; he, forty, a confirmed bachelor, lacking in practiced charm. He called at the Somers Town house that Mary shared with her little daughter, Fanny, and the nursemaid, Marguerite.

He found Mary exasperating at times, demanding and opinionated; yet he was drawn to her striking appearance and brilliant mind. William discovered deep reserves of affection, exciting urges that he had never before experienced. Almost immediately they became lovers.

Gazing up at the portrait opposite his desk, William saw as if for the first time the woman who had been his beloved wife. "Marriage is a law and the worst of all laws," William had insisted, until Mary told him their child was on the way.

He only dimly recalled gloomy St. Pancras Church, but could still feel the touch of his bride's hand as they emerged from the chapel into a spring-damp field of primroses and cowslips. As they walked arm in arm, she assured him that their marriage would change *nothing.* "I will keep my little house and you your lodgings," she promised, adding with an intimate smile, "we will meet in the evenings for meals and other amusements."

William smiled, recalling how brief a time that arrangement had lasted. Within days they had moved together into a larger house, where he still lived—Number 29, the Polygon.

How idyllic it all seemed now, those months the happiest of his life. Mary had been sanguine about her confinement, reassuring him, "At Fanny's birth the midwife said I treated my labor so lightly that I should be making children for the Republic." Again Mary would have no male doctor, preferring only a midwife "to sit by and wait for the operation of nature." Childbirth is a perfectly natural process, she had assured William, promising to be downstairs for dinner the day after the baby's birth.

In reality, Mary's protracted labor lasted late into the night, a dreadful time marked by a violent storm. Earsplitting thunder seemed to shake the very foundations of the house, while jagged yellow streaks crisscrossed the blackened sky. As the storm progressed, so did Mary's labor. At last the midwife descended the stairs to tell William that Mary had born a daughter, but, she admonished, he was not to enter the bedroom until all stages of the delivery had been completed.

William waited patiently as night yielded to dawn. Mary's labor had been only the beginning, a prelude to endless hours of frantic probing and pulling to extract the placenta. Finally the midwife admitted defeat. "You had best call a doctor," she advised the stricken father.

Dr. Poignand did what he could. Rolling up his sleeves, he plunged his hand between Mary's naked legs, slowly, painstakingly removing the placenta piece by bloody piece. There was nothing to block the pain.

When at last William was admitted to her room, Mary was exhausted. "I would have died," she murmured, "but was determined not to leave you."

The next two days had been pure bliss. The horror was over and they had a baby, a new life just beginning. Then, without warning, Mary's condition changed. As William sat at her bedside, Mary began to tremble, her deep, racking shudders increasing until she lay helpless.

Dimly William recollected the nightmare that followed. The stifling September days, Mary blazing with fever, then moments later her teeth chattering violently. Frantic, he had called in doctor after doctor. "Do something," he begged. "There must be something you can do!" Tears ran down his cheeks as he pleaded, unwilling, unable to accept the fact that Mary was dying before his eyes. The last physician left, powerless to do more than prescribe wine to dull Mary's senses and relieve the pain.

Marguerite brought the glass to him, her face blotched from crying. Bending for a moment over Mary's body, she pressed her lips to the clawlike hand resting on the coverlet, then hurried from the room. Dimly William heard the sound of weeping outside the door.

As in a nightmare, he saw himself hold the glass to Mary's lips, fighting to suppress the tears that filled his eyes. Mary's lovely face already resembled a death's-head as she looked up at him. "You . . . are the kindest . . . best man in the world," she had whispered. Then she was gone. William let out a groaning cry and slumped, sobbing, across their bed.

Mary had taught him to love, had opened a heart that had been closed to everything but pure reason. *How,* he wondered, *could he go on without her?*

He forced his gaze away from the portrait. Looking down at his familiar desk, William began to carefully rearrange the stacks of foolscap lying there.

He had, of course, gone on without Mary, muddling his way, writing, lecturing, doing his best for the two little girls—there had never been a question that he would keep Fanny to raise as his own. Still, his best was not enough. He looked up once more at the portrait, sighed softly, then turned away.

Even if what he felt now for Jane was not pure bliss, it would have to do.

THREE

Mary watched from her bedroom window as her papa and Mrs. Clairmont stepped into a hackney carriage. Papa looked nervous, Mrs. Clairmont pleased. Though it was early morning, Mary's Papa wore a frilled shirt, a long-tailed coat, and knee breeches. The ugly goose lady was wearing a fancy purple dress with a broad embroidered flounce at the hem and a turban with a big plume. Mary wondered what secret they shared. Why had Papa not told her that he was going someplace special? She watched nervously as the coach set off down the cobbled road.

It was dusk before they returned. Mary's heart sank as her papa helped Mrs. Clairmont alight from the carriage. Seeing Mary at the window, she smiled. Mary thought of a cat finishing off a bird and could almost see the feathers sticking to her mouth. As though reading her thoughts, Mrs. Clairmont dabbed lightly at her lips with a handkerchief.

"Come down, girls," their father called from the parlor.

Mary exchanged glances with Fan. Her sister's pit marks stood out with sudden intensity. Mary hugged her close. "We have each other," she reminded her.

"Yes," Fan agreed, kissing Mary on the forehead. "We will always have that."

Mrs. Clairmont was still smiling when they reached the bottom of the stairs. "My darling girls," she cried, pulling Mary and Fan to her ample bosom. There was no escape.

Their father hovered nearby. "It's December twenty-first," he said in a proud voice, "not even Christmas, and here I am bringing you the best of all possible gifts—can you guess what?"

Fanny's lip trembled. Mary turned away, lest anyone see her tears. How could Papa do such a thing? She ran from the room, unable to control her sobs. That woman!

Nothing was ever the same again at Number 29, the Polygon.

———

Early one morning the family sat in the breakfast room, snared in a bower of bright pink wallpaper sprigged with ivy. Looking up from her soft-boiled egg, Papa's new wife announced, "I will no longer have Marguerite in my house. She was Mary Wollstonecraft's personal servant and does not respect me as your wife."

Mary's heart caught as she watched her papa put down his fork.

"You are wrong! Besides, the girls adore her."

The new Mrs. Godwin shook her head. "William, she must leave. Am I to run this house, or am I not?"

Papa looked at his plate for what seemed a long time. "Very well, Jane, have it your way."

Hurrying up the steep stairs to Marguerite's room, Mary heard the servant crying softly. Dear Marguerite, who had been with them forever, who had known and loved Mary's mother. Panting from the climb, Mary paused to look about at the Parisian prints that covered Marguerite's walls. *Mother once strolled those streets,* she thought.

"That woman that Papa married says awful things." Mary paused a moment before blurting out, "Was Mother a bad woman?"

Marguerite's brow wrinkled. Her voice, when she spoke, was hesitant, as though choosing each word with care. "Your mother's friends, the ones who read books and tried to make the world better—they admired your mother, loved her." Marguerite paused for what seemed a long time before continuing. "But there were others who did not like her. Some of the things she said and did frightened them. Your mother believed that women have the right to live like men. She felt there should be no differences. Your mother had ideals and lived up to them. Not everyone liked that."

The effort to sort out Marguerite's words made Mary dizzy. All she knew was that Marguerite was her friend and had once been her mother's. "Please, stay with me," she begged. "Mother would want you here with us."

Marguerite blew her nose into a lacy handkerchief. "She would, indeed. I was with your dear mother when Fanny was born. I took care of her when Fanny's father ran off—that dreadful man—I—"

"Dreadful man?" Mary echoed. "What dreadful man? Papa is Fan's father."

Marguerite's hand flew to her mouth; her tearstained face reddened. "*Mon Dieu!* Forgive me! Mary, you must forget what I said. It is a secret."

Mary stared at the servant in dismay. "Is Fan not my sister?"

Marguerite stopped crying and stared into Mary's eyes. "Fanny is your sister, your half sister. She never knew her real father, Gilbert Imlay. He was an American caught up in the French Revolution. Monsieur Imlay and your mother were—oh, you are too young to understand such things."

When Mary started to protest, Marguerite waved off her questions. "It does not matter. Fanny loves your father deeply and thinks of him as her own. You must be a grown-up little girl and promise never, never to repeat this. Do you understand?"

Marguerite's words circled in Mary's head. Fan not Papa's child? How awful for her! No, she would never tell. "Yes," Mary whispered. "It will be our secret."

Housekeepers came and went. Mary would scarcely get used to one before she left or was fired. Their stepmother, mobcap covering her corkscrew curls, swept through the house ordering, reordering, commanding, yelling, screeching, pounding on tables.

The worst part was that the woman insisted that Mary and Fanny call her "Mum." Papa agreed.

Overnight Mary's quiet home grew noisy and crowded. Mum had brought her two frightful children with her. That dreadful Clara was always given the best of everything—including Mary's room. "She has her heart set on it, William," Mum explained to Papa. "You want Clara to feel at home here, do you not?" It was clear that Clara was her mother's darling, but Mary didn't like Clara's brother much better. Charlie was eight, a big brute of a boy who pushed and shoved to get his way.

There were new rules, servants, schedules. Mary's stepmother wanted to change everything, would even have taken down Mother's portrait had Papa allowed her. Again and again Mary heard them arguing, each time louder than before.

The worst change was in Papa himself. In the past, though busy with his books and papers, he had made it clear that Mary was foremost in his heart. She had *felt* his love, or at least thought she had. Now Papa spent more time than ever alone in his study. When at last he did emerge, his attention was handed about like tiny helpings of trifle, divided equally among so many. Mary supposed that was all very fair of him, but she did not care about fair. She was his little girl and wanted to be special.

Mum sometimes gasped when she talked. Fan said it was because her stays were too tight, but as weeks passed, there was no doubt about it, Mum was growing fat. Mary had just turned seven when Fan whispered that Mum was going to have a baby.

A few more months and Mum looked like an elephant. Though she no longer ran around the house pounding and poking into things, her screeching grew even louder. More was demanded of the girls. "Mary, get your nose out of that book and put away the groceries." "Fanny, help me beat these rugs."

If Mum asked Clara to do something around the house, the girl screamed back at her mother. "I will not! You cannot make me." Oh, they were a pair! Mary determined early on that she would do her own share and no more. If Clara refused to sweep the floor or put her clothes away, Mary would certainly not do it for her.

But Fan, poor Fan, was always so eager to please. As the eldest girl, she took on the most tedious tasks—endless silver polishing, dusting, and weeding the kitchen garden. Fan even picked up after Clara. Sometimes Mary felt guilty, but not enough to do any more than necessary.

———

One evening as the children sat with their books before the fireplace, Papa roused them with no explanation and summarily bundled them into a hackney carriage. He was sending them, he said, to Samuel Coleridge's house for the night. The weather outside was dreadful: thunder, lightning, relentless sheets of rain.

Clara had to be pushed inside the carriage. "Why must we do this?" she demanded, kicking at the closed door. "Who knows what kind of mood Uncle Samuel will be in when we get there. He is often kind, but there are other times when I think him about to cry. Mama says he is daft."

Her brother Charlie agreed. "Often he's a fine fellow, full of funny jokes, but I don't like him when he stares into space and won't say anything."

Fan nodded. "Uncle Samuel's moods frighten me."

Mary looked at her in surprise. Samuel Coleridge was among her favorite "uncles," one of the few who still visited regularly since Mum's arrival. "We have never been to his house before. Why are we going tonight?" she wondered aloud.

"I know why," Charlie taunted, "but I am not going to tell you." He leaned back against the cracked leather cushions and closed his eyes.

The hackney's wheels spun through a sharp turn, the iron rims jolting over the cobblestones as the driver urged his team to a quicker pace.

When they reached Uncle's house, the driver accompanied them to the door and banged the big brass knocker. The narrow three-story house was only dimly lit, and not at all inviting. Mary wanted to run back to the coach and hide.

Finally a white-faced Aunt Sarah opened the door and ushered the children inside. After pausing to light a branch of candles, she led them through a stone-floored scullery and down a long, narrow corridor. Their footsteps echoed eerily as Auntie hurried them into the kitchen. It was a large room with a low-beamed ceiling and lots of copper pots hanging about a stone fireplace, where coals still smoldered.

The cook, a thin woman with stringy dark hair, acted like someone not much used to company, but busied herself ladling soup for the children, who seated themselves around the large kitchen table. "Thank you, this is very good," Mary remembered to say. The soup really was good, too, with lots of meat, not just the watery blend of carrots and cabbage she had come to expect at home.

Later, when Auntie led them into the large, high-ceilinged drawing room, she seemed nervous. *Why would someone tiptoe in her own house?* Mary wondered. The Coleridge home was furnished far better than her own. There were large tufted armchairs and gilded clocks and the newest gas reading lamps. Yet, despite the grandeur, something about the place set her to shivering.

Auntie jumped when Uncle Samuel entered the room, his slight body wrapped in a velvet dressing gown, but he seemed pleased to see the children.

Settling into a wing-back chair, brandy snifter in hand, he began to tell jokes. Mary didn't understand any but laughed heartily at them all. Uncle's eyes shone as he talked; his face was florid. This surprised Mary. When she'd seen him last at her home, his manner had been quiet, his dark eyes subdued, almost dull.

Mum had said that she could not for the life of her imagine why Samuel was so often depressed when the rich potter's son, Tom Wedgwood, provided for him most generously. "Imagine the luck of it," she said, "a gift of one hundred and fifty pounds!" Mum thought it would have easily been enough to keep the Godwin family for a year.

Suddenly Uncle clapped his hands, interrupting himself. "I have a treat for you," he announced. "A verse of mine has been newly republished. I doubt that you children ever heard the first version, and now I believe this one is even better."

"Oh, Sam, they are so young," Auntie said, her brow furrowed. "I do not think—"

"Nonsense," he interrupted her. The pupils of his eyes looked like tiny pinpricks. "I have it right here in the desk." As Uncle Samuel bent over the desk, Mary saw his hands tremble.

Watching him pull out several pieces of parchment, Auntie's face clouded. "It's a—disturbing poem."

Uncle countered, "Charlie is certain to like it."

"I will like it, too," Mary assured him, leaning forward eagerly.

"I doubt that." Auntie shook her head. "Wait until tomorrow. Your father can decide. It is time the four of you were in bed."

The storm had grown worse since their arrival. Rain pelted the window and gusts of wind attacked cracks in the casement setting. Uncle's eyes glittered; a vein pulsed in his forehead. "The poem is about a mariner whose ship is blown off course by a fierce storm— just like this one," he told them.

Stirred by Uncle's excitement, Mary turned to him, pleading, "Tell us about the poem, won't you?"

"Yes," the others agreed eagerly. "If you please, sir," Charlie added.

Looking satisfied with himself, Uncle settled into a high-back chair. After clearing his throat noisily, he explained, "An albatross appears and leads the ship back on course, but even as the bird is praised by the vessel's crew, the ungrateful mariner, a navigator who should have known the way himself, shoots the creature with his crossbow."

"Oh, no!" Fan breathed. "The poor bird . . ." Her face had grown sorrowful, but Mary leaned forward, caught up in the tale of the ill-fated ship.

Uncle Samuel's voice deepened sonorously as he recited:

Water, water, every where,
And all the boards did shrink;
Water, water, every where,
Nor any drop to drink.

The wind shrieked around the corners of the house as Uncle continued his tale. The sailors blame the mariner for their tormenting thirst and force him to wear the dead albatross about his neck. The ship encounters a ghostly vessel. On board are Death, a skeleton; and the Nightmare Life-in-Death, a hideously pale woman. The two roll dice for the souls of the crew. Death wins the lives of the crew members and Life-in-Death takes the mariner, a prize she considers far more valuable. One by one all the crew members die.

Mary listened silently as Uncle told how the mariner lives on for seven days and nights, unable to escape the curse he read in the corpses' eyes. At last he can bear it no longer.

I closed my lids, and kept them close,
And the balls like pulses beat;
For the sky and the sea, and the sea and the sky,

Lay like a load on my weary eye,
And the dead were at my feet.

Mary's heart thumped as the awful scene played out before her mind's eye. It was all so awfully scary.

"Now look what you've done, the children are white as sheets." Aunt Sarah rose to her feet, but Uncle seemed to have forgotten them entirely. He sat staring off into space as Auntie herded Mary and the others upstairs. Despite the separate rooms she had prepared, the three girls insisted on sleeping together, and Mary was delighted when Charlie suggested that he spend the night on the trundle beside their large canopied bed. For once she was glad of his company, but, even huddled between Fan and Clara, the bed curtains drawn tight about them, she lay awake for hours. In the moaning wind outside, Mary heard the ship creak, the dead sailors crying out to her.

What a relief the next morning when their new housekeeper arrived to fetch them home, where Papa waited at the door looking very pleased. "I have a grand surprise for you," he said, leading the children up the stairs to the bedroom he shared with Mum. There she was, bolstered by pillows and holding a small baby in her arms. In Mary's eyes, Baby Will looked like any other baby and cried a lot.

———•———

Before long, Papa was back in his study, and now there was even more work to be done. It didn't get easier either. Will was two before he mastered the chamber pot. Fan still bore the brunt of the household chores. Clara was busy with her singing lessons—Mum likened her voice to an angel's. And Mary had her books and writing. She had always enjoyed reading and now, as the months and years passed, found escape in scribbling stories of her own. That and Papa's family tutorials kept her days full.

Each evening, the children were put to bed early because Mum wanted to go to bed early herself. Often troubled by nightmares, Mary took to creeping downstairs to the study, where Papa's circle gathered. Sitting with their pipes and glasses of port, the gentlemen read their stories, poems, and essays to each other or discussed the affairs of the day. They were always deep in conversation, each so eager to get his own point across, that it was easy for Mary to find a hiding place behind a sofa. She listened quietly, loving the heated exchanges that invariably took place. Mary knew that her mother had often spoken out among groups such as this. Mary Wollstonecraft voiced her ideas easily. People listened to her, too. Sometimes what she said made people angry, like the part about women being equal to men, but they listened just the same. *It will be that way for me as well*, Mary told herself . . . *someday*.

One night, Anthony Carlisle, an older man who Mary knew only as a medical scientist, joined the group late in the evening. A short, stocky fellow with bushy muttonchop whiskers, Mr. Carlisle was hatless, his neckcloth unbuttoned. There was an air of excitement about him that set the others to nodding expectantly. Eagerly they cleared space for him in their circle.

"I've just come from Newgate," he told them. "As you know, we've been doing experiments on the bodies of executed prisoners. Tonight"—he paused, looking about the room—"tonight we finally succeeded in passing electricity through the corpse of one of them. Can you believe—the poor creature actually moved!"

Mary's heart quickened at the thought. She knew about electricity, an awesome, mysterious power. Imagine it passing through one's body! If the corpse moved, might it also live? Would such a thing be good? Surely not! The thought of dead men walking among the living made her shudder. Suppose such a creature came to her room, parted her bed curtain. Oh! Mary recoiled in fright, but her mind would not be still. The creature, a monster, would be powered by a fearful essence, something akin to lightning.

After listening to Mr. Carlisle's stories, Mary avoided Papa's study for more than a month. Some things were too dreadful to even think about.

Still, the fearful words echoed in her head: *And the dead were at my feet.*

FOUR

Charles Lamb, one of Papa's most devoted literary cronies, was Mary's favorite "uncle." A gentle, funny man, he never caused her to feel uneasy as Uncle Samuel sometimes did. Uncle Charles read stories to her, and occasionally he and his sister—who was also named Mary—took her to plays and symphonies in London. Mary admired her namesake greatly, for Auntie Lamb was a gentle beauty with a playful sense of humor.

Auntie's inclusion in their outings was rare, however. "She is sad today," Uncle Charles would often explain, or "Our father forbids her to leave the house."

One afternoon, returning from a Punch and Judy show with Uncle Charles, she heard Mum arguing with her father. Silently Mary ascended the stairs to the upstairs parlor, following their angry voices to the open doorway.

"Why do you allow Mary to think herself so special just because her mother was famous?" Mum demanded of Papa. "Infamous is more like it. Everyone knows Mary Wollstonecraft had at least two lovers before she met you."

"Jane!" Papa shook an angry finger at her. "That is quite enough."

"Don't try to stop me, William." Mum held up both palms to silence his protest. "The woman almost drowned herself. Who knows how matters might have turned out if she had not gotten herself pregnant with Mary. Most convenient!"

Papa's face was livid. "Confound it, woman, will you be still!" Mary shrank back but Mum was unstoppable.

"No!" she shrilled. "I will not be still. The way you treat those girls is ridiculous. Why should Fanny be catered to as your daughter when everyone knows she is the bastard spawn of an American scoundrel?"

"Oh!" The word escaped Mary's lips without her even realizing she had said it.

Both adults, facing each other in the small parlor, turned toward Mary in the doorway. Papa looked horrified; Mum's cheeks flamed as red as the flocked wallpaper behind her. "Maybe," she screeched, "it is time your little genius learned the truth. Just because some fool measured her head and said she was going to be smart does not set her apart from the real world."

"Not smart, *brilliant*," Papa bellowed, putting an arm around Mary. "William Nicholson—an illustrious scientist—said her forehead indicated great intelligence."

"A lot of foolishness that you have bragged about ever since."

Mary broke away, fleeing down the stairs. She wanted to hear no more. Flinging open the front door, she saw Uncle Charles still standing by his carriage. He'd been buying violets from the flower woman and was just completing the sale.

"Stop! Please stop! Wait!"

Uncle Charles turned and caught her in his arms as she rushed toward him. "Take me with you," she begged.

"Running away, is it?" he asked, helping her inside the carriage. "What about a little ride around the park first?"

They were past the park and well into the countryside before Mary could bring herself to speak. "Mum says Mother was a bad woman," she said at last.

"She is mistaken. Your mother was by no means bad." Uncle Charles placed both hands on Mary's shoulders so that his eyes were fixed on hers. "Mary Wollstonecraft was brave and brilliant."

They had passed a duck pond and finally a meadow before
Mary asked the next question. "Mum also said that everyone
knows Papa is not Fanny's father. I knew, but thought it a secret.
Fan was such a little girl that Papa is the only father she remembers. Marguerite told me never to tell anyone and I never have."

Uncle patted Mary's hand. "Everyone does *not* know the story
of Fanny's parentage. She was born nearly eleven years ago in
France. We were in the midst of a war, people engrossed with their
own affairs. Anyway, the important thing is that your father loves
Fanny as much as if she were his own."

Mary thought about his words for some time. She felt better, but another awful question remained. Looking up at Uncle
Charles, eyes fixed on his, she asked, "Mum said that my mother
tried to kill herself. Was she that—that—sad?"

The carriage jolted over a mud puddle, throwing Mary forward. Charles steadied her, holding the girl tenderly in his arms.
Why didn't Papa ever do that? Mary wondered. It felt so good.

"Your mother may have been sad sometimes," Uncle Charles
told her. "Everybody has bad times, but we go on and are the better
for it. That's what happened with your mother. Do you know what
she used to say? 'The beginning is always today.' That's something
for all of us to remember."

An hour later, when the wheels clattered over the flagstones
that paved the way to Number 29, the Polygon, Mary's tears were
dry. Uncle Charles had given her a lot to think about.

As the carriage clattered to a stop before her home, Mary
asked one last question. "Why does Mum say such awful things?
Why does she hate me?"

"You are a bright girl, Mary. You should be able to sort that out
for yourself. She is jealous."

"Jealous?" Mary echoed the word. "Why should she be jealous
of me? She has Papa."

"Perhaps, but you are still your mother's daughter. Think about it."

Mary alighted from his carriage feeling happier than when she had gotten in, though still puzzled.

Pieces of the puzzle fell into place a few days later as she sat by the fire, reading. Across the room Mary's stepmother shuffled household bills around the dining table. She was muttering angrily to herself when Clara sidled in. Mary knew right away that Clara wanted something, but Mum smiled just at the sight of her.

It soon came out. Clara had seen some pretty flowered muslin in a shop window, and perhaps Mumsie would buy it, sew a gown. Mary assumed she would; Clara got everything she wanted.

This time, however, the answer was no. "Sorry, sweet one. Look at these bills." Mum gestured at the stacks. "All these bills and nothing coming in." She picked up some of the sheets before her. "Just look at these—the coal merchant, the fishmonger, and our rent is long past due. How am I to pay these?"

"Papa should write a story and sell it," Clara suggested.

Mum shook her head despondently. "That is not as easy as it used to be. Scribble as he will, nothing sells like *Caleb Williams* did, or generates talk in the manner of *Political Justice*." She sighed heavily. "Your stepfather has had his day. Now he's little more than a down-at-the-heels philosopher living on past laurels."

Mary sat openmouthed, the book unheeded in her lap. Clearly they had not noticed that she was there.

"Then why did you marry him?" Clara asked. The girl's lower lip stuck out petulantly. "Surely my *real* father—"

Mum sighed again, put aside the papers. "Your real father was so anxious to be off with his blonde doxy that he left nothing but useless sticks of furniture. It is well that you do not remember those days."

Clara sat down at the table beside her mother. "Then I suppose you . . . Charlie and I . . . we are lucky. Papa Godwin is a good enough man."

"Yes," Mum agreed, "but a fool about money." She flung down the bills in disgust. "Your stepfather has only contempt for tradesmen, calls them 'fawning, cringing creatures centered only in the sordid consideration of petty gains.' That is all fine and dandy for a fancy philosopher, but it is I who must deal with those 'creatures,' who are anything but fawning with me."

Clara's arms went around her mother. "I know that you are the one who must manage everything." She stood back, hands on her hips. "It isn't fair that all anyone ever talks about is Mary's 'wonderful' mother."

Watching silent and unnoticed, Mary felt an unexpected wave of sympathy for her stepmother. Who could blame her for being jealous? *I will try harder,* Mary promised herself.

———————

The next day, while Mary's stepmother sat at the dining table still poring over bills, Willie began to cry fretfully. "Can no one see to him?" Mum screeched in her raspy voice. Mary winced, then caught herself.

The little boy had bumped his knee and sat whimpering on the floor beside a battered hobbyhorse. Mary helped Willie up, then settled him on her lap in a rocking chair. With one arm around the little boy, she riffled through the leaves of a book with her free hand, settling at last on a random page. Willie's whimpers softened; soon he stopped crying entirely, snuggled down, and closed his eyes.

"Where did you get that book?" Mum asked.

"Uncle Samuel gave it to me. He said he bought it as a reminder that poems need not all be scary to be good."

"Indeed. That one certainly seems to have put Willie's mind at ease." Mum reached for the book and flipped idly through the title pages. "*Rhymes for the Nursery*. Do you like it?"

"Yes, very much, we all do—Fanny, Clara, even Charlie has read a few poems. And you see how pleased Willie was."

Mum turned to the poem that Mary had been singing and read aloud.

As your bright and tiny spark
Lights the traveller in the dark,
Though I know not what you are,
Twinkle, twinkle, little star.

Mary watched her stepmother's face as she fingered the book. "A spark—that is what we need," she muttered, perhaps forgetting Mary was there. "It is very dark these days. So, where is the star to guide *our* way? Creditors are closing in. We are but a step away from debtors' prison."

————

Mary woke the next morning to excited voices. When she came downstairs to see what all the commotion was about, heavens above! Mum wanted to start a publishing company. "We will specialize in children's books," she told Papa, who appeared skeptical. "How can we fail with your writing talent, my business sense, and five young readers right here on which to experiment?"

After a day spent browsing through bookstores and libraries, Papa returned both dismayed and encouraged. "There is far too much God stuff about," he said in disgust. "We would be doing a public service to wrest the children's market from mealymouthed spinsters and clergymen. Children should be encouraged to think for themselves. Someone needs to open their minds."

"Absolutely," Mum agreed. "Now all we need is an investor. Can you think of anyone?"

Papa's brow furrowed. "I swear I do not know of a single prospect. My friends are like me, struggling to get by on pamphlet writing."

Mum sat up with a start. "What about Tom?"

"Tom Wedgwood, the china heir?"

"Exactly. He has given more than enough to your fine friend Sam Coleridge."

Papa looked doubtful. "Tom's not very well, you know. Some say he will not last the year."

"Then you had best be off to see him. Get the money now. Perhaps," she added, "we may not even need to pay it back. He can hardly take it with him."

Papa laughed, chucking her under the chin. "Surely you jest. I know you don't mean a word."

But Mum did mean it; Mary knew she did. Maybe her father knew it, too. He went that very evening to pay a call on Mr. Wedgwood. The promise of one hundred pounds that he brought back was enough to get them started.

From then on, Papa's interest—Mum's, too—centered surprisingly on Mary. "All the children read," Mum pointed out, "but Mary's nose is *always* in a book. She is fussy, too; sometimes I have seen her toss a book aside unfinished."

One morning Papa handed Mary a sheaf of papers. "Now, young lady, tell me honestly what you think of this?" She looked down at the words written in Papa's large, strong script. *Fables, Ancient and Modern.*

"But this says 'By Edward Baldwin,'" Mary pointed out. "Why is his name on your book?"

Papa seemed to find Mary's confusion amusing. "You are a big girl, eight now. Surely you must know that not all share my views. Book reviewers call me 'seditious' because I speak out against the king. And everyone knows that I am an atheist. The Goody Two-Shoes who superintend children's schools would be terrified to receive a book written under the name of Godwin."

Mary could scarcely believe that. Her father was the wisest, most wonderful man in the world. Only fools could think otherwise. Still, she was thrilled to be his first critic, a test subject. Papa and Mum watched intently as she settled down to read. At first Mary felt strange but was soon absorbed in the tale of "The Wolf and the Mastiff," in which a starving wolf chides a well-fed but chained mastiff. "Hunger shall never make me so slavish and base, as to prefer chains and blows with a belly-full, to my liberty," the wolf says. She smiled, thinking how much the wolf sounded like her father.

When Mary was perhaps a third of the way through, Mum interrupted her. "Well, girl, what do you think? Do not keep us in suspense. Do you like the fable or not?"

"I love it." Setting the book aside, Mary ran to her father. "I can hardly wait to read the whole book. You wrote a wonderful story, Papa."

He beamed, brushed lightly at the ruffle on his sleeve. "Thank you, Mary, but I did draw a bit from Aesop."

"Yes, but it was you who made the fable come to life."

Mary thought she saw a tear in his eye. Even Mum was pleased and rewarded her with extra pudding at dinner.

At Mum's insistence, Papa's next book, a history of the Greek gods, was dedicated to the headmaster of the Charterhouse School, where Charlie went. The prestigious association had a marked effect on sales and literary reviews. Only the *Eclectic Review* deplored the revealing undress of the engravings and took the author to task for not condemning the baseness of heathen religion. Mum saw to it that he put more clothes on the Olympians in the next edition.

Soon Papa was so involved with the business of publishing that he had little time to write himself. Clearly other writers would have to be hired.

When Mum looked about, her eye fell on Uncle Charles. "That fellow is always scribbling—his fingers seem to be permanently ink stained. He supports his sister and their father with the pittance he makes working as a clerk at the East India Company," she reminded Papa. "Surely Charles could use the money."

Mary liked all her uncle's stories, but *The Adventures of Ulysses* had her hanging on every word. It surprised her to overhear Papa complain, "Your descriptions are far too violent, Charles. Children may read books, but it is their parents who buy them."

Charles finally agreed to remove a particularly realistic description of a giant's vomit. "But that is it," he swore. "Take my work as is, or refuse it."

Mary was relieved to find her father more than eager to take it. Uncle Charles was a favorite. She especially loved his humor and its volatile effect on Mum. Mary would never forget the evening that Uncle leaned over the dining table and blew out the candles just as her stepmother was carving a joint of mutton. After a moment of shocked confusion, the candles were relit only to reveal that Uncle had thrust the joint into his neighbor's arms. The red-faced man clutched the mutton to his chest while Uncle cried out as though horrified, "Oh, Martin! Martin! I should never have thought it of you!"

Mary could hardly control her laughter. Mum was at first speechless; then, hands on her hips, she demanded, "Get out of this house! Get out this minute."

It was only the steady sales of *Tales from Shakespeare* that retrieved Uncle's place at her table. What else could Mum do? The book, written with his talented sister, Mary, had literally sold out in a single day.

Yet Mum had refused to put Mary Lamb's name on the cover—insisting that women's names would not sell books. Mary never believed this excuse. The real cause, she felt certain, was Auntie Lamb's connection to Mary's mother. Auntie was full of anecdotes, telling her that Mary Wollstonecraft had been a heroine to women everywhere.

"You have your mother's smile, I see her often in you," she told Mary one afternoon.

Mary leaned forward to hug her, thinking how fortunate she was to have this clever, lively grown-up for a friend, but her timing proved unfortunate. Mum was standing in the doorway, her frown fearful to behold. Auntie Lamb was never again invited to the Godwin home. Worse yet, Mum prevailed on Papa not to publish any more of Auntie Lamb's work, even with her name omitted.

At first Mary inquired after her, but that only seemed to make Uncle sad. "My sister was once open and sociable," he told her. "She loved people and parties but is now forced to do all the housework herself and take in sewing besides. My family is difficult—they're grim, demanding people. They go out of their way to make life as hard for her as possible. She has grown to hate them. You—you have no idea." Uncle shook his head and would say no more.

A few mornings later Mary heard hushed voices coming from the kitchen. Papa and Mum sat close by the fire, their voices barely above a whisper. "What has happened? Tell me," Mary urged, hurrying to her father's side.

His hand trembled as he brushed a curl back from her forehead. "A servant just brought the news. I do not know how to tell you children. It is a dreadful business." He turned away as if unable to meet Mary's eyes. "Horrible, simply horrible!"

"She will find out sooner or later." Mum shrugged, but Mary saw that her stepmother, too, was greatly disturbed. "It's about

Charles Lamb," she began in a shaky voice. "Or rather about his sister. She has had another of her fits and has been arrested."

"What are you talking about?" Mary wanted to know.

"Your father has tried to keep the woman's sordid past from you, but it's hopeless. Mary Lamb killed her own mother some years ago. Everyone knows the story but you. William wanted to keep it from you—but what's the point? Now she's attacked a servant with a knife. No serious harm done, but there will be a trial. This time Mary Lamb will hang for sure."

"Auntie Lamb!" Mary cried out in alarm. "Is she all right?"

"Oh, she is well enough." Mum's voice strengthened, her usual strident tone creeping back. "None of it's as bad as the last time, when Charles followed a bloody trail into his house. He said it stuck to his boots as he walked. The dining room floor was covered with it, and there, right in front of him, was his mother sprawled across the table, a carving knife stuck clean through her heart. Can you imagine that?"

Mary could not imagine it, nor did she want to, but night after night she awoke screaming as nightmare followed nightmare. How could the lovely Mary Lamb do something that terrible? How could a friend so kind and clever turn into a monster? Could such a horrific change happen to anyone? *Could it happen to me?* Mary asked herself.

There was a trial. Uncle Charles defended his sister. In the end she was not hanged but sent to a madhouse. Some called this a victory, but Mary was not so certain. She wrote to Auntie Lamb secretly at the asylum but never received an answer. Perhaps Auntie never saw the letters. Mary could not ask Uncle; her stepmother had banned him from their home. No more outings, no more giant's vomit, no more disappearing mutton. Uncle Charles, sitting in his house of horror, was as lost to Mary as surely as if a fiend had stolen him away.

FIVE

Aaron Burr banged his silver-tipped cane on the roof, signaling for the coachman to slow his pace. Somers Town looked to be a pretty place, lush with trees and flowing fields. Just an hour's ride from his dingy flat in London, it seemed a different world. Gone were the aggressive tradesmen, the sniveling beggars, and the crush of carriages.

Burr's driver turned onto the Polygon, a stately avenue with three- and four-story houses set back from the road. Most had broad drives bordered with verdant plantings. Number 29, he noted, was the least auspicious. The garden, unlike its neighbors, resembled a jungle.

The coach swung into the drive, pulling to a stop before the entrance. Burr hesitated, distressed at the thought of being disappointed—worse yet, affronted. His exile from family, friends, and country was proving more difficult than he had expected. Jefferson and the others had been harsh indeed.

Of course, Burr had tried to put the best face on his banishment. What better thing than leisure to savor London and the Continent? What he had not anticipated were the subtle snubs. A woman had cut him dead at the theater; a gentleman actually avoided his handshake. Naturally there had been some invitations, but not nearly so many as he might have expected.

Now Burr wondered if he should have sent a note ahead rather than simply driving out to the Godwin house on a whim. Well, so

be it, here he was. Disdaining his man's assistance, Burr flung open
the carriage door.

Thumping his cane on the brick drive, he strode forward
boldly, his gloved palm wrapped loosely against the cane's eagle-
head top. In the States, he had been condemned for his devilish
Godwinism. Surely this was one home where he should be certain
of welcome.

"My name is Burr, Aaron Burr," he told the young thing who
answered the door. Doffing his hat, he bowed slightly. "And who
might you be?" he inquired, one bushy brow raised.

"Mary, sir. Mary Godwin."

"Indeed! You must be the daughter. Your mother was the finest
woman who ever lived."

"You knew my mother?" she asked, eagerness apparent in her
wide gray eyes.

"Alas, no. I merely knew of her, pored over her writings as any
thinking person should. She was a beacon to us all. It is your illustrious father whom I have come to see, William Godwin. May I
present myself?"

Looking past her, Burr glimpsed a medium-sized man with
dark, penetrating eyes, a receding hairline, and gray locks strag-
gling down to his ruffled collar.

"So you are Aaron Burr." The man stepped forward, smiling,
and extended his hand. "I have heard about you . . . many things,
your duel, the exile—"

"I daresay. My reputation seems always to precede me. But I,
too, have heard of you. Since my worst critics in the States accuse
me of being like you, I thought it time we met."

Smiling cordially, Godwin led him through a crowded, cluttered house to a brightly lit study. Every wall was lined with books,
save one. A woman's portrait dominated the space above his host's
desk.

"My first wife, Mary Wollstonecraft," Godwin said in answer to the unspoken question. Did Burr imagine it, or did his host's voice founder?

"I read *A Vindication of the Rights of Woman*, then gave it to my wife and daughter," Burr said. "Such a masterpiece should be required reading for everyone."

"Indeed." Godwin settled into the worn leather chair behind his desk and gestured for Burr to sit opposite him. Burr shifted his cane and lowered himself into the chair. The previous night's brandy glasses still littered side tables; pipe ashes filled trays to overflowing; the air was heavy with stale smoke. Mary appeared with tea and cakes, then sat quietly in the corner, listening as the two men became acquainted.

Burr recognized right away that Godwin had followed his treason trial and was relieved by his host's sympathetic reaction. "It is a sorry thing that a country's former vice president would be tried as a traitor," Godwin said, shaking his head.

"Yes," Burr sighed. "The idea still brings me pain. Some at home actually think—or profess to think—that I conspired with Mexico. In reality, I worked to *acquire* Mexico. It should reasonably be one of the United States, do you not agree?"

Godwin shrugged. "That makes as much sense to me as that other place you have recently acquired—what is the name, Louisiana?" He smiled apologetically. "You must forgive me. When I was a boy, your country was a colony. I am glad you no longer swear allegiance to our king. No one should. If I were king, I would abolish all kings." He laughed, scratching his head. "But your states seem to multiply like rabbits. I simply cannot keep track." He turned to fill his pipe.

Burr sensed that Godwin was not much interested in politics. What could one expect of an avowed anarchist? But soon he found they had much else in common. Both admired the rapturous music of Ludwig van Beethoven, the luminous brushstrokes of the landscape painter J. M. W. Turner, and the poetry of the alchemist philosopher Johann Wolfgang Goethe. What a wonderful time to be alive, each agreed, thrilled by the sublime creations rapidly remaking the world about them.

"Do say you will stay to dinner," Godwin pressed. "My son, Willie, will be preaching tonight."

"Preaching?" Burr repeated, surprised. Godwin was, he had heard, a devout atheist like himself.

"We call it preaching, but it is really declaiming," Godwin explained. "Willie is not yet nine, but when he saw my old friend Sam Coleridge lecture, he was impressed by the crowd watching and listening. Willie, too, enjoys being the center of attention, so I had a miniature pulpit built for him. My daughter Mary writes his speeches." He turned to the girl. "What is it to be tonight?"

Mary's pale face flushed. "The influence of governments on the character of the people."

Oh, poor girl, Burr mused. She must love her father very much. What could he say but yes? Of course he would stay.

At the crowded dinner table, Burr found the Godwins to be a noisy bunch dominated by William's wife, Jane, a short but formidable woman with flashing eyes and good skin. Besides Willie, there were four other children, a mixed bag. Jane's boy, Charlie, the eldest, shared some of his mother's pompous mannerisms but appeared to lack her drive. His sister, Clara, was clearly her mother's pet and knew it, a handful to be sure. Fanny, Mary Wollstonecraft's older daughter, was sweet enough but badly pockmarked. She was soft-spoken and seemed to have inherited little of her mother's brilliance. That had fallen to Mary, the girl Burr had met upon arrival. He was charmed by her quick wit, impressed by her extensive vocabulary. Burr judged the girl to be about fourteen, small, delicate, perhaps too delicate, her face pale, but those eyes . . . so bright and curious.

Dinner seemed a hastily thrown together affair—Mrs. Godwin was clearly not prepared for company. There was scarcely enough goose to go around, and the plum pudding was barely adequate, but no doubt the woman had done her best with what she had.

After dinner the family played similes. "Wise as an owl," Mary said of her father. "Quiet as a mouse," Godwin described Fanny. "Mary is light as a feather," Fanny said. "More like skinny as a rail," Mrs. Godwin countered; her mouth twitched in a nasty smile. And so it went.

Then came charades. Burr and Mary were teammates along with Charlie and Fanny. Mary was the first chosen to select a challenge at random from the other team's hat. Burr found it charming to watch her acting out the puzzle, first unfolding her hands as if they were a book, then holding up two slender fingers. A two-word title? And now the same two fingers. The second word. She laid a finger on Mrs. Godwin's arm. Hmmm, a little word then.

Now Mary was looking about, brow furrowed, as though searching for something. "Lost?" he called out. Mary rewarded him with a pretty smile, then indicated the second syllable of the first word. She knelt down as if to play with something, tossing imaginary objects and then gathering them in. What could it be? Charlie knew.

"Dice," he called out confidently.

"Dice lost?" Burr pondered.

William was laughing. "It is Mary's favorite; I should have known from the expression on her face—*Paradise Lost.* Well done, girl."

Burr was surprised by the animosity in Mrs. Godwin's eyes when she disagreed. "It was not done well at all. We would all have gotten it much sooner if Mary had acted out the beginning first. Is that not the way we are supposed to do it?"

"Not that I have heard," Burr defended the girl. "Besides, what could she have done with *para*?"

Burr read gratitude in Mary's answering smile. Head to one side, eyes suddenly impish, she quoted:

The mind is its own place, and in itself
Can make a Heaven of Hell, a Hell of Heaven.
Better to reign in Hell, than serve in Heaven.

"Very good," Burr complimented her, "but Milton also said, 'Who overcomes by force, hath overcome but half his foe.'"

Resuming her place in the circle, Mary turned her luminous eyes to him. "That may be so, Master Burr, but is it not true that you yourself fought a duel?"

"Mary, you are too forward!" Mrs. Godwin said angrily. "Go to the kitchen and fetch us some cake." The girl was still within earshot when her stepmother commented snidely, "William's friends indulge Mary far too much. She fancies herself superior because studies come easily to her, but she is actually a lazy girl, always dreaming or reading. She scribbles, too; William makes too much of that when there are errands to be done, practical things that matter in *real* life."

The angry tone in Mrs. Godwin's voice, the malicious slant to her eyes made Burr uncomfortable, but Mary appeared unperturbed. She returned shortly, wheeling a tea table with cake, plates, and forks neatly arranged on it. Pausing before her stepmother, she gave her stepmother a sweeping court curtsy. "Will that be all, your grace?"

"Mary!" Godwin admonished.

Burr was surprised. William had smiled benignly throughout the evening, seemingly unaware of the tension between his wife and daughter. Now, when finally roused, he defended his wife.

Withdrawing his pocket watch, Burr checked the time. Enough family life for one evening. Before bidding them farewell, he invited Mary to stroll with him the next day. "We could walk to

Cripplegate, if you have a mind. You can see Milton's final paradise there. I hear there is a bust of him enshrined at the church of St. Giles."

"What about Clara?" Mrs. Godwin quickly interjected.

When Burr hesitated, Godwin broke in. "Clara cares little about Milton. He is special to Mary."

———————

It was a long walk. Burr was eager to reach the shrine, grateful to sink into one of the long wooden pews. At first, awed by the ancient cathedral's vaulted ceilings, they spoke in whispers. Gazing at the poet's likeness, Mary told Burr that the tomb had recently been broken into. One of Milton's ribs had been stolen, the teeth pulled out of his skull, even some of his hair taken. "It seems," she said solemnly, "that no one is safe, even in death."

Burr nodded in agreement. "Chance offers no security. It is the choices we make in *life* that matter. Simple everyday decisions have the power to make us miserable forever—if not ruin us entirely."

Mary turned sideways in her pew to see him better.

"You asked about my duel," he continued. "From what I observed last night, you are attempting one of your own."

Mary's eyes widened in indignation. "You do not expect me to just give in to her?"

"Your position is as precarious as my own. Take my word, a politic approach is always preferable—when possible."

"I have tried that, you cannot imagine how hard I have tried. Mum hates me for no reason at all."

Burr raised a brow. "For no reason? I think not." He took both Mary's hands in his, forcing her to meet his gaze. "My child, I caution you to pick your battles wisely. Let my experience be a warning—even should you win, you may still come out the loser."

SIX

Tears stung Mary's eyes as she glanced about the familiar parlor. The large overstuffed chair where Papa read his paper. The gilt-framed mirror that had once reflected her mother's face. The pictures, vases, and stands that she had touched so many times. Some would survive the move; others would not.

The Godwin family was leaving Somers Town. The thought of forsaking the leafy suburb with all its treasured associations was just too much. Mary leaned her head against the box of books she'd been packing and quietly began to cry.

"Enough of that!" Mum paused in her passage across the room to grab Mary's shoulder and shake it roughly. "We all have work to do, and I won't have you shirking yours. The new tenants will be coming soon, and I mean to leave nothing behind for them."

Mary pulled away. "We can't take the view with us, the green hills sloping down to the river. We can't take the swans or the flowers."

"Are you daft? We're going to London, a city of great opportunity. It will be good for you, good for all of us. Stop your whining and get back to work."

Mum flounced out and Mary reluctantly resumed packing. London might be an exciting place to visit, but who would want to live amidst such clamor? And, as though the noise and congestion were not enough, their London address was to be the worst of the worst. Skinner Street.

"It is a terrible place," she told Aaron Burr, who had been closeted with her father in his nearby study but now paused to chat on the way out. In the past months Burr had become not only Mary's friend, but also a close confidant. "Imagine," she said, "living between a prison and a slaughterhouse!"

His thick gray brows rose quizzically. "The name Skinner is an unfortunate coincidence for a street housing an abattoir."

"That is *not* amusing," Mary chided him. "It's the kind of neighborhood any sane person would flee from, and yet my stepmother has chosen for us to live there. She insists that the publishing house must have a London address. But could she not have picked some other address? Did you know the building was condemned?"

"Your father has made improvements," Mr. Burr assured her. "I rode out to see the house just yesterday. The building is damp, I admit, but there are five floors—plenty of room for everything and everybody. Jane has already established the bookshop on the ground floor, a fine place, too. The windows are low enough for passing children to look in and see the book displays—quite nice, really. The stone carving that your father put over the entrance, of Aesop reading fables to a group of children, sets just the right tone."

"What kind of children are going to stroll by on a street like that?" Mary asked.

Burr patted her shoulder lightly. "I suspect it was the best Jane could find for the price she could afford. Think of it this way: London is a wonderful city. A bright girl—young lady—such as yourself will find much to delight her there."

Mary was doubtful, but what difference did that make? Mum presided as all the Godwin possessions were loaded into three horse-drawn wagons. Sadly Mary placed her own precious treasures—her mother's wedding ring, a note from Papa, and a few scribbled stories of her own—in a drawstring pouch made of tan chamois, which she tucked inside a valise that she would allow no one else to handle.

The house at Number 29, the Polygon, now stood empty. Mum may have seen to everything, but there was much that she had not yet revealed.

As their small parade of wagons rattled through London, vying for space between carriages, chaises, carts, and myriad pedestrians, the neighborhoods grew increasingly shabby. An odor permeated the air, growing stronger with each turn of the wagons' wheels. Mary thought it to be compounded of thick chimney smoke, refuse of all kinds, and excrement, both animal and human. Drawing a scarf over her nose and mouth, she studied the passing scene with growing apprehension. When their driver turned a corner, she gasped. Skinner Street was worse than anything she could have imagined. Offal and blood from the Smithfield Slaughterhouse had been left to putrefy in open gutters, and every kind of trash littered the road.

"I hate it here," Clara proclaimed. "I simply cannot abide it."

"You *will* abide it," her mother replied.

When the wagons came to a stop before a tall, narrow building, Fanny was white-faced, Willie whimpering. Mary looked questioningly up at her father. "Surely we are not to live here?"

"Yes, Mary, I fear that we are."

Moving day was a sorry one, but nothing compared to the day that followed.

———————

Mary woke to the sound of pounding and sawing. What could it be? Climbing from bed, she hurried to the tightly sealed window and shoved it open.

Ugh! Her nose wrinkled. The street below overflowed with stinking filth. The stench was overwhelming. Turning toward

Newgate some hundred yards distant, she saw a small group of men constructing something in the courtyard outside the prison entrance. It looked like . . . Oh, surely not. She turned to Clara, who jostled her. "Could it be—"

"That's exactly what it is," Clara said excitedly, "a scaffold. Have you not heard? Two men are to be hanged this very morning."

The bell at St. Sepulchre's Church tolled, then again, and then again. Below them three men hammered away at a wooden platform. Booths were going up. The street filled before Mary's eyes. She had never seen so many people. Below, men, women, and children pushed and shoved for better views, bartered for crates on which to stand, and finally settled for space to breathe. Raucous vendors angled this way and that, hawking meat pies and ale, tripe and ginger pop. Mary saw posters and flags, miniature scaffolds with hanging effigies. People elbowed and jostled one another. Some bystanders were knocked to the ground. Mary saw an old woman stumble and fall. The crowd knotted over her, tramping and stomping, oblivious. "Stop!" Mary screamed, but no one seemed to hear. "We have got to help her!" she cried, turning from the window.

"Are you daft?" Bustling forward, Mum pushed in between them. Her head beside Mary's, she gave her a disgusted look. "I have locked and bolted the door. You will remain right here."

Just then, the door to the prison swung open. Drums rolled as two inmates emerged, flanked by eight redcoats, muskets in arms. The first prisoner smiled and puffed out his chest, swaggering and raising his bound wrists at friends in the crowd. Two redcoats were forced to drag the second prisoner. Hardly more than a boy, pale-faced, silent, and trembling, he seemed too terrified to move of his own volition. For a frightful instant Mary visualized herself in his place . . . They looked to be about the same age. She shivered involuntarily.

There was a cry of "Hats off!" and then breathless silence broken only by nervous laughter. The first prisoner climbed the ladder to the gallows with a firm step and a smile on his face.

"What did he do?" Mary asked.

"Don't you know?" Again, Mum looked at her as though she were a fool. "That's Sunny Jim Robinson, the highwayman. There are posters of him everywhere. Had a long run, he did. Old Sunny would still be out there if his doxy had not caught him bedding some other tart upstairs at the Cock and Bottle."

"And the boy?"

Mum shrugged. "Stole from his landlord, I'm told. Might as well have killed him while he was at it, the penalty's the same."

Sunny Jim nodded to his executioner, and the two men appeared to exchange a joke. Sunny Jim's teeth flashed in a grin. A hush settled over the crowd as the noose was placed around his neck. Jim raised his bound wrists for a last wave. "Good-bye, ladies, one and all. It was a short life but a merry one."

The hangman swiftly descended the ladder, the crowd so quiet that Mary caught snatches of the chaplain's sonorous words. Sunny Jim seemed to pay little attention. Someone placed a white hood over his head. Mary heard the awful sound of the bolt being slipped. The crowd gasped; the body sank, legs almost still as the rope pulled taut. It was over.

"Cheat!" some cried out in disappointment—there had not been enough of a show to satisfy them. It was a different story with the boy. His legs trembled so badly that two redcoats had to carry him up the ladder. Once at the top, the boy sobbed hysterically. His own water streamed down his breeches as he pleaded with the hangman, the chaplain, *anybody* to save him.

Tears filled Mary's eyes; a lump in her throat felt large enough to choke her. "This is too horrible," she sobbed. She wanted to run away but could not move. The crowd roared with approval as the trapdoor crashed open and the boy dropped through. He twisted frantically, legs kicking wildly in the air. "Die, please, die," Mary whispered. It seemed to take forever.

Later, she learned that the crowd had numbered forty-five thousand. Twenty-eight people had been suffocated or trampled to death and sixty injured. Try as Mary might, she could not get the hangings out of her mind. Though Mum, Clara, and even Fan insisted that the men had gotten what they deserved, she did not agree. Did anyone deserve to climb those stairs knowing there was no return, certain that one's last moments would be spent strangling horribly, twisting at the end of a rope for all the world to see? Mary vowed never to watch another hanging.

She recalled Papa's scientist friend, Anthony Carlisle, who had told of reanimating corpses at Newgate. Was it possible that the two dead men could be brought back to life? Could Mr. Carlisle somehow save the boy, give him another chance?

Even on ordinary days the streets were jammed with traffic to and from the coffeehouse dealers, oil shops, and oyster warehouses that lined the way. Cries of men and animals penetrated the house. Many mornings Mary awakened to the sound of shouting, cursing herdsmen driving their animals to slaughter, and throughout the day she saw fettered prisoners shuffling toward Newgate. It seemed always to be drizzling, and at night a thick, impenetrable fog filled the narrow street. The dampness of the old house crept into Mary's bones. She coughed a lot, and once the coughing began, it was hard to stop. What sleep she managed to get was plagued with horrid dreams.

Despite the unhealthy surroundings, Papa's coterie continued to meet in his second-floor study. The guests professed not to mind the smells, but Mary noticed they each carried a pomander bag when they came to the house, frequently pressing the tiny herb-filled sacks to their nostrils.

One evening Mary chanced to overhear Mr. Burr and Papa in the next room. "William, you have got to get Mary away from here," Mr. Burr was fairly shouting.

The door was ajar; she edged closer.

"Why?" Papa responded. He sounded surprised by the outburst.

"Her education, for one thing," Burr continued. "It is time you gave thought to Mary's future."

"I tutor the girls myself," Papa explained. "They know geography and a little Latin. Enough to get them by."

"That is not enough for Mary!" Mr. Burr made no effort to control his voice. "You need to send her away. That woman you married detests her. Surely you must know that."

"Aaron, my dear fellow, you do exaggerate." Mary heard Papa puff heavily on his pipe. "There is a little dissension between the two, but I am sure that is the case with most mothers and daughters."

"It is more than that," Mr. Burr insisted. "Mary's health is failing. Skinner Street is a cesspool. Newgate reported thirty prisoners dead of typhus this year. This dreadful atmosphere has begun to tell on Mary. Can you not see it?"

A cane thumped for emphasis, and Mary leaned closer, wondering what Papa would say. She was ill prepared for his answer.

"It is impossible, Aaron. I have promised Jane that Clara can go to boarding school. The girl's voice is very pleasant, you know. She needs training. Jane has high hopes for her, has set her heart—"

"*Clara* is going to boarding school?" Mr. Burr sounded furious.

Mary's heart pounded; she had not heard this piece of news.

"You know how determined Jane can be—"

"I do indeed, William," Mr. Burr interrupted him, "but I also know that you have got to do something for Mary before it is too late."

"I wish I could, but . . ." Papa paused a moment. "I have not told you this, Aaron. I was too ashamed. Only Jane knows." He paused again, his voice faltering. "Our—our business is at the bitter end. Despite the success of a few books, the company is failing. It is my own fault. I should never have allowed Jane to talk me into publishing—a damn fool scheme if there ever was one. Half the people in London can neither read nor write. What was I thinking?"

"It is time you began thinking like a father where Mary is concerned."

Papa sighed, his despondence palpable. Mary had heard that sound often lately. "The girl is the least of my problems. Do you not understand, Aaron? We are on the verge of bankruptcy. If I do not get money somewhere, I will have to shut my doors. There is nothing left for us but debtors' prison."

Mr. Burr's voice filled with concern. "I am badly in debt myself, but would fifty pounds be of use?"

"You are a good fellow to offer, but that would not begin to cover it."

"Then what are you going to do?"

Papa's voice lightened. "There is one slight chance. A young lad is coming to pay his respects, a lord—or at least he's in line for a title. He is nineteen, quite wealthy, and admires my work. In fact, he says *Political Justice* changed his life. I think—" Papa broke off. Mary heard a rustling noise and guessed he was fumbling through papers. "I think," Papa resumed, "the young fellow may be interested in helping me advance the causes we both share—liberty and equality, new thought, fresh ideals, all that."

"You would borrow from a mere boy?"

"At his age the money would only go to taverns and whores."

"And just who is this unsuspecting young fool?"

Mary pressed her ear to the wall and heard more paper rustling. Her father apparently was searching for the name. *Papa is wise and good, justified in everything he does.* Who was she to question anything, but still . . . Balancing on tiptoes, she turned to leave yet heard the rest distinctly.

"Yes, yes, here it is," Papa said, as though reading from a letter. "It says here that he is a poet. His name is Shelley, Percy Bysshe Shelley. Ever heard of him?"

SEVEN

Fanny lay awake nights listening to Mum and Papa's frantic, bitter voices. Arguing, arguing—always about money. Newgate was scarcely a block away, and last month Fanny had seen a girl her own age dragged to the debtors' prison in chains. She wondered if the gates were even now poised to clang shut on her family.

Well, not on Clara, surely. Fanny was shocked to learn that her stepmother had scavenged small sums from the household accounts until she'd saved enough to send her daughter to boarding school. She had the tuition paid before anyone knew the money was missing. Clara would depart within a fortnight.

In addition, Papa was sending Mary away "for her health." After some discussion with Mr. Burr, he had come up with a plan. Papa's old school friend William Baxter was a prosperous solicitor residing in Scotland with his wife and two daughters. Mary would live there for a year or two and attend school in exchange for having Baxter's daughters stay with the Godwins on their trips to London.

Papa's letter referred to his home as centrally located, convenient for all the attractions. Fanny doubted that he had enumerated just what those attractions were, because Mr. Baxter had responded with enthusiasm. Mr. Burr had provided the boat fare, and now Mary would be off to Scotland within a week.

Charlie, too, was accounted for—the pittance he earned as an apprentice clerk would see him through. But what of Papa, Mum, and Willie? Fanny hardly dared speculate on her own fate. Once again she was to be passed over. Why was there never anything for her?

Then one morning at breakfast, seemingly out of the blue, a letter seemed to change everything. With a note of pride, Papa removed an embossed page from his waistcoat pocket. "It is from Percy Bysshe Shelley," he announced.

Mum reached across the table and grabbed the paper. "A Shelley!" she fairly screamed. "Is he really one of them? He might be an earl! What does he want? Tell me this minute!"

Fanny leaned forward eagerly as Papa retrieved the letter and read, "'You will be surprised to hear from a stranger, but the name Godwin has excited in me feelings of reverence and admiration. I have become accustomed to considering you a luminary, dazzling against the darkness . . .'"

Shelley, a poet, had published two novels and a pamphlet that he would be sending to Papa, "the regulator" of his mind. The words touched and thrilled Fanny. She knew her father was the most wonderful man in the world; still, it pleased her to have a total stranger agree so extravagantly. Also, it appeared the admirer might be some kind of savior. At least, her parents were pinning their fate upon him. Their arguments had stopped. Conversation now centered on formulating a plan.

"We will invite the young poet and his bride to tea," Mum announced.

"Yes, tea at the first possible opportunity," Papa insisted. "Ask them for tomorrow."

Mum looked about the parlor and frowned. Fanny followed her stepmother's eyes. It was a sorry place—a dark, gloomy room with few windows and floor-to-ceiling bookshelves crushing down like juggernauts. The furniture was battered, the cushions soiled.

"Day after tomorrow," the lady of the house amended firmly.

The invitation dispatched, the Godwin family set to work—not even waiting for an acceptance. There was no time. Many tasks had already been completed when the eagerly anticipated reply arrived. The words, written in purple ink on ivory-coated stock with extravagant loops and flourishes, read simply: "We accept with pleasure." The note was signed "Harriet Shelley." Papa brandished the page triumphantly. Within minutes they were back scouring, sweeping, dusting. Frayed curtains and cushions were swiftly mended, the silver polished until it gleamed. Everyone worked, even Willie. Even Papa!

After much debate, the menu was established. Jane Godwin was adamant: at all costs, a good impression. There would be tiny sandwiches with the crusts cut off—the three girls were up half the night with those—and trifle, rum cakes soaked in sherry and spread with jam and topped with whipped cream. Under Fanny's supervision, the girls baked individual cakes with brandy, raisins, and walnuts, then garnished them with apple jelly. And, finally, the three grand cakes: applesauce, orange, and rum. Fanny breathed a sigh of relief as she surveyed the table. Cooking was one thing in which she could take pride.

All was in readiness when they heard the flower peddler's call in the street below. Clara grabbed her cape and bonnet and dashed down to buy something pretty for the table. One more expense, Fanny worried. They would have to forestall the coal merchant yet another month.

As the door slammed, she turned to survey the room. The house looked as good as it ever could, but her father's waistcoat was snug; his cuffs, despite Fanny's efforts, frayed. Mum's gown was much too tight. Her plump breasts spilled like snowbanks over her décolletage.

Fanny studied Mary thoughtfully. Her sister was dressed in black and looked so tired that Fanny worried she might faint.

"Just what is so special about them?" Mary sounded weary. "Perhaps I will excuse myself. Surely they will not miss me."

"Not if they have a brain between them." Mum glanced up, hands on her hips. "But you are your mother's daughter with those high-and-mighty ways. We need you to impress them."

Papa patted his wife's shoulder. Fanny had seen the gesture often—he was trying to calm her. He turned to Mary, helping her into an overstuffed chair. "Sit here, relax for now, but get up as soon as they come. Shelley can help us, Mary. Save us. Not only is he bursting with idealism, but his ancestors go back to William the Conqueror. Percy Shelley is heir to an estate worth six thousand pounds per annum."

"That is all very nice, Papa," Mary replied, brushing back her fine honey-brown hair, "but what has that to do with us?"

Fanny saw Papa's face turn pink, but only for a second.

Lifting his chin, he began to pontificate: "My contribution to philosophy and literature is clearly enough to entitle me to be subsidized by others more richly endowed with earthly goods. A fervent young romantic such as Mr. Shelley will surely agree that those who have surplus should share amongst the deserving. He is in a position to save our publishing company."

Clara entered just then with tiny pink roses. She had met the Shelleys on the street and was ushering them up from the book-store. With a little curtsy, Clara presented the poet and his wife. The golden-haired Harriet Shelley was beautiful. She wore a ravishing silk gown that clung to her shapely person, and the very latest mode in bonnets, a dazzling confection with a high crown, purple ribbons, and a cluster of curled ostrich plumes.

"Hello," the young poet introduced himself, bowing to each of the women in turn. He was tall but slightly built. His hair was tousled, his mouth tender. Fanny caught her breath as he leaned over her. "I am Percy Shelley, but my friends call me Bysshe." His engaging smile enfolded all of them. "Will you not call me that as well?"

So that is how he pronounces it, Fanny thought. *Bysshe like "dish." How handsome he is.* He had the look of a man who loved the whole world and had no qualms that his affections were fully returned.

Within minutes the poet was chatting passionately with Papa. Both were strong advocates of the Luddite movement. "Ned Ludd is a fine man," Bysshe maintained. "It was only right to tear down those knitting frames. Mechanized looms are putting fine artisans out of business."

Harriet Shelley sat opposite them, resplendent in her purple gown, elaborate blonde pipe curls cascading down slender shoulders. Fanny squirmed, certain that she and her sisters must look like crows in their cheap black dresses.

Fanny rose to heat more water for tea and motioned discreetly for Mary to follow her. She was pleasantly surprised to see her sister looking so much better. The color was back in Mary's cheeks, the sparkle in her eyes. Indicating the striking young man holding court in the parlor, Fanny whispered excitedly, "What do you think of him?"

Mary paused for a moment. "I like him. It matters not how much money he has, there is something sweet about him. His clothes are fashionable enough but so disheveled. I like him all the better for that. It is as though he is not quite of this world."

Fanny hadn't noticed Bysshe's clothes. It was his thoughtful eyes and wavy hair that stayed with her.

"I like him, too." Clara edged beside them into the narrow passageway. "But his wife! All she does is preen in those fine silks and nod her head at his every word."

That was so like Clara, Fanny thought, *always so critical and competitive.* Yet this time she found herself agreeing.

Back in the parlor, Fanny, to her delight, found herself seated beside Bysshe. She turned toward him, heart fluttering. To her surprise, his eyes were fixed on her. Did he see beyond her pockmarked skin? Bysshe smiled, the same warm smile that had first endeared him to her. "Fanny, am I right, the eldest?"

"There are a lot of us to keep straight," she replied sympathetically. "But you are doing well. Yes, I am Fanny and I am eighteen."

"Harriet is seventeen and I am nineteen." His eyes widened as he pointed to Mary, who had just returned to the room with another tray of sandwiches. "How old is she?"

"Mary and my other sister, Clara, are both fourteen."

"Oh, still little girls." He smiled at her but soon got up and walked to the table where Mary stood. Fanny felt as though a warm fire had just been extinguished.

"Who are you, Mary?" she heard him ask. "Are you as pretty on the inside as you are on the outside?" *What a question!* "Are you a reader?" Bysshe persisted. "Do you like to take walks? Perhaps we can take one together."

"Perhaps." Mary looked up at him with a smile that Fanny had not seen before. It was confident and a trifle . . . intimate. Yes, intimate, as though the two of them were the only ones in the room. "That would be nice," Mary was saying. "I am going away, you know. If you are ever to walk with me, you will have to wait."

EIGHT

Depression settled over Fanny like fog. She missed Mary desperately, her loneliness so intense that she even looked forward to Clara's brief homecomings from boarding school. The boys were gone all day. Papa remained closeted in his second-floor study, and Mum busied herself in the bookstore. Fanny wandered aimlessly from room to room, dusting, straightening pillows, putting away Willie's toys.

The one bright spot in her life was Percy Bysshe Shelley, who had settled with Harriet in London. The young aristocrat visited often, sometimes bringing his wife with him. Fanny and Harriet were often left to their own devices as Bysshe and Papa talked endlessly about atheism and the church, truth and government, matter and spirit.

One rainy afternoon as Fanny poured tea, Harriet turned confidential. "Bysshe has always longed for a parent to guide and inspire him." She leaned forward, steepling her small, well-tended fingers. "Now, I believe he has found the wise counselor of his dreams in your father."

Fanny put down her cup as Harriet continued. "My husband and his father, Sir Timothy, were never what one would call close, but when Bysshe's essay, *The Necessity of Atheism*, caused his expulsion from Oxford—well! That was the last straw. Sir Timothy placed all communication between them in the hands of his solicitor. Bysshe was lonely, cut off from everyone, when he came into my life."

A wave of envy washed over Fanny. Why could *she* not have been the woman to fill that void? Surprised by Harriet's candor, Fanny leaned forward, eager to hear more. Despite her spectacular beauty, Harriet was surprisingly unaffected. Fanny poured her guest another cup of tea, deftly turning the pot so Harriet would not see the chip.

Smiling sweetly, Harriet took the faded cup, cradling it in her hands. "Bysshe changed my life, too," she admitted. "I hated school. All those books, and the girls were so unkind. My father is wealthy enough but only a tradesman. The others never allowed me to forget that *they* were landed gentry."

Fanny regarded her companion skeptically. Harriet's bright hair was piled high in soft curls, her shoulders partially hidden by fine lace. It was difficult to accept that this stunning creature had troubles, much less to sympathize. "But you have Bysshe," she reminded the girl.

Harriet nodded happily. "Yes. He saved my life. Truly. If Bysshe had not come along, I do not know what I would have done. And now"—she looked down, a coy smile lighting her face—"perhaps you know. We are to have a child."

"No, I did not know." Fanny's teacup rattled. She blushed at the thought of Bysshe and Harriet naked together.

A wayward thought flashed through her mind. What if Harriet were to die in childbirth? *Oh! What a terrible idea.* Fanny pushed the thought from her head. But still . . . It would be sad, of course, for Bysshe and the child, but she would be there to offer aid and comfort. Is that not exactly what had happened with Papa and Mum? Fanny assuaged her guilt by promising herself she would be the perfect stepmother.

Clara came home from time to time, her whirling skirts and flounced petticoats stirring up a commotion. She was full of French phrases and boarding school airs. "Call me Claire. Claire Clairmont—do you not think it has a ring?" Her cheeks were rosy, unnaturally so, Fanny suspected, and her hair was swept high into an elaborate twist. Claire's bosom was filling out and she flaunted it. Fanny, though four years older, was intimidated by her stepsister's quick confidence and hated herself for her own weakness.

Mary wrote often from Scotland. The Baxter estate was, she said, a place of rugged hills and mysterious caves perched beside the Firth of Tay. Mary described the Baxter family in glowing terms. Mr. Baxter was an expansive, uncomplicated man who enjoyed his wife and children and actually sought their company. Happy and secure, Mrs. Baxter took pride in her girls, an emotion that seemed to encompass Mary as well. Christy was the tolerant, good-natured older sister that anyone might long for.

"In Isabella, who is pretty and blonde and just my own age, I have found my first close friend," Mary wrote. "Here at last is someone in whom I can confide, a special person with whom I can share my innermost feelings. For the first time in my life, I belong somewhere."

These last words cut into Fanny's heart like a dagger. *A special person with whom I can share my innermost feelings? Is that not my role?* Mary's letters made Fanny feel more alone than ever. *Where do I belong? What about me?* she asked herself. *When will my life begin?*

———

Harriet's child was a girl. She named her Eliza, after her older sister. Bysshe called the baby Ianthe after the heroine of *Queen Mab*, the epic poem he had written. Fan wondered if the discrepancy didn't symbolize growing disharmony within the marriage.

If Mum or Papa noticed a rift, they didn't comment. Both eagerly looked forward to Bysshe's twenty-first birthday, when he was to receive his inheritance. There would be a celebration. Fanny fixed pigeon compote, leg of lamb, baked beets with lemon juice, and cocoa flummery with egg whites beaten stiff with costly coconut meat. Papa set aside a bottle of long-cherished brandy. Mum laboriously printed menu cards to inform the guests about the different courses to be served, thus allowing them to plan ahead which dishes might be eaten completely and which merely courteously tasted.

But when Bysshe and Harriet arrived, their faces were downcast. Bysshe's father had connived to withhold his inheritance. Fanny could see that Mum and Papa viewed this action as a personal disaster, but Bysshe was philosophical. "If winter comes, can spring be far behind?" Fanny's eyes filled with unshed tears when he vowed to remain Papa's devoted disciple and promised to borrow money in his own name on Papa's behalf. Bysshe was so dear, so very good and generous.

In an effort to please, Fanny took over the cooking, testing her skills again and again to tempt his fussy appetite. Then one night Bysshe announced that he had stopped eating meat. "Man has no similarity to any carnivorous animal," he informed the Godwins. "We have no claws to hold our prey and our teeth are best served by eating fruits and vegetables." Fanny felt her heart would break as she watched him nibble on browned tomatoes and onion custard.

Dinner conversations mostly centered on books; Fanny had trouble following much of it. No wonder Harriet came less and less often. Papa wanted Bysshe to immerse himself in a breastwork of books. "It is for boarding school misses to read one book at a time," Papa said, encouraging Bysshe to read several at once.

Then, quite suddenly, Bysshe, Harriet, and their new baby left London for Wales. Fanny was stung by their departure. *Was it Harriet's doing? Was she bored with our company?* Summoning her courage, Fanny wrote Bysshe of her family's regret, gently chiding him for leaving without so much as a good-bye. Harriet, whom she blamed for their rude departure, was dismissed as "too fine a lady."

Fanny was excited by Bysshe's speedy response, at first a defense of his wife. "How is Harriet 'a fine lady'?" he demanded to know. "The ease and simplicity of her habits, the unassuming plainness of her thought and speech, have, in my eyes, been her greatest charm." Fanny wondered, *did he deny too much?*

Having laid the issue to rest, Bysshe went on to tease Fanny in his note:

So you do not know whether it is proper *to write to me. I am one of those formidable & long-clawed animals called a* man, *& it is not until I have assured you that I am one of the most inoffensive of my species, that I live on vegetable food, & never bit since I was born, that I venture to intrude myself on your attention.*

Fanny's heart quickened. She was both puzzled and pleased by the letter.

Soon he was back in town but rarely brought Harriet along on his visits. Were they quarreling? Fanny could easily see why.

"She does not understand you, Bysshe."

"No, she does not," he agreed, taking Fanny's hand.

PART II

Soul meets soul on lovers' lips
—Percy Bysshe Shelley

NINE

London, 1814

The coach had barely clattered to a stop before Mary gathered her skirts and scrambled out. Her heart quickened as she ran through the bookshop and up the stairs. Hands trembling, she grasped the knob. The door swung open, and there was Papa beaming down at her.

Mary had been devastated when he summoned her. "It's time you came home," he had written. She had grown to love the Baxter family and adored Scotland, but what could Mary do? Papa must be obeyed.

Looking about the familiar room—papers stacked precariously on battered tables, faded carpets, threadbare chairs, books, books everywhere—she saw that nothing had changed.

"You're early," Mum said without enthusiasm. "You wrote that you were arriving at four. We had planned to meet you then."

"We had a fair wind. I was too eager to be home to wait at the Gravesend dock."

Papa smiled proudly. "So you took a hackney all by yourself, managed your luggage alone? What a brave girl."

"Papa, I'm sixteen."

"I am so happy to have you back," Fanny said, hugging her tightly. "I have been counting the days, the hours." Lowering her voice, she added, "I have much to tell. Something wonderful has happened . . ."

Mary gasped softly at the unexpected sight of Bysshe Shelley, with his dreamy poet's eyes and tousled hair, standing just outside the family circle. He stepped forward, leaning toward her in a way that made their proximity feel startlingly personal. Her heart fluttered as he took her hand.

"Welcome home, Mary. How beautiful you are, even more so than I remembered."

She had forgotten the warmth of Bysshe's voice, soft and gentle. Mary smiled back, drawing confidence from her new frock. The dark, stormy blue-green hues of the Black Watch tartan suited her, she knew. Mary liked the plaid's motto as well: *Nemo me impune lacessit*—"no one provokes me with impunity."

"It is good to be home," she said breathlessly. Bysshe was a daydream transformed to flesh-and-blood reality. Such an attractive reality, but those faraway fantasies had not included Harriet, who smiled sweetly as she moved forward to take his arm.

———————

The Godwin household remained the same hotbed of friction. How different from the Baxter family, who truly *liked* one another. Willie, indulged by everyone, was more fractious than ever. Charlie remained a mischievous tease. Claire, home permanently from boarding school, still had her heart set on being a singer. "Mi! mi! mi! mi!" Her scales rang through the house. Lessons for her meant more tasks for Fanny. "Darling Fan, would you mend this hem? Your stitches are so much finer than mine." "Fan, be a dear and help Mama with the shopping. I would surely go, but señor Passetti is coming to coach me."

"Why do you put up with it?" Mary asked impatiently, but Fanny's soft-voiced reply, "I feel myself a burden," made her sorry to have spoken.

Mum was plumper and a little slower, but her disposition remained unchanged—angry, forever angry. Papa, nearing sixty and noticeably balding, lamented, "Oh, I hate growing old. Why does this ungrateful world refuse to reward my ideas?"

As spring progressed, Harriet took herself and the baby to Bath for a holiday. Her departure puzzled Mary. How could Bysshe's wife bear to be parted from him? But when he engaged rooms for himself on Fleet Street, Mary ceased to think of Harriet. It was a delight to have Bysshe close by.

Day after day, he and Papa closeted themselves with money-lenders. Late one afternoon, Mary saw two of them emerge from Papa's study looking pleased. One paused on the landing to tuck a folded sheet of paper into his wallet before descending the stairs to the bookshop below.

Papa followed on their heels, beaming broadly. Once the men were out of hearing, he whispered loudly to Mum, "We are saved!" Bysshe paused for a moment in the doorway, still gathering papers into his valise. His ready smile was absent, and for once he appeared solemn.

Stepping forward, Mary asked, "Bysshe, what does this mean?"

"It means, my pretty Mary, that your father's creditors have agreed to a post-obit bond sale." When she looked at him quizzically, he explained, "I have borrowed money against my future inheritance to assist your father now, when he needs it."

"But at what cost to you?" she persisted.

The smile she loved returned. Bysshe touched her shoulder. "This is the least I can do for your father. William Godwin is a

living treasure. It is my obligation to free him from paltry con-
cerns. At whatever cost to myself."

Bysshe dined daily with the Godwins. Mary watched him
admiringly, every expression that crossed his face, every gesture
of his hands. He ate little but talked profusely. He wanted nothing more than to reform the world and spoke eloquently against
social tyranny, favoring in its place atheism and the rights of
women. Bysshe was everything Mary admired: an intellectual, a
radical, and an activist. Her parents doted on his every word. She
doted, too, but struggled not to show it. Bysshe's manner was so
provocative. Mary blushed when she felt his eyes on her and speculated, *Does he also dream of me?*

———————

Late one afternoon, as the family left the dining room, Bysshe
put a hand on Mary's shoulder, drawing her into the back parlor. Suddenly it seemed the chipped glass beads hanging from the
candlesticks, the worn carpet, everything about the familiar space,
was rendered in brilliant clarity.

"Sam Coleridge told me a charming tale this afternoon . . .
about you."

Mary looked up at him in surprise.

Bysshe's full lips curved in a smile. "Sam remembers a tiny girl
with long curls escaping her nightcap, luminous gray eyes wide
with fright at his *Rime of the Ancient Mariner*."

Mary shivered. "I remember it, too! 'And the dead were at my
feet.'"

Bysshe studied her. "I can see the other world has a strong hold
on you."

"Do not laugh at me." Her fingertips ached to touch his lips.

"Laugh at you! That same passion got me expelled from Eton."

"Eton!" she exclaimed. "I knew you had been sent down from Oxford, but Eton? Did your paganism begin in the cradle?"

"Very near." He nodded, smiling at her. "I have always loved books on ghosts and witchcraft. One night I drew a circle on the ground, set fire to alcohol in a saucer, and then began an incantation: 'Demons of the air, demons of the fire . . .'"

Mary shivered again, drawing closer to him. "What happened?"

"The headmaster burst in, fairly exploding with fury. He accused me of raising the devil and sent me packing."

She smiled back, thinking how much alike they were in their dark fantasies. "What was your boyhood like?"

"Miserable. Mother may have been the prettiest girl in the county, but it was clear she admired fighters, not lovers. I fear it disgusted her to see me go off into the forest with a book under my arm rather than a gun."

Mary longed to put her arms around him but said instead, "And your father?"

"Sir Timothy is a pompous ass. I doubt that he ever possessed an original thought. Quite unlike *your* father, who has the greatest mind of our age."

Mary nodded. Wonderful as Papa's mind was, she longed more for his company than his thoughts. Could she describe, even to Bysshe, her childish delight on the rare occasions when Papa had drawn her to his knee or stroked her head? "Perhaps if Mother had lived . . . Do you know what *Gentleman's Magazine* wrote of her when she died?"

When Bysshe shook his head, Mary quoted from memory: "'Her manners were gentle, easy, and elegant; her conversation intelligent and amazing, without the least trace of literary pride; and, for soundness of understanding and sensibility of heart—'" She broke off, unable to go on. "How could Papa have forgotten her so easily?"

"He could never forget your mother," Bysshe soothed, "but it must have been difficult for him to be left with two small girls."

"Perhaps, but *Mum*?"

"My poor little Mary." Bysshe's arm stole about her.

It took several heartbeats before Mary forced herself to move away. "You have everything . . . wealth, the promise of a title. Whereas I . . ."

"Nothing is as it seems." He reached out, taking her hands in his, drawing her back toward him.

Mary pulled away, not knowing what to say, and was surprised to see Fan watching them from the hall, her scarred face white and still. Mary beckoned, but the girl shook her head and retreated. Pulling away from Bysshe, Mary walked toward her, but by the time she reached the end of the passageway, Fanny was gone.

TEN

London sweltered in an untoward heat wave. After the clean, sea-swept breezes of Dundee, Skinner Street was more unbearable than ever. Mary found it well-nigh impossible to abide the stench from the sewer ditch, an inescapable odor that permeated everything. If this was May, what would August bring?

Papa rarely emerged from his study; Mum's ranting increased tenfold, a screeching counterpoint to Claire's endless scales. Voice of an angel, indeed! In the past Mary and Fanny had enjoyed quiet talks of books and social foibles, but now Fanny seemed unwilling to talk with her about anything. What was the matter?

Puzzled, Mary recalled her return from Scotland, when Fanny was full of whispered promises of an exciting secret, veiled hints that had gone nowhere. Now her sister appeared petulant and vaguely accusatory.

Mary took refuge in the pages of her mother's travel memoir, *Letters Written During a Short Residence in Sweden, Norway and Denmark*. Late one afternoon, as Mary ran a linen handkerchief across her damp forehead, a single paragraph caught her eye:

> *It appears to me impossible that I shall cease to exist, or that this active, restless spirit, equally alive to joy and sorrow, should only be organised dust [. . .]. Surely something resides in this heart that is not perishable, and life is more than a dream.*

The words spoke to Mary as never before. For years she had sought solace at her mother's grave. Now, with Bysshe's exciting, yet disturbing, presence absorbing her life, she craved nurturing and guidance. Rising from her chair, Mary pulled a light pelisse about her muslin frock. Walking softly through the house and down the stairs, she passed unnoticed. Only Fan, sitting by a window in the bookstore, regarded her curiously. Mary nodded, smiling, but did not invite her company.

Dusk was falling as Mary stepped out onto the street, her favorite time of day. Shafts of sunlight faded slowly to gray, subtly muting the ugliness. How good to be out of the house and away from all of them. Stepping carefully, she made her way through streets overflowing with filth. The alleys through which she passed were a haven for vagabonds, but she knew her way and walked untroubled.

The first star climbed the sky as she approached the entrance to St. Pancras Church. Mary struggled to imagine the spring morning sixteen years earlier when her parents recited their vows. Resentment wrestled with longing as she reflected that had her mother lived, there would be no Jane, no combative stepsiblings vying for the affection of her adored father.

Passing the churchyard, she moved on toward the cemetery. There were no more streetlamps to guide her, but Mary knew the way. The rusty gate creaked open, and she walked softly among the tombs. An owl hooted; all else was still. At last she reached her mother's grave, marked by two willow trees that Papa had planted years before. Kneeling beside the cool stone, she traced the words:

MARY WOLLSTONECRAFT
GODWIN
Author of
A Vindication
of the Rights of Woman

Born 27th April 1759
Died 10th September 1797

A sense of familiarity enfolded Mary like welcoming arms. How many times had she sat before this simple monument, pouring out her heart in the hope that love could transcend death?

Mary needed her mother badly. There was so much she longed to share: frustrations, dreams, and sadness. What was Mary to do? She could not remain at home, not with Bysshe there much of the time. Each day her feelings for him grew stronger. He was forever finding ways to be alone with her, something she could not allow; yet it was difficult to evade that which she most desired. Mary must leave, no question about it. A governess position had been offered her, but the children were odious, their mother a veritable dragon.

"Is there nothing more for me?" she asked aloud, her voice a pleading whisper. "Mother . . ."

A twig snapped nearby. Mary stiffened. Had she imagined it? A form appeared out of the shadows. She stood up, suppressing a gasp, and willed her voice not to quaver. "Who is it?"

"It is I."

"B-Bysshe?" Was it joy or fear that caused her body to tremble?

"Of course it is Bysshe. How could you come here without knowing that I would follow?"

Mary stared indignantly into the darkness. How dare he follow her to this sacred place? "I have come here many times knowing that no one would follow, no living person."

"What a fey spirit you are." Emerging from the shadows, Bysshe pulled a silver tinderbox from his pocket and struck it with a piece of flint. Flame flickered in the growing darkness. Lighting a candle, he placed it beside the tombstone, then took off his coat and spread it on the ground, gesturing for her to sit beside him.

Mary's resentment melted when he took her hand. A violent quiver moved through her. Bysshe's face, so close to hers, was clear skinned, his blue eyes bright inside the flickering circle of light. She had dreamed of being alone with him but was now overcome with shyness. They were silent, staring into each other's eyes. Mary started to back away.

"Oh, not so easy, Mary. I've finally caught up with you. Don't you know, you're in the lion's den. I am a Leo, you know."

Mary suppressed a smile, almost a giggle. She struggled to clear the air. "Claire told me about the letter you wrote to Fan," she said at last, her voice hardly more than a whisper.

"Really! It was merely a friendly note. She was lonely, with you in Scotland and Claire away at school. I thought to cheer her."

"I don't understand what's happened to Fanny. She was all aflutter when I returned, but then she changed, she . . ." Heaviness fell over Mary like a cloak, smothering her pleasure at his nearness. She recalled Fanny's unaccustomed melancholy. "Oh, Bysshe, I begin to understand. Fanny loves you and now . . ." Mary hesitated, her heart pounding. "Surely nothing has passed between you?"

He picked a violet from beside the grave, soft and scented, and handed it to her. "Do you think I would be here if it had?" The rising moon fell silvery across his pale skin.

Mary leaned back against the cold marble tombstone. "I don't know." *What would Mother think of him?* She searched Bysshe's face intently in the flickering light. "I hardly know you at all, and what I do know . . . is Harriet."

Bysshe shook his head and dropped the earth he'd been idly sifting through his fingers. "Can you imagine daily life with a woman who is always pretty, always bright, always blooming, never a hair out of place, never a flaw, never an idea, a single thought of her own—a woman with as much brilliance as a pink-and-white flower?"

"And yet," Mary reminded him, "*you* selected that pink-and-white flower to be your wife."

"It was never an act of passion. Her father insisted upon sending her back to a school where she had been miserable. Harriet was desperate enough to threaten suicide. Now she has no interest in anything but the latest fashions and playing the coquette. She has made herself quite at home in Bath. I hear she finds the attentions of a certain Major Ryan most attractive."

"I can't believe it!" Mary moved closer to him, unable to stop herself. "No woman could prefer another man to you."

"I assure you she does," he said. His fingers caressed Mary's shoulder, moving downward to the fastening of her gown. "Harriet is vain and frivolous—very different from you. She cares nothing for ideals, nothing for poetry."

"I care for ideals and poetry, but I care more for you." Mary was as surprised by her words as Bysshe appeared to be. Her arms assumed a will of their own, stealing up around his neck.

Bysshe held her back. His eyes, intent on Mary, glittered in the dark. "I have nothing to offer you. I can never be free of Harriet."

Harriet! Why even consider her, a woman too foolish to understand and appreciate this wonderful man? Surely a meeting of body and spirit meant more than a mere piece of paper. Passion, terrifying in its intensity, surged through her. Mary's heart raced. She longed to feel his body, taste his skin.

Bysshe cupped her face in his hands and kissed her. Mary tasted his tongue against her lips, thrusting deep and sure. The beat of her heart quickened and her skin tingled. She returned kiss for kiss, pulled him closer, as they removed the clothing that separated them. His hand found her breasts, taut and desirous of him. Bysshe's hand moved down to part her legs. He was patient, finding his way through the silk to her skin. She felt his hardness. Stiffening in pain and fear, Mary cried out. The thought of her mother's deathly remains, her very essence, so close, a witness, thrilled Mary. *Mother, are you pushing me toward him? You are dead and I alive, so alive.* And then, thrusting herself upward into his maleness, she thought no more of death.

ELEVEN

Shadows crept from the encircling tombs. Shivering deliciously, Mary and Bysshe talked in excited bursts, halting only for lush, lingering kisses. They had been lovers for a fortnight, their trysting place the graveyard where Mary's mother lay, complicit in their joy. The future stretched endlessly, theirs to do with as they pleased. Rules were made for others, they agreed.

"We can go anywhere, do anything," Bysshe said, wrapping his cloak tighter about Mary, drawing her close as he leaned back against the now-familiar stone marker.

"Anywhere," she repeated, her hand moving tenderly over his lips.

Bysshe kissed her fingers one by one. "Let us leave tonight— now," he said. "I shall hire a coach to take us to the sea. We will sail at dawn for Calais. A day or two there, and then on to Paris and finally Switzerland. I must show you Mont Blanc. Come with me now."

Mary's heart pounded with excitement, but she shook her head, countering instead: "Tomorrow. We shall leave tomorrow. Tonight I must tell Papa the happy news, Papa and Fanny. Will you not come with me? Surely you, too, wish to take your leave of them."

"Yes," Bysshe agreed. "Our union is so right, so in accordance with your father's views. I shall cherish his blessing."

They rose reluctantly, gathering up Bysshe's cloak and Mary's picnic basket. "I shall miss this place," Bysshe murmured, burying his face in her unbound hair. "How magical that the sacred resting spot of the woman I have admired above all others should be the altar of our love. Only to think that I have won the daughter of such a creature."

Mary turned to face him, raising her lips for another kiss. "I should like to tarry longer."

He slid one of his hands through her hair and kissed her urgently, as though trying to swallow her whole. Mary gave in to it, his breath in her throat. "The sooner we go, the sooner we can begin our new life together," he reminded her.

Fear's chill crept down Mary's spine. Bysshe made it all sound so easy, but she knew their situation was tenuous. She backed away, looked up into his eyes. "What about Harriet?"

Bysshe smiled. "She will understand," he assured her. "What we felt was never love—there was nothing of the passion that you and I share. Harriet and I are merely friends." He paused, musing, then confided, "I have often thought of starting a commune for other like-minded souls. Harriet and little Ianthe shall be the first, but others will follow. What a felicitous band we shall be, a beacon to the world. Why should free souls such as ourselves be bound by outmoded standards?"

Mary took another step backward. "Do you mean that Harriet and her child would live with us? Oh, I do not think—"

Bysshe stopped her with a quick kiss. "It was merely a thought, an idea to consider in the far future. For now I want nothing more than to be alone with you."

"I want it to be that way, too, Bysshe," she said, looking into his eyes. "Always."

The Godwin family was seated at the dinner table when Mary entered with Bysshe. The small room with its dark, paneled walls seemed smaller still with the faded damask drapes pulled closed to keep the insects out. Despite the heat, a wrought-iron chandelier blazed with candles.

Bysshe's eyes sparkled as he took Mary's hand in his. "Good evening to you all. May we intrude with a joyous announcement?" Turning toward Papa, he continued, "I hope, sir, that you will forgive me for stealing Mary away. She and I are sailing to the Continent tomorrow."

Mary looked from one family member to another. Fanny's face had gone chalk white. A fork slipped unheeded through her fingers, clattering to the floor. Mum pulled off her spectacles and glared, for once seemingly at a loss for words. Claire sat perfectly still.

Papa, in the act of carving a slice of cold mutton, slammed his knife down with such force that the platter cracked. "I assume," he said, swinging around to face Bysshe, "that you still have a wife and child?"

Bysshe's eyes widened with surprise. "You of all people must understand how trivial such conventions are when compared to true love. You, who have often called marriage a prison! It was in *Political Just*—"

"Don't tell me what I wrote!" Papa roared. "Mary is my *daughter*. Do you think for one moment that I would permit her to ruin herself by running off with a married man?"

Studying her stepmother's horrified expression, Mary felt certain that she could read the woman's mind. *How can we survive without Bysshe's support?* Rouge blazed against pasty white cheeks as Mum addressed Bysshe. "Surely you would not desert your responsibilities?"

Bysshe turned to her. "Would you, my lady, 'chain one who lives, and breathes this boundless air, to the corruption of a closed grave'?"

"Don't quote your damned doggerel verse to us!" Papa bellowed.

"Mother lived life in her own way," Mary reminded him.

"And all of London thought her a whore for it," Mum countered, satisfaction in her voice.

Mary's face flamed; she fought her impulse to respond to her stepmother, turning instead to her father. "Mother wrote that girls should be taught to think for themselves."

"Yes," he snapped, "but she also wrote that they were to learn restraint and submission."

Anger, pain, and confusion warred within Mary. "While practicing neither," she persisted. How could Papa ignore his own words and the biography he himself had written of her mother?

"That is enough, Mary!" Papa cut her off, turning back to Bysshe. "Good God, man, what can you be thinking? Would you compromise my innocent daughter—the girl you claim to love? How dare you take advantage of my friendship in such a manner!"

There was an awful pause. Mary looked from one man to the other. Bysshe's eyes were wide as he stared at her father. Papa's face was red; a vein pulsed in his broad forehead.

Rising to his feet, he faced Bysshe. When he spoke at last, his voice was controlled. "One thing is clear," he said, "you must do what is best for your wife and little daughter—not to mention the child that is on the way. Leave Mary alone!"

Mary felt as though struck by a lightning bolt. A lump rose in her throat, choking her. "Child that is on the way?" Unshed tears stung Mary's eyes as she turned to face Bysshe.

"I meant to tell you, Mary. I fully intended—" Bysshe broke off, his clear skin a deep pink.

She watched, trembling, as her father coolly surveyed the man she loved. Mary caught her breath, stunned by Bysshe's betrayal of the love that they shared . . . and yet, she reminded herself, the intimacy had occurred before Harriet went away, before the consummation of their own feelings . . . She adored Bysshe. What difference did one more child make?

"It is time," her father said, "that you took your leave."

"Does that mean, sir, that I can never return to this house?"

"No, my son." Papa's voice mellowed to that of a fond and understanding parent. "I was young once. I remember the sudden passions of youth, as well as the follies."

Mary breathed a sigh of relief, but her father was not yet finished.

His eyes on Bysshe, he continued: "As time passes we learn to control one and avoid the other. Of course you may come back, nothing can change the deep bond of friendship that I feel for you. The doors of this house will always be open to you so long"—his voice deepened, demanding now—"so long as you promise never, *never* to see my daughter alone. Do you agree?"

Bysshe stared miserably at the silver buckles on his shoes, then raised pleading eyes. "I love her."

Papa faced him, arms folded across his chest. "If in truth you love Mary, you must forsake this course, which can only result in her misery and disgrace."

"Very well." Bysshe's voice was barely more than a whisper.

"Speak up, lad. I cannot hear you."

"Very well."

"Then I think it time for you to return to your lodgings and pen a note to Harriet. She has tarried too long in Bath. This sorry business would never have happened if she had been in her proper place at your side."

Bysshe nodded but turned his gaze back to Mary. "Darling . . ." he ventured.

She looked away, unwilling, unable to meet his eyes.

"Mary will continue to be your friend, your dear little sister, but nothing, *nothing* more." The gravity had returned to Papa's voice as he tapped Bysshe's shoulder. "Go, son, there is nothing left to be said."

Bysshe picked up his summer cloak, bowed to Mum, and hurried from the room. No one spoke as the door closed behind him. Mary strained to hear the echo of his descending footsteps on the stair.

Finally the lingering stillness was broken by Papa, who leaned forward, looking straight at her. "Now, my girl," he said, his hands clamped down upon her shoulders, "you and I are going to my study for a little talk. Like it or not, you are going to tell me just what the devil you have been doing."

TWELVE

Claire stood in the hallway, ear pressed against the wall as she listened to the shouts and cries—Papa Godwin furious, Mary close to hysteria. Mama finally retired to bed, but Claire adored drama and was not about to miss a thing. Here, at last, was a real one unfolding in the very next room.

Mary's voice, at first calm, grew increasingly frantic. *So, the little witch can cry. Bysshe's graveyard consort is mortal after all. She will not get her way either. Papa Godwin will see to that.* Mary must promise to never see Bysshe alone, to refrain from writing to him, and to absent herself from the house whenever possible when he was present.

Claire gloated. *How very satisfactory!* Something stirred behind her and she turned to discover Fan. The little mouse had stolen from bed and was listening, too.

Mary's sobs carried clearly. "Oh—oh—if I must." The words sounded as though wrenched from her very soul. A door slammed.

"It's over," Fan whispered. "Mary has given up."

"Perhaps." Claire shrugged. "For now, anyway. I would never give Bysshe up. Would you?"

"No, never, not even for Papa."

Claire watched the conflict play out over the course of the week. Mama stood shoulder to shoulder with Papa Godwin. "Mary has always been sly," she announced one morning at breakfast. "It is high time the lazy girl gives up poetry and philosophy and becomes of some use to the family. In the fall she will become a governess. In the meantime there will be no more sitting in the study while the men talk. Mary must clear the supper dishes and manage Willie's bedtime."

A plan evolved as she and Papa Godwin talked. Not surprisingly, Harriet had learned of Bysshe's indiscretions and returned to London. It had not taken Mama long to acquire the address of the town house that Harriet was renting. Papa Godwin and Mama were in agreement. Mary was to go there immediately and allay the young wife's fears.

Shaking her finger in Mary's face, Mama commanded, "You are to assure Harriet once and for all that you are no threat for Bysshe's affections. Convince her that there is not and never has been a romance between you and her husband."

An unlikely task, Claire thought, snickering.

Mary looked from one to the other in horror and pleaded not to be forced into a confrontation with her rival. Little good it did her! Claire saw that Papa Godwin was inflexible. "What if Harriet were to take her case to Sir Timothy?" he demanded to know. "What would her father-in-law think of such goings on? Not only would Sir Timothy be furious with his son, but he would blame you, Mary—blame our whole family. What if he were to disinherit Bysshe? Then where would we be?"

"I cannot do it, Papa," she answered, her voice little more than a whisper.

"You must do it. You *will* do it. Go now and change your clothes."

Sitting unnoticed in a corner, Claire watched with pleasure as Mary reluctantly retired to her room. The little know-it-all was finally getting what she deserved. How tasty. Claire followed her a few moments later and knocked softly on the door.

Mary stood in her shift before a battered armoire. Eyes red and swollen, she regarded the few dresses hanging there. "None is half so grand as anything in Harriet's closet," she lamented.

An understatement, indeed, Claire thought, but she reminded her stepsister, "You are supposed to be acting the penitent. Perhaps your black dress and bonnet would be best."

"If I am penitent, it is only because Papa demands it. I am *not* in mourning. I will not wear that ugly dress or the gray muslin with the white collar either. She will take me for a nun."

Not likely. "Why not the blue silk?" Claire suggested. "Mama gave me a pretty blue bonnet for my birthday. It has a bow in back and a feather in front. The hat would look stunning with your gown if you would care to wear it."

Mary's tremulous smile emboldened Claire to go further. "Perhaps it would be less trying for you if I accompanied you to Harriet's home."

Eyes wary, Mary studied her. "Why should you wish to come?"

Why, indeed? Claire was bored to death reading about life; she wanted to live it. If, for now, her exposure must be vicarious, at least it was firsthand, far superior to a silly novel. "What are sisters for? You need comfort and I should like to give it. Are you not about to enter the enemy camp?"

"I'm afraid the battle is over and I have lost. Papa will never allow—"

"Papa!" Claire's feelings bubbled over. "What does he care about you or anyone else as long as he gets his money? The man is a hypocrite, pure and simple. He writes that marriage is the worst of all bondage and proclaims to all who will listen that love should be free and unfettered, but now he carries on as though he had never preached in favor of the very thing you wish to do." Hands on her hips, she demanded, "What does Bysshe think?"

Mary shook her head. "I do not know. I have not seen Bysshe, but I assume that he is as bewildered as I." Her brow furrowed. "But to call Papa a hypocrite, to suggest that money . . ." Mary stopped, at a loss for words, then continued. "His reaction is difficult to understand, but you must know that Papa is the finest man in the world."

"And Bysshe?"

"Bysshe is the man I love. There will never be another for me, but I must give him up."

Claire suppressed an impatient sigh. In truth, Mary seemed almost as great a fool as Fan. What a relief when Papa Godwin appeared in the doorway a few minutes later. He was so eager to see Mary on her way that he had hired a hackney carriage for her, something he rarely did even for himself.

————·•·————

Silent in the hackney, Mary seemed oblivious to the passing scene, the frustrated cries of coachmen, and the clatter of horses' hooves on the cobblestones. Occasional tears slid down her cheeks, though Claire could see she was trying hard to control her feelings.

Mary blotted her eyes and blew her nose as they turned onto Knightsbridge Road. "Oh dear!" she exclaimed as they pulled up before an imposing brick building with a columned portico, French windows, and two wrought-iron balconies. "I never thought till now that Bysshe might be there, too. I should hate to see him with *her*. How am I to talk with her with him there?"

"It is certainly possible," Claire said, picking up her reticule. "Papa told Bysshe to go home to Harriet. Your job is to reassure her that he will stay there."

"Oh, I know, I know. Do not remind me." Mary adjusted the folds of her pelisse and climbed out of the chaise.

Claire followed her to the building's entrance. A footman in red-and-gold livery answered their knock and bid them wait in the foyer. Claire thought it all quite grand: black-and-white marble floors, a glittering crystal chandelier above a graceful curving stairway. She wondered if Harriet would even admit them.

Mary must have had a similar thought. "Perhaps Harriet is not at home to us," she suggested. "I came here, I tried. Surely that will satisfy Papa. Do you not agree? It is not my fault if Harriet refuses to see me. Let us go home." She turned toward the broad white door.

Mary did not get her wish. The footman returned almost immediately and asked that they follow him.

Icy-faced, her once-slim body swollen with pregnancy, Harriet Shelley awaited them in her drawing room. Claire thought her a far cry from the soigné creature who had swept into their Skinner Street house a year before and eclipsed them all. Harriet's hair was disheveled, her eyes red and puffy, her drawn face white.

The three women stared back and forth at one another. Finally Claire broke the silence. "When is your baby due?"

"In four months." Harriet's hand strayed across her belly.

Claire's eyes wandered around the room, noting that the furnishings were in utter disarray. Portmanteaus and valises were strewn all about, their contents spilling across the Turkish carpet. A painting leaned against the wall; large boxes and several crates remained unopened.

"As you can see," Harriet explained, as though reading Claire's mind, "I have only begun to unpack. The furniture was removed from storage just this morning. Bysshe was to have met me here. We were to build a new life together, but he has not come. Perhaps you know something about that." She swung around to face Mary, who lingered in the doorway.

Mary took a step forward, her face ashen. "I know nothing of Bysshe's whereabouts." Voice firmer, she continued, "I have not seen him in nearly a week and that is how it shall remain. I am aware that I have caused you grief and for that I am truly sorry."

"Sorry!" Harriett exclaimed, her creamy skin reddening. "Do you imagine that 'sorry' is some magic word that makes all the world come right again? Does it in any way make your conduct less abhorrent?"

Claire watched her stepsister's jaw tighten as she looked down. Slowly Mary raised her eyes to meet Harriet's. "No, I realize not. Nothing can change what has happened, but I am here to say that it will not happen again."

"Then that almighty father of yours had best put a leash on you."

Claire saw Mary swallow, visibly struggling to keep her voice calm and measured. Her face flared red. "There is no need of that," she said at last. "I have promised Papa never to be alone with Bysshe, and I shall keep my word."

"Your word! Is that so sacred?" Harriet's eyes dismissed Mary contemptuously. "Just what is so special about you, other than that your name is Mary? A Mary whose only claim is to be the daughter of a whore who had no better sense than to tell the world about it. Pray tell, what did my husband ever see in you?"

Harriet stepped forward, as did Mary. The two glared into each other's eyes, breathing in the same air, until Harriet broke the silence. "Men will say anything to have their way, but of what importance is that? You think Bysshe loves you because he may have said something of the sort. But don't you realize that every-thing he ever said to you he has already said to me, many times? I am his wife. I have given him a child and carry another. It will be a son—I feel certain of it—the heir to the Shelley title. What have you to say to that?"

Mary tossed her head. "*I* am the one he loves. You can never take that from me."

Claire, looking from one woman to the other, saw Mary's eyes turn to silver daggers. This meeting was not going at all the way that Mama and Papa Godwin had planned. Claire knew that she and Mary should leave, but before she could move, Harriet lashed out and slapped Mary across the cheek. So swiftly that it seemed to be part of the same furious movement, Mary grabbed a fistful of Harriet's hair and yanked her head sideways. Claire could scarcely believe her eyes.

Who was this livid stranger? Claire had never seen Mary like this, her face red, her teeth clenched in fury, gasping loud breaths, deep and uneven. Claire thought only of Mama's anger. What if something happened to that brat Harriet was carrying? Sir Timothy would surely see to it that the Godwins never got another cent. "Stop this!" she screamed, pulling her stepsister away from Harriet. "You have got to stop!"

Slowly the color receded from Mary's face. When she spoke, her voice was once more cool and self-contained. "Yes, we had best return home."

Claire and Mary were silent as the carriage jolted back the way they had come. Mary sat with her head tilted back against cracked leather cushions, staring out the window. Claire envisioned the inevitable scene with Papa. He would demand to know what had happened. Oh, this was so exciting!

Heart pounding, Claire watched Mary with eager anticipation as they entered the bookshop, where the whole family stood assembled. Papa Godwin and Mama were white-faced. Fan sobbed uncontrollably. Claire frowned in confusion. How could they possibly know what had just transpired?

Claire's breath caught, but Papa's question took her by surprise. "Does Harriet know?" he demanded, his voice tense.

"Know what, Papa?" Mary looked at him, a quick, startled glance.

"This lad has just come from Bysshe's lodgings," Papa Godwin explained, pointing to a thin young fellow who leaned against the door, his frail shoulders heaving as he struggled for breath. The boy looked frightened, worse than frightened, grief-stricken.

"My master—Master Shelley—took laudanum—a whole bottle of it," the boy stammered. "He was a good master, too, generous and full of jokes, but he said if he couldn't have Miss Godwin, he did not want to live." Sobbing, he raised his head to address Papa Godwin. "The doctor says it's hopeless."

THIRTEEN

"Hopeless!" Mum screamed. "What has that fool done this time? We will never see another pence!" She grabbed her cloak from its peg by the door and threw it about her shoulders. "We must go to him at once."

Papa, behind her, pushed past Mary and Claire and donned his greatcoat.

Mary stood frozen in the doorway, the servant boy's words ringing in her ears. Bysshe loved her that much! It was beautiful and so romantic, but then she imagined him lying pale and still. "No!" she cried aloud. "It is not true." She would not allow it be true. "I am going with you."

"No, my girl." Papa grasped her firmly by the shoulders, moving her back from the passageway. His eyes fixed on Mary's, he spoke emphatically. "You and Claire will stay here and mind the shop—you, too." He pointed to Fanny, who watched white-faced from the landing.

"But I want to help Bysshe," Mary cried, clinging to her father's arm.

"You have done quite enough already," Mum snapped, giving Mary a shove that knocked her back against a counter. Mum yanked open the door, pulling Papa and the boy after her.

From the window, Mary watched them climb into a job-chaise. In a trice they were trotting down the narrow street.

Tears coursed down Fanny's face. "This is your fault," she sobbed at Mary. "Everything was fine until you came home."

Stricken, Mary, too, began to weep. Claire drummed her fingers impatiently on the windowsill. "Oh! Will you two stop! Your fussing helps nothing."

"What do you know about it?" Mary exclaimed. "Mind your own business!"

The day faded to late afternoon; not a single customer entered the bookshop. As the bells of St. Sepulchre chimed four, a post chaise came into view at the far end of the cobbled street. Mary ran to the window, Claire following close at her heels.

The carriage drew near, pulling up before the house. As the driver scurried around to open the door, Mary caught her breath. The descending figure was not Papa. Her eyes opened wide at the sight of the dapper man dressed in a tasseled and corded greatcoat and sporting a shallow-crowned beaver hat. Spying her face in the window, he smiled brightly and twirled his gold-topped cane. Had it been two years?

"Uncle Aaron!" she cried, flinging open the door and running into his arms.

Of all Mary's "uncles," Aaron Burr had always been the best listener. Now, seated beside her in Papa's study, he nodded patiently as she described her lover's talent and brilliance.

"Bysshe is a revolutionary as well as a poet," she told him. "His epic poem, *Queen Mab*, is a masterpiece. It calls for all of us to serve one another, to live and love freely. He writes pamphlets as well as poetry, he—he—" As Mary paused for breath, tears spilled from her eyes. "That wonderful man may be dying this very minute. Perhaps he is already dead, and all because of me."

"Because of you? Really!" Uncle Aaron leaned forward, propping his cane between his legs. "That would indeed be a tragedy," he agreed. "But Mary, whatever the young man's fate, you must think of yourself. This paragon has a wife already, does he not?"

Mary set her teacup down indignantly. "Well, yes, I explained that—that inconvenience. But Harriet does not deserve him! Bysshe is dazzling and wonderful. He wants to change the world. Harriet does not understand him at all!"

Uncle Aaron nodded and contemplated his cup for a moment. "And of course you do."

Noting his sharp-edged tone, Mary looked up. Was he laughing at her? How could that be! Uncle had always been her friend, her partisan. She would have spoken but for the sound of a carriage below. Mary jumped to her feet and rushed down the stairs, pausing only once to glance back at Uncle, who followed, grasping the banister as he descended the steep, narrow passage to the bookstore below.

Mum strutted into the bookshop like a preening goose. Papa stood just inside the doorway. He looked exhausted. Mary hurried to his side and helped him to remove his greatcoat.

"Bysshe is all right," he said, forestalling her questions. "But what a miracle! Your stepmother very likely saved his life."

"That I did," Mum agreed, her flushed face smug. "When we arrived, the doctor had given him up for dead, but I wouldn't hear of it. I pulled that lad right from his bed and forced him to swallow tea—cup after cup of it. Your father and I dragged him across the room, back and forth, back and forth, for hours. Bysshe is very weak, but out of danger."

"I should have been there with you," Mary said. "My place is with Bysshe."

"Mary, Mary," Papa said with a sigh. "The world is not a romantic novel." His face suddenly brightened as he looked past her. "Aaron!" he exclaimed, extending his hand. "What an unexpected pleasure, but my dear fellow, you've come at a dreadful time. A young fool's folly is tearing our family asunder."

"A fool's folly! Is that what you think?" Pain and disappoint-ment squeezed Mary's heart. "Is that all we mean to you?" she asked, staring up at her father. "Yes, I suppose it is."

"What else am I to think? You are a couple of silly children who care only for yourselves."

"The only thing *you* care about is Bysshe's money."

"How dare you speak to me like that!"

"I dare because I hate you!" Mary screamed the words. Turning on her heel, she ran up the stairs to her room. Once inside, she flung the bolt and threw herself onto the bed, sobbing.

A few moments later there was a soft knock on the door.

Mary buried her head in the pillow.

The knock was repeated, firmer this time. "It is Uncle Aaron. I have stopped in London only to see you. I sail tomorrow. I am going home at last."

Going home! That means his exile is over. Mary cringed with shame. She had not asked her friend a thing about himself. He had allowed her to rattle on without saying a word. She hurried to the door. Pulling aside the bolt, Mary stepped back to face him. "I must look a fright."

"Tears will do that," he agreed, smiling. "You must put a stop to them. Let us talk a bit, and then I will be on my way." He pulled up a chair and sat down, facing Mary, who perched on her bed.

As she struggled to choke back new sobs, Mary's words rang in her ears. "I don't hate Papa at all," she admitted. "I love him. What I said—I am so ashamed. It is only that much has happened all at once; I have been so frightened. What if Bysshe had died? It would have been all my fault."

Uncle Aaron patted her hand gently. "You and Bysshe are both very young. At this moment, love is everything, yet I wonder if either of you even knows the meaning of the word."

"Of course we do!" Mary looked up in surprised indigna-tion. "Bysshe and I have each read Papa's book about his life with

Mother and every one of their letters to one another. We feel that very same way about each other, but Papa cares nothing for us. For him, it is all about money."

Uncle Aaron shrugged. "Money matters, of course. Your father must have it if he is to keep the publishing house going, keep his family going. William has given much to the world."

Mary opened her mouth to speak, but Uncle put a finger gently across her lips. "I have a far deeper concern. You speak often of your mother, yet, if you are so familiar with her story, do you think your father—or I—would want you to feel the social ostracism that Mary Wollstonecraft experienced? Would you really wish this Harriet person to be discarded in the same manner as your mother? Think of it, a deserted woman with a young child?"

Mary didn't want to hear such things, didn't want to think about them. How could Uncle Aaron know—how could anyone else know—how she felt? Loving Bysshe was at once heaven and hell. One moment she felt hot, amorous, full of hope and enthusiasm; the next she was filled with despair that seemed unbearable.

"You do not understand," she said at last. "You are talking about old-fashioned conventions. This is the nineteenth century. Bysshe and I are different."

"Really?" Uncle Aaron raised a sleek, dark eyebrow threaded with silver. "Just how different? Bysshe Shelley appears to be a very emotional young man. I would say his actions have already proved him to be naïve and unstable. What he has done to his wife, Harriet, he could as well do to you."

"No, no!" Mary put her hands to her ears. "Papa is wrong. You are wrong." Anger quickened her heart. "Bysshe would never desert me. It is different between us from anything he may have had with Harriet. He has said many times that my thoughts alone can waken his energy. Why, just listen to this and decide for yourself."

Mary drew a letter from beneath her pillow, smoothed the page carefully, and read aloud: "'My mind without yours is dead and cold as the dark midnight river when the moon is down. My understanding becomes undisciplined without you.'"

She sat back, triumphant, and looked at Uncle Aaron. "Could the man who wrote that to me ever be unfaithful?"

Uncle Aaron smiled gently and took her hands in his. "Of course he could—your Bysshe has already proved his perfidy; but for your sake, I fervently hope that it will not happen again."

"It shall not," Mary answered firmly. Her voice dropped to little more than a whisper. "Bysshe will be true, he must be true." She looked into Uncle's eyes, searching for encouragement. She had wanted to share a secret with him, but now thought better of it.

FOURTEEN

The bells of St. Sepulchre tolled four as Mary descended the stairs. On the landing opposite her father's door, she paused. *Papa, Papa, will you ever forgive me?* For a second Mary longed for him to appear in his nightgown and cap. He would quickly put a stop to her madness. For surely it was madness . . . a glorious madness.

A fortnight had passed since she and Bysshe had last seen one another, but using Claire as a go-between, they managed to communicate through notes. "I want to take you away with me," he had written. Mary shivered with excitement. Married or not, she could not imagine life without Bysshe. They were born to be together. Then she thought of Papa . . . and Fan. Both would be shocked, dismayed, deeply hurt. She would miss them sorely. Occasionally Mary thought of Harriet, but those qualms were easy to banish. Harriet was a spoiled rich girl who had proved herself unworthy of Bysshe.

Mary's heart quickened at the thought of darling Bysshe waiting just outside the bookshop. Holding tight to her bag, she tiptoed past the familiar shelves and counters. The door bolt was in her hand; she raised it slowly. The floor creaked. Someone was there, standing behind her in the darkness. Stifling a scream, Mary jumped back as a figure detached itself from the shadows.

"Do not be afraid. 'Tis only me," a woman's voice whispered.

The window beside her emitted a fragment of light from the streetlamp outside. Dimly she discerned Claire's form and saw that her stepsister carried a traveling bag.

Mary gasped. "What are you doing here?"

"I am going with you."

"You are not!"

"If you do not take me with you, I shall scream," Claire threatened.

Mary shrugged, trying to assume a calm she did not feel. "Scream, then. I have made it this far. Bysshe is outside, and in an instant we will be on our way."

"I can help you," Claire persisted. "Really, I can. You speak no French. Bysshe's professors taught him Latin and Greek. What good will those do? I won a prize for my French at boarding school," Claire reminded Mary in a smug voice.

"We will manage," Mary responded, her tone as icy as she could make it.

Claire took another step forward. "Please, please do not leave me behind. You cannot be so cruel! It will be deadly here without you."

Claire's voice was rising. If someone upstairs were to hear them arguing, they would be discovered instantly; Mary's grand adventure would be over before it even began. It was best to get Claire outside where Bysshe could deal with her. Warily, she opened the door.

Mary's lover waited beside a coach. She ran forward, flinging herself into his arms. Bysshe covered her face with kisses. They clung to one another until he looked up in surprise. Knowing that Bysshe had spied Claire behind her, Mary waited for his anger. To her dismay, he merely laughed. "Well, why not? The more the merrier. My intent has always been to form a community of like-minded souls. Claire will be the first."

"But Bysshe"—Mary took his arm, remonstrating—"surely not now. This is *our* trip."

"We have no time to tarry. She is here and ready. We may as well take her." He nodded to the postilion to secure their bags to the carriage roof, then helped Mary and Claire inside. Soon they were clattering away over the cobbles. As they rounded the Old Bailey corner, Mary leaned out the window for a last glimpse of Skinner Street. *Papa, Papa, why must it be like this? Am I leaving you forever?* Another turn and they were headed down the old Roman road toward Dover. Claire settled into the seat opposite hers, tucked her feet up, and was soon fast asleep.

With Bysshe's arms around her, Mary struggled to expunge thoughts of Papa from her mind. What a dreadful thing to have stolen like a thief in the night from her father's house. Visions of his pain and anger left her ill with guilt. *What else could I have done?* Mary wondered. Without her father's consent, she could be pursued and wrested from Bysshe's arms forever.

Mary's ears strained to catch the rattle of pursuing coach wheels. But the streets were deserted, the air oppressively still. The carriage, a post chaise drawn by four horses, was cramped and stuffy. Ten miles an hour was considered a good pace, but Bysshe, determined to exceed it, called out frequently for the postilion to go faster. Waves of fear, fatigue, and excitement swept over Mary as they jolted and swayed.

It was four in the afternoon when he helped her to descend the carriage in Dover; they had been traveling for twelve hours. Mary's legs would scarcely support her.

Bysshe found a bench overlooking the wharf and settled Mary there, surrounded by their bags and bundles. Claire stood idly as he haggled with sailors and customhouse officers, finally hiring a small boat and two hard-faced seamen to take them across the water.

Mary surveyed the craft dubiously, measuring it against the vast expanse of sea before her. "It looks awfully little. There's scarcely room for us."

Bysshe gave her a comforting hug. "I know, dear one, but it is all they have available, and we must sail with the tide."

As the summer sun dipped below the horizon, they glided out from the white cliffs, single sail flapping idly in a flagging breeze. Exhausted, Mary sat on the hard deck, dozing against Bysshe's knees. Finally, just as the moon came up, a heavy swell set in along with the draft the sailors had been waiting for. A breeze caught the sails as lightning lit the dark horizon.

"Calais or Boulogne?" the surly-tempered captain growled.

"Calais," Bysshe ordered. Mary didn't care where they went. She was already miserably seasick.

At dawn the wind changed abruptly. Without warning a violent Channel storm broke, lashing the small boat. Mary, Bysshe, and Claire huddled together in the center, hoping their combined weight would maintain balance as the craft listed heavily to one side and then the other. Often the open deck was only scant inches above the water's surface. Waves swept over them, soaking their clothes. Wet to the bone, Mary coughed and sputtered, salt filling her mouth and nostrils as the spray washed over her.

The boat rocked so violently, she was certain that they would capsize at any moment. None of them could swim, not that it would have mattered in this sea.

The captain, standing at the tiller, swore frightfully at his mate. "Ned, you damned bastard, I told you to drop the jib."

The boat pitched sideways, throwing Claire against the rail. Bysshe lurched across the slippery deck to steady her, but lost his footing. Mary grabbed at him, catching the ankle of his boot as he went over the side, waves engulfing his body.

She clamped both hands around Bysshe's boot; it was soaked, her fingers wet and slippery. "Help! Help me," she shrieked, her voice lost in the wind. Mary clung for dear life, though his weight dragged her forward into the roiling waves, farther, farther. She could not save herself and hold on to Bysshe. *At least we will die together. I will not let him go alone into this terrible depth.*

At that moment, a hard body pressed against Mary. Ned, at her back, steadied her, reaching around to place his strong, firm hands beside her small, frail ones. Together they grasped Bysshe's leg, pulling hand over hand. Barely able to keep his head above the water, Bysshe was a dead weight.

"Ned, you damn fool, get back here!" the captain roared. "Do you want to capsize us?"

Mary's heart pounded. Ned could not leave her now!

He did not.

Pounded by wind, the boat rocked like a toy. Waves washed over the open deck as Claire and the captain struggled to maintain balance from the opposite side. Mary pulled with all her might. Suddenly the craft flipped upright and she lost her grip on Bysshe. For a terrifying instant it seemed that he was gone. Then Ned lunged forward, almost toppling into the sea, and caught Bysshe's leg just as the poet's head disappeared into the waves.

Slowly, slowly they pulled Bysshe closer, until at last they could firmly grasp his lower legs. After a seeming eternity, Bysshe was able to pull his body around and, despite the wind and waves, grasp the side of the boat.

Mary could not believe her joy when she and Ned finally pulled him over the gunwale into the boat. She had wrested her lover from the sea. Bysshe was alive and hers once more. The captain wrapped a blanket around him and held a flask to his lips. Bysshe coughed and sputtered but managed to swallow a little.

Trembling, close to tears, Mary whispered, "I thought I'd lost you. Were you badly frightened?"

Bysshe looked at her, his eyes wide, bewildered. "Yes, at first I was . . . terribly, and then . . . then it was as if the sea were holding

me, embracing me as a mother might. I was not afraid then. I felt—
oh, Mary, if it had not been for the sight of your lovely face above
me, I might have ceased to struggle. It seemed right that I was
there. I felt at home in the sea."

His words, so strange, sent a chill through Mary's body. What
was Bysshe thinking? "Say no more." She covered his face with
kisses. "This is your home; *I* am your home."

It seemed to her that they had no sooner pulled Bysshe aboard
than the wind changed and was blowing them fast into Calais.
Mary smiled as the craft hove surely upon the sands. They were
safe and the sun was shining in France.

FIFTEEN

Mary propped herself on one elbow to gaze at Bysshe's sleeping face. How handsome he was in the pale morning light, soft brown hair falling across high, delicate cheekbones. How vulnerable! Yesterday she had nearly lost him. Today the terrifying memory of his near drowning rendered her lover all the more dear.

Stretching languorously, she relished the feel of the feather bed. Until now, she and Bysshe had shared merely a few stolen hours, precious but painfully brief. How delicious to lie naked in a bed. For a whole night! This was their first morning together.

It will always be like this, she promised herself. Together forever. Nothing, no one could keep them apart now. Bysshe's eyes opened as he reached for her, trapping her legs between his own. They exchanged a long, lingering kiss. He pushed her onto her back and softly caressed her breasts with his fingertips. They lay there for a long time looking at each other. She held him so tightly that she thought their bodies might break, and when their lovemaking culminated, Mary cried. She was not used to crying. The tears ran down her cheeks. It terrified her how much she loved Bysshe, how much he drew her outside of herself and into him.

As his body moved again over hers, Mary heard knocking at the door.

"Ignore it," Bysshe murmured, his lips brushing Mary's throbbing throat.

Knocking turned to frantic pounding. "Let me in! Let me in!" It was Claire.

Bysshe's hands drifted back to Mary's breasts. "She will go away."

Anger and frustration washed over Mary as she sat up. "Claire will *never* go away."

Bysshe got out of bed, grabbed his discarded nightshirt from the floor, and slipped it on. Mary pulled the coverlet around her naked shoulders as he unbolted the door. Claire rushed toward them, white and shaking, dressing gown awry. Her long dark curls hung in tangles.

"The hotel clerk came to my room," she exclaimed, tears streaming down her face. "He says an 'angry lady' is here to see me. It must be Mama. Who else could it be? She has come to take me home, to take us all. What shall we do?"

Beneath Mary's rage and panic, a trace of sympathy seeped in. The poor woman, that awful boat ride . . . Mum had followed them so quickly and, apparently, come all alone. Mary supposed that the captain had told her of their whereabouts. It was he who suggested the hotel to Mary.

"Then we had best go downstairs." Bysshe looked about for his clothes and found them on the floor, entangled in Mary's.

Before he could fully dress, Mum's plump form appeared in the open doorway. Mary could scarcely believe her eyes. It was a Mum she had never seen before: face pale and drawn, hair undone, gown muddy and torn. Seemingly unaware of her unkempt appearance, she looked swiftly from one to the other of them. Her eyes blazed as she turned to Bysshe. "So this is how you abuse my husband's friendship."

Mary's brief empathy for her stepmother faded instantly. How dare she talk in such a way to her Bysshe?

When he spoke, his voice had a hard, flat edge that Mary had never heard. "Go to the lobby," he ordered. "We will speak there. Mary and I will dress and then join you."

Ignoring him, Mum shifted her gaze and pointed an angry finger at Mary. "You were his willing accomplice, were you not? You should be ashamed. Mary Wollstonecraft would be proud of your scandalous behavior, but decent people will despise you."

Bysshe's face flamed. "Never, never speak of Mary or her mother in that manner again!"

Mary sat straight up. "Really, Mum! Just who are you to speak ill of anyone? Where would you be without my father's assistance?" Conscious that the covers had slipped down, exposing her naked breasts, she grabbed at the sheet.

"Oh, do not bother to cover your insidious flesh for me!" Mary's stepmother spat out the words. "It matters not what you do. Stay with him. You two deserve each other. You are beyond redemption! Your own father has disowned you. Whatever dreadful fate awaits you will not be half enough."

She advanced toward Claire, putting a plump arm protectively around her daughter. "My darling girl, I am glad to see that no harm has come to you. I know you never meant to run away. You are too good, too innocent to have left home on your own."

Claire looked down at her bare feet, avoiding her mother's eyes as the woman continued. "This is all Mary's doing. She persuaded you to run away with her, but it is not too late to rectify that mistake. Pack your things, we will leave on the next boat. Hurry! No one must ever know of your part in this folly."

Furious as Mary was at her stepmother's intrusion, she wanted to hug her. Was she finally to be free of Claire? Mary turned eagerly toward her stepsister, but Claire said nothing. Eyes downcast, she backed away from her mother's harangue. Mary's breath caught.

Mum's color heightened, two bright spots flaming against her pasty skin as she stared at her daughter. "Is that how you treat me after all I have been through these past twenty-four hours? Bysshe and Mary have made social outcasts of themselves, but those wicked fools at least have each other. What will you have if you throw your lot in with them? Are you content to merely live in the shadow of adulterers? Surely you will come home with me and enjoy a life worthy of your talents."

Mary watched Claire's face closely but read only uncertainty. What was wrong with the girl? Could she not recognize the logic in her mother's words? Claire would return to London—she must. Her constant intrusion was not to be borne. Mary's heart raced as she waited.

Claire looked hesitantly at Bysshe, a question in her eyes. She reached toward him, her hand faltering.

He returned her gaze, brows raised. "Well, really, Claire, is there any doubt as to which path you should take? Do you imagine for a moment that a few singing lessons are worth the forfeiture of a lifetime of freedom and adventure?"

Mary gasped. "Oh, Bysshe, no! Claire belongs with her mother. That is best for her. Surely you can see that . . . And you and I . . . our life together is only just beginning.

Bysshe looked at her in surprise. "My dear, are you not being a trifle selfish? Claire, too, deserves happiness. The decision must be hers."

Mary's heart plummeted as Claire moved toward Bysshe.

"You had best leave, madam," Bysshe said. "Your daughter has chosen to travel with us."

In that moment Mum seemed to expand beyond herself. The woman cried out in anger, great sobs of fury shaking her wide body. Mary had never seen her so furious as she glared at Claire. "Is this all I mean to you?"

Claire looked down at the floor, avoiding her mother's eyes. Tears trickled down her cheeks, but she said nothing.

"Oh!" Mum exclaimed, her hands turning to fists. "You do not know all that I have done! It was for you—you—so that you could be a great singer, a grand lady. And now here I am, after traveling alone to Dover, frightened to death of the highwaymen, and then . . . and then"—she struggled for breath, fighting to control her tears—"that terrible boat! William was furious when I left. 'Let them go,' he said, but I have traveled night and day. It was for you, Claire. How can you turn your back on me now?"

"I am sorry, Mama. Truly I am," Claire said, moving forward, taking her mother's hand.

"We are all sorry for your distress, madam," Bysshe interposed, "but you can see that your daughter has her mind made up. She is welcome to continue on with Mary and me."

"Oh, no! Bysshe, you cannot mean it!" Mary's heart beat so fast, she thought it would burst. *What is he thinking? Is our life together so unimportant to him?* Bysshe merely frowned at her, his face registering irritation. *Bysshe is everything to me. How can we be so divided on this all-important issue?*

Mum straightened her shoulders. Taking a step back from Claire, she removed a handkerchief from her reticule and blew her nose. Mum stared long and angrily into each of their faces before finally announcing, "Do not imagine for a minute that any of you will *ever* set foot in my house again."

Turning on her heel, she left the room. Mary heard her stamp down the stairs, and then there was silence. Mum's disappointment could scarcely have been greater than her own.

SIXTEEN

Paris at last! Mary was ecstatic. Small matter that the journey from Calais was exhausting, two wretched days in a jolting carriage driven by a surly postilion. They had stopped only to change horses. But now, settled into their tiny rooms at the Hôtel de Vienne, Mary came alive. The thin carpet was worn, the pink-and-lavender flowered wallpaper faded, but she and Bysshe were alone; night had fallen. Claire was out of sight on the other side of the wall. The wall was thin as paper, but still a wall.

After all her longing and frustration had come this wonderful gift of privacy. Mary and Bysshe made love in all sorts of ways, experimenting to see what matter of coupling brought them closer. Mary fancied herself a love goddess, offering all of herself to Bysshe, eagerly complying with anything, everything to satisfy his ardor and her own.

Finally Mary could stand the doubt no longer. Lying beside Bysshe, her voice hardly more than a whisper, she asked, "Was it like this with Harriet? Did you do—all—all that we have done with her?"

Bysshe laughed and pulled her closer. "Never. You and Harriet are nothing alike. She was mostly concerned with not getting her hair mussed. It was like sleeping with a monument. You, my marvelous Mary, are wild and free, filled with passion and imagination and eager for every experience. I cannot get enough of you, my queen of earthly delight."

A sense of adventure intoxicated Mary as a new world of promise opened before her. She thought often of her mother and tried to picture the Paris of her day, a city alive with soldiers, tricolor flags, and rolling drums. Mary was aware that her mother had experienced her greatest joy in Paris. Mary Wollstonecraft had, like her, been passionately in love. Now it was Mary's turn.

Grateful that Claire was a late sleeper, Mary saw to it that she and Bysshe were out early. Paris was their private preserve to discover as they wished. When they visited the newly reopened Louvre, Mary imagined her mother walking there with her lover, Gilbert Imlay, among the first public visitors after the Revolution transformed the royal collection into a museum for all. Mary could almost see them strolling down the same corridors, admiring the same masterpieces. Knowing that Fan had been born in Paris, Mary felt a twinge of guilt at the thought of her sister languishing at home. She wondered, too, about Fanny's father. What sort of man was Gilbert Imlay? Had Imlay been gallant? Handsome? Had he paused to pay homage to the marble nymphs from ancient Greece? "Their breasts are no more lovely than your own," Bysshe whispered in Mary's ear. Had Imlay paid the same kind of compliments to her mother?

When they explored the Tuileries Garden, Mary imagined her mother walking before her. *Liberté! Égalité! Fraternité!* Mary could almost hear the rallying cries, see the royal palace pillaged and burned, the king conveyed to his execution in an open carriage— his own—accompanied by an honor guard. *Mother was here, she saw it all,* Mary thought again and again. What an adventurous life! Mary smiled, certain that her life had taken on a wild and wonderful new direction of its own.

On the morning of August 4, Mary reminded Bysshe that it was his birthday. He smiled, bemused. Now twenty-two, he professed to have forgotten the occasion. "Really, I thought my birthday was the twenty-seventh of June."

"How can that be?" she asked. "You once told me—"

"The twenty-seventh of June was the day you first said you loved me, the night we first made love." He took her into his arms, kissed her neck, and sank his teeth into her skin, sucking so hard, Mary knew he would leave a bruise. She didn't stop him, wanted his mark upon her.

Like Mary, Bysshe was ecstatic much of the time. But she knew he also worried. Their plan to journey on to Switzerland had run into obstacles centering on money. Impatient to run off with her, he had neglected to visit his London solicitor; now they were rapidly running out of funds. Upon reaching Paris, Bysshe had written an imploring note to his publisher, Thomas Hookham, asking for a loan to tide them over. Not only did Hookham refuse to help, but his letter was bitterly critical. He castigated Bysshe, calling his elopement "unconscionable."

Mary handed the letter back to Bysshe. "I wonder if Mr. Hookham's been talking with Papa."

"Or Harriet," Bysshe responded glumly.

In desperation, he sold the pocket watch and chain that had been given to him as a boy by his beloved grandfather. The proceeds kept their party of three going for a few days, just long enough to arrange for their passports and secure a loan of sixty pounds from the bank. "We'll have to walk." Bysshe smiled cheerily. "It won't be difficult—I've engaged a friend to help us. Come meet him, he waits just down the street."

Dutifully Mary put her arm through his as they traversed the narrow cobbled street. Realities that she had first eluded were closing in. France had so recently been a country at war. Though not under direct attack from the Russians, Paris was swollen with casualties. So many crippled men, so many orphaned children, all trying to sell whatever they could. Bysshe bought two apples, the most he could afford. Bruised and soggy, they were scarcely edible. Mary speculated that the glorious Revolution of her mother's time had not gone so well after all. Napoleon had not conquered Europe, but in fact had retreated from Moscow. The French Revolution had promised so much—representative government, the end of aristocratic rule—but delivered very little.

Hurrying to elude the beggars, they were breathless by the time they reached the large wooden building that appeared to be Bysshe's destination.

Mary was growing worried. "This looks like nothing more than a stable."

"Exactly, my dear," he said, leading her inside. "And here is our new friend, Henri."

Mary's heart sank as she looked into the large eyes of a diminutive donkey. "Henri?"

"He will be our companion along the way to Switzerland," Bysshe explained, "the bearer of our bundles."

Mary considered how little walking she had actually done in London and that her shoes were cheap and flimsy, scarcely more than slippers. She looked up at Bysshe, who was obviously pleased with himself. Mary forced a smile. "Henri will be a fine addition," she said, taking his arm.

"We will leave early tomorrow morning," Bysshe announced as they strolled back to the Hôtel de Vienne.

Mary glanced at him in surprise; their time in the capital had been short. Bysshe was smiling brightly. Her apprehensions faded. They were moving on, beginning a new life together. Of what matter was anything else?

SEVENTEEN

"*Vous êtes fous!*" The concierge of the Hôtel de Vienne looked incredulous. "*Comprenez?* Do you understand me?"

Bysshe looked up from the bill he was tallying. "What are you saying?"

"Do you not read the papers?" The concierge stood back to survey them, red-faced, hands on hips. "France has lived with war for twenty years. Millions are dead—God alone knows where it will end. Those bloody Cossacks—dirty dregs of the Russian army— will never leave. What they can pillage from us is the best they have ever had in their lives, but we French are starving. Brigands and deserters are everywhere. What can you be thinking! Three children and a donkey traversing a massacre!"

Bysshe and Mary exchanged glances. She saw excitement in his eyes, knew it mirrored her own. *Fous*, crazy, what did it matter? They were going! "If *you* want to go home, Claire . . ." Mary smiled.

"Go home! And miss Switzerland!" Claire picked up her bag and marched outside to where Henri waited with their other baggage.

<hr/>

From Paris, the three walked steadily southeast across the recently devastated countryside, sometimes covering as much as ten miles in a single day. The sickening odor of putrid flesh hung in the air.

Dead and dying horses lay by the road, blood and intestines draining from bloated bodies. A few poor creatures tried to follow, pulling themselves up on broken, trembling limbs only to fall back helplessly.

Abandoned tables, chests, broken toys, and crockery littered the roadways, and from time to time, they saw crumpled human bodies, once a severed arm. Mary clenched her teeth to keep from crying. Perhaps Bysshe and Claire did the same. No one spoke.

They passed ruin after ruin, most of them humble cottages burned to the ground. Frightened by the sound of gunfire, their small party took cover in one such hovel. The odor of burnt flesh permeated its smoldering walls. Stomach heaving, Mary rushed outside, vomiting again and again. She would take her chances in the open.

At night they stayed at post stations that were increasingly filthy and ill stocked, their greedy managers often hostile. One evening the travelers had nothing for dinner but sour milk and stale bread with rancid butter. In Guignes, they slept at an inn hastily vacated by Napoleon three months before. Bysshe was thrilled by the connection, his eyes shining with admiration. "Napoleon is a man among men. His ideals, his daring, will live forever."

Mary stepped back, staring at him in dismay. "What sort of liberty is this? Where is the 'brotherhood' among dead people? Is Napoleon not responsible for this devastation? He caused this massacre by invading Russia, and now the Cossacks have turned his invasion around. It is only right that he was forced back into France, but look at the desolation around us!"

Bysshe stared at her, eyes wide. "Mary, Mary, what is the matter with you? Do you not understand! History is being made before our very eyes. We are living it."

How could the man she loved admire such a fiend? Mary turned away, saying no more lest their happiness be marred. But living in history, indeed! The countryside was strewn with battle-weary

French soldiers poised to renew war or enforce peace—they knew not which—and populated by frightened inhabitants who viewed the small party of English youths with wary distaste.

Surrounded by gruesome tragedy, Mary felt ashamed of the small problems besetting their party. They seemed so inconsequential in comparison, yet how much longer could she go on?

Reaching into Bysshe's knapsack, Mary carefully removed his knife from its scabbard. Forcing herself, she approached a soldier's corpse lying by the roadside. One leg had been blown away, the other still bore a boot. At first gingerly, then with all her strength, she pulled the boot from his foot.

"What are you doing?" Bysshe and Claire asked, almost in unison.

"The sole of his boot appears to be in good condition," Mary explained. At first she felt like a ghoul, carving through the leather. *But he is dead and I alive.* To stay that way, she must deal with the problems at hand. Mary had cuts and blisters; the soles of her feet were bare and bleeding. Carefully she inserted the leather into what was left of the bottom of her slipper. Slipper! How foolish they had been, so ill prepared. She and Claire wore their best dresses, now dusty and torn. Mary resolved to search the next corpses they came upon for a small pair of boots.

A few moments later Bysshe slipped on a string of intestine lying on the road and badly sprained his ankle. The recalcitrant Henri turned traitor, refusing to carry him. What could they do but bid farewell to Henri and exchange him for an expensive mule, which proved almost as intractable.

That night in their room, Mary clung to Bysshe. "Are you sorry, Mary?" he whispered in her ear.

"Never once," she assured him, yet Mary worried constantly. She had missed two menses and was often ill. Was she carrying his child? She understood the problems that beset Bysshe and saw how hard he tried to conceal the pain in his ankle. It was best not to add yet another burden. If nothing changed, she would tell him when they reached Switzerland. All would be well then, she felt certain of it.

Despite the exhausting days and devastating sights, their nights together were blissful; her skin tingled with pleasure at his touch. To Mary, this was the supreme affirmation of life. Again and again, she marveled at the pleasure Bysshe evoked in her and took pride in her power over him.

One night, just as Bysshe's lips moved down between her breasts, a wild shriek cut through the darkness and a body flung itself upon their bed. Mary screamed in terror. She and Bysshe untangled their limbs and sat up. It was Claire.

"I cannot stand it!" she sobbed. "Rats are in my bed. I felt their cold paws on my face. Please, please, let me sleep in here with you."

What could Mary say?

They traveled eastward, Claire more often than not sharing their bed. Sometimes Mary thought of home, clean clothes and bedsheets, decent food. She longed for her father and missed Fan. But Bysshe was her life and he was here beside her. Their love would never change . . . If only it were not for Claire, who was never far away.

Then one day, through a space in the trees they glimpsed the breathtaking sight that they had eagerly awaited. Hill after hill formed a craggy outline, and beyond, towering above, the snowy Alps. Though awestruck by the grandeur, Mary felt overwhelmed by the force and menace in that gigantic mass. Could her feelings be captured in words? She vowed one day to try.

Bysshe pointed to a sign; they were but six miles from the Swiss border. With their new home now so near, Mary felt her spirits rise. Claire, who claimed to be half Swiss, pointed out the differences she discerned from the French. "Look how clean the people are," she said. "Much more industrious and friendly."

Mary had to agree that the Swiss children were plump and rosy, but then their home had not been the last haven of starving French soldiers or the focal point of avenging Cossacks. There was another pleasant difference. The Swiss greeted the travelers with friendliness rather than suspicion. That night they slept in a snug inn—two rooms with thick walls between them, and crisp, clean sheets. Mary locked the door. She and Bysshe were truly alone. If there was a heaven—as an atheist's daughter, Mary wasn't sure—this was it, paradise.

———•———

The next day's problems, however, were very much of this earth. No letters awaited Bysshe at the *bureau de poste*, and they were dangerously low on funds. While Claire and Mary waited outside on a wooden bench, Bysshe appealed to the town banker. His letter of credit was now soiled and crumpled. Could the banker read it, let alone believe this bedraggled young man to be the heir apparent he claimed to be?

To Mary's immense relief, Bysshe returned with thirty-eight Swiss francs, enough to buy carriage tickets to Lucerne and keep them for a time in Switzerland. At six the next morning, they were on their way.

Pressed close in the crowded carriage, Bysshe and Mary talked of poetry. As they crossed a meadow, he quoted a verse of his own:

Thou wert my purer mind;
Thou wert the inspiration of my song;
Thine are these early wilding flowers,
Though garlanded by me.

But Claire was not to be ignored. "Are the lambs not adorable? What pet shall we get when we reach our new home?"

Bysshe was patient. He liked to play the teacher, and Claire was an eager pupil. She chattered on and on. Mary's spirits no longer soared at the craggy peaks and rock-scarred slopes. The stony monoliths closed in. The constant swaying of the carriage made her queasy. Mary chewed on a slice of dry bread, hoping to subdue the rising wave of nausea. *Would this journey never end?*

Three more days of travel and they reached the shores of Lake Lucerne, where Bysshe booked rooms for them. The lake outside was turbulent, with choppy waves breaking again and again on the shore. It was romantic as long as Mary kept her eyes closed and listened to the water. When she opened them, she saw the dirty room with its grimy walls and lumpy, coarse bed, greasy from the unwashed bodies of previous occupants.

"We have to get out of here," she insisted the next morning. "Bysshe, you must find us a place of our own."

Dutifully he set out but soon returned, frustrated, miserable, his swollen ankle throbbing.

It was Mary who finally found them a home. Not much—two rooms in a large, ugly house that someone with a sense of humor had named The Chateau. Bysshe and Mary would have one room, while Claire would sleep on a daybed in the other, which would also serve as a sitting room and tiny kitchen. Bysshe rented it for six months at one louis per month.

They settled in. This was their dream. Surely other like-minded people would follow them to Lucerne. It would not be long before scores of writers, poets, and artists of all kinds arrived.

In the meantime, Bysshe and Mary began work on a novel, *The Assassins*. Writing with Bysshe was glorious. Their ideas flowed easily together, for it was their own story they told, the drama of Bysshe and Mary played out in a Utopian paradise where life is gentle, love is free, and illegitimacy unknown. Every baby was a wanted baby. It was in writing about such a place that Mary summoned the courage to tell Bysshe about their own child.

She feared his reaction. Bysshe already had one baby in London and another soon to be born. Given their life and finances, it was hardly the time, yet she could no longer hide the truth from him. Mary watched Bysshe closely.

His face clouded—but only for an instant. Then he took her in his arms, a warm smile on his lips. "It is *our* child, Mary, conceived out of our love."

Mary breathed an inward sigh of relief. This was the reaction she had dreamed of yet feared she would not hear. Nothing could part them now.

EIGHTEEN

The next day, Claire woke bored and restless. "I am tired of all this," she announced to Mary and Bysshe. "What am I to do when you are writing? A baby will make it all the more boring. We are already so poor. How will we manage? I want to go back to England."

Bysshe looked up, startled. "Go back?"

Mary's heart pounded with excitement. She took his arm. "Why shouldn't Claire go? She knows the way. Give her some money and let her be gone."

Bysshe looked stricken. "There's very little money left. What would happen to a girl traveling with no funds?"

Mary turned to Claire, exasperated. "Coming with us was your idea," she reminded her. "Now you will have to make the best of it."

Claire began to cry. "You are too cruel, both of you. We have seen Switzerland. Must we stay forever? You can write your silly novel anywhere."

Bysshe stood looking from one woman to the other. "This was our plan—Switzerland was to be the center of our commune. We have to begin somewhere." He took Mary's hand in his. "Tell me truly, Mary, what do you think?"

What did she think? Mary glanced around the room. The apartment that had taken almost all of their money was ugly, the view from the small windows oppressive. Their dreams of founding a commune now seemed unrealistic. Who would want to come here, and how could they feed any who did? Was there a chance that Papa might forgive her if they returned? Surely he must know how much she loved him. Then, too, there was Fan. How pleasant it would be to enjoy her easy company again.

Still, none of this would have been enough to turn Mary from the dreams she shared with Bysshe. It was only the thought that, once in London, Claire would go home to her mother that tipped Mary over the edge of decision. For all Mum's angry words, she adored her daughter and would surely take her back.

Mary squeezed Bysshe's hand. "We will come back to Switzerland someday. I know we will. But for now, I should like to have my baby in London."

Their mode of travel was quickly decided upon. Barges plied the Rhine from Basel to Rotterdam. They were slow, cumbersome, uncomfortable, sometimes even dangerous. Unfortunately, a barge was all they could afford.

Few but students and peasants traveled in this manner, and they, for the most part, were a rough and dirty lot. Mary fled their vulgarity below deck, but the tiny cabin she shared with Bysshe and Claire was close and smelly. Feeling queasy, Mary made her way back onto the deck, where Bysshe sat listening to Claire's latest nightmare. The girl had taken to having them nearly every night. Invariably, Bysshe had to soothe her to sleep. *Enough!* Mary wanted to scream.

The deck was crowded: nursing mothers, pushing and shoving children, men clinking their steins and singing raucously. The very air was tainted by beer, sweat, and vomit. Mary walked farther down the deck but found no available seating. What would it be, the stuffy cabin or Claire's nightmares? Two young men spared her the decision. Rising from their deck chairs, they bowed stiffly. "I am Heinz Muller," the taller one introduced himself. His accent was thick—German, she imagined.

"And I am Johann Schmidt," the other added. "We study at the university in Heidelberg." The two were the most presentable passengers Mary had yet seen on board, clean shaven and not too shabbily dressed. She guessed them to be only a year or two older than herself.

"Fräulein, there is a place for you," Heinz said in thick, halting English. He indicated a cozy nook out of the wind and splattering rain. The bench cushions looked almost clean. "You can see the river without the splash."

Mary smiled, thanking them as they bowed again and backed away. She pulled a book of poetry from her reticule and began to read. When she looked up a few minutes later, they were gone.

The barge docked at Darmstadt on August 30, Mary's seventeenth birthday. She had looked forward to exploring the city with Bysshe. If only Claire would leave them alone. The three of them had taken refuge from an intermittent drizzle under the roof of a small beer garden. There was a music hall across the square. Perhaps Claire would amuse herself there for an hour or so?

She appeared shocked at the suggestion. "Oh, no, I would be afraid without Bysshe—without the two of you. Besides, I am reading *King Lear*. It frightens and confuses me. Bysshe, if you could explain this part." Claire had brought the book with her and held it out to him, page open.

Impatiently, Mary rose from the table, assuming that Bysshe would stop her. Instead, he bent his head over Claire's book. Mary moved to the door, her heels clicking angrily. Two passengers from the barge were looking out onto the street. Johann and Heinz. They smiled and bowed.

"The rain. It is beginning to clear." Johann spoke the words carefully. He seemed eager to practice his English.

"*Ja*," Heinz added, turning to Mary. "We take a carriage to give a—a good view of the stones—the fortress. Would you not come with us?"

She shook her head. Leaving with two strange men was unthinkable; still, Mary longed to get a closer view of the castle ruins she had seen from the barge.

"It is not far," Johann urged.

"We will return in one hour," Heinz added. "It is only a few miles."

Mary glanced over her shoulder at Bysshe and Claire, who were clearly engrossed in conversation. They had not even noticed she was gone. Mary shrugged. Why not? She had had enough of being ignored. This was her birthday! Why not an adventure just for her?

Once inside the carriage, she wondered at her actions and eyed the students warily. They were studying her as well, possibly as surprised as she at such impulsive behavior. Mary smiled and they smiled. Soon they were practicing words and phrases on each other, their English far better than Mary's German.

Before long the carriage stopped. The students helped Mary to alight, and they made their way onto a low stone abutment overlooking a tributary of the river. "Look there." Johann pointed.

Following his gesture, she saw a stone fortress towering above the Rhine. Fallen to ruin, it still looked imposing, with large battlements, turrets, and towers. "Oh, I should like to see the inside," Mary exclaimed.

"*Nein*, you would not." Heinz shook his head. "A monstrous thing happened at the fortress."

"Monstrous? Really?" Clearly they were trying to intrigue her—and succeeding. "Tell me about it," she urged.

Johann leaned closer. "A young man lived there years ago," he explained. "His name was Konrad Dippel and he was a kind of— how do you say—rogue. Herr Dippel left home to study medicine."

"A rogue, you say," she prompted. "How so?"

Heinz picked up the story. "The young Herr Dippel left his university and returned home to—to pursue his *Wunsch*, his passion."

"His passion?" Mary echoed. She felt a faint chill at the base of her spine.

"Dippel was an alchemist," Johann explained. "Do you know this word? He tried to make the *Zaubertrank*—how do you say— potion? He made a potion." Johann paused, his eyes intent on hers as he struggled to express himself. "This potion, it was for making *lang Leben*—a long life. In Darmstadt, they said he looked for body pieces, dug them out of their graves to grind into *der Eintopf*, his evil stew. The townspeople said he did the unspeakable."

Unspeakable? Mary leaned forward eagerly. She remembered her father's friend Anthony Carlisle. Had he not experimented on prisoners at Newgate Prison? Mr. Carlisle had also hoped to bring back the dead. Such an exciting possibility! "Was there not something admirable about the young man's daring?" Mary asked. "Is it wrong to want to push back the limits of nature?"

"Ah, *nein*, Fräulein!" Heinz broke in. "You will not think it good when you hear what happened. One night there was a great storm, thunder rolled down from the mountains, lightning struck the castle again and again. It was as though sent by God himself. *Ach!* A fearful thing! The next morning the young scientist was found lying dead beside his cursed vials. Yet even that was not the end. Villagers say Dippel's troubled spirit haunts the fortress still. They say tombs were destroyed, bodies stolen."

Shivering, Mary looked up at the ruin towering above them. "The fortress does lend itself to legend."

"Tragedy, *jawohl*, but not legend," Heinz replied. "Those things happened in my great-grandfather's time, 1734. Though the fortress is, as you see, deserted and fallen to ruin, it still belongs to a branch of Herr Dippel's family."

"Really!" Mary looked up at the bastion in wonderment. "Let's climb up and go inside. Who knows what we may find . . . body parts, vials, perhaps even the remains of the potion."

The two men looked uneasily at one another and then back at Mary. "*Nein*, Fräulein," Heinz said. "It grows late."

"*Ja*," Johann agreed, "we must return to the barge." He politely took her arm as Heinz led the way down the hill to their carriage.

Reluctantly Mary complied. As she was about to ascend into the carriage, Mary took a last look at the citadel. "What is the name of this place?"

As Heinz took Mary's hand to help her, he glanced back nervously. "They call it Castle Frankenstein."

PART III

I have drunken deep of joy,
And I will taste no other wine to-night
  —Percy Bysshe Shelley

NINETEEN

Alighting from the hackney, Tom Hogg paused to look with surprise at the narrow street before him. The buildings were nothing more than tenements. What could Shelley be doing in a place like this? Tom's cane hit the street with a thud. Gloved palm wrapped loosely around the griffin's head, he waved the driver away. Since Oxford, he and Shelley had had their share of ups and downs, yet nothing as low as this. Tom shrugged his broad shoulders. His mission was to talk sense to his friend. Surely one venue would do as well as another.

That business of abandoning Harriet—the splendid girl he himself had long fancied—for some conniving strumpet could not be ignored. It was up to Tom, Shelley's closest friend, to set things to rights. Why, if he had not been in York studying for the Bar, none of this would have happened. Leaving Harriet to run off with some girl—two girls, it was rumored—to the Continent was unthinkable. But now, Tom was relieved to hear, the ill-starred trio was back in London. Their sojourn abroad had lasted a scarce six weeks. Surely Tom was the very one to sort it out, to send the two girls packing and see to it that Shelley returned to his true love, the deserving Harriet.

Tom looked dubiously at the street before him. It was no more than a path of mud and refuse. Sewage ran in rivulets from the surrounding courtyards and alleys. He heard a shriek from an upstairs window patched with rags. The sound of blows and curses followed. Tom stepped over the prone body of a drunken woman, legs covered with her own filth, and hurried on.

When he at last reached the address he was seeking, Tom found the building no worse nor better than its grimy neighbors. Though in good form, Tom was winded by the time he reached the garret apartment. He was also shocked. What was his friend doing in such a place? Tom knocked tentatively. There was no answer, but he sensed a presence on the other side of the door. He knocked again more firmly. "Shelley!" he called. "Shelley, are you in there?"

He was rewarded by the sound of a bolt being pulled back. Slowly the door opened to reveal a young woman.

"I am Thomas Hogg," he said, removing his hat. "Shelley and I are old friends. We went to Oxford together—" He paused, stunned by the woman's large gray eyes. Tom thought he could drown in their depths.

"I know exactly who you are," she informed him, a smile brightening her pale face. "Bysshe has spoken of you often. I am Mary Godwin."

Shelley's mistress was not at all what Tom had expected. She was perhaps not a classic beauty in the manner of Harriet, but her face was nevertheless pleasing. Quite pleasing. Miss Godwin had a slim, graceful nose and high cheekbones. When she smiled, as she was doing now, her teeth were neat and white. He could not get enough of looking at her.

With some embarrassment, Tom realized that he had been staring. It was as though there were just the two of them in the whole world. "I am honored to meet you." He heard his voice as if from a distance.

Mary took Tom's topcoat and gestured for him to take a seat in the room's one sturdy chair. At first she appeared lighthearted, but as the moments passed, Mary grew quiet. "I—I wish I could offer you tea," she said at last. "But we have no flint left to light the fire."

"I can fix that," he said, jumping up. "I always carry flint to light my pipe, and if you've a bit of paper, we can get something started in the grate." Mary scurried about, finding old parcel paper and a bit of newsprint. There were a few lumps of coal in the grate, and with a little effort Tom got a small fire ready for Mary's copper kettle. Soon she was busy assembling the tea things.

"How is Shelley?" he asked, leaning back in his chair.

"I do not know," Mary answered, her voice grown soft.

To Tom's surprise and dismay, he saw tears form in her eyes.

"Whatever is the matter?" he asked, taking her hand in his. It was icy. No wonder; the room, a shabby place with worn furniture and faded draperies, felt glacial. Tom longed to retrieve his topcoat but didn't want to embarrass her. If only he might wrap it around her slender shoulders.

Mary gently withdrew her hand and busied herself pouring tea. "It has been so long since I have seen him," she explained. "Not since Sunday, almost a week."

Tom frowned. "I do not understand." *How can he bear to be parted from her?*

"He has no choice," Mary said, as if in answer to his unspoken question. "Bysshe fears debtors' prison. We returned from the Continent with nothing. There was not so much as a halfpenny to pay the hackney driver. That surly fellow finally agreed to take us to Bysshe's bank, but when we got there, we found that Harriet had closed every one of his accounts. Was that not dreadful of her?"

Tom did not know how to answer that. He avoided her gaze by setting down his teacup, nearly spilling the contents. "What did you do?"

Mary's face flushed. "What could we do? My stepsister, Claire, and I—Claire is away now tending to an errand—waited in the hackney with our bags and a very angry driver while Bysshe pleaded with Harriet for money. Poor Bysshe, it must have been terrible for him. She misunderstood at first and thought he was returning to her. When Harriet at last realized that I was waiting outside, she became quite furious and threatened to have him thrown out. Finally she agreed to part with a few paltry shillings, and thus we were able to pay the driver and secure these dreadful lodgings."

It was so shocking a tale that Tom scarcely knew what to say. "What of your family—your father?" he ventured at last.

Mary's eyes filled with tears that she struggled visibly to control. "My father refuses to see me and has related our story to others in the most cruel and unforgiving terms. People believe me to be depraved. This very day I received a note from a dear friend with whom I lived in Scotland for two years. She has been forbidden to ever see or correspond with me again."

Tom fought the desire to take her in his arms. "You must be very lonely."

"I have always been lonely," Mary said at last. "These months with Bysshe have been the happiest of my life. Nothing else matters, though the absences are hard to bear. I see him only on Sundays."

"He has returned, then, to Harriet?" Tom could think of no other reason for Shelley's not being with her every moment possible.

"No!" Mary looked at him in angry astonishment. Tom was pleased to see the color return to her face. "It all began a fortnight ago," she explained. "The charwoman brought up a letter 'from a young lady refusing to give her name.' We hurried to the window and saw my sister, Fanny, looking up from the street. When she saw us, she turned and ran. Imagine, my own sister! Fan lives in terror of my father, who says he will cast her out if she communicates with us."

"Why did she come, then?" Tom asked. This was surely a dreadful affair.

"Fan brought us a letter of warning. She had learned that bailiffs were looking for Bysshe. His publisher—you know Thomas

Hookham, do you not? That dreadful man has given them our address. My father knows all this but will not lift a finger to help. He thinks it a fit punishment for my disobedience."

Tom reached absently for his tobacco pouch. "I understand now. You see Shelley here Sundays when arrests are illegal, but is it not possible for you to meet him in secret at other times?"

"Occasionally, but we must be very careful. I fear that I am being watched. If they should follow and catch him—" She gestured hopelessly. "For the most part we content ourselves with notes."

Tom watched with interest as she took a letter from the bodice of her blue paisley gown and handed it to him, still warm from her body.

"'My dearest love,'" Tom read. "'Why are our pleasures so short and so often interrupted? How long is this to last? Meet me tomorrow at three o'clock in St. Paul's. Adieu, remember love at vespers before sleep. I do not omit *my* prayers.'"

Tom looked up, puzzled. "What does he mean by prayers? Shelley is an atheist."

Mary hastily retrieved the note. Long honey-colored hair curtained her face as she folded the page hastily. "Oh! That is not the note I meant to—" Her face had turned a deep pink. "It is merely a little game we play."

Game? Tom enviously conjectured on its nature.

There was an awkward silence. Tom did not know what to say. He was relieved when Mary spoke, urging, "Tell me about your days at Oxford. Bysshe speaks of them with fondness."

Tom puffed on his pipe, savoring thoughts of those halcyon days . . . How well he recalled his first visit to Shelley's room. The floor, every chair and table, littered with books, boots, papers, pistols, phials, crucibles. "Shelley had an electrical machine," he told her, "and a solar microscope."

Mary smiled sadly. "Bysshe sold his microscope only last week."

"Did he now? What a pity. He was always fond of it, the infernal electrical machine as well. I shall never forget that first evening when Shelley attached himself to the apparatus and bade me grasp the handle. I cranked and cranked until his wild locks bristled and stood on end."

"Oh!" Mary cried. "You might have killed yourselves."

Tom changed the subject. "I worked with him on *The Necessity of Atheism*, you know. The pamphlet was talked into being during our morning walks. We used to stroll along the river, Shelley stopping often to launch his paper boats into the stream."

Mary smiled. "He still indulges in that pastime. But what of the pamphlet?"

"It had been published scarcely twenty minutes when a fellow at the New College chanced to spy it in the printer's window. His little group of classical Christians abhorred Shelley already for his long hair, his eccentric dress, and what they had heard of his experimental science. All they needed was an excuse to be rid of him. Shelley was expelled."

"It changed the course of his life," Mary murmured. She carefully placed her teacup back down on the small, rickety table before her. "The expulsion was bad enough—but the rift it caused with his father . . . Sir Timothy has still not forgiven Bysshe."

Tom nodded sympathetically. He longed to kiss Mary's white fingers one by one. "I wrote a note to the master condemning the expulsion."

"What a fine friend you are!" Mary exclaimed, her eyes fastened on him admiringly.

Tom's pulse beat faster. "Much good it did." He smiled ruefully. "The next thing I knew, I was hailed before the same court, my audience an even briefer period. The Master expelled me as well."

"Oh! Poor Tom, what happened next?"

"For a time Shelley and I occupied lodgings together in London, but when Father cut off my funds, there was nothing left for me to do but study for the Bar. Once I had passed, Father used his influence to get me a position at York. Shelley was left at loose ends. Before long he was writing to me of Harriet."

It was an awkward subject, one that Mary quickly changed, talking instead of the book she had begun to write, *History of a Six Weeks' Tour through a Part of France, Switzerland, Germany, and Holland*. When she handed him a few pages, Tom saw that it was a kind of travel memoir relating the course of her astonishing trek. He was captivated by the writing but wondered how readers would react to the candid account of her elopement, not to mention the positive references to the Enlightenment philosopher Rousseau. He thought it best to say nothing.

Tom sat for a time nodding absently as he followed not so much Mary's words, but the play of expressions across her face. She was absolutely entrancing. How lovely she was with her fine, fair hair and liquid eyes, her swan-like throat, her graceful sloping shoulders. At last he grudgingly rose to his feet, bowed to Mary, and bid her farewell.

"I should love to continue our conversation," she said, walking with him to the door. "Won't you come again?"

"I would like that very much," he said before reluctantly closing the door.

Outside the wretched tenement, Tom wanted desperately to talk to someone about Mary. But whom? The matter was delicate, intimate. Then he thought of his literary friend Thomas Peacock. Peacock shared Tom's affection for Shelley. Yes, he decided, Peacock was the very one.

Tom went directly to his friend's set of rooms, but when he attempted to explain his fascination for Mary, Peacock proved cynical and contentious. "You must find the lady quite remarkable to shift your allegiance so completely. I recall how smitten you were with Harriet."

"Ah, yes," Tom agreed, "but that was before I met Mary. I suggest you reserve your judgment until *you* have had that pleasure." Avoiding his friend's amused scrutiny, Tom turned his attention to a decanter of port before them. Studying the amber liquid, he mused, "Yes, Harriet was—*is*—lovely, spectacular, really. Mary cares less for fashion. She is witty and—"

"Dangerous," Peacock interrupted. "Mary Godwin is a witch who has apparently ensnared you as well as our friend Bysshe."

"Dear Peacock, you sound like my family vicar." Tom shook his head impatiently. "He is forever warning me against women of opinion, women who live impulsively, making their own decisions."

"Really!" Peacock raised a brow. "The slipper appears to fit. Does that not describe Mistress Godwin?" Peacock leaned forward confidentially. "I, too, have met her."

"What?" Tom sat up, startled. "When was this?"

"Possibly a week ago. It seems the lovebirds had met secretly in a park but could not bear to separate. Bysshe took her to some dreadful hotel in White Chapel. The innkeeper was suspicious of a couple with no luggage and refused to serve them a meal unless they paid in advance. Bysshe was unable to do that—he had spent everything on the wretched room. In desperation he sent a note to me. Unfortunately I had nothing in my purse to give, but the next morning I took them some cake. It was all I had in the larder. When I entered the room, I found Bysshe reading his poetry to Mary. They appeared oblivious to everything but each other."

"Did you not think her marvelous?"

"Perhaps," Peacock considered. "She is unusual looking, attractive enough, and, I agree, quite bright."

"Mary will distinguish herself," Tom said. "I am certain of it." He stopped, unwilling to acknowledge even to himself that Mary's most appealing quality was the vulnerability he sensed beneath her cool, self-possessed facade.

"Stop dreaming," Peacock chided. "Your time is wasted. For better or worse, Mary Godwin belongs to our friend Shelley. You cannot hope to pry her loose."

"I would not presume to." Tom drew thoughtfully on his pipe.

TWENTY

Tom Hogg blinked at the brilliantly lit foyer. Say what one might about Peacock—that he was cranky, conceited, pretentious, all those things—the man certainly knew how to give a party. Candles everywhere. Peacock's expense for tallow alone must be preposterous.

Tom heard the welcoming sounds of music and laughter in the rooms beyond. As a servant relieved him of his hat and cape, Tom paused before a gilt-framed mirror to survey himself, a well-clad figure in dove-colored breeches and a silver-buttoned jacket. He smiled, satisfied.

Tom had avoided seeing Mary, yet his thoughts returned to her time and again. *Move on,* he had told himself a hundred times; a man forgets one woman with another. It was this very reasoning that had brought him out tonight. If he were ever to forget Mary Godwin, Peacock's soiree was the place to begin. Tom surveyed the scene: the natty elegance of yellow breeches, the bright splash of military tunics. Better yet, the lure of satin and velvet, women everywhere, sparkling eyes, lustrous curls coaxed into enchanting cascades, silky gowns framing silkier bodies. And, oh, the breast-works! The drawing room was filled with extravagant creatures.

A violin played the opening notes of "The Beaux Delight," signaling an end to the orchestra's short break. Tom's wandering gaze explored the room, looking longingly for Mary. No woman present possessed her inner glow. No one could stir his heart as she did . . . Tom's eyes opened wide at the sight of a familiar face.

Bysshe Shelley! That scoundrel! What was it about him that women found so irresistible? Tom glanced eagerly around the room. *Surely Shelley would not have come without Mary.*

A red-liveried servant paused with a drink tray. Tom took a goblet of champagne, all the while studying Shelley. The man's fortunes must have improved if he was out in public. No bailiffs, but no Mary either. Where was she? What was going on?

Tom followed the music into the adjoining ballroom. A row of older women sat at one end, each with her lorgnette poised to survey the swirling scene. Their gray heads came together often, doubtless to share gossipy tidbits. Nearby, a cluster of young girls giggled shrilly at nothing other than their own giddiness.

Guests were lining up along the center of the parquet floor. A country dance began: lines of men and women performing elaborate steps for each other, first advancing, then retreating. A winsome lady with pale curls passed directly in front of Tom. His eyes followed as she whirled before her partner, a big fellow in a red cavalry uniform. The woman reminded him of someone.

When the dance ended and the violins shifted into a waltz, Tom strode to the lady's side. Bowing low, he asked for the next dance and was rewarded with a soft-spoken yes. Tom took her arm, leading her onto the dance floor.

"Sir, you are staring at me," she said, stepping back but clasping his hand tighter.

With an accomplished flourish, he began the requisite series of steps. "I cannot help myself. You are most charming."

"Such flattery is untoward, sir, as I do not know you." She tilted her head. "Are you a literary man like our host?"

"I should like to be, but at present I am merely a lowly law clerk. Tom Hogg, at your service."

As the woman chattered on, Tom realized what had drawn him to her. This pretty young thing bore a slight resemblance to Mary. The realization brought his thoughts back to Shelley. Tom could hear him laughing as though he had not a care in the world. But then, Tom allowed, Shelley had always been a merry fellow.

The sound of violins drew him back to the present. The dance was just concluding. His partner regarded him, a slight frown between her brows. Tom bowed as she dropped a quick curtsy and hurried off to join the rapidly forming line for a quadrille. Not a good sign. Tom realized he would have to try harder if he were ever to quell his feelings for Mary.

Shelley and Peacock were standing in the doorway, seemingly lost in conversation. Shelley's head was bent attentively, long hair falling across his forehead. He has changed little, Tom thought, sipping his champagne. Good stuff. Peacock had laid in the best.

Watching the animated play of expression on Shelley's face, Tom remembered Harriet pounding on his door some three weeks before. He had scarcely recognized her. Harriet, face pale and drawn, blue eyes swollen with tears, was heavy with child. She clung to Tom as he ushered her into his flat, worrying that she might deliver at any moment.

"You cared for me once. Will you be my friend now? Please!" Harriet's voice caught; Tom feared that she would cry.

"Of course I am your friend." He pulled out a chair for her by the fire.

Harriet had shaken her head impatiently. "There is no time. I want you to come with me now to William Godwin's house. He is the only one with any control over Bysshe or that dreadful girl. I cannot . . . simply cannot go alone. Please, you are Bysshe's good friend. Will you not come with me?"

Tom considered it a fool's errand, but what could he say? Harriet's coach waited outside; the postilion let down the steps for them.

"What can Bysshe see in her?" Harriet demanded of Tom again and again as the carriage bounced and jolted over the cobblestones toward Skinner Street. "Mary's appearance is quite ordinary." Harriet began to sob. "Surely you can say something to Bysshe . . ."

"When has he ever listened to me—or to anyone?" Glancing at Harriet's pale face, Tom had felt compelled to add an assurance that he did not feel. "Shelley admires Godwin, looks up to him. Perhaps the man may be of some influence. I shall try."

Heart filled with misgiving, Tom helped Harriet to descend from the carriage on Skinner Street. The poor girl teetered clumsily. Tom wondered if he might have to carry her. Glancing through the shop window, he saw a man with a lofty brow and a short, portly woman stacking books.

The woman hurried forward as Tom opened the door to the bookstore. "May I help you find a book?" When Harriet pushed back the hood of her cloak, the older woman gasped. "My dear girl, I did not know you. I am so sorry, this must be a dreadful time."

The man stepped forward, extending his hand to Tom. "William Godwin, sir." Turning quickly toward Harriet, he took her arm and led her to a chair.

"Is there nothing that you can do, sir?" Harriet asked. "Will you not speak to Bysshe? He admires you so." She hesitated. "Perhaps you might also speak to your daughter."

"Never." Godwin stepped back, shaking his head. "I have disowned Mary . . . I had to, though it broke my heart."

"Then there is nothing . . ." Harriet's voice trailed to a whisper.

Her voice still lingered in his ears. Tom shook his head to clear it. He stared blankly at the tray of drinks a servant held before him. Flutes and basses now amongst the violins. Somewhere the savory smell of roasted lamb. The crack of billiards. Cries of men, a game of chance going on in the next room.

Tom glanced again at Shelley. He stood beneath a chandelier illuminated by a dozen glowing candles. Their eyes connected and Shelley abruptly took leave of Peacock and strode forward. "My dear friend," he said. "I did not know until now, but you are the very person I most want to see."

Tom braced himself for a request. Shelley's snug breeches were a trifle shiny, his cravat frayed, and, worse yet, there was a small hole in his waistcoat. In their Oxford days the two had readily come to each other's aid when one was short of funds, pooling resources and possessions without thought. Now Tom considered his own situation. His father, though a prosperous country gentleman, was not overly generous. Tom's allowance, when compared to that of his friends, was meager. Just how much could he afford to give?

To his surprise, Shelley threw back his head and laughed. "Oh, Tom, Tom. You have not changed a whit. I can still read you like a book."

Tom felt his face flush but looked straight into his friend's amused blue eyes. In spite of everything, Shelley was still his friend, perhaps his dearest. "Tell me what has happened? How can I help?"

"The problem is not financial," Shelley said as they stepped outside the circle of candlelight cast by the chandeliers. "At least, money is not my deepest concern. Eluding bailiffs keeps me on my toes, yet I always seem to manage."

"Then it must be woman trouble." Tom hesitated for a moment. "I . . . had occasion to meet Mary. It seems that you now have two wives, if one is to count Harriet. You are still married to her, are you not? I grant you that Mary is fetching—no doubt about it—but Harriet, you must admit, is glorious."

"Indeed," Shelley agreed matter-of-factly. "Harriet is a gorgeous animal." He pushed back a lock of hair. "But Mary is the companion of my soul." Looking down at his scuffed leather boots,

Shelley murmured, "But Mary is currently with child and often feels ill. Besides"—he looked up defiantly—"a man cannot spend *all* his time with a single woman. There are so many, and each offers unique inspiration. Love is meant to be free. Mary's stepsister, Claire, though lacking Mary's brilliance, is full of energy and good spirits. She is dark, rather exotic, and quite friendly. Claire never questions anything I say or do and always understands and appreciates me."

"Imagine that!" Tom placed his half-filled glass on the table. "Are you telling me you now have three wives?"

Shelley ignored the question, confiding instead, "Claire and I have splendid times together, but Mary tends to be lonely when we are out and about. And when we are at home, Claire and I can hardly . . . Well, you do understand, I am sure. What is Mary to do while I'm with Claire?"

What indeed? This was a bit much even for Shelley. What a fool that man could be! "You could always leave Mary."

"Leave Mary!" Shelley exclaimed, astonishment in his eyes. "I would never leave Mary. I love her."

Tom floundered. "Well . . . well . . ."

"I thought you would feel so, Tom." Shelley laughed lightly. "You always were a broadminded fellow. Surely you can see that someone needs to pay Mary the attentions she deserves."

Tom downed the contents of his goblet in one swallow. "Good God, man!" His heart pounded. Was it possible that his wildest dreams were about to come true? "Please excuse me if I have misinterpreted you, but—but are you . . ." Tom paused, faltering. "Shelley, can it be that you are asking me to become your mistress's lover?"

TWENTY-ONE

Trapped with Claire in a frigid garret, virtually deserted by Bysshe, Mary thought often of Aaron Burr and longed for the sight of that kind, wise man, the champion of her childhood.

"I am different, Bysshe is different," she'd assured him. Now Mary remembered the skeptical tilt of Uncle Aaron's glossy brow. He had called Bysshe naïve and unstable. *"What he has done to his wife, he could as well do to you."*

Mary had scoffed at the idea. Now she sighed, thinking of the changes taking place in her body. Her breasts—Bysshe had called them his fragile peaches—now overripe. And her belly! Once smooth and flat, it grew larger every day. Still, Mary was amazed that it grew at all. The vegetable diet that Bysshe insisted she adhere to left her ravenous.

Yet bouts of hunger were the least of it. Mary's nights were fraught with dreadful dreams centered on the impending birth. Fear was Mary's nighttime companion, never leaving her side until she rose at dawn, exhausted. Mary's mother had died giving her life . . . Was this to be her fate? Was it a terrible obligation that she would be forced to pay? Only lucky women survived childbirth, and Mary had never felt lucky.

As Uncle's words echoed in her head, Mary realized that there was no one to whom she could turn. Papa had abandoned her. Charles Lamb and Samuel Coleridge, bound by loyalty to him, avoided her. Aaron Burr, a breed apart, was a sea away.

Mary longed for Aaron Burr. What she got was Thomas Hogg. Tom was twenty-two, Bysshe's age, but so unlike him. Though tall and not unattractive, Tom lacked her lover's charm. He was quiet and unassuming, his manner mild, his ideas expressed tentatively. At first she thought Tom dull, but as time passed, Mary came to appreciate his thoughtful introspection. Tom's quiet curiosity masked a keen intellect. In some ways they were much alike.

Tom had not only begun to practice law but was writing a novel. *Where did he find the time?* she wondered. He was often at her side, calling daily at her lodgings.

His attentions, coming at a time when Mary sensed Bysshe's affections were straying, touched an aching heart. Days passed without communication. Mary's only consolation was that Claire appeared as uncertain as she. At least he was not sneaking notes to her.

One winter day followed another, and then late one evening a liveried messenger knocked at their door. The letter he carried, addressed to Bysshe, bore the Shelley family crest but was written in Harriet's hand. It was as though a knife had pierced Mary's heart.

"Break the seal," Claire urged, eagerness lighting her eyes. Mary wanted desperately to comply. What did Harriet want of him? Surely anything that concerned Bysshe concerned her as well. Yet despite her own desire, Mary refused.

The next morning, she was up at dawn. With some effort she pulled on a frock—Bysshe's favorite. Mary's heart tugged when she remembered his hands trailing down the soft blue muslin. Now it was so tight she wanted to cry. Pulling a pelisse about her, she set off, determined to find him and deliver the letter.

Mary picked her way carefully, for the roads were filled with chaises, carts, wagons, private coaches, and sedan chairs. Fog shrouded Fleet Street like a heavy mantle as she walked the length of it, up one side and down the other, past bright and gaudy shop fronts lit by flares, pushing her way into countless pubs, where the smell of unwashed bodies and stale ale nearly overwhelmed her. Bysshe was nowhere to be found.

At last, exhausted, she turned back to her lodgings on Church Terrace. It was late afternoon. Mary had gotten little sleep the night before; now perhaps she could lie down. As soon as she entered, though, she found two bailiffs waiting in the doorway, hoping to surprise Bysshe. She caught her breath, relief mingling with fatigue. At least now she knew he was not in debtors' prison.

"You are wasting your time," she told them. "I have not seen Mr. Shelley in more than a fortnight."

The two men eyed her suspiciously, then looked at each other. They were a miserable pair, shivering in their thin, threadbare uniforms. Mary took pity on them. "Have a cup of tea and then be on your way," she said, shrugging off her coat.

They accepted the invitation eagerly. The tea was hot, the biscuits stale but edible. They tarried for more than an hour. Finally the two were persuaded to leave. Listening to them stride noisily down the steep, dark stairs, Mary sighed with relief.

Once the door slammed, Claire handed her a letter. "This arrived just after you left," she said.

Mary's breath caught as she studied the tightly folded missive. It was addressed to Bysshe and bore his publisher's crest. A bill of exchange! Perhaps it would be enough to allow Bysshe to come home. Rising quickly, she put on the shawl that she had so eagerly discarded. "I shall go back to Fleet Street. I will search and search until I find him."

Tired as Mary was, the thought of Bysshe's pleasure kept her going. She could imagine his eyes lighting at the sight of the letter. A steady ache in her back throbbed as she retraced her steps to Fleet Street, peering again into each establishment in the hope of spotting Bysshe. Hacks and delivery wagons clip-clopped up and down, sharing the road with glittering barouches driven by stiff-liveried footmen, their occupants so elegant and indolent. To Mary, they were a world apart.

The wind had picked up and the big shop signs swung and creaked overhead. Mary paused to peer through the leaded window of the King's Brew. She wasn't surprised to find the establishment filled almost to capacity, every table taken, people—mostly men—standing shoulder to shoulder. The smell warmed her as she pushed open the heavy door. Mary thought a coffeehouse a good place for Bysshe, snug and toasty on a winter day, but with none of the enforced bonhomie of an inn. He could simply sit alone and ruminate.

Threading her way through the crowded room, she caught fragments of many conversations. Mary's papa called coffeehouses "penny universities," but they were more than that. With many cutthroats about, travel across London was difficult and sometimes dangerous. Barristers and businessmen frequently found it convenient to set up shop in neighborhood coffeehouses. Here clients were advised, deals finalized.

The dark-paneled room was thick with pipe smoke, the smell of damp wool and sweat so strong it made her queasy. Men herded together, talking, laughing, sometimes shouting to make a point. Mary was about to turn back when a space opened before her. There, across the room, was Bysshe seated in a back booth, staring into a mug, seemingly oblivious to it all. His hair was mussed, his cravat lopsided, his waistcoat unevenly buttoned. His treasured meerschaum pipe, carved in the shape of a mermaid, lay unheeded on the table. Was he composing a poem? Mary saw a few crumpled sheets of scribbled paper before him. She had crossed the room and was standing at his side before Bysshe chanced to look up and see her. With relief, Mary recognized eagerness in his eyes. He jumped to his feet, hugging her close. Although it had been only a fortnight, it seemed years since she had last felt his arms about her. Bysshe was happy, too. He kissed her again and again, seeming not

to care who saw them. A man who'd been seated beside him reading a paper got up and, with a flourish, offered his seat to Mary.

Happily, she sat down beside Bysshe, who kissed her once
again. "How are you?" he said at last, but before she could answer
the question, he asked another: "How is Claire?"

"She is fine," Mary told him, adding quickly, "and so is Tom.
He comes to see me every day and stays late into the night."

"Splendid! You have found yourself a true cavalier."

"Tom is more than that," Mary said, looking up at him. She
had thought to make Bysshe jealous. Foolish dream! He appeared
delighted by the idea of their growing friendship.

Bysshe hugged her again. "What a merry time the four of us
will have once I have finally settled this nonsense with my creditors and can at last come home."

Mary's heart sank. Were Bysshe and she so very different? She
resolved not to think about that; she must not mar the moment.
Seeking to change the subject, Mary asked if he had written any
new poems.

"New poems!" he flared, glancing down at the discarded
scraps of paper on the scarred table. "How can I write when I must
constantly flee from pillar to post?"

Nodding sympathetically, she handed him the letter from
Hookham. "This, I hope, will contain good news."

Bysshe eagerly tore open the missive. "Good news, indeed!
It's a promissory note, my royalties from *Queen Mab*." Waving his
arm, he signaled to a serving man. "Coffee for my lady, and see that
your master cashes this note."

Bysshe took Mary's hand and kissed the palm tenderly. "Oh,
you are cold. It is bitter out, but the coffee will warm you. How are
you feeling? Well, I hope." Bysshe did not like to discuss ailments
other than his own.

The young lad was back quickly enough with the coffee and
a bag of silver coins. When Bysshe poured them out on the table,

Mary saw that there were not half as many as she had hoped. Were there enough to keep them even a month?

"There is something else," she said, reluctantly removing the other letter from her reticule. "It appears to be from Harriet."

She watched him unfold the paper slowly, taking pleasure in his seeming apathy. Quite suddenly, his bored expression changed. His face flushed with pleasure.

"Glorious news!" he exclaimed, pressing the letter into Mary's hand. "Harriet has had a son. Father will be delighted." He hugged Mary excitedly. "Is this not wonderful news? I have an heir."

Wonderful? Was it not over between Bysshe and Harriet? What about her own baby? Mary was struggling for something to say when Bysshe spoke again. "Hurry, drink your coffee. I must be off to Tom Peacock's."

"But why?" Mary asked, trying not to look as forlorn as she felt. "I have only just gotten here."

"I know, dear." Bysshe patted her hand absently. "But Peacock is certain to have a quill and ink ready. I must write announcements to all my friends acquainting them with the news." He tucked the letter proudly into the pocket of his waistcoat. "Marvelous tidings, are they not?"

"Yes, yes, of course, marvelous," Mary agreed, draining the last of the coffee. She rose, staggering slightly as she reached for her pelisse.

"Here, take this money," Bysshe said, counting out more than half of it. "I will give some to your father as well. I'm sure his debts are pressing as ever. Perhaps this will help to change his feelings toward you."

Mary shrugged. "Do I have a father?" She no longer blamed Mum for her father's coldness. William Godwin was a slave to no one but his own greed and bitterness. The loss of the man who Mary had adored all her life had made her even more dependent on Bysshe, but now . . . what remained?

Perhaps a little of her sadness penetrated Bysshe's joy. He leaned forward, taking her hand. "Mary, Mary, is this a time for pessimism?"

She forced a smile, then preceded him through the crowded room. Her ears rang with raucous laughter, shouted toasts, the clatter of mugs and glasses. Was everyone in the world happy but her?

Outside, night had fallen and it had begun to rain. A parting kiss, and they turned and went their separate ways.

TWENTY-TWO

Mary longed to hail a hackney carriage but forced herself to walk back to Church Terrace. Bysshe might consider the money he had just received sudden riches; she knew better. It would soon be gone, and then what? The fear of debtors' prison was never far from her mind. Would her child be born there?

The rain turned to sleet. Mary was soaked to the bone by the time she pushed open the battered wooden door and climbed the five flights of stairs to the one-room garret shared with Claire. It was always dimly lit, for they could afford few candles. Reluctantly, Mary turned the doorknob.

Claire merely nodded, but Tom Hogg's face lit immediately at the sight of her. Such a dear friend! There he was kneeling before the fire, stoking coal. The hearth had been cold and gray, the wind moaning fitfully through the stone chimney, when she left. Tom must have brought the coal. Who else? She and Claire had scarcely a farthing between them. Now, here was a blazing fire filling the dreary room with warmth and light.

Tom jumped to his feet, boots thudding softly across the ragged carpet. He removed Mary's damp cloak and pulled up a chair for her beside the fire. "Look what we have for you." He gestured toward a basket on the table.

"Chicken!" Nothing had ever looked so delicious.

"I know," he said apologetically, "that Bysshe has asked that you forswear meat, but . . . possibly just this once . . ."

"Yes! Yes, just this once." Mary had scarcely realized how hungry she was until then, so occupied had she been in simply shoving one heavy foot before the other. It had been a dreadful day, but now her spirits rose at the warmth of the fire, the smell of good food, the sight of Tom and Claire busy setting forth what seemed the greatest of feasts. Stewed fowl, a salad of leeks, and roasted potatoes. And, finally, three oranges. How good Tom was to have provided this bounty.

Smiling, he placed a glass of wine in Mary's hand. She took a sip and then another. Though slightly bitter, it warmed her body. Looking up into Tom's eyes, which gazed at her so intently, she saw herself reflected. Face flushed, she turned away and met Claire's appraising gaze.

"You were gone a long time. Did you find Bysshe?" she asked.

Mary nodded, not wanting to talk about it. She reached eagerly for a chicken leg.

Claire would not be put off. "And the letter. What did Harriet have to say?"

"Her child is born, her *legal* child." Mary raised her glass. This time she took a gulp. "Bysshe is ecstatic." And why wouldn't he be? Charles, his infant son with Harriet, was heir to the Shelley title and estates. *But what about my baby?* Mary's unborn child was illegitimate.

In an instant, it seemed, her insides rebelled against the wine. Mary ran to the sleeping alcove, where she vomited her stomach's meager contents into a chipped bowl. Mary lay for a time on the cot she shared with Claire, staring up at the sloping ceiling only a few inches above her head. They had but one blanket. The mattress was filled with straw. Only a curtain divided the space from the rest of the small room.

She could hear Tom and Claire discussing her in muffled tones. Too ill to rejoin them, she listened dully to their conversation.

"Poor Mary," Tom whispered.

"Poor Mary, indeed!" Claire snapped. "I am so tired of hearing 'poor Mary.' You have no idea how dull it is here. Mary is forever scribbling. She vows she will be a writer like her mother. We have hardly money enough for candles, and there she is buying paper. I hear nothing but the sound of a quill scraping, unless she has her nose buried in a book. She likes that new lady writer, Jane something, and says her novel will be a classic. *Pride and Prejudice*, what a silly name!"

"But you need not stay," Tom reminded her.

"I have nowhere to go but Skinner Street," Claire told him, her voice lower now. "When I ran away with Mary, I thought it would be a grand adventure." Claire sighed petulantly. "And so it was for a time, but now life is so drab. It's fine enough when Bysshe is here and when Mary deigns to give us a moment alone together, but those times are rare."

"Then why not go home? Surely your parents—your mother, at least—would forgive you."

"I suppose, but think how deadly it would be for me. How could I endure it?"

How am I to endure you? an indignant Mary wondered. She rose, moving to the doorway to watch them. Most agreed that Claire was pretty. Bysshe certainly admired her. Did Tom also find Claire engaging? Hoping that she did not look as wan and miserable as she felt, Mary forced a smile. Shoving the curtain aside, she entered the room with a brisk step. "Since my pregnancy, spirits seem to have a bad effect on me," she said, shrugging slightly.

In an instant Tom was at Mary's side, gently leading her back to the chair by the fire. "Take a little bit very slowly. It will warm you."

She nodded gratefully. "You are so good."

"No more than you deserve." He took her cold hands in his warm ones.

Claire broke in: "I do not like the name Tom, and Hogg is even worse. Neither suits you."

He nodded at her. "I care little for them myself."

Mary paused for a moment, thinking about the problem. "I have an idea," she ventured. "What about Alexy for a name?"

"Alexy? The hero of my novel? Mary, you *are* adorable."

Claire made a face. "Is that not the silliest thing—a grown man changing his name."

"It has not been so long since you yourself settled on Claire," Mary reminded her. "Your name used to be Clara, if you will recall."

Claire bristled. "Clara was such a tedious name! Not at all right for me. Claire is so light, so fair, so French." She tossed her head, raising her chin proudly. "Claire Clairmont is a name destined to mean something. Just you wait and see."

The newly christened Alexy and Mary exchanged amused smiles as he laced her tea with a few drops of brandy.

———·+·———

Alexy, Alexy, what would I do without him? Mary asked herself. A question followed by another: *What should I do* with *him?* Mary could not say that she was not flattered by his constancy. Alexy was the bright spot in her life. He came daily, staying long into the night. Alexy amused Mary, causing her to laugh when no one else could. They chattered endlessly, speculating about Beau Brummel's influence on the Prince Regent and, most recently, Tom Peacock's incarceration in debtors' prison. Often he read chapters from his novel, *Memoirs of Prince Alexy Haimatoff*. It was a romantic tale. She rather liked it.

One day, as Mary and Alexy sat with their heads together reading the *Times*, an item jumped out at them. Sir Bysshe, her lover's grandfather, had died. Surely this must foreshadow some rise in their fortunes.

Mary could not wait to tell her darling the news, and this time searched no farther than the King's Brew, where Bysshe sat with a tankard of ale and a book of verse. As she expected, he was hardly saddened by the news. Despite his father's influence to the contrary, Bysshe would surely inherit something from the estate, and at least a few creditors could be forestalled.

Bysshe left immediately, taking Claire—Claire!—with him to Field Place for the reading of Sir Bysshe's will. Mary was furious.

"The trip is far too taxing for you to take in your present condition," he explained. "And I want company on the road, someone to talk with in the coach. It is a two-day trip, you know."

"But you cannot take her with you to Field Place," Mary reasoned.

"Hardly." He considered a moment. "I will find rooms for Claire at a nearby inn."

So there Mary was, alone in the tiny garret with Alexy. There was no doubt what Bysshe expected her to do with him. But what did she *want* to do? Mary could not say that it was not comforting to feel herself once again the object of a man's desire. She stared at Alexy as if for the first time. He was an average sort of person, not portly, not lean. His hair was light brown, his eyes a gentle blue, his smile genuine. He was taller than Bysshe and broader through the shoulders.

When Alexy stepped forward, reaching for her, she did not resist. Slowly he began to remove her clothing: her gown, her petticoat and chemise, and finally her under drawers. She wished it were dark so that she might hide herself. Her breasts were swollen, her belly curved, but, surprisingly, Tom seemed to like those things. He could not, in fact, get enough of them.

"Mary, Mary, I have loved you so long," he breathed into her throat. Mary's arms, seemingly of their own volition, stole up about his neck.

She supposed one might say he tended to her needs. Her body responded readily enough. It had been long, far too long, since she and Bysshe had been alone together. Tom's hands, his mouth knew all the right places to delight her. As though from a distance, she heard a voice—her own voice—crying out in pleasure.

But no, it was not the fierce, heedless passion that she had experienced with Bysshe. It was more like something she imagined a much older person might feel. The threat of disenchantment lurked just outside their circling arms. And so, in the thrall of desire, they moved cautiously, careful neither to hurt nor be hurt.

TWENTY-THREE

Having at last come into a portion of his legacy, mortgaged though it might be, Bysshe was not about to practice discretion of any kind. His new home had silvery-blue draperies and Axminster carpets, crystal chandeliers and an antique tapestry. The house at 41 Hans Place was spacious, so spacious that Bysshe wanted Tom to move in with them.

Bysshe remained delighted with his lofty experiment in free love, but Mary was disenchanted. She determined to set matters straight with Tom—Mary no longer thought of him as Alexy—before he became a member of their household. Sitting down at her new mahogany writing desk, she picked up a quill. The message began easily enough; the words flew: "I know how much & how tenderly you love me, and I rejoice that I am capable of constituting your happiness."

She sat looking at what she had written. Well, yes, she was pleased to have made him happy, but how far did she want to go with that? She must not get his hopes up any higher than she had already. Tom was a good friend, the best, but would never be more to her than that.

Picking up her quill again, Mary wrote more slowly: "We look forward to joy & light in the summer when the trees are green, when the sun is bright & joyful and when I have my baby. With what exquisite pleasure shall we pass the time." Yes, that was the right tone. Let him know that she would no longer have time for him, that soon she would have someone else to consider.

But that was not enough. Tom must know where matters stood. Whatever romantic feelings she had felt for him had dissipated. Her love for Bysshe was what counted, and it must be made clear. She wrote on: "My still greater happiness will be in Bysshe—I love him so tenderly & entirely."

Folding the paper carefully, she sat for a time staring at it. The missive was meant to put a permanent end to her affair with Tom. And that was all well and good, but did she want to banish him completely? Not really . . . Was Tom not a comfort? As her pregnancy advanced, Bysshe and Claire continued their romance. Was a mere friendship with Tom so wrong?

----·----

It was an awful time for Mary, marked by frightful dreams of her mother's death shortly after her own birth. Thoughts of her imminent childbirth continued to terrify Mary. Doubtful that she would survive, Mary was obsessed by fears of the unknown. At best death would bring oblivion, at worst . . . Mary dared not speculate. And what of the baby? Was that infant soul destined to feel the same loneliness, the same sense of abandonment that had clouded her own childhood? She longed for a woman's counsel.

Mary had inquired for midwives and interviewed a few; one rather pleased her. Susanna was old, about fifty, Mary imagined. She talked of presiding at many births with terrible mishaps. Yet weren't Susanna's claims never to have lost either a mother or a baby reassuring? She would surely know what to do if things went wrong.

Bysshe scoffed. "A midwife! Surely we can do better than that! When the time comes you will have the finest doctor that money

will buy." He patted Mary's arm reassuringly, then hurried off to
Fleet Street with Claire at his side.

*At least he feels something. He cares enough to want the best for
me,* Mary told herself.

When the first pains came, she did not recognize them for what
they were. It was February and the baby was not due until April.
Tom was spending a holiday with his father in Scotland, Claire
had gone to visit a friend from boarding school, the maid was on
holiday, and the cook off tending an ailing child. Bysshe and Mary
were alone. "Oh! I must have twisted my back," she told him.

Bysshe shook his head. "That's how Harriet's pains began
when Ianthe was born." Face gone pale, he hurried to the window
and called out to a passing boy. Tossing the lad a coin, he told him
to fetch a doctor right away. "I'll give you three times this when
you come back," he called after him.

Mary was horrified. Not the finest that money could buy, but
anybody the lad was lucky enough to find. Moaning softly into
Bysshe's shoulder, she struggled to remain calm. She smiled; this
was not so bad. Then another pain snatched the smile away and
her breath with it.

Bysshe pulled her up from the couch where she had been lying.
"You will need to walk a bit. It's said to make the labor go faster."

"Will it be long?" Mary asked after another spasm gripped her,
and then another.

"Don't think of that. Think only of our baby coming."

*But why so soon? Is something wrong with the baby? Or is it me?
Is something the matter with me?*

The afternoon passed into twilight. When Mary was so weary
that she could no longer put one foot before the other, Bysshe
allowed her to lie down. Poor man, he looked so tired. Then
the real pains began, screaming pains. Sometimes it was hard to
remember the child. There was only pain. Mary cried and fought,
but it went on and on without seeming to go anywhere. Where was

that doctor? She and Bysshe were alone, he beside her, trying so hard to be calm. His eyes betrayed him. He looked terrified. "Am I going to die?" Mary cried out. "Don't let me die!"

Bysshe was trembling when he took her hand, holding it tightly as the night wore on. "That's right, just a little bit more," he encouraged her from time to time. His face was white, his eyes wide with terror.

"I cannot do this," Mary gasped, exhausted. "Help me! I cannot do this!"

Then another pain tore into her, the worst yet. She screamed until she could scream no more. *I'll die now,* Mary thought, and hoped it would be soon. "Push," Bysshe urged, but she had no energy left. Bysshe held her, his sweaty face against hers. As the baby began to emerge, she felt as though her body were breaking open. Surely her pelvic bones were splintering. It was only when the baby was out that she groaned, an ugly sound that seemed scarcely human. The smell of blood—fetid, yet sweet—filled the room. It was over. Bysshe, his face white and drawn, was beside her, holding something dark and shriveled. Was that *creature* her baby?

They heard pounding at the door. At last, the doctor. He was a disheveled old man reeking of alcohol. "You were fortunate," he said, his dirty hands moving over Mary as he cut the cord. "It was apparently a short labor, and now here is your little girl."

Short! It had not seemed so. But that was over now. Mary held out her arms. The baby opened her mouth and wailed. *Her first cries. I have given my baby life,* Mary thought joyously, but then a chill passed through her body as she looked down at her baby girl's fragile form. *So small. So very, very small.* As Mary rocked her daughter tenderly, she felt the infant's spirit clinging tenuously to her own. With all her heart Mary willed her baby to live.

She was rewarded. The tiny girl thrived through that day and night and the next day, too. Mary's spirits rose as she nursed the baby, her tiny, perfect fingers wrapped around Mary's own, her milk giving the infant life.

The following day Fan came to call, her hair damp from the winter rain. How good to see her sister at last. It had been months since her last furtive visit, but now Fan had braved Papa's wrath to see her tiny niece. The next morning she was back, this time with Charlie. No word from Papa, but Mum surprised Mary by sending baby clothes.

"Do you think I might name the baby Mary—after my mother?" Mary asked Bysshe. He sat on the bed beside her and took the baby into his arms. "It is a lovely name, the best." His face was anxious as he studied the sleeping infant. "The doctor warned me that it is unlikely that our little girl will live. Let's not name her—not yet." The words struck fear into Mary's heart, but when Bysshe and Claire went out to buy a cradle the next day, her hope was restored.

Mary had her dearest girl for ten days.

On the eleventh morning, she awoke to find the baby's face a gray blue. Mary cried out in horror. *No, no, it cannot be!* She would not let it be. For hours Mary rocked her little darling, holding the baby against her heart. Her daughter's body was rigid, like a block of ice. Frantically, Mary pressed her nipple into the baby's mouth. Surely the strength of her love could call the baby back. It did not. Again and again Mary breathed into the tiny mouth. She had helped to create the child's life; why could she not restore it?

At last a white-faced Bysshe took the baby from Mary. There were tears in his eyes. Tom went out to make arrangements. Mary found it too awful to think about her baby girl alone in the dark, cold ground. Oh, she could not let them take her away! Mary did not know what happened next. It seemed for a time that it was she who had been buried. She existed in darkness, scarcely aware of the steady murmur of voices, people talking to her and about her.

"You can always have another," Claire cheerily suggested.

Another? When her arms still ached for the one she had lost? How could Claire dismiss so casually the dear creature she had held for so brief a time? "Stop!" she sobbed in fury. "Do you not understand?"

Bysshe took Mary tenderly in his arms but echoed Claire's words. "When you are stronger, there will be others."

Others? The lost one had been the product of their first passion, their innocent idealism about the world and each other. The tiny, precious babe had been born of their very souls. No other baby could take *that* child's place.

Days and nights passed as Mary sat locked within herself, silent and alone. Finally one morning, Bysshe shook her gently, raising her chin so she would look into his eyes. "I am taking you away," he said. "It will be a holiday, just the two of us." He bent and kissed her tenderly, but Mary turned away. Kisses made babies and babies could kill. If they didn't break her body, they would surely break her heart.

Mary remembered little of the days that followed. There was a long coach ride with a troublesome woman trying to engage her in conversation, then a small cottage, gulls crying, the scent of seaweed, Bysshe's voice droning on and on. Perhaps he was reading to her.

Then one afternoon she awakened as from a dream. She was sitting in a rocking chair by a window. How many hours had she spent there, staring at the ocean, yet seeing nothing? Far off in the distance, she distinguished a tiny figure, a man walking on the beach. As he came closer, she saw that it was Bysshe.

Mary rose from the chair, hurried about the room. When Bysshe arrived at the cottage, Mary was waiting. She had found a pretty frock tucked away in a trunk and had placed a flower from the garden in her hair.

Bysshe searched her face, his hopeful smile broadening. "Mary, my darling, have you come back to me? You were gone so long."

"Yes," she whispered, her hand reaching out for his. "Yes, I have, but I want *you* back, too. *All* of you."

———•———

Those were happy days for Mary. For Bysshe as well, she felt certain. It was their true honeymoon, for at last they were alone together, free to discover each other as never before. Bysshe and Mary walked and talked and read together. And, yes, they made love—many times. But it was different. Bysshe was different. Patient, gentle, he seemed as eager for her pleasure as for his own. It was not long before Mary knew that she again carried his child. *Am I ready to risk my heart again?*

Yes, Mary decided. Love was worth the risk.

She and Bysshe remained in their little seaside cottage four months. It was William Godwin's pressing demands for money that pulled them back to London. Mary wondered aloud, "What a strange man, my father. He refuses to recognize me, yet importunes my lover at every opportunity."

On their last morning at the cottage, Mary and Bysshe watched the sun rise over the sea. A new day. It was time, Mary realized, to begin a new life as well. It was May. A whole year had passed since her return from Scotland. What a year! Love and joy beyond belief, but also disillusionment, destitution, and great sorrow. Mary had learned much of life that she would have preferred not to know, but there was no going back. She must make the best of things and move on.

"Bysshe." She turned to face him. "Our life is going to be different now. It *must* be different. Tom is a fine man, my closest friend." She paused to frame her words slowly and distinctly. "But in the future that friendship can never be more than platonic. I have told Tom that, and now I am telling you. He must leave our home. What happened—what happened before—is over. Forever."

She searched Bysshe's face anxiously. What she wanted to convey was so contrary to his ideals of a free and unfettered life. She prayed that she would not lose him. "It will not happen again," she said, "not with Tom, nor any man but you."

There was silence that seemed to go on forever. Mary wanted to say something to break the awful quiet but realized that she had already said it all. What was Bysshe thinking?

At last, he took her hand in his. "I understand." Bysshe's voice was little more than a whisper, but his eyes met Mary's as his full lips framed the words.

"And," she continued, gazing back at him, "I love only you and will always love only you. Can you not say the same to me?"

"I love you, Mary. Of course I love you. You must know that."

"Then Claire . . ." She paused, her heart pounding. "Claire must leave, too. She and all her possessions must be gone from our home before we set foot inside." Mary held her breath, watching his face, waiting.

Bysshe looked at Mary for a long moment. At last he spoke. Taking her shoulders in his hands, he stared deeply into her eyes. "It will be as you wish, Mary."

PART IV

Love will find its way
Through paths where wolves fear to prey
    —Lord Byron

TWENTY-FOUR

"I have found the perfect abode for you," Bysshe announced to Claire. As quickly as that, she was turned out of 41 Hans Place. Bysshe's solicitor had procured rooms for her in the seaside hamlet of Lynmouth.

"I live in a state of tranquility," Claire boasted in a letter to Fanny. "It is wonderful indeed to escape from the turmoil of Mary's passion for Bysshe." She went on to describe her cottage covered in jasmine and honeysuckle in the midst of a countryside tailored for delightful walks.

Claire slammed down the quill. What a cad Bysshe was! He had granted her a small stipend, then dumped her in the middle of nowhere. Lynmouth was exile, pure and simple.

But there were other occasions when Claire thought of him with longing. She would take out the copy of *Queen Mab* he had given her and read the inscription:

Do I dream? Is this new feeling
But a visioned ghost of slumber?
If indeed I am a soul,
A free, a disembodied soul,
Speak again to me.

It was then that she coaxed from her memory every kiss, every caress, bringing them forward like precious keepsakes. She thought

ANTOINETTE MAY

178

of his fingers laying claim to the part of her that had always been so private and shivered with pleasure.

Merely being part of Mary's adventure had never been enough. Claire wanted to *be* Mary, the brilliant one, the Godwin girl that everyone looked to and admired. For a time Claire's efforts to separate Bysshe from her stepsister had seemed to succeed. But now what chance had she? At seventeen, Claire saw life stretching endlessly before her, arid and hopeless.

As summer turned to fall, she walked the headlands daily, doing her best to ignore the suspicious stares of farmers ploughing the nearby fields. Claire knit six scarves, then tried a sweater and quickly abandoned it. Each day she made several eager trips to the post office. Charlie wrote infrequently; he was apprenticed now to a printer and lived in a loft. Dear Fan—Claire had come to think of her stepsister as "dear"—wrote nearly every day. Nothing interesting, but at least it was mail. Sometimes Fan sent books. Desperate for something to fill the evening hours, Claire devoured one after another. She identified readily with Robinson Crusoe, a castaway on a remote island. The people of Lynmouth seemed scarcely more hospitable than cannibals.

Pamela, or Virtue Rewarded gave her food for thought. Pamela's master holds her prisoner in his castle. She loves him but refuses to give in to their mutual desire. Many considered the novel licentious; Claire thought it silly. Why wait for anything one wanted?

As months passed, desperation swept over her. If Claire had remained at home, she might have had a grand career as an opera singer. Instead, disowned by her parents, she was solely dependent on Bysshe's largesse. If his stipend should end—as it might at any time—where would she be? Then one day the taciturn postmaster handed her a letter. Claire's heart caught at the familiar handwriting. Did Bysshe want her back? She scanned the page rapidly. Apparently so, but not for the reason she had hoped. Mary's baby was due within the month. "She will have need of you," he wrote.

Claire had no illusions. Bysshe intended her stay to be a brief one. In no position to bargain, she still tried. "I will come," she wrote him, "but only if you promise to secure lodgings for me afterward in London, somewhere near Drury Lane. I will *not* return to Lynmouth."

His answer was brief: "Have it your way."

———————

Mary was delivered of a son, full-term and healthy. To Claire's surprise, they named the baby William. Papa Godwin continued to be dreadful, refusing to have anything to do with Mary and seeking out Bysshe only to plague him for money. Oh, well, none of that was her concern. She had enough to do with the baby—rocking him endlessly, seeing to his linen changes.

All the while Mary and Bysshe were so pleased with each other, so close. Bysshe seemed scarcely aware of Claire's existence. She was amused at first but soon irritated by the fuss they made over their little "Willmouse." Babies all looked the same to Claire. Still, she sometimes wondered . . . what would it be like to have a child of one's own? As always, Mary had everything. She intended to hold on to it, too. Mary was scarcely on her feet before Bysshe moved Claire into rooms he had found for her a short block from the theater district.

Left to her own devices, Claire went to the theater often. She was happy merely to watch from the pit—what else could she afford? Wearing her one party dress and a castoff cape of Mary's, she saw two favorites, *The Merry Woodman* and *The Rustic Revel*, again and again. The spectacle enthralled her: false noses, beards, and hair; trapdoors and sheep's blood spurting from concealed bladders. Yet even this paled beside the sight of elegantly clad gentry in their curtained boxes.

Frequently she saw the Prince of Wales, plump and red-faced in his striped waistcoats and flamboyant collars, beside him the still-beautiful Mrs. Fitzherbert. Theirs was indeed a love story— the beautiful commoner, the wayward prince—though Prinny, as everyone called the Regent, seemed an unlikely hero.

Looking up one night, Claire's eyes fixed on a figure in a box near the Regent's. It was Lord George Gordon Noel Byron, England's most glamorous celebrity. Bysshe and Mary were besotted with the peer's poetry and were forever quoting him. Now there he was, sitting alone, gorgeous as a god. Even from a distance Claire could feel his power, sense his charisma. She liked his dark curly hair, too. The cut, a trifle long for fashion, might appear foppish on anyone else, but he was so strong, so virile. His eyes were deep-set, his nose distinguished, some might say stern, his lips sensual. Claire wondered how they might feel on her own. Other women watched him, too—beautiful, worldly women. He could have any of them.

Claire knew all about Byron. Everyone who read the broadsheets did. Publication of his epic poem *Childe Harold's Pilgrimage* three years before had rendered the young lord an overnight success. But that was barely the half of it. The handsome nobleman was a notorious libertine. As if his affair with Lady Caroline Lamb wasn't scandalous enough, there was rumored incest with his married half sister and now the recent separation from his wife. *Well, let them talk,* Claire thought. He was the most celebrated bard in the land—Bysshe, in comparison, a mere nobody. Claire imagined herself on the lord's arm, everywhere envious eyes fixed on her.

Later that night, back at her lodgings, Claire sat for a time before her small desk. Her heart quickened as she picked up a quill. Claire's hand trembled at first, but at last she wrote with painstaking care:

An utter stranger takes the liberty of addressing you. If a woman whose reputation has yet remained unstained, if without guardian or husband to control her, she should throw herself on your mercy, if with a beating heart, she should confess the love she had born you for many years, if she should confess the love, should return your kindness with fond affection and unbounded devotion, could you betray her, or would you be silent as the grave? I am not given to many words. Either you will or you will not. Do not decide hastily, and yet I must entreat your answer without delay.

Claire signed her name with a flourish. The note was a masterpiece; she would have a messenger boy deliver it to him at the theater.

Claire waited anxiously for a reply. A day passed, then another. Nothing. She felt foolish and then frightened. So much was riding on this. She could not allow herself to become discouraged. Perhaps he had not even gotten her note. Quickly she penned another, this one to his home.

Lord Byron is requested to state whether seven o'clock this evening will be convenient for him to receive a lady to communicate with him on business of peculiar importance. She desires to be admitted alone and with utmost privacy. If the hour she has mentioned is correct, at that hour she will come.

She gave her note with a coin to a newsboy. "Stay for a response and I will tip you double," Claire instructed. She had not long to wait. Claire's pulse raced as she broke open the seal and read:

Ld. B. is not aware of any "importance" which can be attached by any person to an interview with him, and more particularly

by one with whom it does not appear he has the honor of being
acquainted. He will however be at home at the hour mentioned.

———————

The mansion at 17 Piccadilly took Claire's breath away, a lofty
structure with a white portico and broad steps flanked by massive
Corinthian columns. Even the hackney driver appeared impressed,
coming around to help Claire descend and taking her hand as
though she were a grand lady. The implied homage pleased Claire
so much that she tipped him half a crown before realizing it.

Lord Byron opened the door himself. Where were the servants? Her heart quickened. Were they to be alone? His eyes swept
over Claire before meeting hers. One dark brow lifted. "Who are
you?" he asked. "Who sent you here?"

Claire forced herself to meet his gaze. Byron was dangerously
attractive in his finely cut red coat. She tried not to stare at the way
the lord's breeches hugged his thighs, looking instead at his dark
hair, thick and glossy. She imagined it would feel like silk.

"I am Claire Clairmont," she told him. "No one sent me. I am
here because I want to be."

"Indeed." He watched her steadily, carefully. She stared back,
her heart pounding.

"Did you write those notes yourself?"

In his eyes she read a kind of lazy amusement that embarrassed
her, made her feel helpless and tongue-tied, but a little angry, too.
"Of course I wrote them. Who else?"

"They were damned clever."

Claire flushed with pleasure. "Thank you, m'lord." She dropped
a small curtsy.

"Come inside. Let me have a look at you."

Byron was only a few inches taller than she but carried himself
with distinction. Well . . . except for the limp. It was said the lord's

right foot was deformed. He disguised it well, walking with a rolling gait, but Claire could imagine how he hated it.

Silently he led the way to a study off to the side of the entryway. It was clearly a man's domain, the furniture oversized and sturdily built. She saw books everywhere, nothing new in that. What she was not accustomed to were the multitude of marble statues, nymphs and satyrs, each cut with painstaking detail. Voluptuous breasts and penises everywhere. Embarrassed but also curious, Claire scarcely knew where to look. Turning away, she started at her own mirrored reflection. A graceful, curving figure in white muslin, small, dark curls bobbing against a background of crimson drapery. Claire smiled.

Byron moved to a console table by the window, where decanters of liqueurs and crystal tumblers waited. Pouring two rations of a rich amber liquid, he handed one to her, then downed the contents of his own in a single swallow. Claire caught her breath as she felt the impact of his eyes on her, cool and appraising. "How do I know you were not sent here by my enemies?"

Claire gasped. "I represent only myself. I cannot imagine you having enemies."

"I have many."

"Then perhaps I am naïve, my lord."

"I doubt that, my lady."

"I am not a lady," Claire answered with a smile. "Perhaps you will discover that for yourself." She suppressed a nervous shiver.

Then the question she had been waiting for: "Why have you come?"

"You are a director at the Drury Lane Theatre," Claire responded, proud of her clear, strong voice. "I want to be an actress." She added, with only the slightest quaver, "Surely you can advise me and perhaps"—she hesitated—"put in a word for me."

The lord withdrew his pocket watch as if to check the time. He shrugged impatiently. "I am to dine with friends—"

Claire moved forward, cutting him off before he could dismiss her. "Perhaps we could talk another time." She looked up at him imploringly. "We could go out of town to some quiet place, perhaps a little country inn where you are unknown." Claire gulped and swallowed hard. She felt his eyes following the working of her throat. A hot current flowed through her.

He studied her a moment, his eyes cold, wild, and blue. "You must know that I am legally bound to Annabella. I could never make an honest woman of you, should I even care to."

"I have no need of that," she assured him. "You will see I am quite without convention."

"Indeed." His arms encircled her, his lips sealing hers. From shoulder to thigh, he pressed against her. Claire's hands clenched and released at her sides, then reached up for him.

Byron stepped back, holding her at arm's length. "Don't fall in love with me," he warned gruffly. "Nothing can come of it."

TWENTY-FIVE

Claire's visits to Mary and Bysshe's new home at 41 Hans Place were surprisingly infrequent. Mary wondered about that, but not often. Claire had vanished into her beloved theater district. Mary was happy for her, happier still for herself.

Then one morning she heard impatient pounding at her door. Claire was back, ebullient, looking for all the world like a cat with a newly captured bird. What was Claire up to now?

Mary hadn't long to wait.

"I have taken a lover," Claire informed her as soon as she'd settled herself on the velvet settee. "He's a poet. You may have heard of him." She paused for effect. "George Gordon, the Lord Byron."

Mary's mouth gaped. No wonder Claire preened; she had captured a rare bird, indeed. Byron was famous beyond belief, so famous that she—indeed, all of their literary circle—scarcely considered him a man at all. Lord Byron was a god.

She stared at her stepsister in disbelief. Claire had been known to stretch the truth, even, if it served her purpose, to fabricate. Mary listened skeptically as the story unfolded.

"He must have seen me in the audience at the theater," Claire explained, "because just before the third act, an usher came to me with a note. The Lord Byron was inviting me to have dinner with him after the play."

"And you agreed?"

"Of course," Claire said, tossing her dark curls.

"You were very bold."

"No bolder than you with Bysshe," she retorted. "How is this different?"

"Lord Byron is different. Surely you have read Lady Caroline Lamb's memoir. She called him 'mad, bad, dangerous to know.' Lady Caroline is a woman of the world. If that was *her* experience, what can you expect?"

"*Lady!*" Claire retorted. "She is a trollop. Did you know that Caroline Lamb sent him a lock of her hair?"

"What is so unusual about that? Many women do it."

"Not from her head, you goose! From down there." Claire pointed to the folds of her gown. "Who do you know who's done that? It's really true, he showed it to me."

"What!"

"Do not be so shocked, my dear. He is accustomed to such things. Lady Caroline simply does not understand him. No one does. The women he has known before have been most unkind. Why, his very own mother is responsible for his deformed foot. It was her vanity, insisting upon wearing stays when she was carrying him, that caused it. Imagine!"

"If true, that is very sad, but it does not change a thing. He is married," Mary reminded her.

"What difference does that make? They no longer live together." Claire rose impatiently and began to pace the room. "Bysshe is married to Harriet. I will console my poet as you do yours. Console and inspire him."

Yes, Mary realized, Claire the aspiring actress knew the part well. She had been understudying it for more than a year. Yet surely Claire must see the difference between the two men. She was rosy with excitement, yet her eyes avoided Mary's.

"Why have you come?" Mary asked.

"Georgie—Lord Byron's close friends call him Georgie." Claire tossed her head, preening once again, then paused, faltering. "He admires you and Bysshe very much."

"Admires *us!*" Mary sat back in surprise. "How is he even aware of us?"

"He has read *Queen Mab* and likes it. He says that Bysshe is quite talented, that one day his poetry will be read everywhere. I have told him about you as well and, of course, he knows of and respects your parents."

"Well, that is very nice, but . . ." Mary's voice trailed off. *What does Claire want?*

Claire looked down, pink cheeks reddening. "He does not believe I know you," she said, her voice barely above a whisper.

"Not know me?" Mary exclaimed. "That is absurd!"

"No, it's not absurd. People lie to him all the time." Claire's eyes flashed. "You do not understand. People will say anything to Georgie, do anything to get what they want from him. It has made him suspicious of everyone. Even me. He believes that I made up my connection to you to impress him."

"Then I am sorry for you, but what has that to do with me?"

Claire widened her eyes, pleading. Mary knew the expression well. It was usually reserved for Bysshe. "You must come to tea," Claire urged. "Let him meet you. Please do this for me. It will help in so many ways. I am . . . shy with him, awkward. I do little more than sit on a stool at his feet."

In the carriage riding to his home, Claire was uncharacteristically quiet. After an inordinate amount of time looking out the window, she turned reluctantly to Mary. "You are pretty and clever." She spoke the words softly, hesitantly. "He will no doubt fall in love with you and be lost to me forever."

Mary suppressed a smile. If she desired such a dalliance, it would serve Claire right, but Mary did not. Surely not with a man of Lord Byron's reputation. She loved Bysshe and would have no other, but mischievously, Mary remained silent. Claire would have no reassurance from her.

"Why are you so lacking in confidence?" Mary asked at last. "It is most unlike you."

Claire looked away. "*He* does it to me." Her words were soft, barely above a whisper. "I feel so awkward, I can only watch him and listen silently to every word he utters."

Mary studied Claire. "You are lovers," she said at last. "Do you never converse?"

"Not often," Claire admitted, eyes downcast. "It seems we hardly say more than, 'Does this feel good?' or 'Would you like me to do that?'"

Mary thought of herself and Bysshe, often talking the night away, and felt sorry for Claire, possibly for the first time in her life.

———

Whatever Mary may have expected, Lord Byron was not it. At eight-and-twenty, he was well built and handsome, no one could deny that, though his features were strong, almost harsh, seared by disillusionment and cynicism. Then he smiled, a most charming smile that drew her close.

To Mary's surprise, Lord Byron bent over her hand like a courtier, then took it gently, leading her into the drawing room. "Go see what the housemaid's up to, she is late with the tea," he instructed Claire with a casual wave of his hand. "I shall have a few words alone with this lovely lady."

"Yes, m'lord," Claire replied with a mock curtsy, but her cheeks flamed red as she turned on her heel.

"Come this way," Byron said, taking Mary's arm and tucking it into his own.

Two suits of armor guarded the entryway to the boldly impressive drawing room. It was hard for Mary not to stare at the vast fireplace fashioned to accommodate several tree trunks, or the massive array of pikes and shields mounted above it. Across the room was a colossal marble-topped refectory table, surely centuries old, pushed against tall windows draped in red velvet. Lord Byron gestured for her to take a tufted chair, then lounged back on the silken couch, arms stretched above his head.

In the midst of this grandeur, Lord Byron talked admiringly of her parents' work. "*Political Justice* seared my mind," he said, picking up a well-worn copy from a marble-topped side table. "And *A Vindication of the Rights of Woman* was a daring manifesto. I cannot say that I agree with its premise, but I recognize the genius from which it sprang."

"Really? I can scarcely imagine that the rights of women are of much import to you," she answered.

"You misjudge me."

They paused, taking each other's measure. *He's undressing me in his head,* Mary thought, and rather enjoyed the notion. She met his bold blue eyes and smiled. "Take care your attentions don't hurt Claire. She has already been estranged from my father—the only father she has ever known—because of my elopement with Bysshe."

Byron shook his head. "I cannot understand your father. His was the most radical of all the tracts to come out of the Revolution. Marriage, he said, was a travesty for thinking people."

"Yes, but what he writes as a philosopher and what he feels as a father are quite different. Bysshe and I—Claire, too, by association—discovered this to our great dismay."

"I am sorry to hear that." Byron looked at her almost, Mary speculated, as though he meant it. "But," he continued, "I promise no longer to be a distraction to your sister. I am leaving soon for the Continent and will never return to England."

Mary looked at him in surprise. "Does Claire know?"

"If she would but listen. I have told her from the beginning. My own life is chaos. Society chooses to misunderstand my feelings for my beloved sister, Augusta. Only recently I took her to a party that Lady Jersey had given for me—for *me*—was I not entitled to bring whom I pleased? Apparently not, the guests walked out en masse.

"My Francophile politics are equally unpopular," he continued. "My defense of Napoleon—'freedom's son'—is too much for those fools. Last week I attended the House of Lords—my rightful place—but only one member so much as spoke to me.

"Yes," he concluded, taking a pinch of snuff from the silver box tucked into his waistcoat, "it is time I left London for good."

Mary breathed a sigh of relief. "Claire will be very disappointed."

"She'll get over it. If there is one thing of which I am certain, absence is a sure cure for love."

At that moment Claire entered the room, followed by a sullen housemaid wheeling a carved mahogany tea cart. Claire regarded them suspiciously, but Byron appeared not to notice. He bantered easily, talking of the theater, the newest books, the latest antics of the Regency court. Claire's hot, hungry eyes never left his face.

Byron's conversation drifted to Bysshe and *Queen Mab*. "He's good—very good. *Queen Mab* is a stunning creation," the lord said, turning to Mary. "I like his theme of revolution well enough, but disagree with his philosophy. Your Bysshe sees social change as a two-pronged revolt powered by nature and human virtue."

"Of course." Mary shrugged, smiling. "That's what it is. But agree or not, you have no idea the pleasure it gives me to know that you are even aware of *Queen Mab*. Bysshe set the press himself and ran off but two hundred and fifty copies. It is his soul's work. The world is changing before our eyes, factories springing up everywhere, young men walking away from land their fathers farmed for centuries. New inventions are created daily, or so it seems, but how are we to control them?"

Claire looked from one of them to the other, her dark eyes wide. "I don't understand this talk at all. *Queen Mab* is about a fairy queen. It's but a tale."

Lord Byron glanced at Claire as though she were a child; then his eyes fixed again on Mary. "It appears your Bysshe seeks to offer humanity a road map."

Mary, too, ignored Claire. "You understand then that the world Bysshe envisions—that we both envision—cannot come from violent revolution. It can only be achieved through nature's evolution, through ever-greater numbers of people becoming virtuous and striving for a better society."

Byron shook his head. "Understanding and agreement are very different, but"—he paused to smile at her—"nonetheless stimulating. I wish, dear lady, that I could meet your Bysshe and talk with him about these matters, but I fear that is not to be."

He rose to his feet and once again bowed over Mary's hand. "I have agreed to meet friends," he explained. "I can hardly be tardy for my own farewell dinner."

"Farewell dinner!" Claire echoed. "Whatever are you talking about?"

"Claire, Claire, if you would but listen! Mary will tell you the details." Byron walked Mary and Claire to the portico, then hailed a hackney and paid the driver with a flourish.

As the carriage rumbled down the cobbled street, Claire looked at Mary in angry resentment. "What is this about Georgie leaving?"

"He's planning an extended trip to the Continent. It's possible that he may never come back."

"Well, we'll see about that!" Claire said with an impatient sigh. "You were both just awful, talking about those silly ideas as though I were not even present."

"You wanted me to meet him. Did you think we would not talk?" Mary sat back, hoping to avoid one of Claire's tantrums. Her mind whirled with thoughts of the infamous Lord Byron. Once an adored member of society, he had held the House of Lords enthralled with his speeches. Only recently Byron's epic poem *The Corsair* had sold ten thousand copies on its first day of publication . . . At the same time so much evil was spoken of him. Dreadful things. How could the same man be party to both?

Finally Mary leaned toward Claire. Her voice scarcely more than a whisper, she asked, "Those stories they tell . . . the incest, that he loves both men and women, that he—he buggered his own sister . . . can they be . . . is any of it true?"

Claire raised her head, meeting Mary's gaze. "Some of it, I suppose." She shrugged. "Yes, you might as well know—it's all true."

TWENTY-SIX

Claire had succeeded again. She had talked Mary into a debacle. Why, Mary wondered, had she allowed it? *What is the matter with me? When will I learn?*

It began with Claire's insistence that she and Bysshe needed a holiday. "He is tired—anyone can see that," Claire said. "And you"—she turned to Mary—"you look so pale. A change of scene would bring color to your cheeks." *Where was this coming from?* Mary had wondered. Was Claire angling to live at Hans Place as a caretaker in their absence? Not likely! They would never get her out. Claire would stick like glue.

Mary had drawn a sigh of relief when Bysshe shook his head, but after a few days of Claire's importuning, she saw him weaken. Really, could she blame Bysshe? Papa's constant demands for money must be wearying, and the lack of interest from his publisher was depressing as well. One morning Bysshe put down the book he'd been reading and looked at Mary. "I know you have always dreamed of Italy. What about it, Mary? A villa by the sea ..."

"Yes," Claire chimed in. "You could sit on the veranda and scribble to your heart's content."

"We have a little money now," Bysshe reminded Mary, his blue eyes teasing. "Why not enjoy it?"

So they would go, but, of course, that was not the end of Claire's meddling. She wanted to travel with them. "Please, please,

please, take me," she begged. "It has been such a long, hard winter. You cannot leave me behind."

Well, yes, Mary could have, easily, but Bysshe intervened. "Claire can take care of Willmouse while you write."

They began to make plans, to talk enthusiastically of the upcoming adventure. Then, almost overnight it seemed, Claire lost interest in Italy. She wanted instead to visit Switzerland.

"Why?" Mary asked. "Have we not been there?"

"It will be even better this time," Claire said, her eyes on Bysshe. "Remember the snowcapped mountains, the lake glittering in the sun?" She turned to Mary. "Willmouse will adore Switzerland. It will be warm and gorgeous there. He will thrive."

A fortnight out of London, their small party reached the Alpine foothills. Rising from a desert of silent snow, the heavy coach inched its way toward Geneva. Warm Switzerland, indeed! As it turned out, the spring of 1816 was the worst that anyone in the region could remember. Swiss astronomers were predicting the end of the world by mid-June. The sight of Claire sitting opposite her in the coach caused Mary's chest to tighten. Why had she allowed that dark gypsy to reenter her life? Watching Claire fidget nervously, she wondered what the girl was plotting this time.

As if Claire read Mary's mind and sought to avoid the question, she took a small book from her reticule and began to read aloud:

Thou lovedst me
Too much, as I loved thee: we were not made
To torture thus each other—though it were
The deadliest sin to love as we have loved.
Say that thou loath'st me not—that I do bear

This punishment for both—that thou wilt be
One of the blessed—and that I shall die

"Oh!" she broke off, looking from one to the other. "Is that not romantic?"

"Very," Bysshe replied shortly. "Byron writes of love as though he knows it well."

Thoughts of her own love for Bysshe filled Mary's heart as she gazed out on the terrain they had traversed two years before. She turned her head to catch his smile. Their eyes met; Mary knew they shared the same memories. It was a wonderful moment, but also poignant. Life had seemed so carefree then. She could never have imagined the agony of bearing a child only to lose her. Mary felt baby William's warm breath and held him closer.

The pale, hesitant sun sank lower as the carriage reached Poligny. The familiar landscape was ending, the expanse ahead unknown. "Surely we will continue?" Claire asked impatiently as they clambered out to stretch their legs. "We are not to spend the night here!"

Willmouse, now awake, cried fretfully. Mary longed for an early supper and a warm bed, but the drab slate-roofed village looked anything but inviting. Crags overhung the narrow chalets, casting murky shadows. The sense of being locked in by towering, death-dealing peaks was almost unbearable. "What do you think?" she asked Bysshe.

"We will stop for dinner only," he said.

By the time they finished eating, their two postilions were ready with fresh horses. Dusk had fallen. The rain had ceased, but the wind blew fiercely and the serpentine road—bound on one side by a chasm filled with misty clouds—continued, slippery and steep. Crashing thunder sent small avalanches of snow down the sides of the mountain as they climbed, the coach's lanterns swinging heavily in the wind.

They reached the post house in the village of Champagnole just as the town clock struck midnight. Exhausted, Mary watched one of their postilions climb down from the box and knock at the entrance. After an interminable wait, the massive doors swung open, allowing their carriage to drive into a long hall crowded with equipages. Postilions slumbered on bales of hay, oblivious to the newly awakened chickens that clucked excitedly, scattering in all directions. Mules brayed, pigs grunted; the stench was terrible.

Inside the post house, heat from the stove threatened to suffocate them all. Even at this late hour, the small taproom was crowded with peasants who drank beer at a trestle table stretching the length of the room. Privacy was not an option in the adjoining sleeping room, which smelled of beer and sweat and candle wax. Willmouse slept between Bysshe and Mary; Claire lay on a trundle beside the bed. On the other side of her, three male travelers snored lustily, insensitive to the boisterous singing in the next room.

At dawn they were up and on their way. The carriage wheels spun through a sharp turn, the iron rims jolting over cobblestones as the driver urged the team to a quicker pace. Though grateful for the freshly heated brick foot warmers on the coach's floor and the woolen blankets that swathed her body, Mary was soon numb with cold and could see her breath. On one side, pine forests crowded the narrow road; on the other, a precipice dropped to a snowy abyss. As they ascended the mountains, dark clouds unleashed flurries of snow. Occasionally the sun broke through, illuminating towering pines, some wreathed with misty vapor and others dark spires pushing into the sky.

As the day advanced, the weather changed, snow falling so fast that they were forced to halt early in the evening at the village of Les Rousses.

"No!" Claire protested and began to cry. "We must go on."

"Stop your sniveling," Mary snapped. "We are *not* going on." She turned away impatiently and strode into the town's inn, William held tight in her arms. Bysshe followed. Once she'd glanced about, Mary, too, felt like crying; the place was filthy, dust and cobwebs everywhere. She smelled a damp, rank odor and heard a familiar rustling. Again Bysshe and Mary exchanged glances, but this time the memory they shared was anything but pleasant. Rats.

"We must protect William," Bysshe warned, wrapping them both in his arms.

They took turns keeping watch over their baby all through the long night, aware always of scampering feet and furtive eyes gleaming from dark corners.

The next morning, Bysshe hired four fresh horses and an additional postilion to force the carriage through the snow and prevent it from slipping into the chasm. All around them were bottomless gulfs and jagged summits. The road was almost invisible in the vast expanse of white, broken only by isolated crags and monster pines. Watching the relentless flakes pelt against the windows of their carriage, Mary thought no scene could be more desolate.

———

On the last two days of their journey, the weather slowly changed, making their descent easier, though they still needed a drag chain to prevent the carriage from outrunning the horses on the steep mountain slopes. The snowstorms lessened and finally stopped. Rain fell lightly and then not at all. At the next post station they sold their runners and replaced them with wheels. The sun came out at last and they made good time. Night was falling as they passed through the entrance to Geneva, the last travelers to be admitted before the gates swung shut for the night.

The first passerby they encountered was able to direct them to the Hotel d'Angleterre. It was, Claire insisted, a mecca for English travelers. Everyone who was anyone went there.

"But that doesn't mean that we have to," Mary said. "We aren't anybody. We are ourselves. Why not search out somewhere more intimate and less expensive?"

"Oh, no! We must go to the Angleterre, no place else will do," Claire argued. Her voice softened, grew husky as she turned to Bysshe. "It is so right for you, just the place for a poet to see and be seen."

He shrugged his shoulders expansively as he turned to Mary, taking her hand in his. "We can afford a few days at a fashionable hotel."

Mary was not so sure but felt too tired to argue. All she wanted was a quick bite of food and a quiet sleep. The hotel seemed daunting as they drove up. Inside, crystal chandeliers—so many of them—dazzled her. They followed a porter up, up, up a marble staircase that seemed to go on forever. William slept soundly in Bysshe's arms as they climbed, then continued down a long corridor. At last the man stopped, snapped his fingers, and another porter bowed to Claire and opened a door for her. Mary glimpsed a pretty bedchamber tastefully furnished in rose and cream. Claire and her bags disappeared inside.

Mary and Bysshe continued on to the next door. It opened onto a small but inviting sitting room and beyond that a large bedchamber and dressing area. Mary saw a canopied bed, a thick comforter. Beside it was a pretty mahogany crib. Gently Bysshe lowered Willmouse into it; the baby slumbered, oblivious.

Two porters entered, carrying luggage. Their belongings, now so battered, looked all the shabbier in this lovely room, but Mary didn't care. They had at last reached their destination. She turned to Bysshe and found him instructing the porters: cold chicken, strawberries in cream, champagne. The two servants disappeared, leaving them alone.

Mary unwound her shawl and draped it over a chair covered in rose damask. Bysshe's arm encircled her waist. He led her to French doors that opened onto a small balcony. "We have a view of the lake," he told her. "Tomorrow we will enjoy it together. Glancing out, she saw flickering lantern lights leading to a black velvet sea; it looked like fairyland. Mary shivered in anticipation. "Tonight," he continued, "we will enjoy each other."

Mary was not nearly so tired as she had imagined.

———————

The next morning dawned warm and dazzling. Lake Geneva, Mary discovered from her balcony, was as blue as the heavens it reflected. A delicious scent of spring flowers and moist earth filled the air.

Once the favorite of Empresses Joséphine and Marie-Louise, and the haunt of Madame de Récamier, the Hotel d'Angleterre was *très chic*. The *ton* who continued to flock there overwhelmed Mary with their rich silks and lush brocades. The hotel library, lined floor to ceiling with books, contained everything from classics to Gothic romances. Often Mary sat at a polished mahogany library table jotting down her own story ideas with a silver quill, but just as frequently she strolled arm in arm with Bysshe through the hotel's extensive gardens. The Hotel d'Angleterre's lush plantings reached all the way to the lakeshore. Everywhere the scent of roses filled the air.

William, now four months old, blossomed in the late spring sunshine. Each day, Mary spread a blanket for him on the grass and watched with delight as his dear eyes followed the butterflies fluttering by. His cheeks were so full, his eyes big and bright as he wriggled his arms and legs. The world was his to discover.

If thoughts of Harriet and her two small children intruded into Mary's newly found peace, she quickly banished them.

It was a magical time. Claire, though still strained and impatient, appeared engrossed in her own secret thoughts and kept to herself. Bysshe engaged Elize, a Swiss nursemaid, to help care for William. A plump darling of a girl with blonde braids about her head, Elize seemed to really like Willmouse and enjoy caring for him.

In a letter to Fanny, Mary described their days:

We have hired a boat. It is delightful, whether we glide over a glassy surface or are speeded along by strong wind. The tossing of the boat raises my spirits and inspires me with hilarity. Twilight here is of short duration, but we at present enjoy the benefit of an increasing moon and seldom return until ten o'clock, when, as we approach the shore, we are welcomed by the scent of flowers and new-mown grass, the chirp of the grasshoppers, and the song of evening birds.

There was an unreal quality about those first days in Geneva, as if Mary lived in some fabulous dream from which she had no wish to awaken. Then one sunny afternoon, when she and Bysshe returned with Claire from a shopping trip, they saw a coach standing before the inn. It was the largest and grandest that any of them had ever seen—surely the most splendid coach in the world.

The postilion standing guard was quick to inform them that the oversized vehicle was an exact duplicate of Napoleon's personal carriage and had cost the exorbitant sum of two hundred pounds. Eight perfectly matched black horses had maneuvered it over the Alps. Bysshe speculated that the owner must have paid a small fortune in fees at each post station for such an entourage.

A group of curious bystanders crowded around the coach, seemingly awestruck. "Whoever owns it had an easier ride than we," Bysshe commented, pointing out the suspension system of springs. They moved nearer and, when the postilion obligingly opened a door, pushed up close. Bysshe, always so concerned about matters of health, immediately spotted a shelf containing Epsom salts, James's powder, liquid laudanum, and sulphuric acid, plus many other intriguing remedies he did not recognize. Also inside the carriage were not only the standard compass, barometer, telescope, blankets, pillows, and cushions, but also a library, a couch, and a chest for plates and other crockery—everything necessary for the leisure, meals, and study of a gentleman.

Claire dug her nails into Mary's arm before breaking away and rushing into the inn. Bysshe appeared mystified, but Mary did not need to see the large L. B. emblazoned on the door panels to identify the owner. Instantly she understood all. No wonder Claire had been in such a hurry to get to Geneva.

As they followed Claire inside the hotel, Mary heard her address the desk clerk: "I am Claire Clairmont—is there a message for me?" There was nothing. When she pressed for details about the new guest, the clerk informed her that Lord Byron had requested that he and his companion, a Dr. John Polidori, not be disturbed by *anyone*.

Claire, face blotched, eyes brimming with unshed tears, looked as though she'd been slapped.

Since their meeting a few weeks before, Mary had heard a flood of rumors. Byron was said to have swum the Bosphorus, killed an unfaithful Turkish mistress by drowning her in a sack, and lived in a ruined abbey haunted by a hooded monk. Fantastic tales proliferated daily. Swiss newspapers were filled with accounts of how the poet had been denied a visa by King Louis XVIII, who referred to Byron as the devil incarnate—"His Most Satanic Majesty."

Mary's breath caught. Astronomers had predicted the end of the world, and now the Satan himself had arrived.

TWENTY-SEVEN

The twin blues of lake and sky stretched endlessly before Mary. The scene was sublime. Yet strolling the beach with Bysshe and Claire, Mary felt the weight of disapproving eyes. *Well, why not,* she reasoned. Bysshe had deserted his wife and small children only to run off with not one mistress but two. Who could blame the hotel guests for gossiping?

Mary held her head up, her shoulders back, but was relieved when Bysshe found a secluded spot for them to sit. Attendants appeared almost magically, setting up chairs and a colorful sun umbrella. Mary sank down, pulling a book from her reticule. In seconds her nose was buried in *Macbeth*. Let the busybodies stare all they pleased. She had Shakespeare.

Soon the warm sun and soft breezes grew too enticing to barricade behind a book. Mary looked up, sighing contentedly. A sailboat was just coming into view. She watched it draw closer.

As the craft neared shore, Claire gripped her arm. "It's him," she gasped.

Mary sighed again but not with pleasure. Lord Byron was trouble. She knew it.

As he sailed toward shore, hotel employees darted forward into the water to assist him. Conversation ceased and a small crowd gathered. Mary studied Lord Byron's handsome face, his piercing eyes and cynical mouth.

Claire ran forward as he stepped ashore, her arms outstretched, but stopped short of the poet, whose expression had frozen. Mary and Bysshe followed her at a more leisurely pace until they confronted him on the beach. "You have met my stepsister, Mary Godwin," Claire began tentatively.

Lord Byron glanced beyond her to Mary; his full lips parted in a smile as he bowed, amused, cynical eyes penetrating as they swept over her . . . *He sees everything.* Mary flushed but was not displeased.

"And this is Bysshe Shelley, our traveling companion," Claire continued, her voice faltering.

The men eyed each other. Mary wondered if Byron might not be curious about the younger man who, like himself, had created a stir not only with his poetry but also by his manner of living. Their handshake appeared tentative, Bysshe awed, Byron brusque. Nonetheless, they agreed to meet that evening for dinner. "Dr. John Polidori, my companion, will join us," Byron added.

Mary and Claire exchanged glances. What sort of companion?

———

Dining at the Angleterre was a splendid, glittering affair, perhaps a hundred diners served by an army of waiters rushing about bearing steaming tureens of rich sauces and silver trays ladened with lamb cutlets, boiled salmon, and sweetbreads. Mary heard the clink of crystal and cutlery, smelled the mingled scents of rich food, tobacco, and perfume. She hesitated, awed by the finely cut jewels and satin smiles. By the gentlefolk, who, like Bysshe, could trace their ancestry back to William the Conqueror. His world before he met her, a world so different. *Does he miss it? Oh, please, no; let him be content.*

Claire wore a red gown that Mary had not seen before, cut low to flatter her ample breasts. Had Mary been wrong to dismiss

Claire as an air dreamer? Thus far, her scheme appeared to be working.

The evening pleased Mary as well. It began as a contrast between success and aspiration. Byron airily discussed his triumphs: "*Childe Harold* was, as you may know, an overnight success."

Bysshe's admiring eyes shone. "Mary and I loved *Childe Harold*. We read it in a single sitting, then went back over our favorite passages." He paused for a moment. "You were kind to say you had read and enjoyed *Queen Mab*. Perhaps you are the only one. The readership was small."

How could Byron resist such genuine admiration coupled with modesty? He couldn't, Mary found. As the evening progressed and Bysshe, gentle and unpretentious, expressed himself with calm confidence, the balance shifted. Both men were brilliantly intellectual, but while Byron read to dazzle, Bysshe read to know. Mary watched delightedly as the most famous poet in the world listened appreciatively to her lover expound on vitalism, a controversy that divided the thinking world. Bysshe held his own well.

Mary recalled the evening of her fourteenth birthday, when Papa had taken her to hear Humphry Davy speak on vitalism at the Royal Institution. Davy had predicted that man would one day control nature with scientific instruments of his own creation. The idea still intrigued her, its implications causing her pulse to quicken. Doctors frequently dissected corpses in order to study them, but suppose body parts could be reassembled and sewn together. Suppose this pieced-together body could then be animated . . .

She turned her attention back to the conversation. Bysshe was arguing. "Surely you must agree that there is a life force or principle. What else would cause our erections?" When she lowered her gaze in embarrassment, he added, "or Mary's face to flush?"

Lord Byron shook his head. "I would call that a blood force."

"But what animates the blood?" Bysshe countered. "Suppose we could direct it at will?"

John Polidori appeared pensive; he had taken no part in the conversation. Mary studied the dandified young doctor. He was strikingly handsome, with large dark eyes and olive skin. John's curly black hair was cut in the Roman fashion, à la Brutus. His trousers were perfectly tailored, his linen freshly starched with an elaborately knotted cravat. Mary was curious about this fashionably dressed young man.

She wondered if he had yet discovered Byron's relationship with Claire. Clues were imminent. Byron was talking of his estate, Newstead Abbey. "Much of the building is ancient, it is said that Queen Elizabeth—"

"Oh, tell me, is it true the abbey is haunted?" Claire broke in.

"What an impulsive creature," John said in a half whisper to Mary. "Can she not wait to chew her food before blurting into the conversation? Her taste, too, is abominable. Those earrings! Anyone can see they are made of paste."

True enough, Mary thought with a smile, but also a little rude. Had John forgotten that Claire was her stepsister? Perhaps he did not care. Perhaps Mary didn't either. Claire was nothing if not impulsive; let others experience the consequences for themselves.

It did nothing to alleviate John's pique when, a moment or so later, Byron caressed Claire's bare shoulder. Though shocked, Mary felt a moment of relief that they were Byron's hands and not Bysshe's. Claire was well occupied for the time being, at least. But poor John, white-faced, rose abruptly to his feet, turned on his heel, and left the room. Glancing around the large dining hall, Mary saw that he was not the only one who looked askance at their table. Soon, she feared, their party would be the talk of the town.

"Heigh ho!" Claire sniffed, following Mary's eyes. "The Genevans should be grateful to us for livening things up."

Mary had to agree that gossip appeared to be the chief diversion in parochial Geneva, a grim stronghold of Puritanism, where inhabitants sealed their city off from nighttime sin by closing their gates promptly at ten. If their party was to remain, Mary realized, they must find a more private retreat.

———·——

At the end of May the mercurial weather changed again. Confined to the hotel's common rooms by a week of drenching rain, Mary was restless, and even the free-spirited Bysshe fidgeted under the curious stares of other guests. One morning the weather cleared sufficiently for him to take Mary sailing. On the opposite bank of the lake, they discovered a pretty little villa. The owner was happy to rent the place, and the next day Mary and Bysshe, Claire, and Willmouse and his nurse, Elize, moved in.

From the beginning Mary loved the tiny Maison Chapuis. She reveled in the lake and mountain views and was lulled by the strange, strong voices of women singing as they worked in the vineyards behind the house. Abandoned by friends and family, Mary had found her social life in London limited to Bysshe's cronies, the two Toms—Peacock and Hogg. The one disapproved of her, the other, well . . . obviously that had been a mistake. Now here were these exciting new friends who visited every day no matter how foreboding the storm clouds.

Soon Byron, too, was house hunting. "I've found a villa on the lake," he told Mary one afternoon. "It is beautiful, a perfect setting for you. I hope to entertain you there often."

Mary was flattered, even more so when she saw Villa Diodati. The hilltop mansion, with its tiered terrace, classical colonnades, and tall Palladian windows fronting on lake and mountains, was impressive. They were all excited by the acquisition, and everyone but John was delighted by the discovery of a narrow footpath winding down through the vineyard to Maison Chapuis.

The moonlight sails that had delighted Bysshe and Mary now included Claire, Byron, and John. The high, choppy waters excited Mary, excited them all. Lord Byron was especially exhilarated. "I will sing an Albanian song for you," he told Mary one night, throwing his head back to howl in a weird, wild way that he insisted was truly Albanian. "Albe," Mary's nickname for him, was born that magical, moon-tossed night.

At Maison Chapuis, life was simple and pleasant. While Claire slumbered late into the day, Mary and Bysshe rose early, played with Willmouse, and sailed on the lake. In the afternoon an eager Claire, an ebullient Bysshe, and Mary—curious about everything and everybody—climbed the path to Villa Diodati. Their visits lasted late into the night while theories were expounded, poems recited, politics argued. Claire would leave with Mary and Bysshe, walk down to the house, say an elaborate good night, and then steal back up the hill and into Albe's bed.

"Isn't this charade a bit silly?" Mary asked Bysshe one night. "It's all so obvious."

Bysshe merely shrugged.

"What about John Polidori? Do you think the three of them sleep together?" she wondered aloud. When Bysshe refused to discuss the subject, she worried that he might be jealous and took pains to see that their own nights were especially pleasurable, exploring his ears with her tongue, his body with her knowing fingers.

Once, returning from Diodati in the early morning hours, Claire slipped and fell, lost her shoe, and ran home without it. Some officious burgher turned it in to the mayor, and before long the whole town had guessed what was going on. *Poor, sorry Cinderella,* Mary thought. Claire had clearly dreamed of impressing, with an enraptured "bold, bad Byron" dancing attendance. It was not to happen. Albe, instead delighted by his newfound friendship with Bysshe, ignored her much of the time.

Mary was happy, taking pleasure in the growing bond between Bysshe and Lord Byron. It seemed to her a synthesis, the coming together of opposite elements, head and heart. Albe, she knew, saw himself as the center of the universe, a far cry from Bysshe, whose soul was dedicated to the worship of beauty in all forms and who idealized women as a source of exaltation and inspiration. Mary loved Bysshe's rose-tinted glasses, as long as they were trained on her.

How different was Albe, who viewed women merely as attractive nuisances. "It is the plague of these women that you cannot live with or without them," he said to Bysshe, not seeming to care a whit that Mary and Claire were present. "I cannot make up my mind whether or not women have souls. My ideal would be a woman with talent enough to understand and value mine, but not sufficient to be able to shine herself."

Mary thought the struggle to hold her tongue would strangle her, but she remained a silent listener, lest her views spoil Bysshe's pleasure in his new friend. Seeking to change the subject, Mary turned to John. "Everyone talks about vitalism. Albe and Bysshe argue constantly. You're the doctor in our midst. What do *you* think?"

"It was the center of most conversations in Edinburgh," he said with a shrug. "Some of my professors said there was no soul, but others believed even cats and dogs possess them. The respective merits of Alessandro Volta and Luigi Galvani were debated often. I myself am drawn to Galvani's animal electricity theory, but many colleagues are intrigued by the possibilities of the voltaic plates.

If dead frogs can be made to twitch by electricity, perhaps one day . . ." He paused, shrugging.

"I should like nothing more than to see my baby brought to life," Mary told him. "But is it . . . right?"

"The same question has plagued me." John's glossy brows came together. "Is such an idea against God's plan? Isn't it another sort of Tower of Babel?"

Mary sat quietly for a moment, seeking to pull together thoughts that had begun to trouble her. "If I have a god, it is nature—a life force, if you will. Is it right for mere humans to go against something that great and powerful? Should we dare to even think of such a thing?"

Byron looked up from his brandy and stared quizzically at Mary. "My dear girl," he said at last, "it appears you harbor a brain in that pretty head of yours."

TWENTY-EIGHT

Mary was lonely. Bysshe was either walking with Byron in the surrounding hills, sailing with Byron on the lake, or talking endlessly with him on the veranda. Sometimes she sat with them, but both men made it clear that they preferred her to remain a silent listener.

Mary took to walking with John Polidori. Away from the others, she found him an eager conversationalist. John had, she learned, received his medical diploma from the University of Edinburgh the previous year. At nineteen, this was quite an accomplishment. The subject of John's dissertation, *The Psychosomatic Effects of Sleepwalking and/or Nightmares*, fascinated Mary.

She would have liked to confide the dreams that disturbed her own sleep, how often her baby girl appeared in them—not dead, but needing only to be cuddled and caressed back to life. But those dreams were too close to her troubled heart to share. Instead, Mary asked John about the scientific experiments he had made.

"They were mostly on the frogs we spoke of last night," he admitted. "Frogs, I fear, are the martyrs of science."

"But if a frog can return to life through science, the possibilities are limitless," she argued. "Have you ever dissected a human body?"

"Yes, of course, all doctors must, but they are difficult to come by. Most good Christians believe that physical bodies rise from their tombs on Judgment Day to meet the Lord. Dissection makes that rather difficult."

Mary stopped to lean against a country fence. "Resurrection hardly seems necessary if one day humans can be awakened from the dead with a bolt of electricity. Your university is famous for turning out illustrious physicians, but I've also heard that Edinburgh is known for body snatching. Did you ever—"

"No," he answered quickly. "That was not necessary for me."

"Did no one ever try to reanimate the bodies?"

"No, Mary," he replied firmly. "Let us talk of more pleasant things. Did you know that I have been commissioned by John Murray, Byron's publisher, to keep a journal on my travels with Byron? Murray has already advanced five hundred pounds. He wants me to write two plays as well."

"You are very clever—I know you will succeed," she encouraged him.

Sometimes Mary and John took Willmouse with them in his pram. Often they rowed out on the lake. Once they rowed all night. Another night they visited a nearby cemetery, stopping at the grave of a little girl. Mary felt the loss of her own baby girl keenly, a child very likely conceived on her mother's grave. The loss of both her mother and child weighed heavily on Mary, but John did his best to raise her spirits. His humor was arch, but rarely cruel.

No question but that he could make her laugh, but Mary worried, too . . . Could John be another Tom? It wasn't long, however, before she realized that there need be no concern on that score. John had no romantic interest in women whatsoever. "It isn't that I don't like them," he assured her. "I do. They can be charming. *You* are always charming, and I can learn things from you."

She looked at him in surprise. "What sort of things?"

"You don't tell all you know, and that smile of yours is mysterious like the Mona Lisa's. You are always watching and listening. Sometimes I see you scribbling. I should not be surprised to find us all in a book one day." It was John's turn to smile. "Be kind, won't you?"

"To *you*, John," she promised, touching his cheek.

Mary had a handsome *cavaliere servente*, who appeared as delighted with her companionship as she with his. They enjoyed many of the same books, particularly Dante and Tasso, and talked of them while strolling. John took an avid interest in the *ton* and had an endless supply of gossip. He knew not only the Regent's latest escapades, but also those of the Duke of York's mistress, Mary Anne Clarke, who sold military commissions on the side.

What was the Regency coming to? Mary wondered. A king lost in a netherworld of madness while his adult children flitted from scandal to scandal? She relished John's juicy tidbits, and when he made suggestions about her wardrobe, Mary listened. Before long she had ordered two new gowns. One lavender, the other smoky gray. The style—high waisted with narrow skirts—was all the rage and suited her well.

John tutored her in Italian and helped care for Willmouse. He was gentle with the baby and seemed to genuinely enjoy playing little games with him. One day John offered to inoculate William for smallpox.

Mary was shocked at the suggestion. "Surely you would never do such a horrid procedure!"

"I have done it many times," he told her. "Smallpox is at its most virulent in young children."

"My own sister, Fanny, got it when she was a baby," Mary admitted. "She is badly scarred."

"Dr. Jenner's discovery is going to put an end to such tragedies," John said. "Let me vaccinate William. The treatment is harmless and can spare you both much grief."

The idea, so controversial, startled Mary. "No, never," she said, stepping back from him. "I have already lost one baby. I could never risk my little Willmouse."

"Think about it, perhaps you may change your mind."

The next day's paper contained a frightening article. An outbreak of smallpox in Geneva had carried off five children. Mary hurried to William's crib and looked down at him searchingly. Did she imagine it, or was his little face flushed?

That afternoon when John came to call, Mary waited with questions. "I have heard of Dr. Jenner, but thought his remedy a folktale."

John raised an eyebrow. "Folktale? More like folk fact. Dr. Jenner's cure was inspired by milkmaids whose exposure to cowpox made them immune to smallpox." John reached for his bag. "I always carry a vial with me." Mary's breath caught as John removed a small glass vessel from his bag. "It is pus from a cowpox pustule," he explained.

What a dreadful idea! Holding the baby, Mary tried not to shiver as John made a scratch on William's small shoulder. Her darling looked so vulnerable. The next morning a tiny scab formed. A day later William had a small fever. Terrified, Mary ran sobbing to John, who gently reassured her. Soon William's fever passed and his bright eyes were again surveying the world with eager curiosity.

At Villa Diodati, Byron spent the mornings in bed. During his last days in London, he had indulged himself with food and drink to the extent that when registering at the Angleterre, he gave his age as one hundred.

Now, he admitted to Mary, he was trying to revitalize himself through diet, taking nothing but a bit of bread and a cup of tea for breakfast, vegetables and seltzer water at noon, and tea with no milk or sugar at night. The regimen did little to improve his disposition. It was "bugger this" or "bloody hell that" much of the time.

Fierce winds and driving rain put an end to sailing and walking. Byron's third canto of *Childe Harold* was the only work in

ANTOINETTE MAY

progress. Each evening, before saying their good nights, he casually tossed Claire pages to copy for him.

With nothing from Byron but his poetry, Claire, pale and strained, was increasingly withdrawn and often ill. One night, she fled the library, where they had been sitting, her hysterical sobs echoing down the long hallway to the door. Bland-faced, Albe merely shrugged.

Awkward as it might be, Mary determined to pursue the matter with him when next they were alone.

The opportunity afforded itself the following afternoon when there was a lull in the rain. "Let us walk," she suggested to Albe, who stood at a diamond-paned window, staring out through the misty glass.

He nodded, smiling, and a parlor maid hurried to fetch their capes. Delighted by the sudden burst of sunlight, they strolled arm in arm along a white gravel path. Riotous flowers had blossomed seemingly overnight to blur the pristine hedges of trimmed yew. Delicious as it was, the specter of a frantic Claire tugged at Mary's heart. Deeply concerned, Mary felt she could wait no longer.

"Claire is miserable," she blurted out. "Is there nothing you can say or do?"

Albe laughed. "Nothing you or she would approve." Backing off, he held up his hands as though to ward her off. "Don't scold! You know as I do that Claire is a foolish, impetuous girl. I could not help this. In fact, I did all that I could to prevent it. Now I have at last put an end to it. I was not in love, but I could hardly play the Stoic with a woman who had scrambled eight hundred miles to unphilosophize me."

"But you did care about her once, at least a little bit," she reminded him. "Can't you at least be friends?"

"Mary, Mary," he chided. "Surely you know that a mistress can never be a friend. While you agree, you are lovers; when that's over, anything but friends."

Mary's heart quickened. She was angry but also frightened. "Bysshe and I are different, *very* different. We are both lovers and friends and will remain that way—always."

"I sincerely hope so, Mistress Mary. But is it wise to venture all your eggs in one basket?"

Mary looked up in dismay. "Whatever are you saying?"

"I am saying there are many forms of friendship. Why not explore some with me?" He took her hand lightly in his.

Mary's heart thumped. It was as though she stood on the edge of a precipice. "No, Albe. I prefer our present form. Is it not time that we returned to the villa?" Arm in arm, they walked back through the garden.

———

Daily Mary was confronted by a despondent Claire, a petulant John, now more resentful of Bysshe than he'd ever been of Claire, and a distant Bysshe so stimulated by his friendship with Byron that he seemed scarcely aware of her.

No longer was it the idyllic holiday she had envisioned in London. A growing storm outside underscored the sense of gloom and violence within. The Arve and Rhone overflowed their banks and the lake rose seven feet. Bridges washed away, crops were destroyed, roads rendered impassable. People were warned to remain indoors—as if a warning was necessary.

Persistent rain beat against the windowpanes at Chapuis and Diodati, acting on frayed tempers. John and Claire constantly sniped at one another, each vying for crumbs of Albe's attention. Mary attempted to escape into books but could not. One or the other of them was constantly trying to draw her into their quarrels.

For a time it had seemed to Mary that she and Claire were growing closer, but now, perhaps because of Claire's ever-growing disappointments, she bared her claws once again. "What do you suppose Harriet is doing these days?" she asked one evening as the group sat in the Villa Diodati's book-lined library. "Don't you suppose that Bysshe will eventually return to her? Harriet's children are, of course, his *legal* heirs."

A chill snaked down Mary's spine, but her face flushed with anger as she turned to face Claire. "How kind of you to think of me. But with a baby on the way, shouldn't you ponder your own future?"

Frowning, Byron rose angrily. His crippled foot tangled in the carpet, pitching him forward so that he fell, leg splayed grotesquely, across the floor. Mary and Claire rushed to his side, but Albe angrily waved them away. Swearing, he rose to his feet and limped to the sideboard to pour himself a drink.

Bysshe looked up from the book he was reading. "What about a game of cards?" he suggested to John.

"Why not," the doctor replied. Coals crackled in the fire, sending up a spur of sparks as he replenished his glass. The two men sat facing each other, their dark leather armchairs drawn close to the banked fire.

Bysshe shuffled the cards lightly. "What shall it be—quadrille, Pope Joan, faro?"

"Why not whist?" John countered. "We can invite the ladies to join us. Mary? Claire? What about it?"

Most considered whist a rather common, below-stairs game, yet they all played it. Claire was eager. Mary hesitated. John had seemed in a foul mood all evening, not at all the laughing companion of a few days past. Before she could say anything, Albe nodded to a servant who stood in the doorway. In a trice, a small table was set up and two additional chairs brought for Mary and Claire. Albe lounged on a couch across from them.

Bysshe swiftly dealt thirteen cards to each. Claire began, placing a card on the table, the three of hearts. Mary was obliged to follow in suit. Easy enough, her hand was mostly hearts. Bysshe

THE DETERMINED HEART   217

and John each played a heart, John taking the trick. And so it went. The game progressed swiftly, their early banter kept to a minimum as the tension increased. Gloating, John took the lead. Then Bysshe trumped the doctor's knave and played an ace of diamonds.

John set his glass roughly on the table, sloshing alcohol on the cards. "Sir, you are cheating! That ace has been played before."

Bysshe merely laughed. "You are mistaken. Let us go over the tricks and you will see—"

Mary scarcely recognized John. His olive face had turned a blotchy red. Clearly he had had far too much to drink. She reached out, gently touching his arm. John brushed her aside and rose to his feet, eyes blazing. "Are you calling me a liar?" he demanded, his voice blurred. "Sir, this is an insult no gentleman can ignore!"

Mary's heart pounded. Was he actually challenging Bysshe to a duel?

Bysshe laughed again good-naturedly, but Byron rose to his feet. "I recollect Bysshe has some scruples about dueling, but I have none and am more than ready to take his place."

"Oh!" Mary gasped. She rose to confront them. "What are you saying? What is happening to us? All of you—stop!"

TWENTY-NINE

Storms swept the countryside, an atmosphere of violence accompanying the gloom. Night after night, Mary, Bysshe, Claire, and John sought refuge around Lord Byron's great marble fireplace. As thunder crashed around them, they recited poetry or read aloud, the increased proximity bringing the drama between Claire and Byron into ever-greater focus.

Mary watched her stepsister pose, reclining against the brocade couch cushions. In a soft husky voice, her eyes focused on Byron, she recited:

> *My very chains and I grew friends*
> *So much a long communion tends*
> *To make us what we are:—even I*
> *Regained my freedom with a sigh.*

The sleeves of her gown slipped back from her white arms as she stretched languorously. "Of course, I would never seek *my* freedom."

The poem was Byron's. Mary had seen it that morning at breakfast when he had tossed the manuscript to Claire to fair copy. Now, he raised a dark brow. "Are you playing with me?"

"I should like to, m'lord."

After downing the contents of his wineglass in one swallow, Byron set it down on the table and walked across the candlelit room to stand over her. "What if I were to ask you to remove your clothes?"

Mary gasped. He spoke as though she, Bysshe, and John were not present, not watching, not listening to every word.

But Claire seemed not to mind. "There are better places, sir," she told him. "M'lord need only say what he desires, for any of his wishes to be granted."

"You would, indeed, remove your clothes here?"

"And yours as well, if it would please you. But, as I have said, there are better places."

Mary saw disdain in Albe's face as he turned away. Why couldn't Claire see it for herself?

John fared no better in his pursuit of Byron. Whatever their relationship might have been, Bysshe's presence had ended it. There had been no more talk of duels, but the young doctor's piercing glances leveled at Bysshe could as well be swords. Oblivious to the rest of the party, the two poets talked long into the night in a secluded corner of the drawing room.

On other occasions, they attempted séances. Was Byron moving the small table at will, Mary wondered, or was it truly a spirit force that caused the legs to rise and fall in answer to a spoken question? She watched carefully but could discern no movement on his part.

"Will my next poem be a success?" Bysshe asked one night.

The table went wild, the legs tap, tap, tapping until Mary thought they would break.

"There's your answer," Byron cried out, clapping Bysshe on the back.

"If only my baby's spirit would speak to me," Mary half whispered.

"Really! You are too much." Claire's laugh was brittle. "What could she say but 'goo goo'? Of what use would that be?"

"Of more use than your prattle!" Mary snapped.

"Enough, you two," Byron growled. "I'll give you something to improve your dispositions." He crossed the room and returned with a silver flask. "Try this." He poured a reddish-brown powder into Claire's brandy. "It may calm you down a bit." Turning to Mary, he smiled. "Why not take a little laudanum, too? Perhaps you'll have a vision. Who is to say it will not be a true one?"

Mary hesitated. The storm had set her nerves on edge, and she knew laudanum to be relaxing. She lifted her glass to him.

"Save some for me," Bysshe surprised her by saying. He so rarely used laudanum, seldom even drank spirits, but tonight Mary noticed that his face was flushed.

"Shall I read to you?" Byron turned toward his massive bookshelf. "Is this not a night for ghost tales?" Leafing through a rare book of German stories, *Fantasmagoriana, or a Collection of the Histories of Apparition, Spectres, Ghosts, etc.*, he read at random the story of a husband who kissed his bride on their wedding night, only to discover to his horror that she had been transformed into the corpse of the woman he had loved before her.

The macabre tale alarmed Mary. What of Bysshe's love? He was a married man living with his wife when she had met him. Commitment meant little or nothing to him then. What of now? What of his commitment to her?

Looking up, Mary saw that the candles on the sideboard had burned low, leaving the room shrouded in shadows. Claire, for once silent, nodded sleepily in her high-back chair. John sat at the table, absorbed in a game of Patience, while Bysshe sharpened a quill with his penknife.

Albe watched them all like a puppet master. Pouring himself something rich and dark from a crystal decanter, he picked up another volume from a nearby table and turned to Mary. "I understand Sam Coleridge is an old friend."

She nodded, smiling softly, as thoughts of her childhood came to mind. The nights she had stolen downstairs in her nightcap and gown to hear Samuel dramatically intone his poems. How exciting to hear the grown-ups talk . . . but the mariner, his awful deed, his terror and loneliness. *I fear thee, ancient mariner! I fear thy skinny hand!*

Albe riffled through the pages. "Mary will enjoy this poem, I think. She is one of the few women with the brains to appreciate it. The only one in *this* room, surely." Albe pointed to her, his fingers appearing strangely elongated. Mary wished she had not taken the laudanum.

The verse Albe selected was *Christabel*; Mary wondered if "appreciate" was the word to describe her feelings as she listened to the story of a witch who took the form of a beautiful princess seeking shelter in Christabel's father's castle. Assigned to share Christabel's room, the witch slowly undresses before the helpless girl, revealing a serpent-like body. Byron's deep voice emphasized the lines:

Then drawing in her breath aloud,
Like one that shuddered, she unbound
The cincture from beneath her breast:
Her silken robe, and inner vest,
Dropt to her feet, and full in view,
Behold! her bosom and half her side—
A sight to dream of, not to tell!
And she is to sleep by Christabel.

Do I appreciate being frightened? Mary wondered. *Sometimes, surely, and would it not be splendid to possess the power to frighten others with* my *written words?*

Coals cracked in the fireplace, sending up a hiss of smoke. Outside the storm grew worse; wind shrieked at the windows. Without warning, Bysshe leapt to his feet and ran screaming from the room.

Heart madly pounding, Mary rose to follow him, but Albe stopped her. "Wait, Mary, the devil only knows what's gotten into him." Turning his heavy-lidded gaze to John, he ordered, "*Doctor Polidori, this is your bailiwick. See to him at once.*"

John's boots pounded across the parquet floor. Albe stood with his arm around Mary, who began to tremble. Had Bysshe gone mad? What was happening to him? She pulled away and started toward the door, but the sound of returning footsteps stopped her. John was back, half carrying, half dragging a damp and disheveled Bysshe. Someone had thrown water on him, possibly the liveried servant who was now helping to support Bysshe.

Mary rushed forward only to stop short. Bysshe, half drenched, stared at her, his face contorted in fright. Mary's heart was in her throat. Her lover's face was deadly pale, his pupils dilated as he stared at her. Was it the laudanum? He must have taken a very large dose.

"Mary!" Bysshe gasped, looking at her with what seemed to be horror. His hands hung limply at his sides.

She started forward again, her arms reaching to comfort him, but he backed away, eyes wide, terrified as he regarded her. "I was watching—watching you as I listened to the poem. You were someone else, some*thing* else. You were naked, your eyes blazing out at me from where your nipples should be."

Mary's face flamed with embarrassment. The others stared as if she were a monster. Their stunned silence crushed her like a heavy mantle. Finally Byron broke the awful quiet with a sudden challenge: "We shall each write a ghost story." Turning to Mary, he added, "You and I will publish ours together."

Nervous enthusiasm rippled through the room. It would be a contest. They talked at once of skull-headed ladies, ghosts, and ghouls. Bysshe shook his head groggily, but at last even he joined in. Only Mary was unable to think of a theme.

The storm was so violent that she, Bysshe, and Claire remained at Diodati. Mary lay awake most of the night, listening to the great house creak and groan. Eyes seemed to stare at her from beyond the bed curtains. Sleep, when it came, was fitful.

The next day dawned heavy with rain. Mary had scarcely entered Albe's dark-paneled breakfast room before John pounced on her. "I have already begun my story," he told her. "It's about a vampire. What about you? Have you decided on a plot?"

She shook her head wearily. A hearty breakfast of ham, eggs, and pheasant had been laid out on the sideboard. The array of silver utensils set before her glittered brightly in the candlelight. Too brightly. After a cup of tea, she made her way down the muddy slope to Maison Chapuis. She wanted to be alone to think.

Willmouse was wide awake and crowed happily at the sight of Mary. She played with him much of the morning, then spent the remainder of the day closeted in her room. Staring out at the wet, windswept landscape, Mary's thoughts circled wildly. *"You are going to write a story, are you not?"* Albe had asked her at breakfast, a note of skepticism in his voice. Of course she was! It was naught but a rainy night's diversion, but Mary determined that her story would be equal to or better than Byron's or Bysshe's.

That evening Bysshe and Claire preceded Mary to Villa Diodati. It began to rain again, a brisk downpour. Dark was falling as Mary climbed the hill alone, slipping and sliding on the muddy path.

Inside, a fire brightened the long, shadowy drawing room. Candles guttered in their ornate sconces. Drawing closer to the blaze, the group speculated upon the mysterious power of electricity and the experiments of Erasmus Darwin, who was said to have galvanized a piece of vermicelli into life. "Surely that is proof of a life force," Bysshe insisted. Albe would only agree that electricity was a force in itself.

It was midnight when they finally parted. Once home, Bysshe fell fast asleep. Mary lay quietly beside him, listening to the pounding rain. A jagged flash of the most intense light was followed by an immense crackling sound. Outside, crashing reverberations rolled down the mountainsides and onto the lake, echoes reinforcing echoes.

"What if electricity—this lightning crackling across the sky—could create a life force?" Mary wondered aloud. There was no answer from Bysshe. He had slept through it all. Mary listened to his even breathing, then drifted for a time, neither awake nor sleeping. Images passed before her mind's eye. She saw dark shadows across a snow-covered wilderness, a dead boy lying in a forest, and a screaming woman with a noose around her neck.

All receded to be replaced by a student kneeling beside the thing he has created, a form patched together from bits and pieces. A man, yet is it a man? The young scientist pulls a lever, and a powerful engine pours life force into the supine creature. It stirs uneasily. Horrified, the student flees to his bedchamber. He sinks into a deep sleep but is awakened. Something is pulling aside his bed curtains. A frightful creature stands at his side. It looks down at him with yellow, watery, but speculative eyes . . .

———·—

Mary rose early the next morning. Bysshe still slept as she dressed quickly and hurried to the Diodati breakfast room. As she entered, Mary was glad to see a fire in the grate. Albe had just risen from the table where he and John had been sitting. He smiled at her, one dark brow raised quizzically.

Elated at last, she smiled back, bowing with a grand sweep of her arm as a man might. "Good morning to you both." Mary surveyed the well-stocked sideboard. Her appetite had returned full force. She was ravenous. Wielding a pair of silver tongs, she prepared a plate for herself, artfully arranging a freshly baked scone beside slices of shaved ham.

"I have my story," she informed them cheerfully before tucking in to her plate.

Once back at Maison Chapuis, Mary dressed Willmouse, then helped Elize prepare his breakfast. Once the dishes were cleared away, she sat down at the table.

Taking a fresh sheet of foolscap, Mary wrote briskly, "It was on a dreary night of November that I beheld the accomplishment of my toils . . ."

PART V

Her voice did quiver as we parted,
Yet knew I not that heart was broken
From which it came, and I departed
Heeding not the words then spoken.
Misery—O Misery,
This world is all too wide for thee.
    —Percy Bysshe Shelley, "On Fanny Godwin"

THIRTY

Fanny woke at five, ill prepared for the day that awaited her. She heard a quick knock at her door. Without waiting for an answer, Nan, the Godwins' maid, entered, carrying a pitcher of hot, soapy water. "Mrs. Godwin said you was to look extra nice today. Everything just so. I'll be back to help with your stays." She set the pitcher on a low table. "Now hurry along; I haven't much time, what with that fancy breakfast she's told me to fix for those fussy aunts of yours."

As the door closed, Fanny lifted the pitcher and poured its contents into a basin. She cleansed her skin with the perfumed soap that Claire had left behind two years before. She had cherished the small bar, tucking it carefully away in the corner of her drawer. Rarely had the fancy soap been used. Few occasions in Fanny's life seemed worthy, yet she often took the bar out to sniff the fragrance.

Fanny dried off with a threadbare towel. She longed to dust her face with the tiniest pinch of pearl powder or, even better, Pear's Almond Bloom, but those things were not for her. Fanny reached for her bone toothbrush and paste jar and scrubbed vigorously. She had good teeth. What about the tiniest bit of pink carmine on her lips to show them off? She applied the salve carefully. Fanny had taken—borrowed—the enamel case from Mum's drawer. She would have to return it quickly.

She had barely hidden the case before Nan returned to assist
with her corset. Fanny treasured the garment, for it bore the initials M. W. for Mary Wollstonecraft. Her mother, the champion of
women's rights, had struggled with the same stiff-boned corsets
worn by every woman of her day. Fanny was happy styles were
changing, designers drawing inspiration from classic Greek statues. Hoops and flounced layers of petticoats were passé, in their
place waists raised to just below the bosom, skirts allowed to hang
free. Fanny's heirloom corset had been modified, the undergar-
ment now a clever combination of straps, tapes, and laces that separated her breasts, pushing them up and out to create a kind of
trembling, heaving effect that rather embarrassed her.

As Nan helped with her drawers and petticoat, Fanny thought
anxiously of the interview that awaited her. *I must be careful, so
careful. Everything depends on this.*

Nan held up a blue dress. It was old—all her dresses were
old—but Fanny rather liked this one. Hadn't Papa once said the
blue matched her eyes? She tugged nervously at the décolletage,
hoping to show as little of her pockmarked chest as possible, then
put on a pretty plumy bonnet that had once been Claire's, pulling
it low to shade her face.

Fanny turned to view herself in the mirror, then picked up a
watch that Mary and Bysshe had sent her from Geneva. It was a
lovely thing of filigreed gold set with tiny sapphires. Fanny pinned
it to her shoulder, reassured that they must have been thinking of
her when they bought it.

Fan had heard by chance only the previous day of the trio's
return and was determined to brave Papa's wrath and visit them.
Perhaps this time she herself would have exciting news to share. So
much depended on this interview.

Taking the blue gloves that Nan handed her, she preceded her
servant down the narrow stairs. Fanny's heart was thumping. If
only her aunts, Everina and Eliza, would like her. They were alone,

she the daughter of their only sister. Would that not count for something? She had been educated by William Godwin—was that not enough in itself to make her a fine addition to their school?

A chill ran through Fanny at the thought of the interrogation that lay before her. The scandal caused by Mary's elopement . . . How was Fanny to get around that? She pushed open the door. The aunts were sitting at the breakfast table with Papa and Mum. Forcing a smile, Fanny dropped a light curtsy. "I am so very happy to meet you both at long last . . . my mother's beloved sisters."

"I am your Aunt Everina," the tall, thin one introduced herself. She picked up her lorgnette, scrutinizing Fanny. "You don't look a bit like your mother."

You don't either, Fanny thought. Mama was beautiful. She answered instead, "I don't seem to look like anyone. Perhaps my father—"

"We are not here to discuss that scoundrel," her plumper sister interrupted. "I am your Aunt Eliza. My sister and I consider his connection to your mother and your subsequent birth as most unfortunate." She paused for a moment, raising her own lorgnette and leveling it on Fanny. "Nonetheless, we are determined to do our Christian duty," she said at last. "Whatever the circumstances of your birth, you remain our niece."

Setting down her teacup, Everina eyed Fanny speculatively. "I am certain your—er—stepfather, Mr. Godwin, must have told you that Eliza and I have a school in Dublin. After much discussion— and despite the disgrace that first your mother and now your sister have brought upon this family—we decided that we should at least consider the possibility of hiring you. What have you to say to that?"

What had Fanny to say? This was a chance—probably her only chance—to get away from Skinner Street, to not merely read of her sisters' adventures but to enjoy some of her own. Looking now from Everina to Eliza, she wondered if adventure was too much to expect, but at least there would be change.

"I am honored that you would consider me," Fanny answered. She regarded the two more closely. Her mother had founded their school before she was born. Fanny was now twenty-two. Why had they not interviewed her long ago?

"What do you say for yourself?" Everina asked. "What can you do?"

"I know grammar. I could teach that and, of course, composition—"

Before she could continue, Eliza broke in, "A *little* composition only. A lady needs merely to know how to write a proper letter, nothing more. Your mother was forever scribbling. We will have none of that. You can see well enough where it led." The two sisters exchanged glances. "You do realize," Eliza said, "that the purpose of our school, insofar as the female pupils are concerned, is to educate them to be exemplary wives and mothers. No more than that. The things your mother espoused, like social equality with men— we shall not even discuss her thoughts on . . . on other kinds of equality—and full educational rights for women are anathema to us."

Everina looked directly at Fanny. "We have had to overcome a great deal of prejudice because of your mother's conduct. Do you know that no less a man than Horace Walpole called her a 'hyena in petticoats'?"

"Balderdash!" Papa shouted, throwing down the newspaper behind which he had been barricaded. "Walpole was nothing more than a failed politician and a boring writer to boot. Everyone knew he preferred men to women. Who is he to defame the finest woman who ever lived?"

Fan's heart filled with joy. Papa had said all that she had wanted to say but dared not. The job was so important.

Mum stiffened, puffed out her chest. "Really, William, you do exaggerate."

Ignoring her, Everina covered her ears. "I will not hear such talk. What are we to think of a girl who is the product of this household?"

"You are to think that she is the most capable, most agreeable daughter of the woman who started your damned school in the first place and paid its bills till the day she died." Papa turned to Fanny. "My girl, think about it, do you want to work for these two nanny goats?"

The sisters gasped, but Fanny thought her heart would choke her. She wanted to hug Papa but would not. She had been a burden for so long. "Yes, I do," she said, nodding. "It is time for me to go."

"What about her salary?" Mum interjected.

Fanny looked from one sister to the other. Any sum would do. To think that she would actually have something of her own. Once they decided upon fifty pounds, everyone seemed pleased. Fanny most of all.

"You had best tell the maid to get her trunk ready," Eliza said. "We are booked to return on the same boat we came in on and must be ready to sail with the tide."

Mum looked surprised. "Don't you want to stay and see a bit of London?"

"See London! The fog's so thick, we could barely make our way from the carriage to your door."

Fanny's heart pounded. She was really leaving Skinner Street. She would miss Papa, but he would scarcely note that she was gone. Fanny looked about the familiar room, memorizing every detail.

Everina cut into her thoughts. "There is one thing before we go . . . Mary. Despite all that she has done, we do want to see her before returning to Dublin. She, too, is our niece. Her son is our grandnephew. We should like to meet them."

Papa's face reddened. "We no longer recognize Mary and have never seen her child."

"But surely I could take them, Papa," Fanny begged. "We could stop by on the way to the boat." This was a splendid turn of events. The one thing that had given Fanny pain was the thought of leaving the country without bidding Mary good-bye.

Papa sighed heavily. "I've no doubt that Fan knows the way to their home, though I strictly forbade her to go there." He turned, leveling his gaze on Fanny. "Do not think that I was not aware of the letters you two exchanged. Please yourself. You are your own woman now."

Your own woman. Fanny smiled broadly. She could not help herself.

———

The door at 41 Hans Place swung open. A serving maid greeted them with a pleasant smile, but before anything could be said, Mary darted forward to hug Fanny.

"Oh," Fanny gasped. "I have missed you so much!" Reluctantly pulling back, she made the introductions. "These are our aunts, Everina and Eliza Wollstonecraft, come to meet you at last."

They moved into the parlor, where Willmouse crawled eagerly toward them. "Oh, he has grown so much!" Fanny exclaimed, kneeling beside him. "He's not a baby anymore, he's a little boy." She kissed Willmouse's chubby cheek.

"A happy little boy who's anxious to know his Auntie Fan."

Fanny thought Mary very beautiful in her blue muslin morning gown, golden-brown hair falling in soft curls about her face. How could the aunts not forgive her, not, indeed, love her upon sight, and then there was little Willmouse. Who could resist him?

Fanny felt wistful, but happy, too. "I have news for you," she told Mary. "Wonderful, exciting news."

Just then the parlor door opened and Claire rushed in. Fanny gasped. Claire had put on weight. Her breasts, her . . . oh, no!

Everina and Eliza rose as one from their chairs. "I assume that you're the Clairmont girl. We have heard much about you, too much," Everina said, looking Claire up and down. "But no one told us that you were married or expecting a child."

Eliza moved closer to her sister until the two of them stood shoulder to shoulder. "Who may I ask is your husband, the baby's father?"

Claire stopped in her tracks. Gathering her flyaway hair with one hand, she skewered it to the top of her head; with her other, she pulled her dressing gown together. "I have no husband," she informed them coolly. "My baby's father is George Gordon, the Lord Byron."

It was the end of everything for Fanny. She knew instantly.

Eliza eyed Claire contemptuously, then turned to Fanny. "Four pupils were removed from our care following Mary's elopement," she said. "We were hard-pressed to keep the rest. The good Lord only knows what will happen this time. But one thing is certain, we can have no girl from the Godwin house connected with our school."

Fanny rose to her feet. "Please—this had nothing to do with me—I—"

Everina picked up her reticule. "Eliza has expressed our feelings, surely they are clear to you."

That was that. Without a backward glance they were out the door and on their way.

Fanny sat for a time holding Willmouse on her lap. She tried desperately not to cry. Claire was disdainful. "A position with those two ninnies is worth no more than a fart in a whirlwind."

"Oh, Claire, what do you know?" Mary exclaimed. "Fan, this is terrible. I am so sorry. I know it's a dreadful disappointment, but there will be other opportunities. I know there will. In the meantime, why not try your hand at writing? Mother made a living at it, and I've begun a novel of my own. The main character is a monster, but mainly it is about loneliness."

Loneliness! *What did Mary know of loneliness?* Fanny wondered. Mary had Bysshe Shelley and his delightful child as well.

When Claire excused herself to write a letter, Fanny asked Mary about her. "Is it really true that Lord Byron is her lover?"

"*Was* her lover. There was a little something between them in the beginning, but he tired of her. Now Byron calls Claire a cockchafer and will have nothing more to do with her."

"I suppose she will remain here with you and Bysshe."

"I'm afraid so, we can hardly turn her out on the street."

"Claire will manage. She always lands on her feet." Fanny rose from her chair and preceded Mary to the door. When she opened it, she saw her small trunk sitting on the sidewalk at the bottom of the stairs.

"At least you can go home," Mary said. "Papa will have nothing to do with *me*."

Yes, I have a home, but what about a life? Why doesn't Mary ask me to stay?

Outside, Fanny hailed a hackney carriage and signaled to the postilion to help with her trunk. "Good-bye, Mary," Fanny said, hugging her sister tightly. "You have a dear son and your book will be a great success. I know it. There will be more, too, more books and more babies." She gave Mary a quick kiss and stepped unaided into the cab.

"Where to, miss?" the coachman asked.

Where to? Where to? Fanny caught her breath, the path suddenly clear. "To Charing Cross, the coach terminal." The carriage drove off and she did not look back. When they at last reached the station, it seemed incredibly crowded, but Fanny fought her way forward, dragging her trunk as best she could. Careless, confident people dashed this way and that, jostling her and rushing forward without a backward glance. Each of them had somewhere to go.

At last she reached the ticket counter. Again the question: "Where to, miss?"

Fanny looked beyond the agent's shoulder to the printed schedule. The next coach would leave in ten minutes for Bristol. "Bristol, one way with a transfer to Swansea." How fortunate that Papa had parceled out a little spending money. Carefully Fanny counted out the coins.

It was a long ride to Swansea; Fanny had plenty of time to think. As day turned to night, she tried to remember the parents she had scarcely known. Fanny dimly remembered a tall, rugged man who'd thrilled her with stories of his native Kentucky. "I will take you and your mama there," he had promised. Instead, he abandoned them to Paris's coldest winter in history, famine, all the terror and chaos attendant to Robespierre's execution, and a smallpox epidemic. *If I had not been born, would he have left Mama?* Papa Godwin had been so kind, pretending to be her father, imagining that she did not know otherwise. There were so many questions that Fanny would have liked to ask. Now it really didn't matter, nothing did.

At long last Fanny reached Bristol and checked into the Mackworth Arms Inn, a dingy hotel by the coach station. She unpacked a few items from her bag and then sat down at the battered desk. Goose quill squeaking across the paper, she penned two quick notes, one to Papa, one to Mary.

Fanny stared at the bottle beside her. Mary Wollstonecraft had twice attempted suicide. Fanny would succeed where her mother had not. Laudanum had been her friend, bringing solace on sleepless nights. It would not fail her on this last night. Reaching for the bottle beside her, Fanny tipped her head back and drank deeply.

Her last thoughts were of Bysshe.

THIRTY-ONE

The toast was soggy, his eggs underdone. William Godwin frowned at Jane across the breakfast table. Young Willie and a neighbor boy had been playing a card game, but it was not going well. A shouting match had disintegrated into jostling.

"Confound it, where is the maid when we need her?" Godwin demanded. "She needs to clear the table and do something with these dratted boys."

"She cannot be everywhere at once," Jane said.

"Fanny was, or at least seemed to be. It was she who saw to Willie. And Fanny never allowed anything to leave the kitchen unless it was well cooked. We should never have let her go."

"It was an economy measure," Jane reminded him. "You were well aware of that at the time. There's one less mouth to feed now. And was it not you who complained of Fanny's 'weary, woeful ways?'"

"Did I say that?" William wrinkled his brow in annoyance. "Well, perhaps." He thought briefly of his stepdaughter's sweet smile. Sweet, indeed, but rarely seen. William supposed Fan had inherited a melancholy streak from her mother. She, too, suffered fits of depression, but then there had been the other times . . . William thought longingly of his first wife and remembered her words to him early in their marriage: *I want you to be riveted to my heart but not always at my elbow.*

Godwin could imagine their daughter, Mary, saying something like that, but never Fanny. She had not the spirit. In truth,
Fan's mournful looks could be trying. "Perhaps her departure was
for the best." He nodded to Jane. "Fanny must be well content with
her aunts, since she has not bothered to pen us so much as a note."
Putting down his fork in disgust, William picked up the *Times*.

After a while he followed Jane downstairs to the shop. A ship-
ment of books waited to be sorted. He saw Jane sniff disdainfully
at a biography, *Life of Nelson*. Its author, Robert Southey, an old
crony of his, was no friend to her. That scandalous Caroline Lamb
had a book out, too, *Glenarvon*. William scanned it speculatively.
Why couldn't his Mary write a book? He scarcely remembered a
time when the girl had not been scribbling. Might it one day come
to something . . . something lucrative?

Bysshe had self-published a small book, hardly more than a
pamphlet. *A Vindication of Natural Diet.* His wretched paean to
vegetables was a far cry from *Queen Mab*, but William placed the
book prominently. If Bysshe's nonsense sold; they would be the
better for it.

Standing back to admire the effect, William was startled by the
sound of a door slamming. He turned to see the poet himself rush
pell-mell into the shop.

Jane thrust herself forward to block his entrance. "What are
you doing here? Surely you are aware that William refuses . . ." She
paused, face suddenly pink. "Is it about our bills? Fan promised to
write to you just before she left with her aunts. We are terribly in
arrears. Surely you would not want Mary's own father in debtors'
prison?"

"Fanny's most recent missive was not about money," Bysshe
told her. "It is a most distressing note."

William glanced at the mail platter by the door and saw a small
envelope. He'd been in the bookshop a good half hour and not
noticed it.

"Well?" Jane glared at Bysshe, then turned to William. "Don't just stand there looking at each other. What does Fanny have to say for herself?"

"Mine is merely a note. It says very little," Bysshe answered.

William's skin prickled. Something bad had happened. He knew it. Looking down at the thin sheet of paper, he saw the imprint, Mackworth Arms Inn, Swansea. He recognized the small, cramped handwriting, but the words . . .

"I depart immediately to the spot from which I hope never to be removed," William read aloud. "What the devil does that mean?"

Bysshe shook his head. "I know naught, but Mary is quite alarmed, practically hysterical. She fears the worst and is desperate to prevent it. Mary's waiting outside now and insists that we take a coach to Swansea immediately."

"No!" William banged his fist on the table. "That would be most foolish." Striving for a calmer tone, he continued. "The less that anyone knows about this affair—whatever it is—the better. Take Mary home. I will go and see for myself what can be done."

Bysshe looked relieved. "Let me know if there is anything I can do," he said, striding quickly to the door.

William's fellow passengers on the coach ride were a sorry lot, a cadaverous man who coughed incessantly and a heavily pregnant woman with three ill-tempered brats. The coach, battered by wind, lurched constantly. Twice it nearly overturned, tossing the passengers on top of each other. *Why would anyone choose to travel in such weather?* William wondered but didn't ask, not caring to hear their stories.

Finally the coach came to a halt and he looked out. *Bloody hell, this is the end of the world.* The Mackworth Arms Inn might be pleasant enough during the season, but it was winter. Sea and sky blended together into a gray mélange that stretched as far as he could see. Valise in hand, William walked down the gravel path leading to a brick building fronted by a broad veranda. Heavy wind and rain ripped about the white pillars, tearing at the bolted shutters.

The servant who answered William's heavy knock was a mere boy. Eagerly William followed him toward a blazing fire, where a short, plump man stood warming his backside.

"Glad to meet you, sir." The man extended his hand. "My name's Sam Mackworth, and this is my inn. It's good to have you with us, sir. We're a bit quiet right now, most of our guests left right after—" He paused, looking down. "It's this dratted weather, of course."

William took Mackworth's hand and shook it. "My name's Godwin, William Godwin. I've come from London to find my daughter. She is of medium height, dark hair—" William stopped. Mackworth had stiffened visibly and no longer met his gaze. "Whatever it is, you must tell me everything you know. Now."

At last Mackworth spoke. "I'm afraid it's bad news. There was a lady who came here, quiet, respectable-like." He hesitated, swallowing visibly.

William felt ill. He forced himself to ask, "What happened? Is she here? I want to see her."

Mackworth and the boy looked at each other. William knew he wouldn't like whatever they had to say. "Tell me immediately or I will call the police."

"No need for that, sir," Mackworth told him. "We have already done it."

"Then for God's sake tell me what happened."

"The young lady checked in three days ago in the early evening," the boy said. "I showed her to her room, everything seemed to her liking. She didn't want me to bring her anything."

"I want to see her now." William's angry bellow echoed in his ears.

"I'm afraid—I'm afraid—that will be difficult." Mackworth took a deep breath and looked straight at William. "It's as my bell-man told you. The young lady went straight upstairs. The following morning she didn't come down for breakfast or lunch. By teatime, I grew concerned and knocked on her door. There was no answer. Eventually I had the door forced open. There she was lying on the floor, her skin cold as ice." Mackworth paused. "There was no identification other than the initials on her stays, M. W."

Mary Wollstonecraft. Mary's three-year-old daughter hiding behind her mother's skirts. The sweet smile, even then wistful. Such a good girl . . . always the peacemaker between warring family members. William fought to banish the memories. He had other children, each of them much more demanding of his time and affection than little Fanny. *It was not my fault.*

"I called the coroner," Mackworth continued. "It was laudanum. Her body is at the morgue, but I have a letter that she wrote before . . . and a memento in my office. If you will come this way."

Godwin's eyes filled with tears. Little Fanny, the kindest of them all. But surely this was not kind! She had placed him in a most uncomfortable position. His hands clenched angrily and then unclenched.

"Will you be taking the body back with you, sir?" the inn-keeper asked.

"No!" William could hardly do that. His livelihood was dependent upon the flagging success of his Juvenile Library. He could not have the world know that the stepdaughter of William Godwin had taken her own life. "I would have you bury her in an unmarked grave." He handed the innkeeper a few pounds. "See that this is kept quiet."

William looked at the small gold watch that Mackworth handed him. It must have been a gift from Mary. Where else would Fan have gotten it? He took the letter, shoving it into his pocket. It was only in the coach on the way home that William finally summoned the courage to open the letter, a single sheet of notepaper. Hand trembling, he read:

I have long determined that the best thing I could do was put an end to the existence of a being whose birth was unfortunate, and whose life has been a series of pain to those persons who have hurt their health in endeavoring to promote her welfare. Perhaps to hear of my death will give you pain, but you will have the blessing of forgetting such a creature ever existed.

Home at last, he penned a letter to Mary, his first communication to her in more than two years. "Go not to Swansea; disturb not the silent dead. Do nothing to destroy the obscurity she so much desired. It was her last wish. It was the motive that led her from London to Bristol, and from Bristol to Swansea." He was careful not to mention Fanny's name.

William sought at any cost to keep the family tragedy out of the papers. Sadly he confided to friends that Fanny had gone to teach at her aunts' school in Dublin and there contracted a fatal fever. A great tragedy, he agreed, while bearing their condolences with grave fortitude.

Good as William's performance was, the story didn't hold up. Before long everyone knew of Fanny's suicide. "From the fateful day of Mary's elopement, Fan's mind had been unsettled," he was finally forced to admit. "Her duty was with us, but I am afraid her affections were with Mary."

Jane went a bit further. "Her affections were with Bysshe. All three of our girls fell madly in love with the depraved Mr. Shelley. Can it be of any surprise that our eldest killed herself on his account?"

When they were alone, William angrily cautioned her to go no further. "I have always felt that there was something going on between Bysshe and Fanny . . . When he came so often to the house . . . before Mary's return from Scotland. We must never speak of it again, not even to each other."

Two months later Harriet's body was found, battered and bloated, floating in London's Serpentine River.

She left behind two notes. One, written to a girlhood friend, asked, "Is it wrong, do you think, to put an end to all one's sorrows? I often think of it—all is so gloomy and desolate. Shall I find repose in another world? Oh grave, why do you not tell us what is beyond thee?"

To Bysshe, Harriet wrote: "I never could refuse you and if you had never left me I might have lived, but as it is I freely forgive you and may you enjoy the happiness of which you have deprived me."

Upon reading of the death, William immediately sent a message to Bysshe and Mary, urging them to come at once to Skinner Street.

William greeted them cordially. He extended his hand to Bysshe and tried to embrace Mary, but the ungrateful girl stiffened, moved out of reach. She was white-faced and appeared to be trembling. "What is the matter?" he asked.

"What is the matter? You threw Fan away, that's what's the matter. She's buried in an unmarked grave—I cannot even go there." Mary began sobbing. What was William to do?

Fortunately Bysshe took Mary in his arms. She seemed to draw comfort from him. Finally the sobbing stopped.

William struggled to conceal his annoyance and led the way to his study. As always, the portrait of Mary Wollstonecraft held their attention. "Oh, Mama," Mary sighed, "if only you had been here, none of this would have happened."

"Do not be so certain," William countered. "Once your mother told me, 'There is not a subject that admits so little of reasoning than love.'"

Bysshe gave a bewildered sigh. "Why have you asked us here?"

William braced himself and resolved to retain a calm manner. "I assume that you will want custody of your children with Harriet."

Bysshe shrugged. "Of course. I have not only the legal right but a moral one, and Mary supports me in every way."

"Yes." Mary nodded eagerly. "We want to raise Ianthe and Charles with our own little Willmouse. We went immediately to the Westbrook home to get them, but thus far Harriet's father has not admitted us. We are seeking legal action."

"That will net you nothing," William told them matter-of-factly.

"What do you mean? I am their father!"

"Yes, but consider your present living arrangement. To a conservative court, you are living in sin. How will that look compared to what Harriet's established family has to offer?"

"What are you suggesting, sir?"

"There is only one solution. Marriage."

Bysshe bristled. "You know very well that is anathema to both Mary and me. Love and commitment are not something that can be defined in a court of law. Our feelings go far beyond that."

When Mary said nothing, William shrugged. "Then you are unlikely to have custody of your children. You will be lucky even to be allowed to see them. Mary's mother and I married for the sake of a child, and here she is. If you want your family together, you will have to do the same."

William rested his case, omitting the fervent hope that such a bow to convention would loosen up Sir Timothy's purse strings, with subsequent benefit to William himself.

He was hard put to maintain his equanimity when—a scant three weeks after Harriet's death—Bysshe and Mary became man and wife. The couple was married in St. Mildred's Church in London on December 30, 1816. William and Jane were the only witnesses.

Mary wore a lavender gown that quite became her. The bride's cheeks were rosy, her eyes sparkled. Her husband, William noted with some relief, did not look unhappy.

The four had dinner together afterward at a nearby pub. The conversation was at first stilted, but three bottles of claret loosened things up. Bysshe had his arm about Mary. Her head often rested on his shoulder.

"Your husband tells me that you are writing a little book," William ventured to Mary. "Is it a romantic tale?"

"Hardly." She turned to him with a half smile. "It is neither little nor romantic. I am writing of a man and the monster he creates. You might call it a tale of abandonment."

"Really!" Godwin sat back. He hardly knew what to make of that.

Once home, William sat down at his desk and penned a letter to his brother, his first communication in more than a year. He omitted any mention of Fanny's death and was also silent about his year-old grandson, William. His words were entirely of Mary's new station in life.

Her husband is the oldest son of Sir Timothy Shelley, of Field Place, in the county of Sussex, Baronet. So that, according to the vulgar ideas of the world, she is well married, and I have great hopes that the young man will make a good husband. You will wonder, I daresay, how a girl with not a penny of fortune should meet with so good a match. But such are the ups and downs of this world. For my part, I care but little of wealth. It is enough that she be respectable, virtuous, and contented.

William went to bed satisfied.

THIRTY-TWO

Mary seesawed between happiness and despair. Everything positive about her relationship with Bysshe had intensified—their lovemaking, their joy in Willmouse, and their scintillating discussions of poetry, philosophy, and social causes. Everything not so positive—Bysshe's roving eye, his insistence on a meatless household, his total confidence that his way was the only way—seemed less important. The institution of marriage, once decried, was for the most part a garden of earthly delight.

But there were other times when Mary thought her heart would break. She, too, had thrown Fan away. Sometimes Mary wanted to die, to find Fan wherever she was buried and share her fate, whatever that might be. Guilt gnawed at her; she ate almost nothing and slept little. She remembered Fan's still, white face watching in the hallway as she and Bysshe talked—flirted. How dreadful it must have been for her.

As long as Mary could remember, Fan had been there, a loving and protective buffer against Mum's pettiness and her father's wrath. And how had Mary repaid that loyalty? By running off with Bysshe and taking Claire—Claire!—with her. What had she been thinking?

Fan, left behind to deal with the aftermath, had never reproached her. Instead, it was Fanny who walked through the rain to comfort her for the loss of her baby daughter when Bysshe and Claire were off who knew where. It was Fan who had warned

Bysshe of the debt collectors, Fan who . . . Oh, the list went on and on. Was there anything that Fan had not done or tried to do to make Mary's life easier?

And what had she done in return? Nothing. Worse than nothing. She and Bysshe had taken Claire on yet another trip to Switzerland. All the while Fan had written countless letters, loving communications, inquiring about Mary's life and the people she met. Fingering the missives now, Mary realized they were a lonely cry for help. Fan had sought merely a vicarious existence, and even there, Mary had failed her. Finding her sister's letters melancholy, she had sometimes allowed them to go unanswered. Where was the succor Fan so desperately needed? Mary had considered inviting Fan to stay with her, but the house was so crowded with Claire and her expected baby. *I was so thoughtless, so selfish,* she castigated herself. *Why didn't I stop her, hold on to her!*

Mary's conscience troubled her on another score as well. Harriet. Again and again a vision rose unbidden of the sunny, high-spirited young woman who had first visited the Godwin home. Despite Harriet's beauty and fashionable clothes, there had been no arrogance or affectation about her; rather, she had been friendly and open.

The intervening five years had changed everything. Try as she might, Mary could not avoid the reality that Harriet's appalling suicide had paved the way to her own happiness. Because of Mary, Bysshe had abandoned Fan and Harriet.

Mary could do no more than promise herself to be the perfect stepmother to Harriet's children, Ianthe and Charles. Having herself endured a most difficult stepmother, she swore to be the opposite. Mary eagerly looked forward to the court-appointed decision that she felt certain would grant legal custody of the children to Bysshe.

When Claire's baby was born in January, Mary took the occasion to dash off a note to Byron. "Albe, you will be happy to learn that Claire was safely delivered of a little girl yesterday morning at four," she told him. Then added with some satisfaction, "Another incident has also occurred which will surprise you, perhaps. It is a little piece of egotism in me to mention it—but it allows me to sign myself—in assuring you of my esteem & sincere friendship, Mary W. Shelley."

It was a happy moment; Mary felt a new sense of fulfillment and security. But that night she awakened screaming from a frightful dream. Harriet had thrust back the curtains and stood at the foot of Mary's bed, an arm outstretched, pointing an accusatory finger at her. Behind her was another figure. Fan! Her sister was crying softly.

Mary awakened, trembling. "What have I done? What have I done? How can I go on? I am a monster."

Bysshe lay quietly beside her, never wakening. Outside a storm raged, thunder roared. A bolt of lightning lit up the room.

Willmouse was crying, and quickly she was at his side. Yet even as she tended to his needs, remorse swept over her. Fanny would never know the joy of holding her own child. Mary held Willmouse to her, so tight that he began to squirm and cry. Reluctantly she returned him to his crib.

The next day, in an effort to assuage her guilt and pain, Mary returned to her monster. She would pour her energy into completing the novel that she had begun to call *Frankenstein*. The story, begun the previous summer in Switzerland, took shape rapidly.

As though he stood before her, Mary saw young Victor Frankenstein go off to the university like any other lad. Once there, the lure of science ensnares Victor until he is driven to perform unhallowed experiments that challenge the will of God. Frankenstein's monster is nonhuman in his origin and physical appearance, but only too human in his longings, desires, and passion for revenge, which drives him to commit murder.

The regrets that haunted Mary would haunt a reader as well, she felt certain. Who had not experienced such anguish? Mary hoped that readers would look beyond the monster's physical deformity and see not only fearsome power but beauty and tenderness.

Drawing from experience—the loss of her mother and insensitivity of her father, the separation and social ostracism following her elopement—Mary wrote easily of the anguished monster:

> *Oh, Frankenstein. Remember, that I am your creature. I ought to be thy Adam; but am rather the fallen angel whom thou drivest from joy for no misdeed. Everywhere I see bliss from which I alone am irrevocably excluded. I was benevolent and good; misery made me a fiend. Make me happy, and I shall again be virtuous.*

Answering for society and authority, Frankenstein replies: "Begone! I will not hear you. There can be no community between you and me; we are enemies." Mary understood her capricious character well. She hadn't far to look for a model.

She had her story well in hand. Her plot would turn on the strength of sexual desire, the force that brings people together, anchoring them in common humanity. Frankenstein created his monster only to abandon him, but, of course, they would meet again.

The monster begs, then demands: "You must create a female for me, with whom I can live in the interchange of those sympathies necessary for my being. This you alone can do; and I demand it of you as a right which you must not refuse."

At first the creator agrees. Victor Frankenstein pieces together a female monster in his laboratory, but then, terrified of what he has done, tears the body apart in the presence of his first creation. The monster's response, once he recovers from his howls of anguish and despair, is simple: "I shall be with you on your wedding night."

Mary grasped the quill, her hand flying across the paper. The monster's threat was to be carried out during a grim scene where Victor Frankenstein's bride is strangled on her bridal bed. Thus, both creator and created destroy each other's hopes of sexual fulfillment. Their links to human society shattered, they become pariahs, each tortured by the knowledge of what he has done and the thirst to be revenged for what he has lost.

With a satisfied sigh, Mary sat back. Her story's denouement was indeed gruesome, perfect for a horror tale. She had met Byron's challenge head on, never imagining it as more than a rainy night's amusement, but gradually, as the weeks and months passed, her feelings changed. The result of Mary's effort and anguish was a book. Did an effort such as that not deserve an audience?

THIRTY-THREE

Mary and Bysshe had scarcely been married a month before they were invited to a small reception. Mary looked up from her writing to listen to the invitation that Bysshe was reading aloud. "Does this mean that society has at last come to accept us?"

Bysshe scanned the invitation. His mouth curved in a smile. "Perhaps. At least a certain *form* of society. This is from my old friends the Hunts—Leigh and Marianne. You would have met them before, but Leigh has been in prison."

Mary set down her pen. "Really!"

"It's not what you think," Bysshe assured her. "Leigh is not a criminal, at least not in the eyes of people like us. Prinny threw Leigh into Surrey Gaol for two years because of his inflammatory columns in the *Examiner*. Surely you have read them?"

"Well, yes, now that you mention it . . ." Mary thought back to that time—had it been two years ago?—Bysshe on the run to escape debtors' prison, she and Tom Hogg sprawled across the tattered rug of her garret, newspapers spread before them. "I remember a particularly brilliant column on the abolition of the slave trade."

Bysshe smiled again, slipping an arm about her waist. "Leigh's a firebrand after your own heart."

"Does he not own the *Examiner*?"

Bysshe nodded. "With his brother. They even published the paper from prison."

"How extraordinary!"

Mary was eager to meet Leigh Hunt. When he wrote that "the same people who deny others everything are famous for refusing themselves nothing," Mary thought of Sir Timothy and loved Leigh instantly for skewering her father-in-law so perfectly.

At the party Mary found Leigh to be an attractive man. His father was from the West Indies, and Leigh had been raised there. She liked Leigh's exotic good looks, his jet-black hair, olive skin, and thick, expressive lips, but it was his warm smile that pleased her most.

Mary also felt an affinity to Leigh's wife, Marianne, who stood out from the carefully coiffed women about her. Marianne's honey-blonde hair seemed always about to escape its bonds; the same might be said of her lush body. Despite an age difference of possibly a decade, Mary recognized a common bond. Like her, Marianne was newly pregnant and had a husband who fought conventional prejudice with his pen.

Mary longed to become better acquainted, but the four Hunt children were little savages, running everywhere, chasing a large red rubber ball, darting in and around the assembled guests, pushing, stamping, stepping on toes. Neither Leigh nor Marianne took much notice of the commotion. Marianne even smiled benignly at Mary, exclaiming, "Is it not a delight to see such high spirits?"

Clearly it would be impossible to have a private conversation amidst such bedlam. Mary leaned forward, almost shouting into Marianne's ear, "Shall we take tea Wednesday next at Almack's?"

———•·•———

Almack's was a fashionable social club. At night the establishment was given over to supper parties and assemblies. In the afternoon, tea was served. It was a splendid place to see and be seen, but Mary asked the waiter to show them to a quiet corner. The secluded nook, partially obscured from view by an oriental screen, palm trees, and trailing plants, felt perfect for a tête-à-tête. They sat before a carved mahogany table covered by lilac napery and gleaming silver.

At first the two women chatted about the guests at Marianne's party. They were delighted by the young poet John Keats and agreed that he was both handsome and talented, if a bit shy. Mary had been pleased to see her childhood mentors Charles and Mary Lamb after so many years. "Charles was very kind to me as a child," she confided, "and it is wonderful to see Mary doing so well."

"Yes, she is having one of her good times," Marianne observed. "Charles is a most forgiving brother, but who knows when she will have to be confined again. It comes on so suddenly. Such a dear woman, we love her despite her—her lapses."

The women spoke freely of a current controversy, the British Museum's acquisition of the Elgin Marbles. "I agree with those who say Lord Elgin's a thief," Mary declared. "The statues came from Greece and ought to be sent back there."

Marianne agreed. "Perhaps Princess Charlotte will see to that when she is queen. That poor girl—her dreadful father and, imagine, a mad grandfather! Charlotte is the only decent member of the royal family. Marianne removed a silver flask from her reticule and poured a splash into the teapot. "Do you not find that a spot of brandy smoothes the bite of black tea?"

Mary smiled. So that was how Marianne managed to get through the day with those awful children. At last she ventured, "It must have been terrible for you when Leigh was in prison."

"Terrible does not begin to describe it—the awful sound of chains dragging on stone. Those dark corridors, the curses, the crazed laughter. The smells—rat droppings, urine. Mary, you cannot imagine. I took fresh flowers every day, but even that was not enough to dispel the dreadful odors.

"What concerned me most was Leigh's health. Surrey Gaol is so awfully cold and damp. The chill seeps into your bones. Some friend—possibly Lord Byron, he visited often—must have told the prison magistrate about Leigh's racking cough. For whatever reason, he was transferred, given two rooms in the prison infirmary. It meant that I could move in with him."

Mary studied her new friend, admiring Marianne's bravery. "Bysshe told me that you transformed Leigh's quarters."

Marianne smiled as she reminisced. "We screened the barred windows with blinds—you could not see those dreadful gallows—and papered the walls with a trellis of roses. The ceiling was painted sky blue with clouds. Leigh says that colors are the smiles of nature."

"Imagine doing all that in a prison!"

"I did my best—ordered shelves and filled them with books and busts and flowerpots. We even had a pianoforte. Lots of friends came to see us. We had dinners catered. Tradesmen brought in good food and wine. We talked late into the night—much as we do now."

An unaccountable sense of loneliness swept over Mary. "What a wonderful life," she said at last.

———— · ————

Bysshe was traveling about the countryside looking for a suitable home. He and Mary felt certain that once the custody trial was held, Ianthe and Charles would be living with them, so they wanted lots of room.

Feeling hopeful, Mary wrote:

Ah! were you indeed a winged Elf, and could soar over mountains & seas, and could pounce on the little spot. A house with a lawn, a river or lake, noble trees, and divine mountains, that should be our little mouse-hole to retire to. But never mind this;

give me a garden & absentia Claire, and I will thank my love for
many favours.

She was eager to be out of London. Times were turbulent. One
day, while riding to luncheon at the Hunts, her hired coach was
stopped for two hours at St. James Square. All traffic had come to
a halt. London was a city of more than a million souls, and Mary
thought they must all have been out in force that afternoon. The
road was filled with impatient horses neighing and stomping, the
angry curses of their drivers audible above the racket.

"What has happened?" she called out to a man standing beside
his sedan chair.

"Someone threw a rock and broke Prinny's carriage window.
He is furious and has stopped all traffic until the culprit is found."

Soon the Prince Regent will be calling for gag orders and seek-
ing to suspend habeas corpus, Mary thought. She worried for Leigh
and told him so almost the moment he greeted her in his drawing
room. "These are dangerous times. You cannot go around writing
about the monarch's incompetency and moral corruption."

He smiled at her concern. "Why not, pray tell? I've been doing
it for years. Prinny may attempt to stifle the free exchange of opinions in the *Examiner*, but no law can really prevent the spread of
ideas and ideals. Look around."

Mary glanced about her at Leigh's guests, ensconced in com-
fortably worn settees and chairs. Amid a clutter of galley proofs and
trailing flowerpots, a coterie of writers, philosophers, artists, and
journalists drank beer, ate cheese, and argued. Mary Lamb read
an essay while Benjamin Haydon debated atheism with William
Hazlitt and Sam Coleridge disputed poetry with John Keats.

Mary was stimulated by the clash of egos and ideas and flattered by the respect given to her own views. But, as the breakfast
debates, tea talks, home concerts, and supper parties continued,
she came to recognize that the most imminent threat to the literary

salon's stability was closer to home than Prinny's rubber-stamp government.

It was a given that Marianne's younger sister, Bess, competed for Leigh's attentions. Like Bysshe, Leigh made no effort to conceal his attraction to both sisters. It was a familiar story. Mary knew the signs and recognized them immediately: Leigh's arm placed intimately around Bess's waist, the lingering glances, their heads too close while in conversation.

It appeared that over the years a division of interests and expertise had allowed the threesome to maintain an uneasy balance. Marianne was the domestic and maternal one, a natural homemaker and a devoted mother, while Bess added intellectual stimulation, enthusiastically discussing literature and politics, and providing a sounding board for Leigh's *Examiner* columns.

Mary surmised that it had all worked well enough until she arrived on the scene. Leigh was lavish in his compliments regarding her talent and good looks. She was completing a novel, she had a handsome, titled husband, an adorable son. What did Bess have?

Whenever the two were alone, and sometimes even when they were not, Bess made a point of bringing up Harriet's drowning. She talked about Fan's suicide as well, asking endless personal questions. Both subjects were so painful that Mary once burst into tears. Was Bess being deliberately cruel? Fond as she had grown of Marianne and Leigh, Mary's visits tapered off. She didn't need a second Claire in her life.

It didn't take Marianne long to recognize the chill. "Please come to breakfast tomorrow," she pleaded in a note. "We miss you."

Mary had to admit, she missed them, too, and with some trepidation, she called the next morning.

The maid had scarcely shown her inside before a disheveled Leigh rushed forward. "It is good that you are here," he said, taking her arm. "We are in a dreadful state of affairs."

Mary looked beyond him to Marianne, who stood in the doorway, her cheeks blotched with tears. A constable strode about officiously, jotting things in a notebook. She rushed past him to hug Marianne. "What can I do to help?"

Marianne led her into the drawing room, where Bess reclined on a chaise, drinking tea. Bess's face, too, was teary and her hair hung in damp tangles, but Mary thought she caught a look of fleeting satisfaction.

"What has happened?" Mary asked, looking from one woman to the other.

"I could bear it no longer, I simply could not bear it!" Bess rose to her feet and fled the room.

"Tell me! What is going on here?" Mary pleaded.

"It's a frightful business," Leigh said. His face was flushed, his eyes downcast. "Bess . . . Bess . . . This morning she attempted to drown herself in the pond. Fortunately two laborers were passing by and saw her. They pulled her out."

Mary's anguish returned full force. Harriet and Fan had each sought release from nebulous twilight existences. Bess displayed a dark fascination with their fates, asking countless questions. Mary had thought it merely a catty means of driving her away. Had Mary followed her instincts, she would have stayed away, but she hadn't, and now this near tragedy had occurred. It was a foolish grandstand performance—exactly the sort of thing that Claire might do—yet could have been fatal. Mary sighed in exasperation. *Am I once again the displacer? Is it once again my fault?*

THIRTY-FOUR

Mary's quill flew across the paper, imploring Bysshe: "We must move from London as soon as possible."

Mary hoped finding the "right house" wouldn't take too long. Her pregnancy was advancing and the tragic deaths of Fan and Harriet had taken a heavy toll on her. She wanted nothing more than a permanent home, a place where she could feel secure. Did such a haven exist?

Finally, in late March, Bysshe signed a twenty-one year lease on Albion House, a mansion covered with wisteria and built in the Gothic style. Spacious, with large rooms, it had an enormous library facing onto a vibrant garden. Across the road, the Thames wound its way to London, a day's journey away.

"It truly is perfect," he wrote Mary. "This is where my children will become our children; our families will merge. They and their children's children will live on at Albion House for a thousand years. This will be our dynasty."

Mary, though relieved that the waiting was at an end, felt some trepidation. She was ill prepared to be the mistress of a vast estate. There were so many servants to supervise, so much organizing and planning to do. She was a writer, not an executive, her housekeeping skills casual in the extreme. Bysshe, having grown up in great manor houses, would have high expectations.

She strove to put doubts aside, reminding herself that they were at last putting down roots. She was determined that Albion

House would be a happy place. Marianne contributed sculpture, Leigh sent a piano, Bysshe bought a small skiff, and Mary ordered crate loads of books. Bysshe's enthusiasm was infectious. Mary sighed contentedly. Albion House was a place where she and her family could grow and flourish.

Eager as Mary was to show off the place to the Hunts, who lingered in London, she had first to deal with her father and, as always, Claire. Bysshe had not even considered Mary's request that Claire remain in London. She and her baby were staying with the Hunts but would soon be joining Mary and Bysshe in Albion House.

William Godwin appeared early in April sans Mum, who was visiting friends in France. Mary was glad, at least, of that. A few hours later Claire arrived looking fit and happy. Her baby daughter, Allegra, remained with the Hunts. Claire was determined that under no circumstances were Godwin and her mother to know of the child's existence, let alone that the notorious Lord Byron was the infant's father.

Mary had desired so much from Papa's visit, had wanted it to go well, almost as much for Fanny's memory as for her own peace of mind. Fan had, Mary knew, been torn between allegiances. "My heart is warm in your cause," she had written shortly before her suicide, "and I am *anxious, most anxious*, that Papa should feel for you as I do, both for your sake and his own."

But it had not gone well. At the wedding Papa had appeared genial and affectionate. Now Mary realized that his amiability had been all about drawing Bysshe's purse strings closer to himself. During the much-anticipated visit, Papa was stiff and remote with her, yet tenacious in his pursuit of Bysshe's largesse. "Just a small loan," he insisted.

They all knew better.

Mary expected her father to melt at the sight of his one-year-old grandson, whom he had not seen before. Willmouse, who was just learning to walk, toddled eagerly toward this new friend, clutching a toy to share. Godwin ignored him and appeared, if anything, annoyed by the intrusion of a child into his conversation.

Tentatively Mary confided to her father, "I am continuing to work on my novel. I am calling it *Frankenstein*—"

Papa leaned across her to Bysshe. "My *Mandeville* is at the publishing house. It is a novel of the seventeenth century and will, I am sure, be even more successful than *Caleb Williams*."

"Let us hope so," Bysshe muttered to Mary. "Then there will be no more talk of loans."

Her father's visit left Mary deeply depressed, overwhelmed by the certainty that nothing she could do would ever satisfy him.

William Godwin had scarcely departed when Tom Hogg appeared. Bysshe was delighted; Mary not so. Though only a fleeting weekend visit, it seemed too long for Mary. "What a dull fellow!" she exclaimed to Bysshe.

"You liked him well enough once."

"Stop smirking. It was you who pushed me off on him. Anyway, that was a long time ago. Tom was just starting his law practice. He was full of idealism; it was endearing. Now he is a boring lawyer who drinks too much."

Bysshe said no more, merely smiling at her in a superior way. Mary allowed the conversation to rest but speculated privately about the changes wrought by time. How transient was human experience. She had lost so many dear ones. Did nothing last? That night she confided to her journal: "Everything passes and one is hardly conscious of enjoying the present before it becomes the past. Moments of enjoyment live only in memory and when we die, where are we? If only a means could be found to not only create life but sustain it."

She was reading the third canto of *Childe Harold* and missed Albe's flamboyant presence and the stimulation of his intellect. Mary anticipated enjoying his society at some future date but reflected dismally that the encounter would inevitably become just another memory. Death would come one day, and in the last moment all would be a dream. Obsessed with thoughts of life's transience, Mary felt desperate for some measure of immortality.

"Oh, am I not melancholy!" she exclaimed, tossing down the poem in exasperation. Mary blamed her depression on the imminent birth of her child and longed for her pregnancy to be over with.

But the melancholy clung like a wet cloak until Mary concluded that a degree of permanence might be achieved through writing. It was pleasant to imagine her words taking on an independent existence, a life that might endure beyond her own. Smiling at last, Mary returned to the macabre tale that had its inception at the Villa Diodati. Might a monster be her salvation?

Meanwhile, Bysshe began work on an epic poem that he was calling *Laon and Cythna*. "The protagonists are brother and sister," he told Mary late one evening as they sat before a crackling fire. She stiffened, wary of what was to come next.

"They are ardent lovers—as a man and a woman."

She caught her breath. "What are you thinking?"

Bysshe smiled. "I mean to startle readers out of their ordinary lives."

"A story based on incest will surely do that," she agreed. Struggling to keep her voice steady, she continued, "You must know the idea is preposterous. People will hate you! We'll never be invited anywhere. How can you even think of such a thing with the custody hearing coming up? Do you want to lose your children forever?"

Bysshe learned back against the couch cushions, arms crossed behind his head. "Even if I did not have family and position, even if I were not one day to be a baronet, children are always awarded to their father. I have no concern on that score."

"But Bysshe—" Mary started to protest, but held back. Bysshe was so very sure of himself. She knew there was no point in arguing with him. She could only hope that he was right. The timing seemed most ill-advised for such a topic, and soon she discovered that incest wasn't the poem's only unsettling theme. Bysshe's tale of insurrection, though set in the Near East, was clearly modeled after the French Revolution, which still terrified British aristocrats and left many in the middle class feeling uneasy.

She hesitated, fearing that she had said far too much already. Bysshe was an avid critic of her work but had made it clear from the beginning that he wanted no suggestions directed toward his own. Only just beginning to emerge from her depression, she wanted no angry exchanges to set her back.

In May the Hunts arrived. They brought with them not only Bess and their own four children, but also Allegra, a little "cousin" whom Claire had kindly agreed to take charge of for the summer. The charade had been Bysshe's idea and a good one, Mary thought. Some semblance of convention seemed essential to the upcoming custody hearing.

In the meantime, the summer loomed before them, long and lazy. Bysshe's new boat was large enough to transport several adults and a pile of laughing children up and down the river. But for the most part, the Hunts' brood ran wild in the garden, playing endless games of highwaymen and police. Leigh and Marianne seemed oblivious to the din and merely smiled. The racket drove Mary inside to the great library, where she wrote for hours on end.

Claire, besotted with her child, carried the infant everywhere, exclaiming over her every coo and gurgle. "Bysshe, is Allegra not beautiful? Have you ever seen such eyes? Does she not resemble her father?"

Bysshe moved forward on *Laon and Cythna*. Leigh wrote his *Examiner* columns, sending them to London each week for publication. Mary continued to create her *Frankenstein*. She had completed the first draft. It had taken nine months of sustained effort. Now she spent hours on end going over her manuscript word by word, editing and re-editing. Mary's sadness was fading. She was pleased with the book and more confident of the future than she had been in years. *Is this happiness? Perhaps so.*

In the evenings they took turns reading aloud and discussing the day's work: Mary's latest draft, Hunt's newspaper column, and Bysshe's newest verse. They argued politics, too, often heatedly, but everyone agreed that Mary's novel was exciting and innovative. No one had ever read anything quite like it. While they talked, Marianne cut silhouettes of the group, rigging up candles to cast an eerie shadow.

Excited by her novel's promise, Mary was also stimulated by the flow of creativity going on around her. Her editing at last complete, she took up her quill again and carefully fair copied the eighty-thousand-word manuscript. Then, hand still cramped and fingers aching, she set off for London with Bysshe to meet the iconic John Murray, Byron's publisher.

When days passed with no definitive word, Bysshe went home to Albion House. Mary stayed on in London, shopping and visiting friends. One day she walked all the way to Somers Town to sit by her mother's grave. How long since she had done that? *Mother, do you know all that has happened? Do you know all that* will *happen?*

A few days later, feeling lonely for Bysshe and Willmouse, Mary took the next coach home.

A rejection from Murray arrived two days later. That meant more copies to be made, additional submissions to tender. Rejections continued to trickle in.

When Mary began to feel discouraged, Bysshe reminded her of her parentage. "Mary Wollstonecraft and William Godwin set the world on fire with both their philosophical work and their fiction. You are their heir. That is what drew me to you in the first place."

"Really?" Mary smiled at him over her shoulder. "I thought it was something else."

"Well, that too," he agreed with a wink.

As she waited, Mary revisited *History of a Six Weeks' Tour*, a project begun some two years before. Now Mary added descriptions from their more recent trip, a bit of philosophy, and a poem by Bysshe. Among Fanny's possessions she found her own letters to her sister from both trips, carefully tied with ribbon. Dearest Fan had kept them all. Mary's eyes filled with tears.

Later, as Mary read the letters, memories flooded back. How much more vivid was a letter as compared to a journal entry. She would draw from all these sources. Though her pregnancy was well advanced, Mary worked on, determined to complete and sell this new work as well as her novel.

Mary was settled before the massive library table, scribbling away at a great rate, when something brushed her shoulder. Looking up, she saw Bysshe smiling at her.

"How absorbed you are! You didn't even hear me enter the library." Peering over her shoulder, he read aloud:

Mont Blanc was before us, but it was covered with clouds, its base, furrowed with dreadful gaps, was seen above. Pinnacles of snow intolerably bright, part of the chain connected with Mont Blanc, shone through the clouds at intervals on high. I never knew—I never imagined what mountains were before. The immensity of these aerial summits excited, when they are suddenly burst upon the sight, a sentiment of ecstatic wonder, not unallied to madness.

"Mary," Bysshe exclaimed, "that is grand!"

Mary thought he sounded surprised. "Thank you," she said, smiling up at him. "I am glad you like it, but do not think that this will be just another travel narrative about admiring mountains and lakes. I am going to write about politics—the Revolution and Jean-Jacques Rousseau."

"That may be harder to sell," he warned. "People are not accustomed to women writing about politics."

"My mother did it."

"These are different times, I fear."

"Perhaps," she admitted, "but I'll include other things as well, like Henri and the way we were always running out of money." She tilted her head back, laughing at the memories. It all seemed so long ago.

On August 4, Bysshe celebrated his twenty-fifth birthday. On August 30, Mary turned twenty. On September 2, their daughter was born.

"She's a beautiful baby girl," Bysshe said. "Let us name her Claire."

"Claire!" Mary sat up in bed. She could not believe her ears. "Are you serious?"

"Of course, I'm serious. Do you not think it a lovely name?"

"I think it is insulting! There is already one Claire too many."

Mary's pulse raced with anger. *What could Bysshe be thinking? Did he think at all?* "Go away!" she cried.

Bysshe retreated, closing the door behind him, but before long, he was back, seating himself on a chair beside her canopied bed. "What a thing to say—'one Claire too many!'" He appeared shocked at her outburst, but his words were conciliatory. "If you don't care for Claire, what about Mary for a name?"

Mary settled back against the pillows. "Mary was the name we chose for our baby that died," she reminded him. She thought for a moment. "What about Fanny?"

Bysshe shook his head. "That is sad as well. What about Clara? It's an entirely different name from Claire."

Really? Hardly different enough. Mary hesitated, speculating on his motives. *What is going on with Bysshe? Had he and Claire planned this together?* But eventually she agreed. It was in the nature of a peace offering.

THIRTY-FIVE

A week later Mary received word that both *Frankenstein* and *History of a Six Weeks' Tour* had been accepted for publication and would soon be for sale.

She was delighted to have Lackington as the publisher and liked their bookshop as well. With its galleries and circular display tables, it was one of the most popular in London. She had a good contract, too. Her publisher would take all the risk of printing and advertising. After deductions to cover these expenses, the profits would be divided equally.

By the end of the month, both manuscripts were off to the printer.

On October 30, Mary opened the *Morning Chronicle* to see an advertisement for *History of a Six Weeks' Tour.* By November 12, she held a copy in her hands. This was her own creation, as precious to her as Willmouse or Clara, though she would never admit that, even to Bysshe.

History of a Six Weeks' Tour received favorable reviews, and Mary eagerly looked forward to the publication of *Frankenstein* in early January.

Meanwhile, Bysshe encountered difficulties publishing *Laon and Cythna.* Though the book was initially scheduled to be out before Christmas, the publishers were vacillating about the incest theme.

"Poor Bysshe," Mary lamented to Marianne. "He talked so much about 'breaking through the crust of outworn opinions.' Now his publisher insists that he change the book's title to *The Revolt of Islam*. It's a ruse to divert the reader from the brother-sister relationship."

"You realize that I am not much of a reader, but the new title does have a ring to it."

"There is more at stake than the name," Mary admitted. "It is not only the incest they object to. What bothers them most is Bysshe's rejection of God and hell. Besides the new title, they want major changes—twenty-seven substituted pages."

It was a grim Christmas. The sun no longer reached over the roof into the garden. Albion House was well-nigh impossible to heat, and its rooms grew increasingly dark and damp. Mary noted to her dismay that the books in the library were beginning to mildew, Bysshe's *Queen Mab* among them. By now they were all thoroughly sick of Albion House. It was way too much responsibility for Mary. She was delighted when Bysshe put the lease up for sale

On January 1, the three-volume novel *Frankenstein; or, The Modern Prometheus* was published anonymously. "Let the book stand on its own," Mary's publisher had originally advised her. "With your name—a woman's name—on the cover, *you* will become the controversy, not the book. Test the waters first."

Mary had taken his advice and was surprised that, despite the dedication, "To William Godwin, author of *Political Justice*, these volumes are respectfully inscribed by the author," many believed the novel had actually been written by her father. Others surmised Bysshe to be the author. Mary was delighted; her novel was causing a stir.

"Its theme is highly questionable: man's unholy quest for knowledge," one reviewer wrote. "It is more than that," another countered. "*Frankenstein* is about man versus God."

"It is beyond blasphemous," a newspaper columnist said. "It posits the idea that man might create a living entity without God's help at all."

Many writers were suggested as the possible author, none of them female. All agreed that such challenges—some called them scathing attacks—to both science and religion could not possibly have been written by a woman.

Mary looked up at Bysshe from the stack of papers she had been reading before the fire. "I suppose I should be annoyed. I *am* annoyed. I wish I'd insisted on putting my name on it in the first place. Really, to think that a woman could not attempt a scientific theme! But," she admitted, "I'm also pleased that so many are taking my book seriously."

"You've tapped into their secret fears that scientists will go too far—delve into regions unknown to them, to anyone." Bysshe's voice took on a hollow, sonorous tone. "Who knows what hideous creatures may be unleashed into the world." He hunched his shoulders and moved toward Mary, shuffling until he caught her, enfolding her in a playful grip. Mary smiled, resting her head on his shoulder. It was so good to see Bysshe happy.

At just that moment Claire appeared. "Oh! I am sorry to interrupt you," she said, pausing in the doorway. "It is only that one of the servants said that you had received a letter from Albe. He has not written to me since Allegra's birth. I wondered if there was any word about her, about me . . ."

Bysshe sighed softly and stood back from Mary. "Yes, he did write, but you will not like what he said. I myself am shocked by Albe's behavior. He did not mention you, but requests that Allegra be delivered to him in Venice by courier."

"By courier! She is not yet a year old."

"You need not do it," Bysshe told her. "If you prefer, you and Allegra can remain with us."

Stiffening, Mary sought to catch his eye. She had been living for the day when Claire and her child would join Byron. Now here was a letter, and Bysshe had not even shared its contents with her . . .

"So, Albe does not want me anymore. I can no longer pretend—dream—that he does. I will have to send Allegra to him . . . somehow," Claire said, faltering. "I cannot bear the thought of giving her up, but what life can she have as an illegitimate daughter of a penniless mother? He can give her everything, I nothing."

"Then we must find a responsible couple to take her to Venice," Mary ventured. "Elize can accompany them. Willmouse will miss her—she has been his nanny from the first—but it is best that Allegra travel with someone she knows."

Claire's eyes were on Bysshe. "How strange life is. Soon Ianthe and Charles will be returned to your keeping. You will have four children to love, while I may never see my baby girl again."

"You can always visit or, better yet, live close by," Mary said. She was sorry for Claire—it was clear to all that she adored Allegra—but not surprised by Albe's decision. His feelings had been evident in Switzerland.

Mary remembered clearly his words spoken to her late one stormy Geneva night. *"I never loved Claire nor pretended to love her—but, but by God, Mary, a man is a man. If a girl of eighteen comes prancing to your bedside at all hours of the night, there is but one thing to do. And now she is with child and must return to England to assist in peopling that desolate island. This comes of putting it about as a man will, damn it. It is thus that people come into the world."*

Now Mary wanted nothing more than to have the baby matter settled and Claire out of the house before the custody trial. Once Bysshe's children were awarded to him, their family's new life would begin.

That evening they assembled for dinner at the baronial dining table cheerily lit by many candles. The roast stag was tender and tasty, the Hunt children reasonably subdued. During a slight lull in the conversation, Claire's claws came out: "Willmouse will not be such a happy boy when two older children arrive to supplant him and he must wait to be served third."

Willmouse did not hear her; Mary pretended not to. Life was going too well to be disturbed by Claire's pettiness.

Lord Eldon's appointment as chancellor of Bysshe's custody case was an unexpected blow. "Bloody blazes!" Bysshe exclaimed when he heard the news.

"What's the matter?" Mary wanted to know.

"He was a fellow and tutor of University College when I was at Oxford," Bysshe explained. "I always suspected that Eldon was largely responsible for my expulsion."

"Oh, that was so long ago," she reminded him. "You were but a boy. Surely he won't hold a few youthful indiscretions against you." Inwardly she wondered—were Bysshe's chickens coming home to roost?

Mary's apprehensions grew as she sat beside her husband in a crowded London courtroom. Lord Eldon seemed to tower over them, ramrod stiff in his court robes, a purple waistcoat and breeches, lace cuffs, and starched cravat. A sword dangled at his side, and, beneath his black hat, he wore the traditional shoulder-length wig. Her heart filled with dread.

He returned her gaze coolly, regarding her through narrow, speculative eyes. Mary thought his thin lips cruel, his nose hawk-like. Turning away, she noted that the Westbrook clan was out in force.

"They didn't take Harriet back after you separated; why are the Westbrooks suddenly anxious for the children?" she whispered.

"I doubt that they care a fig for the children." Bysshe didn't bother to lower his voice. "It is me they seek to punish."

Lord Eldon banged his gavel twice, effectively silencing the reporters and curious bystanders who jammed the court.

Mary held her breath as his ruling was read slowly, distinctly, and with obvious malice.

"Percy Bysshe Shelley has blasphemously derided the truth of the Christian revelation and denied God as the creator of the universe. This man made friends with a most unsavory character, William Godwin, author of a blasphemous work called *Political Justice*. He then deserted his wife and ran off with Godwin's daughter, and they have since had several illegitimate children. Thus, the legitimate offspring are to be removed from his care."

The courtroom went wild. Many people applauded; some stamped their feet. Mary, turning to Bysshe, saw fleeting expressions of shock and pain. She took his hands in hers while he sat white-faced and silent. At last he turned to her, his face incredulous. "How could this have happened?"

How could you not know? Mary wondered, but said nothing.

Devastated, Bysshe lost interest in writing. His tea sat untouched on the table; his food went untasted. As though the loss of Bysshe's children were not enough, Harriet's creditors dunned him mercilessly for her final bills, and, as usual, William Godwin importuned him for money. Claire railed as well. "If only Byron could see Allegra. I know he would love her." She looked at Bysshe pleadingly. "Perhaps he would even come to love me. Could we not follow him to Italy?"

"We cannot go anywhere," he told her, his face glum. "I am obligated to maintain Albion House." The mansion they had imagined as a haven now seemed an albatross.

They had returned from the trial to a country estate grown hostile and forbidding in the winter chill. The damp and cold exacted a frightening toll on Bysshe's health. He developed a deep, hacking cough and seemed to grow paler with each passing day.

The news that followed them to Albion House was not good either. Despite Bysshe's compromises, readers did not take kindly to *The Revolt of Islam.* Mary worried constantly about her husband. He seemed more frail than ever.

Then, quite out of the blue, their luck changed. To everyone's surprise and delight, Albion House, advertised to no avail for months, suddenly had a taker for the lease.

"That means we can go to Italy!" Claire trilled.

For once the three were in agreement. Sunny Italy.

But first there would be a month in London. Good-byes must be said. They took rooms on Great Russell Street rather than stay with the Godwins. William was driven frantic by their imminent departure and pushed adamantly for Bysshe to leave his money in a joint account in London. Though Mary's heart ached for her father, she agreed with Bysshe that this was a very bad idea.

A round of shopping and farewell parties was marked by one significant ritual. Byron had asked that his daughter be christened, and Claire, eager to comply with his wishes, arranged for a service at St. Giles-in-the-Fields. According to his instructions, the child was to be baptized Clara Allegra with the addition, "reputed daughter of Rt. Hon. George Gordon, Lord Byron, peer of no fixed residence, travelling on the Continent."

Clara Allegra. Mary was surprised by Albe's choice, Claire well pleased. "Perhaps he doesn't completely hate me." Turning to Mary, she added, "Don't worry, we will call her Allegra so there will be no confusion between our little ones."

The morning of the service, Mary took Bysshe's arm, looked up at him, and said, "I want our children christened as well."

His eyes opened wide. "You don't mean that! You could not! I will not listen to such nonsense. What would your father say?"

"For once I do not care what he says. I know not if there is a God, but I do like the idea of a heaven. If there is such a place, I want Willmouse and Clara to be welcome there one day."

"Mary, Mary," he said, shaking his head in disbelief.

"Bysshe! Listen to me! Whether I like it or not, Claire is still with us and my own baby is named after her. I gave in on that. You must allow me my way on this."

His head turned away from the ceremony, Bysshe nevertheless attended it, sitting at Mary's side.

On their last evening in London, the children were put to bed early. It was not long before a weary Claire followed them upstairs. Papa came to dinner but left soon afterward—angry and empty-handed. The Hunts stayed on to chat. It was a bittersweet evening for Mary. Though Bysshe fell asleep midsentence, she wanted to experience every last minute. Who knew when she would see her friends again?

The next day, March 11, 1818, Mary, Bysshe, Claire, the three children, and their nurse, Elize, rose before dawn. As they rode toward Dover, tears formed in Mary's eyes. It was to be good-bye London, yet Italy beckoned. This would be a new beginning.

PART VI

The beginning is always today
—Mary Shelley

THIRTY-SIX

The sojourn began well. Mary thought she and Bysshe had discovered paradise when they happened upon the hillside village of Bagni di Lucca just twenty-eight miles north of Pisa.

Within days they had leased a villa, Casa Bertini, and settled in. "We are surrounded by mountains covered with thick chestnut woods," Mary enthused in a letter to Marianne. "Vines are cultivated at the foot of the mountains. We see fireflies in the evening— somewhat dimmed by the brightness of the moon. Our walks are delightful. We lead here a quiet, pleasant life."

Glancing up from her writing, Mary looked about the garden. It was glorious, bright flowers everywhere. Nearby, Willmouse and Allegra played with Clara, encouraging the playful baby to walk. Seated across from her, an impatient Claire fanned herself, seemingly oblivious to the grape arbor above, the cascading waterfall nearby.

Claire looked sullen. She was, Mary knew, not nearly so pleased with their new surroundings. She still clung to the dream that if Byron were but to see Allegra, he would be captivated. How could he not love the child? How then could he not love her mother?

Bysshe was less sanguine. In a note to Byron, he asked:

Will you spend a few weeks with us this summer? Our mode of life is uniform and much as you remember it at Geneva. Our surroundings are solitary and grand. If you would visit us—and

*I don't know where you could find a heartier welcome—little
Allegra might return with you.*

While they waited for his answer, there was a flurry of letters
from Papa, Tom Hogg, and Tom Peacock. *Frankenstein* continued
to garner favorable comment. The prestigious *Quarterly Review*
professed, "The man who has written the work is a man of talents."
Better yet was Sir Walter Scott's review in *Blackwood's*: "The work
impresses us with a high idea of the author's original genius and
happy power of expression."

Five hundred copies had been printed, and they were sell-
ing briskly to an enthusiastic audience. Many lauded the book
and were all the more excited when word finally leaked out that
she was the author. A reviewer from *Blackwood's* wrote, "For a
man it was excellent, but for a woman it was wonderful." *La Bell
Assemblée* described the novel as "very bold fiction." *The Quarterly
Review* stated that "the author has powers, both of conception and
language." The *Edinburgh Magazine and Literary Miscellany* hoped
to see "more productions from this author."

But reaction was divided. The *British Critic* attacked the novel's
flaws as the fault of the author. "The writer of it is, we understand,
a female; this is an aggravation of that which is the prevailing fault
of the novel; but if our authoress can forget the gentleness of her
sex, it is no reason why we should; and we shall therefore dismiss
the novel without further comment."

Mary was thrilled by the attention but worked to conceal it,
for Bysshe's *Revolt of Islam* remained largely ignored. Though her
husband professed to be happy for her, Mary sensed a growing
gulf between them. "*Frankenstein* is a charming little book," she
heard Bysshe comment to a friend. Her frightful monster *charming*? Really? Mary watched him from beneath her lashes but said
nothing.

When Albe finally wrote, it was to decline their invitation. Instead, he dispatched a messenger to bring the child and her nanny to him in Venice. Two days past her twentieth birthday, Claire waved good-bye to fifteen-month-old Allegra as the child set off with Elize and a courier.

Though Mary had longed for some sort of resolution of Claire's situation, she had grown fond of Allegra. Willmouse missed his playmate, and Mary missed the sound of their happy laughter. She noted another change as well. Without Allegra to look after, Claire's attention moved once again to Bysshe. Mary was watchful, nervous. Bysshe had promised to end his affair with Claire, but that had been three years ago. What were his feelings now?

Elize had promised to write often and with candor. She lost no time in complying. "Lord Byron's behavior is beyond scandalous," she wrote. Elize went on to describe a parade of women—grande dames, illustrious courtesans, and harlots off the street—who shared his great bed overlooking the Grand Canal. It was the lord's pleasure to outwit both zealous fathers and jealous husbands, taking whatever woman caught his fancy. He cared little, had no shame, and reveled in his notoriety.

Byron drank prodigiously but ate almost nothing. Elize said he lived as though his strength were boundless, but it was not: he had collapsed the previous night in the midst of a grand ball. Doctors diagnosed him with exhaustion, fever, and venereal disease, and warned the lord that he was killing himself.

Then came the worst letter of all. Elize claimed that Byron had sworn to make Allegra his mistress as soon as she was old enough. Albe's affair with his sister was well known. Why not his daughter? Claire was hysterical.

"He was clearly joking. He cannot mean it," Mary attempted to assure her.

"He does mean it," Claire cried. Tears streamed down her face. "I must go to Venice immediately."

"I will take you," Bysshe responded quickly.

Far too quickly, Mary thought. "Surely there is no need for that," she told him.

Bysshe looked at Mary in surprise. "She cannot make the journey alone."

Within a day he had hired a one-horse gig and they were off, leaving Mary behind with Willmouse and baby Clara. Mary's beloved Casa Bertini turned dark and tomb-like overnight. Awakened by frightful dreams, she felt pain and death lurking nearby, as if waiting . . . For whom did they wait? She buried her head in a pillow, stifling her cries. The children must not hear, must not feel the dread that enveloped her. It was the first of many dark nights.

"If you love me, you will keep up your spirits," Bysshe wrote her from an inn en route to Venice, "and at all events tell me the truth about it, for I assure you I am not of a disposition to be flattered by your sorrow though I should by your cheerfulness." He went on to describe his breakfast with Claire. They'd had figs "very fine, & peaches whose smell was like one fancies of the wakening of Paradise flowers."

Well, is that not nice, Mary thought, the pages of the letter, so eagerly yearned for, falling unheeded to the floor. *How pleasant to know that he and Claire are having such a grand time!*

Bysshe's next letter informed Mary that he and Claire had reached their destination. He was writing from Venice, that fabled city of which Mary had only dreamed. Venice, with its infamous gala balls and masquerades where night turned to day and there was no sense of what hour it was or even what day of the week. Oh, yes, Mary knew all about Venice.

Bysshe also wrote that Albe had appeared delighted by his unexpected arrival, but when Bysshe attempted to bring up the subject of Claire and Allegra, his host's mood abruptly changed. Lord Byron was vehement in his expressions of hatred for Claire. He detested his former mistress and swore never to see her again. "I will not allow her near me!" he had said, banging his fist on the table. With this in mind, Bysshe felt he could not possibly reveal the truth—that Claire was at that moment waiting impatiently in a nearby hotel.

Instead, Bysshe told Mary, Albe had insisted then and there on taking him on a gondola ride, proclaiming, "I must show you the sights."

What sights? Mary wondered. Where had Albe taken Bysshe? Knowing Albe as she did, it might well have been a brothel tour. Her husband's letter contained no clue. Rather, he described how he had at last succeeded in persuading Albe to allow Claire to see their child. The stipulation was that it must be in some distant place where Albe could not possibly lay eyes upon Claire himself.

"Where is she now?" Albe had abruptly asked. In a panic Bysshe had covered up one deception with another. Claire was with Mary, Bysshe told his friend; they were traveling together to the medieval village of Este, where he was to meet them upon leaving Venice.

"Este?" Albe had repeated thoughtfully. "I own a country villa there, Casa Cappucini. It is built on the ruins of a Capuchin monastery, a charming place. I shall have it made ready for you at once. Spend a few days here with me and then join the women in Este. I will arrange to send Allegra there. It will be a short reunion with her mother, but nonetheless a reunion."

Well, really, this was too much! Mary was furious. Why had Bysshe not told the truth? Why did he have to involve her, to involve their children in this ridiculous charade? With an exasperated sigh, Mary picked up the letter again and began to read.

Pray come instantly to Este and bring Willmouse and Clara. I shall be waiting there with Claire & Elize. You can begin packing directly upon receiving this letter & employ the next day in that. The following day get up at four o'clock and go by post to Lucca where you will arrive at six. Then take a vetturino for Florence to arrive the same evening. From Florence to Este is three days by vetturino. Este is a little place & the house found without difficulty.

Oh dear, Mary thought, putting down the letter. *Vetturinos* were such rickety conveyances; they frequently tipped over. It would not be easy traveling so far alone with two small children. Mary picked up little Clara, cradling the baby in her arms. Small-boned with fair, almost translucent skin, she looked like a fragile doll. Clara had been an easy child from the beginning, docile and sweet, yet alert and filled with eager curiosity. Not quite one, Clara was teething. As Mary studied her daughter's face, she noticed a slight flush. On closer study, Clara did not look well. Mary's instinct was to delay the trip. Yes, Bysshe's integrity was at stake as well as Claire's happiness, but were these considerations worth risking her baby's health?

Mary sat for a time rocking her daughter while thinking of Bysshe and Claire alone together . . . Lately there had been something . . . different . . . something vaguely unsettling. Yes, he had promised to end their affair, but what good was that? Bysshe was mercurial. Did his word count for anything?

––––––––

Mary spent her twenty-first birthday packing. Clara seemed her sparkling, happy self again. Surely Mary had only imagined a fever. On the evening of August 31, three days after receiving Bysshe's letter, she arrived in Florence. Here Mary encountered passport trouble and was held up an entire day. Willmouse was clingy and fretful, not his usual happy, outgoing self at all, and Clara seemed subdued. Mary began to worry. The journey was a dreadful mistake.

The muggy summer weather, the dust, and the flimsy *vetturino* were taking their toll on Clara. It seemed to Mary, now terrified, that her little girl weakened with each hour. By the time they reached Albe's Villa Cappucini in Este, Clara had developed a bad case of dysentery.

"I am glad you've come at last," Bysshe said, helping her from the hired town carriage that had brought her and the children from the terminal. "Claire is not well."

"*Claire* is not well!" Mary straightened her tired body to confront him. "Will you look at this baby, *our* baby? She refuses to nurse and has lost so much weight in the past six days that you will not know her. Clara is desperately ill."

As they entered the palatial mansion, Mary saw nothing of Claire but thought she heard someone retching violently from behind a closed door.

"What is the matter with her?" Mary asked.

Bysshe shook his head, looking worried. "She is violently ill and bleeds profusely. Now she is deadly pale. The baby can go along on her doctor's appointment tomorrow, but you will have to rise at half past three in order to get there in time."

"But Bysshe, Clara needs to see a doctor now." Mary struggled to hold back her tears. Surely he did not understand; she must reason with him. "Our baby is gravely ill."

"Don't work yourself up." Bysshe sounded almost exasperated. "Children often fall sick here in summertime."

"Yes, and many of them die." Mary fought to remain calm. "You don't understand how serious this is."

"You are the one who does not understand, Mary. Please try to keep your voice down. I told you, it is Claire who is dangerously ill. I fear that she will bleed to death. Do you think I would have delayed taking her to a doctor if there were any nearby? There is nothing to do but wait. Take Willmouse and the baby upstairs, put them to bed. Lie down yourself. All I need is to have *you* get sick."

———————

At three the following morning, Mary brought Clara to Bysshe. He appeared more relaxed and greeted her with a smile. "Claire is better, the bleeding has stopped." Mary saw his face whiten at the sight of the baby's wizened form. It was as though he were seeing her for the first time. Had he paid no attention the night before?

"We must take her to Venice immediately," Bysshe announced.

"Venice! That's so far. She's been so shaken up from all the jolting, the dust—you have no idea what it was like. What about the doctor here? The one that Claire's going to?"

"I fear he is not good enough," Bysshe admitted. "Albe has a splendid doctor by the name of Aglietti. This may be Clara's only chance."

"Oh, no!" Mary clung to the baby as Bysshe put a light cloak about her shoulders against the early morning chill. "What about Willmouse? And Claire?" she asked as he hurried her down the marble stairs.

"Claire will be all right. And I have given instructions for a servant to care for Willmouse. He will be fine."

More dust, more jolting, more heat. By the time their coach reached the environs of Venice, where travelers needed to board gondolas to cross the lagoon into the city, it was five in the evening. Almost immediately they were surrounded by some twenty or so gondoliers, all offering their services. Mary's senses were assaulted by strident cries until Bysshe selected a boat and they stepped into

it. Scarcely had they settled into the gondola before Clara suffered a convulsive fit. Terrified, Mary held her closer, murmuring
endearments into her small ears.

Once they'd reached the city, Bysshe stopped at the first inn
they came to, hurrying Mary and the baby into the dimly lit, dirty
lobby. "Stay here, it will be easier on Clara," he advised her. "I will
find Albe's doctor and be back as soon as possible."

In an instant he was out the door, leaving Mary alone with
her desperately ill baby. Mary had never felt more helpless and
alone. No one came near her. No one offered succor. Mary sat
alone, rocking Clara, staring deeply into her eyes, hoping by sheer
force of will to bring some animation back into the still features
that reminded her so much of Bysshe. Mary's efforts were in vain.
Clara's small, shrunken body was failing. Mary watched with horror as the baby's eyes rolled back into her head.

By the time Bysshe returned with the doctor, there was nothing that anyone could do. Clara was dead.

"Our child died of a disorder peculiar to the area," Bysshe
wrote to friends back home.

But Mary knew better.

THIRTY-SEVEN

Claire discovered a pleasant irony in playing lady of Byron's manor. He might profess to disdain her, but here she was—mistress of his vast estate, Villa Cappucini. Claire took pleasure in the light, spacious rooms and spreading gardens with their bountiful fruit trees and grape-laden vines. And then there were the servants, a retinue of them, catering to her every whim.

Bysshe, Mary, and Willmouse had joined Byron in Venice, while Claire remained at the villa in Este with Allegra and her nanny, Elize. Claire thought it sad that baby Clara had died—she had been a sweet, charming child, to be sure. Yet the passing was no one's fault. Certainly not Bysshe's, much less her own. Mary must get over it, move forward with her life, and stop blaming people for a random misfortune. It had been weeks since Claire had received even a line from her.

Instead it was Bysshe who wrote, "This sudden tragedy has reduced Mary to a kind of despair. All this is miserable enough—is it not? But must be borne. Meanwhile forget me and relive not the other thing. Above all, my dear girl, take care of yourself."

Claire sighed impatiently. Grand as her surroundings might be, the fact remained: she was living again in exile while Mary and Bysshe were in Venice doing all sorts of amusing things with Byron. Claire thought with longing of the bright Venetian light on the Grand Canal and the soft lapping sound of gondolas, then reminded herself that Villa Cappucini was the safe haven she desperately needed.

Claire had tried to abort her baby, had nearly died from it, but the attempt had failed. Now she considered this a sign that her child was meant to live and felt a little smug at the prospect. Perhaps her role in life was to bear the babies of the world's two greatest poets. Was there not something grand about that? On the other hand, what good was grand if nobody knew about it? She was lonely at times, but not really unhappy. It was a delight to have Allegra with her again and the prospect of a new baby was exciting. But what of Bysshe? It would seem that his main concern was protecting his precious Mary.

The autumn season was mild. Claire sat in the dappled sunlight reading, knitting, dreaming. Then one day in October, Bysshe paid her a surprise visit. He had come alone to Villa Cappucini, ostensibly to sort out books and papers. Claire was delirious. It was difficult to contain herself in front of the ever-watchful Elize.

"You look lovely," he said once they stood together in the drawing room with the door firmly closed. "Very robust." He eyed her belly thoughtfully. "Are you recovered from your—your—?" He paused, seemingly at a loss for words. "I would never have expected—wanted—that of you. Surely you know that?"

"I suppose, but tell me, tell me true, are you not just a little sorry that my attempt failed?"

"Since you put it that way, I will confess. Its success would have made life less complicated." He took her hands in his. "What matters finally is your well-being."

Claire sat on the chaise longue and then reclined, aware that the rosy pink cushions flattered her. "I am well enough. Sometimes even just a bit . . . happy." When Bysshe said nothing, she continued. "Tell me the news. Is Mary any more reconciled to Clara's passing?"

Bysshe settled himself opposite her in a large baronial arm-chair. "She is trying, but it is a daunting task. Clara was the third child Mary has born and the second to die. Then, too, there were the . . . unfortunate circumstances. Though she says nothing, I sense that she is angry as well as miserable." He paused, fumbling for his mermaid pipe and flint. "Mary has always been subject to depression. It appears to run in her family. I find it difficult to imagine the great Mary Wollstonecraft taking her own life, but she tried twice—and, of course, there was Fan."

"Poor Bysshe, this must be hard on you," Claire sympathized.

"You have no idea. Happily Mary now has an admirer. The Chevalier Mengaldo secured an introduction as soon as he heard that she was the author of *Frankenstein*. He is an ardent fan and calls often. He escorts her to the opera and to plays."

Claire looked up in surprise. "Are they lovers?"

"Unfortunately not."

She chuckled, shaking her head. "Oh, tell me that you would not be just a little jealous."

Bysshe straightened in his velvet-tufted chair. "When have I ever been jealous? You look skeptical, but be assured, I am *never* jealous. I want my women to enjoy themselves as I do." He paused for a moment, lost in thought. "Even if I were inclined in that direction, I would still be happy about anything or anyone who could cheer Mary up."

"Really?" Claire raised a delicate brow. "Tell me about this chevalier."

"He is gallant, brave, I am told."

Bysshe tamped his pipe, and Claire caught the faint scent of old leather and spice. She loved it.

"Mengaldo fought and was decorated for his part in France's war against Russia. He, like Mary, is an aficionado of ghost tales. They share that and a love of the theater.

"Mary keeps busy in other ways as well. She spends as much time with Willmouse as possible. We have rented a villa in Naples, and Mary has a household to run. She has started writing a new novel, and Albe has given her the manuscript of his latest poem, *Mazeppa*, to fair copy it."

Claire's chest contracted, but she kept her voice even. "Ah, yes, the great Albe. What of him?"

"He remains a genius, but is becoming something of a fiend. Believe me, you are well out of it."

"He loved me once," Claire said. She rose from the couch and left the room but swiftly returned carrying a small, intricately carved box. "He wrote this for me long ago. I have always kept it hidden." Taking out a folded piece of paper, she explained, "Albe used to admire my voice. I sang for him often. That all seems so long ago, but what can it be . . . three years?"

Reluctantly Bysshe took the paper she pressed upon him and read aloud:

There be none of Beauty's daughters
With a magic like thee;
And like music on the waters
Is thy sweet voice to me:
When, as if its sound were causing
The charmed Ocean's pausing,
The waves lie still and gleaming,
And the lull'd winds seem dreaming.

"You see, however he may feel now, he did care once." Claire paused for a moment, her eyes searching Bysshe's. "You cared for me, too, I think. You sent this shortly after you and Mary were married." She handed him a second sheet of paper.

Claire watched intently as he read the note. She knew its contents by heart.

Thank you my kind girl for not expressing much of what you must feel—the loneliness and the low spirits which arise from being entirely left. Nothing could be more provoking than to find all this unnecessary. However, they will now be satisfied and quiet.

"I assume 'they' refers to Papa Godwin and Mother."

"Of course." Bysshe sucked thoughtfully on his pipe. "William believed—or professed to believe—that marriage would ensure my custody of the children. As you know, it did not—"

Claire leaned forward to touch his arm. "But how do *you* feel—how do you feel now?"

"You know very well how I feel about institutions." He moved his arm away from her ever so slightly. "Marriage is surely one of them. But the fact is that I love Mary. I have always loved her."

Claire struggled to keep her voice light, though her heart pounded. "So if you have not come for me, I assume then that you are here because of Allegra. What of her? What of my little girl?"

Bysshe looked away for a moment and then met her eyes as though forcing himself to do so. "That is why I have come. Albe insists that I bring her to him."

Claire caught her breath. It was the news that she had dreaded. The idyll with her little girl had been far too happy to last. Claire thought of the games they had played, the pleasure she had taken in brushing Allegra's long curly hair, the stories she had read to her. "But what of his threats? He said he would have his way with her."

"Albe was only joking. He likes to shock people, surely you have seen that. His villa in Venice is filled with pets of all kinds— dogs, cats, even monkeys. He is always kind and gentle with them. Would he be less so to his own child?"

"Can I not go with her? Allegra is not even two."

Bysshe rose. Standing behind Claire, he placed his hands on her shoulders. "You know better than that. Albe has made his feelings all too clear. He cannot abide having you in the same town with him. He has asked that I bring Elize with me as well. I am to take them to him in Venice."

Claire fought to hold back the tears. It was all so final. Would she ever see Allegra again? Steadying her voice, she asked, "Will you and Mary remain in Venice as well?"

Bysshe shrugged. "I thought you knew, Mary and I plan to spend the winter in Naples."

Claire looked down. Her voice scarcely more than a whisper, she asked, "What of me—what of *our* baby? It is due around Christmas."

Bysshe stared at her a moment, a very long moment, it seemed to Claire, then shrugged again. "Oh, what the devil! Come along with us to Naples."

THIRTY-EIGHT

Mary thought Chevalier Mengaldo attractive, for an older man. She was flattered by his attention, and their conversations had slowly begun to raise her spirits, for they found many interests in common. Indeed, they often sat with heads together, exchanging ghost tales.

She was drawn to the optimism inherent in such tales. The very idea that a spirit had thumbed his nose at death and then come back to show off to mere mortals appealed to Mary. She saw a ghost tale as both a clue and an invitation to a world beyond her own reality. Mary wanted so much to believe that no one *really* died.

Yes, Mengaldo was a good companion. Sometimes he even made Mary forget her anger toward Bysshe, but the longing for her darling baby Clara . . . that would never go away. Eventually Mengaldo was able to persuade Mary to leave Willmouse with his nurse and the housemaid while they went to the opera and the theater. She had been studying Italian for several hours each day and could at last understand what the performances were all about. After a time she came to enjoy the outings.

One evening he arrived at her home dressed in his blue-and-gold hussar's uniform with a short cape and a black mask. Quite dashing, really. Mengaldo looked at Mary quizzically. "Tonight is Prince Renaldo's masked ball. Surely you have not forgotten?" In his hand was an ebony scepter to which a second mask was fastened. When he held it out to Mary, she saw that it was filigreed gold with pearls rimming the eye slits.

She demurred. "It is very beautiful, but I have no gown fine enough to wear with it."

"Surely that is not true." Mengaldo studied her for a moment. "Perhaps something crimson. I have never seen you in that shade and should like to."

"I do have a crimson gown," Mary admitted. "I have never worn it. The dressmaker had just completed it when . . . when . . ." The words caught in her throat.

"You must wear it for me tonight."

Mengaldo looked so happy, so expectant, so very pleased with himself. How could she not agree?

"It will take time for me to dress," she warned him. "You may grow tired of waiting."

"You will always be worth waiting for."

When she at last appeared before him, Mengaldo's eyes lit appreciatively.

Soon they were settled into his elaborate gondola, she a cloud of cascading crimson. It was a muggy night, the air humid and rank, but a full moon reflected on the dark water as the two gondoliers guided them down the Grand Canal toward the prince's splendid mansion. The boat had a cabin complete with damask cushions to recline upon and windows that could be closed with horizontal shutters. "We call them Venetian blinds," Mengaldo explained while adjusting one for Mary.

The ball was to be held in one of the splendid mansions that extended over the Grand Canal. The gondoliers skillfully steered their craft between massive pillars to a broad marble stairway, where they were greeted by waiting footmen.

Curiously she ascended, hurrying ahead of Mengaldo to the grand ballroom on the second floor. There Mary paused, stunned by the splendor before her. The room was like a multifaceted jewel. All about her champagne spouted from glittering fountains banked in dazzling ice sculptures. Numerous mirrors framed in gold reflected crystal chandeliers and sconces supporting more candles than Mary had ever seen massed together in her life. Scents assailed her from every direction—exotic perfumes, savory meats, and polished leather.

Mary scarcely knew where to look. The room was filled with masked men and women who whirled and twirled to the music of a full orchestra. She saw devils and queens, highwaymen and fairy princesses, gypsies and pharaohs. Mary and Mengaldo danced briefly, but soon she was claimed by another and then another. Mary shook her head to clear it and looked up into a pair of penetrating gray eyes. The man before her was a good six feet tall, with curling raven hair that just cleared his collarbone. He had wide, square shoulders and long, lean legs. His face was crudely handsome, his skin tanned to a tawny gold.

"Where is your mask?" she asked him.

He raised an eyebrow, thick and silken. "Do I need one? What you see is who I am."

Mary's heart quickened as she studied him. "Really?" She cocked her head to one side. "You look like a pirate."

His lips curved in a smile that displayed white teeth. "You are most astute, madam. I *am* a pirate."

Mary continued to study him, curious. He met her gaze, eyes intent on hers. For an instant time stood still. As they whirled past a mirror, Mary caught a glimpse of a radiant woman she scarcely recognized.

Someone else claimed Mary, and they spiraled together in the new dance that had taken the country by storm. Many called the waltz "riotous" and "indecent," but not Mary. She loved it, loved even more the face-to-face style of dancing. Still, the unaccustomed three-quarter time forced her to concentrate. Thoughts of the dashing stranger were swept away, but in the gondola going home, she remembered him. "There was a man at the ball that I have not met before," she said, turning to Mengaldo.

"There were more than one hundred gentlemen at the ball this evening."

"Well, this man was a bit different. He was not wearing a mask or a costume, yet there was something most flamboyant about him. He seemed pleasant enough, but he looked like a brigand and said he was a pirate. Do you know the man I mean?"

"He *is* a pirate." A frown creased Mengaldo's broad forehead. "The name's Trelawny, Edward Trelawny. He is a rascal to be sure. There are all sorts of rumors. Trelawny is said to be a buccaneer, a smuggler. Indeed, he is a brigand of the worst kind."

"He sounds like Byron's *Corsair* come to life." Eyes closed, Mary quoted:

Not thou, vain lord of Wantonness and Ease!
Whom Slumber soothes not—Pleasure cannot please—
Oh, who can tell, save he whose heart hath tried,
And danced in triumph o'er the waters wide,
The exulting sense—the pulse's maddening play,
That thrills the wanderer of that trackless way?

"Oh, my romantic girl." Mengaldo sighed. "Try to remember that life is not a poem."

Well, Mary knew *that*.

———•———

The next morning Edward Trelawny presented himself at the lodgings where Mary awaited Bysshe's return. When a servant removed his cape, Mary noted that Trelawny wore tight, perfectly tailored trousers, a fashionable cutaway coat, and immaculate linen. She liked his dashing, debonair appearance. Bysshe cared so little about such things. Her husband's expensive clothes were always badly wrinkled and often stained.

"I hope you will forgive me for arriving unannounced," Trelawny said, taking her hand and kissing it. He stared hard at her, a look that warmed her body and brought a swift, rising sense of excitement.

"Oh, it is far worse than that." She stood back, smiling as her eyes met his. "We have not even been introduced."

"But I have heard all about you. Consensus has it that you are as witty as you are lovely."

"And I have heard about you as well . . . not so lovely." She led the way into the drawing room, where a fire burned cheerfully in the grate.

"You should not believe all you hear."

"Why not?" Mary surprised herself by asking. Life had been so very sad of late. If tall tales would amuse and entertain, what was the harm? "It's so dreadfully wet and dismal outside. Would you prefer coffee—perhaps with a little brandy in it?"

"I knew you were a lady after my own heart."

"That may be, but you must also know that I am married?"

"Yes." Trelawny leaned back with a sigh. "I took the trouble to learn that unfortunate detail, but I am told that your husband is away, perhaps even astray."

"He remains my husband."

At that moment there was a commotion in the anteroom, bags thumping, servants scurrying. Mary rose to her feet as the door flew open. There was Bysshe, cheeks flushed, shoulders slumped. Behind him stood a white-faced Claire, who appeared to be a good seven months pregnant. Mary's heart constricted; blood pounded in her ears as waves of shock, pain, and embarrassment swept over her.

She searched Bysshe's face, but he would not meet her gaze. Mary's voice, when she found it, was icy. It mattered not that

Trelawny was present—she had to know the truth. "The child Claire is carrying, I assume it is yours?"

Bysshe was silent. Face flushed, he stared at the floor.

Instead, it was Trelawny who spoke. "Bysshe Shelley, I presume? Edward Trelawny at your service." He bowed slightly, then turned to Mary, adding, "Even as an outsider, I can see that you have much to sort out." He took her hand and kissed it. "Goodbye . . . for now."

THIRTY-NINE

It was a wretched holiday season. The journey from Venice to Naples was made all the more difficult by Mary's refusal to speak to either Claire or Bysshe, who, in turn, spoke little to each other. They all reserved their conversation for Willmouse, whose happy, chattering presence was the only thing that made life bearable. Mary's thoughts were never far from Trelawny. She wondered where he was and what he was doing. Would they meet again? *Should* they meet again?

Once in Naples, Bysshe found a pretty apartment that raised Mary's spirits a notch. Number 250, Riviera di Chiaia, had tall, wide windows offering a spectacular view of the Royal Gardens and beyond to the ever-changing waters of the bay. Three days before Christmas Mary and Bysshe made a pilgrimage to Pompeii. They marveled at the statues and mosaics, many still intact, and picnicked beside a crumbling temple.

Sitting on a grassy knoll near the forum, they listened to the subterranean thunder of Vesuvius, its distant peals seeming to shake the very air and light of day. In awe, they drew closer to each other. Mary wondered if Bysshe remembered, as she did, the monumental mountains and deep, ice-encrusted crevasses of Switzerland. Did Bysshe still marvel at the might and majesty of nature? Mary could not bring herself to ask; he seemed so far away. They returned home to Claire, forlorn and very pregnant.

Five days later, her baby girl was born at home. A doctor attended the birth, assuring Bysshe that mother and child were doing fine.

Whatever Bysshe's thoughts, he did not share them with Mary. It was a miserable time for everyone. Mary could not bring herself to even look at the baby. She closeted herself in the bedroom that she had shared with Bysshe. He was now exiled.

"Go away! Take Claire with you, Claire and your damned brat!" she cried, then flung herself, sobbing, on the bed. Life seemed unbearable.

A day and a night later, Mary entered the drawing room, dry-eyed and with an ultimatum. "You have a choice to make," she told Bysshe, leveling a finger at him. "You know as well as I that if Claire remains here with the child, the whole town will know of it. If your father finds out, he could take little Willmouse to raise himself. You could lose him as surely as you lost Ianthe and Charles. Make a decision now and act on it."

Claire rushed into the room and stood looking from one to the other. "But what about me? What about *my* child?"

Mary assumed that Claire had been listening outside the door and answered coolly. "That is for Bysshe to decide." Glancing up at him, Mary challenged, "What will it be, Claire's child or *our* child?" Her eyes locked on his. "You cannot have both."

Bysshe looked away, unwilling, or perhaps unable, to meet her gaze. "Mary, you must believe, I never wanted this . . . never meant for it to happen."

"I do believe you, Bysshe, but 'this' is the way it is."

Angry tears streamed down Claire's face as she glared at Mary, fists clenched at her sides. "Where is all your fine talk of free love now?"

"That was five years ago," Mary reminded her. "I was a girl, filled with my mother's brave ideals. In the end my mother wanted security just as I do. I have lost two children, I gave up the father that I loved, my childhood home. Now all I want is to live in peace with my husband and our remaining child."

"I want peace, too!" Claire exclaimed, hands on her hips. "Albe has taken my darling Allegra from me. Who knows if I will ever see her again! Now I have been given another child, another chance. Do you want me to give her up, too?"

"That is entirely up to you. I ask only that you take her out of my home."

"It is Bysshe's home, too, and Bysshe's child." Claire turned anxiously toward him. "You said you loved me."

"No, Claire, I did not."

"Well, you have often said you adored me. Is that not the same?"

"Not . . . really." Bysshe looked down at his scruffy boots and then back at Claire. "I do adore you in a way. How could I not after all we have shared these past five years, but love . . ."

Adore. How well Mary knew those grandiose phrases that Bysshe loved to throw about. She could easily imagine him saying, "I adore you" to Claire. She wanted to strike them both.

The next day Bysshe left the apartment first thing in the morning. "I have a few errands to do," he explained to Mary.

When he did not return for lunch, she wondered what he was up to. Mary glanced suspiciously at Claire but saw that her stepsister was rocking her baby by the fire, completely absorbed.

When Bysshe finally returned late in the afternoon, he appeared weary but strangely pleased. "Why were you gone so long?" Mary asked, looking up from the book she had been reading to Willmouse.

"You may not like this," Bysshe said, sitting down opposite her. "But you must hear it nonetheless. I have been registering Claire's baby." He ran his hand nervously through his hair. "It had to be done, Mary. It's the law here."

"I suppose so." She hesitated. *What now?*

"I registered her as Elena Adelaide . . . Shelley. And I gave your name and mine as Elena's parents."

"That is really too much!"

Bysshe smiled sheepishly. "I thought you might be pleased. Willmouse will have someone to play with."

Dumbfounded, Mary stared at him in disbelief. "Do you imagine Claire's child a replacement for our Clara?"

"Well, not really . . ." He paused, pushing back a lock of hair that had fallen over his forehead. Finally he met Mary's angry eyes. "What was I to do? The only alternative was to have 'Illegitimate' stamped on the child's birth certificate. Would you really want that?"

Why should I care?—the words sprang quickly to Mary's lips. But then she looked at the tiny infant sleeping in Claire's arms. None of this was the baby's fault. No, she did not want an innocent child branded a bastard. "Just get them out of here," she said at last.

Bysshe turned to Claire. "Suppose I were to find lodgings for you and Elena, something pleasant, perhaps a cottage overlooking the sea."

"And then where would you and Mary go?" Claire wanted to know. "Somewhere far away and exciting, of that I am certain. I have been twice exiled. I hate it! I dread to be alone, and even if that were not the case, I am tired to death of the Bay of Naples."

Mary was adamant. "Then think of another place, any place. Go there and take your baby."

Bysshe's glance shifted uncertainly from one woman to the other.

The solution arrived the following morning in the form of yet another woman. Bysshe answered a knock at the door to find Elize standing on the step, a portmanteau in her hand.

"What are you doing here?" Claire demanded to know. "You are supposed to be caring for my Allegra in Venice."

"It pained me terribly to part from Allegra. I love her like a mother—as you love her, m'lady—but Lord Byron has placed her in a convent."

"A convent!" Claire gasped. "Allegra is little more than a baby!"

"Yes, I am told she is by far the youngest girl there, but Lord Byron's newest *lady*, Countess Teresa Guiccioli, says his palazzo is no place for a child. I must agree."

Claire turned to Bysshe. "Now my little Allegra has neither a father's love nor a mother's. Is there nothing that I can do?"

Bysshe shook his head regretfully. "You know as I do that a child belongs to its father—every child but mine, that is. At least you can take consolation in the fact that Allegra is being taken care of. The convent way is not our way, but I think it superior to Byron's way. We must accept that this development is for the best. Perhaps our luck is improving."

He turned back to the nanny, still standing in the doorway. "Come in, dear Elize, and sit down. It is good to see you again." He glanced at her valise. "Are you traveling? What are your plans?"

"I have no plans," she told him, her eyes downcast. "My position as Allegra's nurse ended when she left Venice. When I heard that you were here, I came to tell you the news, with the hope that you might know of work for me."

"Indeed, we do." Bysshe smiled. "It happens that Mary and I have decided to move north to Rome. Claire has had another baby. Would you consider staying here with her as housekeeper and Elena's nurse? Keep our housemaid if you like. You would be in charge."

Elize hesitated; the feathers in her bonnet fluttered as her eyes roamed the room.

"As you can see it is small but very comfortable, a charming place, really."

"Yes, very charming," Elize agreed.

"There will be no scandal," Bysshe assured her. "Elena has been registered as the child of Mary and me. No money problems either. I will see to it that you are all well cared for."

Claire began to cry. "But I hate Naples."

Bysshe shrugged. "Then come with us if you like."

Mary's breath caught. *Oh, no, this cannot be.* She turned to Claire. "Do you really want to be separated from both your babies?"

Claire hesitated, her eyes on Bysshe.

"Really, Claire, your place is here with Elena," he said at last. "Elize will take good care of you both."

"No! Do not leave me behind!"

Mary gasped. "Would you really leave your baby?"

Bysshe shrugged. "It's up to you, Claire."

Elena Adelaide Shelley was duly baptized February 27, 1819. The next day Mary, Bysshe, William, and Claire left Naples. Elena Adelaide remained with Elize.

FORTY

As Mary traveled northward to Rome, the promise of spring found an echo in her heart. Leaning out the coach window, she saw verdant young grass and wildflowers of all kinds and colors poking up their excited heads. Some of the pain at Clara's death slowly receded. Bysshe was beside her; Willmouse snuggled on her lap. Spring was the season of promise, her favorite time of year. She smiled, reassured that the two loves of her life were close, with yet another on the way. Yes, she had forgiven Bysshe. If life was to be bearable, she had to move forward.

Of course, Claire, too, was close by, but this time she had promised, in exchange for traveling with them from Naples, to find a position for herself in Rome. She would seek employment as a companion, possibly even a governess. Mary would see to it that she made good on that promise.

Thrilled by her first glimpse of Rome, Mary struggled to describe her impressions in a note to Marianne. "Rome has such an effect on me that my past life before I saw it appears a blank, and only now do I begin to live." Brave words. Mary did her best, saturating herself in Roman art and culture and studying Italian with a vengeance. With his little hand clasped in hers, Willmouse accompanied Mary to her favorite sites—the Trevi Fountain, the Sistine Chapel, and the Galleria Borghese. At three years old he was a delightful companion, curious about everything and friendly to everyone.

Though Mary remained annoyed that Claire was still with them, she knew that her stepsister was honestly trying to find a full-time position. At present she worked at a temporary job, teaching English to an Italian family. It kept her out of the house much of the day. There was one thing of which Mary was certain: Claire and Bysshe were each making a concerted effort to avoid the other.

Mary had fallen in love with Rome and was greatly stimulated by the eccentric set of expatriates she encountered daily. Still, she could not shake a sense of impending doom. Something awful was going to happen; Mary felt it but spoke to nobody of her fears, lest giving voice to them would call these evil premonitions into being.

I have nothing to fear, everything around me is perfection, she reminded herself. It was a kind of mantra she repeated countless times. Yet, as the days grew increasingly warm, she was forced to face the reality that the hot, muggy Roman summers could be hazardous for small children. She suggested that they travel north to Tuscany, but Bysshe and Claire wanted to go south to Naples to see Elena. Mary would have none of that. Was it not enough that Elize sent them weekly reports?

At an impasse, they did nothing. The truth was, no one wanted to go anywhere. Rome was too much fun. April passed and most of May; then on the twenty-sixth, Willmouse fell ill. The whole household descended into panic, but in a day or two the child was his cheerful self again.

Nevertheless, they had all been badly frightened. There was no question but that they must leave the hot, humid city immediately. "Naples will be hot as well," Mary argued. Bysshe, even Claire, agreed; they would seek summer refuge in the cool recesses of Bagni di Lucca. Claire dutifully wrote friends of friends seeking summer employment there and was accepted. Their departure was planned, arrangements quickly made. Bagni di Lucca was a highly social resort. Mary looked forward to it and thought she might

even do a little entertaining. The change would be good for all of
them, they agreed.

Then, on June 2, Willmouse suffered a sudden relapse. Looking
up at her from his little bed, the child's eyes, usually so bright with
joy and curiosity, were listless. He coughed incessantly while his
temperature soared. Mary went rigid with terror and disbelief. Was
she about to lose yet another child? It was worse than that. This
was *Willmouse*. It was Willmouse's presence that kept at bay Mary's
ever-present fear that her losses were retribution for the pain that
she had caused others. She had stolen Bysshe from Harriet, perhaps from Fan as well. Nothing could change that; nothing could
make it right.

"Bysshe, get a doctor," she ordered, her breath coming in gasps.
"Fetch him yourself, bring him back quickly."

"It is just a light fever, I do not think—"

"You do not think?" she screamed. "You do not care! We have
already lost Clara. Is that not enough? Please go. Now!"

Bysshe reluctantly set aside the book he had been reading and
rose to his feet. Then, at last meeting her frightened eyes, he hurried from the room.

It seemed an eternity to Mary, waiting by Willmouse's bed, but
when Bysshe returned, she realized that he had been gone scarcely
an hour. At his side, a bit out of breath, was Dr. Lombarti, a short,
stocky man with thick gray hair and a pince-nez clipped to his
nose.

"You need have no fear, signora, your little boy is in good
hands," he told Mary.

His voice was strong, his manner assured, but Mary thought
she detected a fleeting look of concern in the man's dark eyes.

Dr. Lombarti settled in and remained in almost constant
attendance. Mary watched in horror as her darling boy began to
convulse. "Oh," she sobbed, "this is just like Clara. I cannot bear it."

"Nonsense," Bysshe chided her. "You heard the doctor, it's nothing. Willmouse will be well in no time." Confident words, but his face was anxious as he took a seat beside her.

Mary clamped a handkerchief to her mouth lest the child waken and see her crying. She and Bysshe sat at Willmouse's side for three consecutive days and nights, determined to wrest their little angel from death's grip. They spoke little and rarely looked at one another, marking only Willmouse's obstructed breathing, the heaviness of death that weighed on his precious eyelids.

Willmouse died quietly. His small body, so white and still, was laid to rest the following day in the Protestant Cemetery.

Willmouse had been Bysshe's favorite, most beloved child. Claire loved him, too. Who could not? They were all distraught, but Mary, who had only just begun to recover from the loss of Clara, was devastated. Willmouse had always seemed to her like a bit of Bysshe in miniature. Now it was as though some of her feeling for her husband had died with their child. It was all so cruelly unfair. Mary struggled to suppress her bitterness but some spilled out.

"We chose Italy for Bysshe's health," she wrote to Marianne, "but the climate is nowhere near warm enough to benefit him and yet it is that same climate that has destroyed my two children.

"I no sooner take up my pen than my thoughts run away with me and I cannot guide it except about *one* subject and that I must avoid. I shall never recover from this blow. Everything on earth has lost its meaning to me."

Mary was twenty-one. She had lost three children, two within eight months. A fourth baby stirred within her but brought no joy or consolation. This new being seemed merely a reminder of the transience and futility of life. How could she ever give her love to another child?

William Godwin had paid scant attention to his grandson in life; perhaps it was too much to imagine that he would feel grief at his namesake's passing. Still, Mary had hoped that her father might show some semblance of empathy.

He did not.

Picking up the letter she had discarded, Mary smoothed it out and read again:

> *What is it you want that you have not? You have the husband of your choice, to whom you seem to be unalterably attached, a man of high intellectual endowments, you have all the good of fortune, all the means of being of use to others, and shining in your proper sphere. But you lost a child: and all the rest of the world, all that is beautiful, and all that has a claim upon your kindness is nothing because a child of four is dead.*

Mary was too full of sorrow to be angry.

Bysshe folded his arms around her. "It is time we left Rome," he said. "We must move on and begin a new life."

Mary nodded, looking up through tear-dimmed eyes. Together they began to pack their books and clothes, but when they got to Willmouse's toys, Mary thought her heart would break. The little tin soldiers that he had played with so often, the cunning puppets that were his favorites . . . Overcome by memories, she began to sob. "How are we to part with this?" she asked, holding up a worn shoe scuffed by his small foot.

"Somewhere there is another child in need of it," Bysshe told her.

Another child who would live to manhood, another child who would have a life, while for Willmouse, it was over.

Mary, Bysshe, and Claire traveled by coach to Leghorn. It was a dismal journey for them all, but they were rewarded by a light, airy house by the sea. Nearby, peasants sang as they worked, and at night, a waterwheel creaked as it irrigated the land. Bright, sunny days alternated between storms of majestic terror, the likes of which Mary had never experienced.

Bysshe was trying to help her, to help himself; dimly Mary was aware of this but could not stifle her grief. They had often been described as a brilliant couple—and, indeed, their intellectual bond was strong—yet both knew that a vital physical attraction was the glue that had held them together during the past five years.

With Willmouse's passing that drive had dissipated in Mary. Sometimes she went through the motions of lovemaking to please Bysshe, but on other occasions could not even do that. Her sexual rejection of him was unfair, even cruel, yet after the loss of three children, how could she accept physical intimacy as a creative fulfillment of their love? Rather, it had become to her a travesty of life, a lure and prelude to more death and despair.

One morning Mary woke to find a poem on her pillow.

My dearest Mary, wherefore hast thou gone,
And left me in this dreary world alone?
Thy form is here indeed—a lovely one—
But thou art fled, gone down the dreary road,
That leads to Sorrow's most obscure abode;
Thou sittest on the hearth of pale despair,
Where
For thine own sake I cannot follow thee
Do thou return for mine.

But how could she return to him with a heart hardened to stone? The poem seemed to her cold, unfeeling. Did he care so little for their precious boy? How could he imagine that their life could go on as it had before?

To Marianne, Mary wrote: "Hunt used to call me serious. What would he say to me now? I feel that I am not fit for anything & therefore not fit to live."

It was Leigh who replied by return post, telling Mary how much she and Bysshe were missed by their London friends. Mary smiled at the memory of happier times. She considered Leigh's suggestion that it was time she returned to writing. A bit of a story tugged at her tired brain.

Bysshe was working hard on a long poem, *The Cenci*. It was to be a tragic drama in five acts. He seemed absorbed, almost happy, if that were possible. Glancing over his shoulder, she read a verse:

> *that fair blue-eyed child*
> *Who was the loadstar of your life.*

And another declaimed:

> *All see, since his most swift and piteous death,*
> *That day and night, and heaven and earth, and time,*
> *And all the things hoped for or done therein*
> *Are changed to you, through your exceeding grief.*

Again Mary wondered at Bysshe's ability to use his grief for the loss of his son in the composition of a poem. To her it seemed incredibly callous, yet was it possible that writing could bring her solace as well? She sat down at her desk, confronting quills, a pot of ink, and a stack of blank paper. Slowly, word by word, sentence by sentence, she set to work again on *Mathilda*, the novel she had begun a few months before. Often she wondered if she had the courage to finish it, for the theme was obsession. Mary was attempting to put into words not only the loss of her beloved children but also a rationalization of her relationships with her father and husband.

She was hard at work when the next blow fell. Word arrived from the British Consul in Naples that Elize had given over the care of Elena to foster parents. The circumstances were murky, but one thing was certain—the child was dead. Elena Adelaide had been but eight months old.

Bysshe was devastated. "My Neapolitan charge is dead," he told Mary. "It seems as if everything I love is tainted and ultimately doomed."

Claire was inconsolable. If she had remained behind with her child, this might not have happened. Her obsession with Bysshe and her sense of entitlement must certainly have contributed to the tragedy. Still, Mary tried her best to comfort Claire and Bysshe. She had resented their daughter; perhaps, if truth be told, hated her, but that seemed long ago. A child's life, whatever its history, deserved to be treasured.

It was decided that they would move to Florence for the birth of the baby that Mary, half joking, called her "new work, now in the press." Secretly she was not nearly so sanguine. The child she carried, a tiny soul gestated in such strain and suffering . . . might it be a . . . monster? Mary shuddered involuntarily, then quickly promised herself to be a better parent than her Dr. Frankenstein. At the same time she wondered if she could really love this new baby. Could she—dare she—risk her heart again?

FORTY-ONE

Heigh-ho the Claire & the May
Find something to fight about every day

Claire scribbled the verse in her journal and sat back to look at it. What more could she add? The five months following Willmouse's death had been well-nigh impossible. Mary had been off in some twilight world of her own with naught to say to anyone. Why Bysshe stayed with her was more than Claire could see. She had much to say to him on the subject, but Bysshe would hear none of it. His manner was gentle, almost malleable; yet there remained issues on which he would not budge.

The new baby's birth in November caused all their spirits to rise. Mary's labor was short, a scant two hours. Claire thought it almost unseemly the way the child fairly slipped into the world.

Afterward, Mary had propped herself up on her elbows, gasping. "Let me see it, let me see it!" Her eyes were wide, almost fearful.

"You have a fine healthy boy," the doctor said, handing the infant to Mary.

"He is normal," Mary whispered. "Normal."

Well, what was she expecting? Claire wondered.

Claire thought the baby, named Percy Florence, pleasant enough. He was alert and lively from the first, though Claire thought his nose near as big as Papa Godwin's. Percy was never allowed to cry. Mary scooped him up the moment he awakened

and carried him everywhere with her. Claire thought it all a dreadful bore, though sometimes late at night she crept into Percy's room
to stare at his sleeping form. Her thoughts strayed then to her own
baby, Elena, lost to her forever. And what of Allegra? Would she
never see her again? Why must Mary be the one to always have
everything?

As the days passed, tensions dissipated. Then, quite suddenly,
the armed truce between Claire and Mary ended. It was Claire herself who literally opened the door to new trouble. In the absence
of the butler, she had rushed to answer an angry pounding at the
front entrance. Flinging open the door, she was surprised to confront Paolo Foggi, a manservant who had worked briefly for the
Shelleys while they were living in Naples. The nerve of the man,
coming to the front door! What was he thinking?

"What are you doing here?" she asked. "What do you want?"

"You will know soon enough," he growled. "It is your brother-
in-law that I want to see."

Claire's nose wrinkled. Paolo reeked of wine and sweat. He was
a burly man, thickset with a large belly and dirty, unkempt hair.

"Who is it—" Bysshe stood now at Claire's shoulder. "Well,
hello, Paolo. What takes you so far from home?"

"Business with you, m'lord."

Bysshe's brow wrinkled. "I know of no business that we might
have. You were paid in full when we left Naples."

"Not quite." Paolo allowed himself a satisfied smirk. "Not quite,
that is, unless you want your fancy friends here to learn what you
were up to with this lady."

He said the word "lady" with such contempt that it fell like a
blow. Claire felt pressure behind her eyes and opened them wide.
She wanted to cry but would *not*, not in front of this—this lout.

"Go inside," Bysshe directed her. "Stay with Mary. Keep her
away."

"If you think you can keep your wife from finding out about your bastard, think again," Paolo muttered.

"Go inside, Claire," Bysshe repeated. "I will join you shortly." To Paolo, he said, "You were a fool to come here, my wife knows everything there is to know."

Claire retreated into the house and nearly collided with Mary, who stood in the marble entryway, baby Percy crowing loudly in her arms.

"What's going on out there?" Mary asked. "I heard loud voices."

Claire shook her head angrily. "I know not, but there is a dreadful man outside who has come to make trouble."

The two women waited apprehensively in the foyer. It was not long before Bysshe came back inside.

"That blasted fool wants to blackmail me," he told them. "It seems that Foggi is now married to Elize and that she has told him everything."

"You mean about you and Claire . . . and Elena?" Mary asked.

Claire exploded with anger. "It was that lout's wife who turned my poor child over to strangers. Elize might as well have killed Elena herself, and now here is her husband with the gall to attempt blackmail! How dare he!"

"How dare *you*!" Mary interjected. "You might have stayed in Naples and taken care of your own baby. Perhaps then she would be alive today. Instead, you chose to force yourself into my home. Now it is I who must bear the brunt of even more unpleasantness—all because of what you and Bysshe have done."

Percy, perhaps aware that his mother's attention was no longer fixed on himself, began to wail at the top of his lungs.

Claire watched the color creep up Bysshe's neck and into his cheeks and knew that she, too, was blushing. Mary, always so holy. Claire could not, would not, listen to another word. Quietly she turned and, without a backward glance, walked to her room, closing the door behind her. At least she could no longer hear that blasted baby.

The next day Bysshe went to see Benito Filiberti, the most acclaimed attorney in Florence. Claire and Mary waited nervously but said not a word to each other. When Bysshe returned, they searched his face anxiously for clues. He appeared sanguine. "My instincts were true in registering Elena as the child of Mary and me," he told them. "There is no one who can prove otherwise. Paolo Foggi is a troublemaker but can do nothing. Signor Filiberti will see that a restraining order is placed on him, but he advises that Mary and I leave the city as soon as possible."

Claire gasped. "But what about me?"

"Signor Filiberti and I both think it best for you to remain here in Florence—at least for the time being."

Claire saw a pleased expression flash across Mary's face and hated it. She turned to Bysshe. "Where am I to live? What will I do?"

He smiled reassuringly. "That can all be arranged."

And so it was. Signor Filiberti had a friend, Antonio Bojti, a distinguished Florentine doctor. Claire would live with the Bojti family as a paying guest. Bysshe and Mary proclaimed it the perfect solution and set off for Pisa the following week with baby Percy in tow.

At first even Claire conceded that there were advantages to the new arrangement. The Bojtis had a charming villa in the prettiest part of Florence. Signora Bojti, a German, taught Claire to speak her native language, while Claire instructed the children in English.

The Bojtis were an attractive, popular couple, much sought after by the Florentine social set. It was easy for them to introduce Claire into the city's more rarefied circles. She attended luncheons, teas, dinners, even grand balls. There was satisfaction to be found from meeting people on her own—not merely as an appendage to the Shelleys. Still, Claire was often lonely. These socialites were strangers who knew nothing of her separation from Allegra or the death of baby Elena. She could derive no sympathy from them, and, of course, it had to remain that way. Any knowledge of Claire's troubled past would mean her total expulsion from Florentine society.

She spent much of her time wandering the streets. Claire's one true friend was the journal to which she retreated each night to pour out her heart. Claire's quill moved across the paper as she recalled the day's walk in vivid purple ink. She paused in her writing and sat back in her blue velvet wing chair, glancing around at the room with its warm tones of mauve and rose, the four-poster bed curtained in lacy white. It was a lovely room, the Bojtis lovely people, but it was not her room, nor they her people.

Claire picked up her quill and continued to write: "Must I always live in exile?" She wrote many letters to Byron, pleading to be allowed to see Allegra. Finally she addressed a nagging fear that plagued her. "I can no longer resist the internal, inexplicable fear that haunts me that I shall never see her again." Byron ignored that letter as he had all the rest.

⸻

In midsummer, Claire went to Leghorn for a brief holiday. Somehow Bysshe contrived to meet her there. It was August 4, his twenty-eighth birthday. Claire chose a gown green as the sea for the occasion. It was cut low enough to show a glimpse of her frothy white chemise. Together they strolled barefoot on the beach, then dined at an outdoor café. Finally the last sips of wine had been drunk. Bysshe fixed his sky-blue eyes on her brown ones. They sat silently, taking one another's measure.

"I should like to stay the night," he said at last. "Soul meets soul on lovers' lips. It has been so very long. I should like to sleep with you."

"Sleep, yes." Claire nodded. Suppressing a sigh, she continued, "I would like very much to hold you in my arms for a whole night, but no more than that. I cannot risk another baby, another broken heart."

Bysshe nodded regretfully. "I understand."

Claire stared at him speculatively. Obviously Bysshe had not told Mary that he was stopping in Leghorn to see her. What else was he not telling? And then she knew. Seething, she confronted him. "You are on your way to visit Byron, aren't you?"

Bysshe smiled sheepishly and shrugged.

"How could you!" she cried, flinging down her fan. "I was a mere child when Byron seduced me, and since then he has treated me with nothing but contempt. He stole my darling girl from me and has her—not even four yet—locked up in a convent. Do you care nothing for what he has done to me? How can you still be his friend?"

Bysshe merely shrugged again. "That is how things are."

Furious, Claire stalked off, leaving Bysshe sitting by himself at the table, but once back with the Bojtis in Florence, her one small happiness was again derived from his letters. What else did she have?

At first Bysshe wrote often, missives clearly not intended for Mary's eyes. Once when Mary had seen him writing and guessed the intended recipient, she insisted on reading the letter and adding a note of her own. Later he penned an additional message. "I wrote to you a kind of scrawl the other day merely to show that I had not forgotten you," he explained, "& it was taxed with a postscript by Mary. It contained nothing that I wished it to contain."

Bysshe appeared bored with the domestic life. A man admiring of his poetry had suggested a trip to Egypt and Syria. "How far all this is practicable, considering my finances, I know not yet," Bysshe admitted. "I know that if it were, it would give me the greatest pleasure, & that might be either doubled or divided by your presence or absence."

Claire gasped with pleasure at the suggestion. The trip was alluring, if far-fetched. Most important was the implied possibility. Would he consider leaving Mary for her? Claire's heart filled with hope, her mind with daydreams. Then came a bit of chance gossip. Bysshe, it was said, was making a fool of himself over Emilia Viviani, the daughter of the governor of Pisa. He had written an extravagant poem to her, a paean to her beauty and nobility.

Before long Bysshe's letters dwindled. Claire began to fear not only for the loss of his affections but his financial backing. What if he were to cut off her stipend?

Claire was frantic. Then at last, a letter. In it, Bysshe poured forth a glowing description of a literary community that he and Mary planned to form in Pisa. Leigh and Marianne Hunt were coming from England. Others would follow. He and Leigh planned to publish a journal, which Byron promised to finance. There was no talk of Claire becoming part of this illustrious group, but Bysshe did invite her to Pisa for a brief holiday. Very brief, as she was to leave before Byron arrived.

With much enthusiasm, Mary and Bysshe showed her about their small but comfortable villa. There were smart new furnishings, a few good paintings, and best of all, many of the large windows faced out on the Arno. Mary pointed out the Palazzo Lanfranchi just across the river. Claire thought it very grand. "That," Mary told her, "is where Albe will live. We expect him soon."

Claire studied Mary. Was she gloating? Probably inside, but she said nothing. Neither spoke; too much had been said already.

When Bysshe handed Claire into the post chaise that was to take her back to Florence, his smile might merely have been that of a friendly stranger. She settled into the stuffy coach and opened the window against the cigar and pipe smoke that filled the interior. About a mile down the road, the chaise encountered a caravan passing in the opposite direction, first a deluxe traveling coach followed by wagons piled high with luggage, then a dozen horses, and finally, a parade of rolling cages housing a menagerie of exotic animals. Claire needed no one to tell her that it was Lord George Gordon Byron and his entourage on their way to join the Shelleys in Pisa.

Claire sensed instinctively that this outrageous traveling train, glimpsed from the window of a public coach, was her last sight of the man who had changed her life forever. Was Bysshe lost to her as well?

PART VII

Man's love is of man's life a thing apart,
'Tis woman's whole existence
    —Lord Byron

FORTY-TWO

With Claire settled at last in Florence, Mary found herself alone with Bysshe for the first time since their arrival in Italy. Who was this man? Who, in fact, was she? Surely they were not the same couple that had once eloped to France, dodged bailiffs, and spent passionate Sundays together in bed. How very long ago that seemed.

Though she could not bring herself to express it in words, the loss of Clara and William had changed everything for Mary. She longed to share her feelings with Bysshe but could not; they were too raw. Bysshe, too, seemed wary of acknowledging the distance that had penetrated their lives together. Instead, his response to the impasse was to send a flurry of invitations to their London friends.

For Mary it was far more difficult. Percy's birth had brought her back from a despondency akin to death, but she could not rid herself of the feeling that life was vengeful and capricious. The stunned joy, the loneliness, and the fatigue of new motherhood was a constant reminder of how much her happiness depended upon a single fragile life. This impossibly small, yet ever-demanding creature was the core of her existence.

As always, Mary also sought solace in writing. This time her subject would be a historical novel based in Italy, the country she had come to love. The specific time and place, fourteenth-century Lucca, would be the challenge, the research required for such a book massive. But was that not exactly what she needed—a subject that would engage her spirit as well as her brain? Her fascination grew as she perceived medieval history mirrored in the sweeping changes shaking the world around her. Unlike *Mathilda*, which had been primarily about human relationships, *Valperga*, her current project, was Mary's response to the social and political turmoil erupting across Europe at the onset of the 1820s.

She was coming out of her lethargy, beginning once again to feel confident about both herself and her work, so it hurt terribly when Bysshe referred to her narrative as "raked out of fifty old books." Did he not understand the arduousness of research? This was yet another barrier between them.

Mary plunged deeper into her story, striving always for perfection. *Valperga* was fiction, requiring vivid characters as well as colorful facts. She was casting about for subjects when signora Aldina, a neighbor, suggested they visit the gardens of the chiesa e convento di Sant'Anna. "They are very beautiful," she explained, "but rarely open to the public."

Signora Aldini, a short, plump woman in her forties, wore her hair in a tight bun. She had a keen sense of humor, spoke excellent English, and was eager as a girl to share the city's gossip.

Mary had readily agreed to the outing, but as they approached the convent, she stared warily at the medieval church buildings. The cold stone walls looked grim and foreboding. The pope, only recently restored to office, was said to be a zealot who favored a return to the Inquisition. Mary shivered, thinking of the poor souls who might be interrogated inside.

"Is it not lovely?" signora Aldini exclaimed as they passed through the massive iron gate.

"These gardens are lovely," Mary carefully agreed. In contrast to the austere church buildings, the convent grounds were magnificent. Mary scarcely knew where to look. She was surrounded by exquisite marble statuary, splashing fountains, trailing wisteria and honeysuckle, roses of every hue, blossoms everywhere. The scent was exquisite.

Rounding a hedge of trailing morning glory, Mary spied a young woman entering what appeared to be a chapel, prayer book in hand. Head bowed, she looked the picture of devotion. "How pretty she is! What would a girl like that be doing in a convent?"

Signora Aldini was quick to explain. "She is Emilia Viviani, the governor's daughter. I shall be happy to introduce you. Emilia is a bright girl and sociable; she would very much enjoy meeting an English writer." Signora Aldini smiled, a knowing gleam in her eye. "You are quite right, a convent is scarcely the place for her."

"Then why—"

"A jealous stepmother."

Well, Mary knew all about jealous stepmothers! She decided to meet Emilia and learn her story firsthand.

The medieval Convent of St. Anna, Mary discovered, doubled as an exclusive boarding school. The nineteen-year-old Emilia was a student, not a postulant. In fact, once they were introduced, Emilia laughed merrily at Mary's mistaken conclusion. "No, no, no! I could never be a nun. The Lord has not called me, and I am sure he never will."

Surveying the young woman standing before her, Mary felt inclined to agree. Emilia seemed very much of this world. She was extraordinarily pretty with skin like porcelain and large, heavy-lidded eyes that gave her a sleepy, almost voluptuous appearance.

"Won't you sit beside me?" Emilia asked. Signora Aldini nodded pleasantly to the two younger women and strolled off by herself along a sunlit path. Smiling eagerly, Emilia took Mary's hand and led her to a secluded bench. As they sat together in the convent's carefully tended rose garden, Emilia poured out her heart. "My father is a tyrant," she complained. "He and that dreadful woman he married are keeping me here against my will. I sleep in a tiny cell at night, and I have nothing to do but needlepoint.

There are no books in the library save religious ones. My life is a nightmare! I wish I were dead!"

Mary recognized a bit of the actress in her companion but remained sympathetic. "How long must you stay here?" she asked.

"Until they find a husband for me."

Mary looked up from the small bouquet of pink and peach roses that she had gathered. "You are not allowed to choose your own?"

"Of course not. It is possible that I may not even meet my husband until we stand before the altar to recite our vows. He will, I am certain, be a rich old man, white-haired and decrepit." Large tears spilled down Emilia's ivory cheeks as she began to cry.

Sympathies aroused, Mary did her best to cheer the girl. She visited often after that and brought Emilia novels to read. It wasn't long before Bysshe noted her numerous excursions and began to question her. Mary's answers clearly appalled him. "How could it be that such an innocent creature is the object of social and financial barter?" he asked Mary indignantly. "Can she do nothing for herself?"

"Signora Aldini says that Italian girls are almost never allowed to pick their own husbands," Mary explained. "Apparently Emilia's story is not unusual. Many families place their daughters in convents while suitable marriages are arranged."

"That is unthinkable!" Bysshe wandered off, shaking his head in disbelief.

The next thing Mary knew, her husband had sought and somehow been granted permission to visit Emilia himself. "She is a tragic captive," he told Mary after his first visit, "a victim of parental and religious oppression." Mary knew from experience that both forces were particularly abhorrent to him. It didn't surprise her that he was soon wildly infatuated.

At first Mary was mildly amused. It was all so typical of Bysshe. Emilia was beautiful, unobtainable, and had plenty of time to write flowery, flattering, and increasingly coquettish letters. She was also, Mary quickly realized, a natural flirt. Perhaps the governor was wise to keep her under lock and key.

Bysshe loved to see himself in the guise of a romantic rescuer. Had he not saved Harriet from the boarding school she hated? And the elopement from Skinner Street, was that not a form of rescue? Annoying as it was to Mary, she recognized that Bysshe provided a buffer for Claire against Byron's callous treatment. Wouldn't he just love to somehow save Emilia from an arranged marriage to a man old enough to be her father?

The chances of the friendship going beyond a flirtation seemed impossible and that, Mary believed, was its primary charm. Bysshe did not have to *do* anything but write romantic notes, hold Emilia's hand, and vow undying love.

Absorbed as she was in writing *Valperga* and caring for Percy, Mary was at first only dimly aware of deeper attitudinal changes. Bysshe had always been eager to read his new work to her but now seemed evasive. He was writing, he said, an epic poem that he called *Epipsychidion*, or "concerning a little soul."

A "little soul"? Mary suspected that the subject was Emilia and wanted to know more. One night as he sat in their lofty library, quill flying as he bent over a sheet of paper, she slipped into a chair beside him.

"Will you not share what you have written?" she asked.

Dropping his quill, he moved his hand to cover the paper. "It is a meditation on free love."

"But that is nothing new," Mary protested. "You and I have always agreed that free love is but a realistic view of the natural needs of men and women."

"It is more than that," he told her. "Free love should lead to true love or universal love. Before, I wrote and spoke of social necessity, but love should go much deeper than that. Free love is a moral and philosophical duty."

"I see," Mary replied but was not at all certain that she did.

He nodded his head dismissively and Mary left the library, hurt and confused.

Later that night, after he had gone to sleep, she crept back. Bysshe's papers were neatly stacked on the library table. On the top was a short poem. Avidly, Mary read:

> *I never was attached to that great sect,*
> *Whose doctrine is, that each one should select*
> *Out of the crowd a mistress or a friend,*
> *And all the rest, though fair and wise, commend*
> *To cold oblivion, though it is in the code*
> *Of modern morals, and the beaten road*
> *Which those poor slaves with weary footsteps tread,*
> *Who travel to their home among the dead*
> *By the broad highway of the world, and so*
> *With one chained friend, perhaps a jealous foe,*
> *The dreariest and the longest journey go.*

A jealous foe! Was that how he saw her? Did he really view their marriage as a home among the dead?

Bysshe proceeded to immortalize Emilia in *Epipsychidion*. Mary was never supposed to see the poem; he had planned to request that it be published anonymously, but of course she did see it. Emilia was immortalized as "youth's vision thus made perfect," as a "Seraph of Heaven! too gentle to be human."

Well, really, what could Mary say to that? She lived in the real world and knew it. Of course she was not perfect. Who was?

The next part of the poem pleased her even less, for she recognized it immediately as a portrait of herself.

> *The cold chaste Moon, the Queen of Heaven's bright isles,*
> *Who makes all beautiful on which she smiles.*

That wandering shrine of soft yet icy flame
Which ever is transformed, yet still the same,
And warms not but illumines.

It was a terrible blow. The moon had always been Mary's private touchstone. "I feel it is friendly to me," she had once confided to Bysshe. "It brings me insight and sometimes luck." Now it was as though he had used the moon against her and was telling the world that his wife was cold and impassive. Mary wanted to tear the poem into shreds and longed to beat her fists against Bysshe's chest. She did neither, reasoning that the obsession with Emilia would soon dissipate. Before long their life together would return to normal.

In September of 1821, Emilia married, as she herself had predicted, a wealthy Italian nobleman. Indeed, he was twice her age, but still under forty, tall and broad shouldered with thick red hair. Quite attractive, it was said.

Mary was pleased to pass on to Bysshe the rumor that Emilia was soon leading her bridegroom and his mother "a devil of a life." Signora Aldini whispered that Emilia had taken up the habit of praying to a saint. Very devout to be sure, except that with each new lover she changed her saint.

But by that time it really didn't matter. Bysshe's fascination with Emilia had already faded. Mary, snooping once again, read a note to his publisher meant to be included with the manuscript of *Epipsychidion.* "It is a portion of me that is already dead," Bysshe had written. "The person whom it celebrates was a cloud instead of a Juno. I think one is always in love with something or other; the error, and I confess it is not easy for spirits encased in flesh and blood to avoid it, consists in seeking in a mortal image the likeness of what is, perhaps, eternal."

Mary smiled wryly. Emilia merely a cloud? So much for Bysshe's grand passion. But how long would it be before he once again donned rose-colored spectacles and beheld yet another paragon?

FORTY-THREE

Bysshe's next "perfect woman" introduced herself as Jane Williams; but, strictly speaking, Williams wasn't her name. She and her companion, Ned Williams, weren't married, because Jane's real husband was in India.

By the time the couple joined the Pisan circle, Jane and Ned had been living together for two years and had a son and baby daughter. Mary and Bysshe agreed that Jane was quite pretty, exotic really, with her bangle bracelets and glossy dark hair set off by paisley scarves and shawls. She seemed pleasant enough, if a little slow. Tall, open-faced Ned, on the other hand, exuded high energy and intellect. He was an enthusiastic reader and an aspiring writer. Mary especially liked his lively nature and thought him the picture of good humor.

Sometimes the two couples explored river walks and mountain paths together, but mostly they just talked. Though Jane was the only one in the group not writing something, she had a musical talent that charmed them all. Jane sang in a low, husky voice, accompanying herself on a guitar that Bysshe bought for her. Before long, Bysshe forgot his earlier opinion that Jane was dull. Instead, he saw her as gentle and serene, the epitome of all that was desirable in a woman.

Seven years with Bysshe had taught Mary both independence and fortitude. She was developing friendships on her own and pursuing new interests. Occasionally she even went to church, creating quite a stir among the congregation in view of her husband's avowed atheism.

When Mary developed a fascination with the Greek language, Prince Alexander Mavrocordato, an exiled Greek patriot, was only too pleased to tutor her. A man of action, just thirty years old, he came every morning to impart his language. Mary was drawn to his flashing eyes and was challenged by his penetrating intellect. She liked him and was flattered that he liked her even more. The opportunity to study with him while indulging in a mild flirtation eased Mary through this otherwise difficult period.

Bysshe seemed less pleased. Mavrocordato was dashing, well connected, and closely involved with the political upheaval of Europe. The prince's attentions and Mary's pleased acceptance of them clearly irritated Bysshe. Though used to sharing his own affections, sharing Mary's was something else again.

One morning Alexander greeted Mary with a delighted smile. "I have just learned that Greece has declared her freedom. Before the week is out, I will be on my way to join the struggle against the Turks."

Mary's sadness at her friend's imminent departure was balanced by excitement. Yet another Mediterranean country was rebelling against imperial rule! She shared Alexander's liberal politics and was deeply stirred by his upcoming adventure. That evening at dinner, she eagerly poured out the news to Bysshe. "Alexander is about to sacrifice family, fortune—everything—for the hope of freeing his country. Such a man will succeed, I know it."

Bysshe nodded distractedly. "Well, that's all very grand, I'm sure, but while he's off in Greece tilting at windmills, I will be building a community of intellectual exiles right here. We already have Jane and Ned and Byron and that new mistress of his, Teresa Guiccioli—did you know she was a countess? Leigh and Marianne will be sailing from London most any—"

Bysshe did not say a community centered about himself, but Mary easily guessed his intentions. "Tilting at windmills!" she interjected. "Alexander will be fighting for a better world, a free world."

"Then let us hope he does not kill himself in so doing." Bysshe turned back to the poem he was writing.

While he waited for his group to assemble, Bysshe's interests continued to center on Jane. He made no effort to disguise his attraction. At first Ned had been flattered by the poet's attention to his beautiful companion, but lately he'd begun to worry. "Don't you think that Bysshe and Jane are spending a bit too much time together?" he asked Mary.

Ned's bright blue eyes were clouded as he searched her face. Mary could well understand his pain. Ned and Jane had been an adoring couple. It must be difficult for him to see her head turned in such an obvious fashion, to watch her drawing closer and closer to the charismatic poet.

"It would do no good to try to keep them apart," Mary warned him. "Bysshe will have his way. And then it will be over."

Mary was less sanguine than she sounded. With Bysshe focused on Jane, and Mary's close friend and confidant Alexander on his way to Greece, the holidays had been dreary indeed. Then, on January 4, the picture altered dramatically with the reappearance of Edward Trelawny. As abruptly as he had departed, Trelawny was back in Mary's life. Only the day before, he had chanced to run into Ned, an old friend from India, and Mary's name had been mentioned in passing. Trelawny lost no time securing an invitation for himself. The sight of him filled her with the same irrational excitement she had felt the first time she had seen him. His eyes seemed to glisten with delight as they looked down at her. Mary felt a warm glow of pleasure go all through her body at their expression.

Trelawny was much as Mary remembered—a dark giant of a man with a mass of curly hair and white teeth gleaming through his curly black beard. He was, she knew, an adventurer who could turn his hand to anything—boats, horses, guns, writing, and most probably, women.

That night Mary entrusted her opinion to her journal.

Trelawny is a strange web which I am endeavoring to unravel. He is extravagant, partly natural and partly perhaps put on, but it suits him. There is an air of extreme good nature about him, especially when he smiles, which assures me that his heart is good. He tells strange stories of himself—horrific ones—so that they harrow one up. I believe some of them, as for the rest, who knows? I am tired of the everyday sleepiness of human inter-course & am glad to meet with one, who among other valuable qualities, has the rare merit of inciting my imagination.

Might it come to something more? He regaled her with the latest news about London and Paris: the new books, operas, bon-nets, marriages, murders, and other marvels. They attended a costume ball and danced until three in the morning. She gave a series of supper parties that Bysshe professed to abhor. Trelawny was delighted to serve as host, and, in turn, he delighted guests with amusing anecdotes and salty sea tales. The winter of Mary's discontent was over.

More and more she was coming to see Trelawny as a catalyst. The Pisan exiles, as they called themselves, had come together ini-tially with the idea of publishing a journal. Freed from England's strict libel laws, their publication would unleash upon the world a fresh spirit of independence and progressive ideas, but given the delayed arrival of Leigh, the ideas were merely bandied about at the dinner table, on shooting expeditions, or in the billiard room.

Then one evening as the two couples were discussing the journal at dinner, Trelawny entered the room and placed a package on the dining table. It was, he said, a gift for Bysshe and Ned. Hurriedly removing the wrappings, they discovered a model of an American schooner. "I know just the man who could build a life-size version of this for you," Trelawny announced. "His name is Dan Roberts and he is a fine seaman."

Bysshe and Ned seemed to go wild with excitement at the prospect. That night they talked of the sails, the stern, and the bow. Trelawny wrote a note to his friend Captain Roberts, asking him to begin work immediately. Mary walked with him to post it the following day. He was tall and striking. Mary noted the many glances turned their way and felt proud, as though an exotic beast strode beside her. One that she alone could tame.

That afternoon Bysshe and Ned set off by coach for La Spezia. They were delighted by the idea of their families spending the spring and summer together by the sea and spent two days sailing around the small Bay of Lerici looking for suitable houses.

Mary enjoyed quiet dinners with Trelawny and playful days with Percy. She had sent early copies of *Valperga* to friends in London to read and was greatly pleased by their enthusiastic reactions. Even her father liked it. He was sorely in need of funds, he told Mary. The lease was up on the Skinner Street house. Awful as the place was, he was about to be evicted, turned out on the streets. What was to become of him? Mary resolved to do her best by consigning her book's royalties to him when it was published.

All that really mattered was that *Valperga* would be a success and little Percy a sturdy, thriving two-year-old. Claire was finally somewhere else. Mary's friendship with Trelawny was an ongoing delight, and Bysshe seemed happy enough with his boating plans and flirtation with Jane. Perhaps that was the most she could ask—they were together, yet enjoying separate lives.

Then the blow fell. Mary returned home from a walk carrying a bouquet of spring flowers. Bysshe stood white-faced in the
doorway.

"What is it, dear?" she asked, the smile fading from her lips.

"Albe was just here. He is distraught. A terrible thing has
happened."

"Not Allegra!" Mary gasped.

Bysshe frowned curiously. "Why would you ask that?"

"I had a letter from Claire yesterday. She has had a premoni-
tion of doom and is desperate to see Allegra. Claire's frantic. She
talked of kidnapping the child from the convent."

"Poor girl, I wish she had. A message arrived but an hour ago.
A fever raged through the convent. Dear little Allegra took ill. She
died of typhus fever."

The flowers slipped unheeded through Mary's fingers. Allegra
dead! That dear, bright, and pretty five-year-old lost to them forever. And Claire, poor Claire. Only another grieving mother like
herself could completely understand such a loss. *But I have Percy,*
Mary gratefully reminded herself. Claire had no one.

FORTY-FOUR

There was no question but that Claire would join Mary and Bysshe in Pisa. Deep as Mary's antagonism ran, it was not enough to counter Claire's bereavement. Violently angry one moment, emotionally devastated the next, she could not be left alone. Claire had lost her only remaining child. What could be more awful than that? Mary suffered deeply for her stepsister and went out of her way to be kind and thoughtful.

"It was that wretched convent," Claire said again and again. "I had a feeling—I *knew*—it would be the death of Allegra. The place was a pesthole. The nuns never bathed the children. The good sisters thought bathing the whole body indecent and immoral. You can imagine how that evil place stunk to high heaven!"

Mary wondered, not for the first time, about the nature of God. If there really was one, why could he not have done something for the poor children inside a convent built in his honor? Why had he taken her three babies and now Allegra? There were no answers. She put her arms around Claire and held her close.

One thing that might be said of Allegra's tragic death: it had brought a sense of closure for Claire. No longer was she beset by evil premonitions, nor was she driven by a nagging urgency to protect her daughter. The frantic, fruitless one-way correspondence with Byron was at an end.

Byron! Mary was still angry. Only the day before, she and Bysshe had received a most defensive letter from him. "I do not know that I have anything to reproach in my conduct," Byron had written, "and certainly nothing in my feelings and intentions towards the dead."

But, possibly in acknowledgment of Mary's insistence that the convent had been totally unsuitable for Allegra, he had added, "It is a moment when we are to think that, if this or that had been done, such an event might have been prevented."

Well, think he should! Mary knew that Byron had never even visited Allegra at the convent.

———

As the days passed, Bysshe and Ned continued to search for homes on the Bay of La Spezia, some fifty miles north of Pisa, but could find only one available, Casa Magni, some three miles from the village of Lerici. Until something else could be discovered, they would have to share it. Claire would live with them as well; she was still too distraught to be left alone.

"The place is wild and wonderful," Bysshe told Mary. "You are going to love it."

Perhaps so, she speculated. Mary was certain of one thing: she loved seeing him so full of enthusiasm. Happily she threw open the shade and turned to Jane. "Is it not wonderful to sit with the windows open wide and no smoky fire in the grate?" Surprisingly Jane had turned out to be something of a friend despite Bysshe's continued infatuation. He was attracted to so many women. Mary could scarcely hate them all.

She was excited by the prospect of a move to the seashore and began to long for the sparkling waves and olive-covered hills of La Spezia. The Bay of Lerici was said to be beautiful. The few travelers who went there raved about the intense blue of its waters, the pink color of the sand, the sunbeams that glanced off the sea to dance along the cliffs. "If April proves fine, we will fly like swallows," she enthused.

The Shelley party arrived by coach in the midst of a horrendous thunderstorm. Casa Magni, the home that Bysshe had leased for them, clung to a cliff just above the waterline. That night, with the surf thundering against the foundation and the ocean spray rattling the windows, Mary thought it more like a ship at sea than a house on land.

The next day two small boats arrived. Sailors unloaded boxes, trunks, and articles of furniture on the tiny beach. Everyone helped to carry their belongings up through the lapping surf, but the business of actually moving in was even more difficult. Despite its rather grand name, Casa Magni was originally built as a boathouse. The ground floor was damp and muddy—uninhabitable. The five adults and three children would have to crowd into three bedrooms the size of closets on the floor above.

Claire would have none of it. "This place is far too depressing," she announced the following morning. "I want to go back to Florence." All agreed that she should not travel alone, so Bysshe offered to take her back to the Bojtis.

Mary thought they should all go back to Florence, indeed go anywhere rather than remain where they were. The thought of living in such close quarters troubled her. Jane said nothing; she simply looked from Bysshe to Ned. Both men had plenty to say. They were delighted by the bay and could not wait to settle in, get a boat built, and go sailing. What difference did the house make? The two set off the next day.

Despite her earlier anticipation, Mary detested the damp, dilapidated villa, the ever-present odor of dead fish and seaweed, the oppressive heat, and, most of all, the awful desolation. It didn't help that she was pregnant and not feeling at all well. Surveying the house, she prayed that she would not have her baby there. The ground floor consisted of an open stone portico with seven

roughly whitewashed arches and a flagstone floor running back
into the building. The edge of the flagstone had a low wall, which
formed a small jetty. Often the sea splashed to the very foot of the
portico and carpeted the flagstones with sand and sea creatures.

Above the portico was a terrace running the length of the
building and fronting on the bay. Inside, a large room was reached
by a rear staircase. Off this central chamber were the three small
rooms. The ones to the left and right faced the sea. Bysshe immediately chose one of these for himself—he had trouble sleeping and
wanted to be alone. Mary and little Percy would have the other.
The bedroom left to Ned, Jane, and their toddlers, two-year-old
Edward and fourteen-month-old Rosalind, was at the back of the
house and faced into a dense forest.

"When Bysshe comes back, we'll teach the children to swim,"
Ned suggested. "They're never too young to begin."

"Unfortunately Bysshe does not swim," Mary told him.

Ned looked at her in amazement. "How can that be?"

"I cannot answer that. He has always been drawn to water and
boating but has refused many offers of swimming lessons. Perhaps
you will be the one to persuade him. For now, would you watch
Percy for me? I'm going to try to find something for dinner."

Mary took the string shopping bag from its hook and started
down the stairs. The errand was tedious at best. It was difficult to
find food in the two tiny villages far down the beach on either side
of them. The poverty of the people was beyond anything that Mary
had ever seen; yet the villagers did not seem unhappy. Whether
they went about in dirty content or contented dirt, she was unsure.
Mary only knew that she herself was miserable.

Mary did her best to achieve her own kind of disorderly order
out of the chaos around her. She also tried to ignore the raucous
villagers who came each night to drink, swim, sing, and dance on
the small beach below their house. Mary was learning, or trying to
learn, to live day by day, but what she could not do was thrust aside

a sense of impending tragedy. The dreadful house was so isolated, the surroundings—rugged beach backed by dense forest—too savage. Mary could not get Claire's premonitions of Allegra's death out of her mind. She watched Percy constantly, worried over every sneeze or sniffle. She could not lose him, too.

Mary longed for Bysshe's return, but when he came, it seemed the distance between them had only grown wider. Bysshe was delighted to be back in Lerici, a place he found vivid and joyous. "I wish this summer would never pass," he said again and again. "I wish we would never leave."

Mary scarcely knew how to answer him. She could talk easily enough with Bysshe about poetry, philosophy, or politics but was unable to communicate any of her inner feelings. Locked in fear and depression, she existed in a twilight region.

The days dragged by as Bysshe watched anxiously for the arrival of the ship that Trelawny was having built for him. Late one afternoon as the sun began to set, Mary stepped onto the terrace and stood beside him. "What are you going to name the boat?" she asked.

"Albe wants to call it the *Don Juan*, but I don't care much for that. What do you think?"

Mary struggled to keep her voice light. "Why not something with some spirit to it, a name that's lilting, maybe a little ethereal, mystical—something that embodies you?"

She was pleased to see Bysshe smile. "That sounds better." He put an arm lightly about her. "Have you any ideas?"

Mary liked the feel of him close to her. It had been so long . . . She thought a moment, and then a chance remark came to mind. *"Bysshe comes and goes like a spirit, no one knows when or where."* Something like that . . . but what? And then it occurred to her. "What about *Ariel*?"

"Oh, I do like that!" Bysshe smiled down at her, his arm tightening.

ANTOINETTE MAY

And then Ned came out. They talked a bit about the name—
Ned liked *Ariel*, too—and stood silently for a time looking out at
the sea. It had been a warm, pleasant day, but now a storm was
brewing. Waves crested and crashed hard against the pillars below.
They were going to go in when Bysshe gave a low cry. "Did you see
that?"

"No, what? Where?" Mary and Ned responded almost in
unison.

"There, there!" Bysshe pointed. "Do you not see?"

Mary followed the direction of his hand. "Who? What?" She
saw nothing but roiling water.

"There it is again!" He leaned forward over the rail, his eyes
fixed on the angry sea. "There! Do you not see her? It's Allegra,
she's rising out of the water. Her hands are clasped . . . as though in
joy. She is looking at me. Her face is radiant!"

"Allegra!" Mary gasped. What had come over him? Shivering,
she leaned over the balcony beside him and peered out to sea. "I
see nothing but water."

"Nor do I," Ned agreed. "Really, Bysshe, you must be mad."

Bysshe silenced him. "Quiet! Be quiet!" His eyes were
anguished. "Surely you see her, hear her. She—" He stood still, his
face transfixed as though in awe, and then turned abruptly and
headed back into the house.

Mary rushed after him. "Darling, what is it? What did you
hear?"

Bysshe looked away, his tortured eyes not meeting her gaze.
His voice was hardly above a whisper. "Allegra was calling me to
come to her."

FORTY-FIVE

On May 12 the *Ariel* sailed into the small cove in front of the Casa Magni. Only it was not the *Ariel* at all.

"*Don Juan!*" Mary exclaimed, staring at the name emblazoned on the sails. "That name better suits a coal barge than a yacht."

"Apparently Trelawny and Captain Roberts yielded to Byron's wishes," Bysshe replied, his voice angry as he stood beside her on the terrace. "I shall see to that."

Mary knew that her husband had come to feel overshadowed by the other poet. Bysshe had written little of late, complaining, "I have lived too long near Lord Byron, and the sun has extinguished the glow-worm."

"It will be all right," she insisted. "You and Ned can remove the name easily enough."

And so they tried for twenty-one days, scrubbing the sails with a combination of turpentine, spirits of wine, and buccata. All to no avail. Bysshe flatly refused to sail under the title of Byron's poem. He ordered that section of sail cut out altogether and a new patch put in by a local sailmaker. It bore the name *Ariel*. Yet try as they might, Mary, Ned, Jane, even Bysshe found themselves referring to it as the *Don Juan* until finally the name stuck and the boat was never called anything else.

"The important thing," Mary reminded Bysshe, "is that she is a stunning ship—truly elegant." As Trelawny had pointed out to her, the craft was twenty-four feet long but slim, with twin mainmasts,

schooner-rigged with topsails and an assortment of jibs. Whatever
the name, Bysshe's boat was a true water spirit. Indeed, Bysshe for-
gave Captain Roberts the name when he discovered that there was
no craft that could match her for speed.

Only Trelawny, who had stayed behind to help, had reserva-
tions. "You need to take on more hands," he warned.

"We have Charles Vivian—he helped to sail the ship here from
Genoa," Ned reminded him.

"Charles is but a lad. You need at least one more capable hand."

Ned was indignant. "As if three seasoned salts were not enough
to manage an open boat!"

Trelawny was not convinced. "If we had been in a squall today
with the main sheet jammed, and the tiller put starboard instead
of port, we should have had to swim for it."

Bysshe shrugged lightly. "Not me! I should have gone down
with the boat."

Mary looked from one man to the other. It was true that the
Don Juan sailed well in good weather, but Trelawny was right. In a
strong breeze she heeled dangerously and took on water. Trelawny
was forced to return to Pisa on business, but Mary was relieved to
see Ned haul the boat out of the water and go to work on her. He
built a new framework on the stern, cleaned and greased the hull,
then added more pig-iron ballast and stored it in the hold to make
the *Don Juan* steadier in a breeze.

The Bay of Lerici dazzled in the changing light, and the hours
spent skimming the azure waters were pure magic. Tanned and
healthy, delighted with the *Don Juan*, his "perfect summer play-
thing," Bysshe's muse returned. An idea begged to be set to words.
Mary was delighted to see him jotting down the lines of a poem.

When Mary went sailing with Ned and Bysshe, she was pleased
by Ned's efforts to teach Bysshe the rudiments of helmsmanship.
Unfortunately they were to little avail. Bysshe rarely looked up
from his notebook. When the ship came about, the boom nearly

knocked him into the sea. It happened more than once, but Bysshe always returned, unfazed, to the work he called *The Triumph of Life*.

———————

Spring turned to summer, wrapping the days in baking heat. A stifling stillness settled over the bay; sun shimmered on the rocky beach. Percy and the Williams children turned fretful, Jane petulant. Mary's pregnancy was not going well. The persistent smell of dead fish didn't help. She hated the house, its setting, the villagers, but worst of all was the continued sense of impending calamity that she could neither define nor shake. Mary's only moments of peace were on board the *Don Juan* with Bysshe. Her head on his knee, her eyes shut, she felt the wind and their swift motion, alone together. Often Mary's mind drifted to memories they'd shared on the water: the rough voyage to Calais, gliding down the Rhine on a barge, skimming across Lake Geneva with Albe. But those were other times, she and Bysshe different people.

At night thunderstorms rumbled up the coast and exploded across the bay. Mary was not surprised when Bysshe told her at breakfast that he had been having bad dreams. One night he awakened Mary by sitting down on her bed. She put out her hand to touch his arm and was surprised to find him trembling. "What is it?" she asked.

Bysshe's voice was shaking, too. "Jane and Ned . . . they came into my room. Their bodies . . . were lacerated . . . covered with blood. Bones protruded from their skin. It was hideous!"

"How awful," Mary said, drawing him closer. She ran her fingers through his hair as she might Percy's. "Wake up, darling, you are dreaming."

He shuddered. "Jane said, 'Get up, the sea is flooding the house and it is all coming down.'"

Mary realized that he was sweating and got up. Grasping the pitcher by her bedside, she poured cold water into the basin and dampened a cloth, pressed it to his brow. "Dear one, what a terrible dream! No wonder you were frightened, but that is all it was—a dream."

"No," Bysshe persisted, "it was real. They or some form of them were in my room." He paused for a moment as though gathering his senses. "There was something else . . . I got up and went out on the terrace. I thought it would calm me. I had just lit my pipe, and suddenly out of nowhere I saw myself."

Mary shook her head. "I do not understand. What do you mean, you saw yourself?"

"I saw myself. *Me.*" He paused, thinking. "Or perhaps it was my counterpart. I know not, but there I was, looking directly at myself or a mirror image, except that there was no mirror."

Mary shivered. Was Bysshe going mad? What should she do? Was it best to humor him? "What did the man—you, I mean—say?"

"It was a question: 'How long do you mean to be content?'"

"Is content not a good thing?" Mary asked.

"Not if it means stagnancy."

"I do not think the message meant stagnancy," Mary told him. "I believe it means that you are on the verge of creating something wonderful and new."

At least that was what Mary hoped it meant. What was going on in Bysshe's mind? And what of this vision of Allegra? If he was to see a vision, why was it not Willmouse or little Clara? "Get under the covers with me. I'll rub your back until you go to sleep like I used to. He—you—won't be back tonight."

The next morning, Trelawny arrived unexpectedly for a short visit. Mary felt better at the sight of him. Trelawny always knew how to take charge of things and make them right. If anyone could handle the situation, he could. She had slept little the night before and lay on the couch chatting with Jane and Trelawny, who stood together at the window. Mary was pleased that her friend had come for a visit, but the conversation was idle and she had begun to drift into sleep when Jane startled her awake. "That's strange!" she exclaimed.

"What is strange?" Trelawny asked.

"It is Bysshe, did you not see him? He passed in front of us on the terrace—twice."

"I did not notice, but it hardly seems strange," Trelawny answered.

"But twice he walked in the same direction. How could he have gotten back without our seeing him?"

"Good God!" Trelawny said sharply. "I saw nothing. Could he have leapt over the wall?"

Mary jumped to her feet, and the three of them rushed out onto the terrace. Bysshe was not there; nor was he—they were glad to note—on the ground some twenty feet below. As it happened, he was out on the *Don Juan* sailing with the young lad, Charles Vivian.

What am I to make of these strange happenings? Mary wondered as she recorded them in her journal. She was not unduly concerned about Bysshe's dream. He was by nature fanciful; it seemed not too surprising that he would have bizarre nightmares every now and then. Mary was far more concerned that Jane, who was so very unimaginative, would have beheld a vision in broad daylight.

The next day, as Trelawny was leaving, Claire returned unexpectedly. She had grown tired of Florence and offered to help Jane oversee the children. For once Mary was actually glad to see her. The recent unexplained happenings, added to the stress of the place itself, were becoming too much for her. She had started to bleed. Was she about to lose yet another child?

After a day in bed, Mary felt better, her hopes running high, but a week later, a massive hemorrhage began at eight o'clock Sunday morning and continued unabated for seven hours. The pain was almost unbearable. Once she cried out for Bysshe, but he was sailing with Ned and could not hear her. Between Mary's fainting fits, Claire and Jane plied her with brandy and vinegar. A doctor had been sent for; but there was no sight of him. The baby was dead and everyone expected Mary to die as well.

Once Bysshe finally returned, he demanded that buckets of ice be brought from the village. When they arrived, he filled a large tub with them. Mary shrieked when she realized what he was going to do. "No, no, no!" she begged.

Mary kicked and screamed as he tore at her gown and dragged her toward the water. She shrieked until she thought she had no voice left when he plunged her into the frigid tub. The shock was so extreme that she lost all sense of pain and seemed to float above herself. She saw Claire and Jane below her pulling at Bysshe and heard their angry shouts. Mary felt her spirit poise to leave her body but was unafraid. She felt certain that it would be well received by a beneficent and gentle power. She had no fear, but also no active wish to live. She floated serenely, open to whatever might happen.

Late in the evening the village doctor finally found his way to the remote Casa Magni. "The ice was the only thing that could have stopped the bleeding," Mary heard him say.

Mary closed her eyes, feeling that a decision had been made for her. She hoped it was the right one.

A few nights later, Mary, still ill and very weak, was awakened by Bysshe's screams. He rushed into her room; his face in the dim candlelight was red and contorted. He's dreaming that same terrible dream, she told herself, and tried desperately to awaken him. Bysshe continued to shout fiercely and pace about the tiny room. Terrified, Mary jumped out of bed and ran across the hall to the Williamses' room, but weakness overcame her and she fell to the floor.

Ned jumped out of bed and ran onto the landing, where he confronted Bysshe. Slowly the ranting ceased; Bysshe stood quietly. "What is going on here?" Ned demanded to know.

"He was asleep, dreaming some terrible dream," Mary explained.

"No," Bysshe countered. "I was not asleep. I saw a vision of my own body. I was watching myself bent over Mary's bed strangling her."

Mary felt as though a sword had been plunged into her heart. So much remained unsaid between them. Could the barrier ever be breached? What could be the meaning of such a dream? Did Bysshe hate her?

The next day Bysshe seemed his usual self. Holding up a letter that they had received a few days before, he announced to Mary, "Leigh and Marianne have left Genoa. They should reach Leghorn by July first. I mean to meet them there as a surprise."

"Oh, no, please!" Mary said, then caught herself.

"I'll only be gone a few days, less than a week," he assured her.

The dread that had clung to her over the past few weeks seemed overwhelming. Was it merely anxiety stemming from her pregnancy and miscarriage? How silly to allow that to influence their lives. Perhaps a short separation would do them good. The *Don Juan* was Bysshe's toy, his newest love. Nevertheless, Mary reminded him, "You've never sailed so far."

"I will take Ned. Captain Roberts, too, if it makes you feel any better."

Mary hesitated. Captain Roberts had built the boat. Bysshe and Ned had competently sailed it for weeks. What more could she say? Mary touched his cheek softly and then turned away. Bysshe would do exactly what he wanted to do.

———·—

July 1 dawned bright and clear; the wind was blowing strong from the west, the best possible slant for a sail to Leghorn. A broadly smiling Bysshe hugged Mary and promised to be back in a few days. She, Claire, and Jane stood on the terrace, still waving as the *Don Juan*'s topsails disappeared from view.

FORTY-SIX

For Mary, Jane, and Claire, the days dragged, hot and oppressive. The men were due back in less than a week. Every passing ship seemed to bring a message from an impatient Ned. "I am tired to death of waiting," he wrote Jane. "This is our longest separation ever and it seems a year to me."

Bysshe wrote Jane as well. "I fear you are solitary & melancholy at Villa Magni. How slow the hours pass, & how slowly they return to pass so soon again, & perhaps forever, in which we have lived together so intimately, so happily. Adieu, my dearest friend—I only write these lines for the pleasure of tracing what will meet your eyes."

He wrote to Mary in a less poetic vein. "How are you, my best Mary?" he asked. "Write especially how is your health & how your spirits are, & whether you are not more reconciled to staying at Lerici at least during the summer."

Bysshe went on to say that they had enjoyed an easy sail to Leghorn, but once there, things turned stormy. The Hunts had left London expecting to launch a journal with Byron. After a wretched voyage from England, they had arrived at Pisa only to find Byron bored with the whole idea. Instead, he was thinking of taking his mistress, Teresa, to America, to Switzerland, to England—he hadn't yet decided where. But there was no question, the last thing he wanted was a destitute Leigh with his pregnant, sickly wife, Marianne, and their six unruly children.

Bysshe had, he went on to tell her, been faced with the challenge of reconciling Byron and Leigh, the twin poles of his intellectual existence, into a creative partnership. He had determined to rescue the journal, Leigh's only means of economic survival in Italy, and had somehow succeeded.

In a triumph of diplomacy, Bysshe not only forged an alliance between the two men but got the journal named and the first issue planned. It would contain poems—by Byron and himself—a short story by Mary, and articles by Leigh. Bysshe was justly proud but remained dubious of the future. "It will be called the *Liberal,*" he wrote Mary, "but how long an alliance between the wren and the eagle may continue I will not prophesy."

Ned wrote Jane that they and their cabin boy, Charles, would be home Monday, July 8. The women waited impatiently. Then, early Monday morning, Mary was awakened by the crash of thunder. Rain splashing against her window sounded more like hail. Surely the men would not attempt to sail home in weather like that.

Tuesday passed as the sea continued to batter Lerici. Jane thought the same storm must be engulfing Leghorn. "It is wise for them to wait there, do you not agree?"

Mary nodded. Surely Bysshe and Ned knew what they were doing, but the wait was hard to bear. The awful fear, the sense of doom that had centered on little Percy, now transferred itself to Bysshe. *How is he? Where is he?*

On Wednesday the storm dissipated and a felucca arrived from Leghorn. When a sailor told Mary and Jane that the *Don Juan* had sailed on Monday morning, they did not believe him. Surely the man was ill-informed, but the day passed without another boat in sight. Thursday dawned calm and clear.

The waiting, the uncertainty was frightful. Why were the men not home by now? Then, on Friday, a boat arrived with a letter from Leigh addressed to Bysshe. Mary feared that something was wrong. How could a letter to Bysshe arrive before he did? Seeking to read it alone, she hurried out onto the terrace. The sea, so cruel a few days before, stretched before her like an azure carpet.

With trembling fingers, she broke the seal. "Shelley Mio," Leigh had written, "pray let us know how you got home the other day with Williams, for I fear you must have been out in the bad weather and we are anxious." The letter slipped from Mary's fingers.

"What is it?" Jane asked. "What does he say?" She grabbed at the fallen paper. Looking up at Mary, Jane began to cry.

Mary grasped her shoulders. "We know nothing for certain. We must take a coach to Pisa immediately. Leigh or Albe will have news by now. We'll ask everyone. Our men are alive somewhere. Plans change, you know that." Still weak from her miscarriage, Mary found the strength to rush back to her bedroom, grab a small portmanteau, and throw a few things into it. "Hurry," she called over her shoulder.

Claire helped them both and offered to stay behind with the children. "Please, please," she begged. "Send word to me just as soon as you know something, anything."

"We will, I promise," Mary said, giving Claire a grateful hug.

Once in Pisa, the women went directly to Palazzo Lanfranchi, Albe's villa. A beautiful dark-haired woman opened the door. "Where is he?" Mary cried.

"Mary! What is it?" Albe appeared at the door. "You look as though you had seen a ghost." Taking her by the shoulders, he searched her face. "Rather, it is you who looks like a ghost. What is the matter?"

"We are looking for Bysshe." Mary spoke carefully, her eyes fastened on Albe's, hoping, hoping.

He shook his head. "I don't understand. I thought Bysshe was with you. He left here Monday. It was a bad day, I would not have sailed, but he and Ned were determined."

Mary fought hard to keep her voice calm. "If you and Leigh know nothing more, I must go on to Leghorn. Trelawny and Dan Roberts will know what to do."

"You can't go now. It's after midnight," Albe told her. "Stay tonight with us. Leigh and I will go with you to Leghorn first thing tomorrow."

Mary shook her head; a large lump filled her throat and she could barely speak. "I must go on to Leghorn now."

Byron loaned Mary his coach and two postilions; Jane insisted on accompanying her. Within minutes they were riding on into the night. Dawn was breaking as they rode into Leghorn. Eagerly the women went from inn to inn, until they finally tracked down Captain Roberts and Trelawny at an outdoor café. Mary held fast to the chair back as her eyes met Dan's. The two men rose to their feet, but at first Trelawny would not look at her.

Certain now that her worst fears were true, Mary forced herself to ask. "It has been five days since they left here, where are they?"

Dan shook his head doubtfully. "The weather was foul Monday. I warned them against sailing, but they were adamant. It was noon when they walked onto the pier, and Bysshe was impatient to cast off. The weather seemed to have cleared a bit, but I still didn't like the look of it."

"Then why did they not stay?" Mary cried.

"At first Ned wanted to," Trelawny said, "but Bysshe would not hear of it. The breeze was coming steady out of the west. At that rate, he said, they would be home by seven. His work with Leigh and Byron was done—he was eager to be on his way."

Five days ago. Mary's eyes filled with tears. She fought to keep her voice steady as she asked, "Trelawny, why did you not sail along side? I see Albe's boat anchored here." She gestured toward the wharf. "The *Bolivar* is so much larger and stronger than the *Don Juan*. With you sailing it and a few crew members—"

"Forgive me." Trelawny shook his head. "Can't you imagine how that thought has tortured me? I am so sorry, so very, very sorry." His gray eyes were dull with sadness as he looked at her. "When I saw that they were determined to go, that we could not dissuade them, we readied the *Bolivar* to sail alongside them."

Dan Roberts leaned forward and took Mary's hand in his. "We put up the sails and hoisted the anchor chains. Our two ships heeled and headed out of the harbor side by side."

"But what happened?" Mary and Jane asked, almost in unison.

"The guard boat signaled us to halt. The health officer demanded clearance papers. He was ready to fire on us," Trelawny explained. "Bysshe and Ned had them, but we did not. It all happened so fast. We had not known in the morning that we were going anywhere and had no reason to file."

"So it all hinged on that, something so little . . ." Mary's voice trailed off.

"When I saw Bysshe wave good-bye, I walked down the pier to the lighthouse and climbed the tower," Dan told them.

"What did you see?" Mary gasped out the words.

"A brewing storm was sweeping toward shore." Roberts looked down, not meeting her eyes. "The *Don Juan* was directly in its path, bucking through rising waves."

"Was there nothing more?"

"The sky was darkening. I could barely make out the ship. Soon everything was blackness."

"You're both talking as though that was the end," Mary protested. "Why should it be a foregone conclusion that the boat went down? The *Don Juan* could have gone aground somewhere."

"Mary, Mary, that was the first thing I thought of," Trelawny said. "We took the *Bolivar* out the very next morning. I dispatched couriers up and down the coast and posted a reward. I was told that a water keg and some bottles of water had washed to shore near the small fishing town of Viareggio. So we went there. No question, the bottles were from the *Don Juan*, but I continued to search. We have gone out every day. We were about to start again when you arrived."

"They were just bottles," she argued. "Ships have been blown far out to sea and still been recovered. They may have been driven to Corsica or farther up the coast, even to Nice." She stared into Trelawny's eyes, begging him. "You can't just give up!"

Trelawny took her hands in his and kissed them. "Let me take care of you. You have traveled far, you have been up all night. You're both exhausted, hungry, too, I should imagine. Let me take you and Jane back home to Casa Magni. Dan will continue the search, and I'll join him when I get back."

"I can't—I will not—just give up," Mary cried.

"You must for now," Trelawny told her. "I will take you home. Wait for me there. I promise I'll search to the ends of the earth until they are found."

What could Mary do but agree?

Sailing to Lerici, she stared out at the vast sea and a voice within cried out, *This is his grave.*

Reaching their destination at last, Mary, Jane, and Trelawny threaded their way through a crowd of wildly dancing peasants who were celebrating some sort of feast day on the small beach before the house. Casa Magni was dark. Inside, they found the children sleeping. Claire sat close by, reading by candlelight. She looked up, her eyes filled with hope and then fear. "Is there any news?" she asked, her voice barely above a whisper

Mary shook her head, unable to speak.

At dawn Trelawny departed for Leghorn, returning the next evening at seven. Looking up at him, Mary had no need to ask, and yet she did. "Is there any word?"

Grim-faced, he told them that the bodies of Bysshe, Ned, and young Charles had been found. They had washed ashore. The wait was over.

The *Don Juan* had gone down in the Gulf of La Spezia under full sail. Why were the sails not trimmed, both he and Dan wondered aloud. People in the coastal towns speculated endlessly, but no one knew what had happened. When the bodies had washed ashore, they were badly decomposed. Trelawny first examined Ned's body, which had been partially eaten by fish. He identified it by a black silk handkerchief with the initials EEW. One of Ned's boots was off and his shirt was pulled partly over his head, as if he had been stripping to swim for it.

Bysshe's body, discovered six miles up the beach, was also badly mutilated, but Trelawny easily recognized the familiar double-breasted jacket and nankeen trousers. In one pocket was a soggy volume of Sophocles; in the other, doubled back as if hastily thrust away, Keats's *Lamia*.

Charles Vivian's body was the last to surface; only his skeleton had survived the sea's ravages.

FORTY-SEVEN

They came to watch Bysshe burn. Villagers stood back, respectful and silent, awed by a pagan ceremony forbidden by their faith. The day was hot and breathless. The sea hissed against the shore, a yellow ribbon rimming the cobalt Mediterranean.

Heat waves danced above the sand, the air so thick it felt like warm rain. Medals dazzled in the Italian sun. Debonair officers in scarlet regimentals and well-fed dignitaries in wilted cravats sweated beside ragged urchins. Curiosity drew them close as they awaited a macabre postscript to a mad poet's life.

Mary stood close to the bier, her face illuminated by morning sun. A slender figure in a black silk gown, she drew attention, heard the whispers of the townspeople. Ignoring their inquisitive glances, Mary stared at the shrouded form before her, remembering her lover, her life. Bysshe had blazed across the firmament like a comet, leaving in his wake a trail of poetry and passion, lust and longing, children, miscarriages, and suicides. Was this really the end?

Many times he had stood beside her on the beach, tall, thin, beardless, in his only slightly worn black jacket and trousers. *I should have kissed him longer.*

Because Mary wanted the funeral to be a simple rite resembling the pyres of ancient Greece, Trelawny found a black iron furnace with an open hearth and erected it on the sand. Bysshe's body lay surrounded by stacked driftwood. When it was uncovered, she gasped in horror. Lime thrown into the makeshift grave had stained his skin indigo. A sweltering breeze blew in from the sea, carrying the odor of decayed flesh. Mary put her handkerchief to her nose. She feared that she would faint.

A thin, transparent shroud exposed Bysshe's sea-ravaged body. For a second Mary's eyes closed, unable to bear the sight. Trelawny had brought salt and frankincense for the flames, and oil to pour over the body. He stood beside Mary, the mountains behind them, the sea before, waiting for the final scene to play out.

Now Trelawny signaled to ignite the flame. Mary's breath caught. Behind her, Albe sighed heavily. Breaking away from the group, he kicked off his boots, shucked off his clothes, and plunged naked into the sea. Byron's *Bolivar* was anchored three miles from shore. He would make it easily, but Mary's Bysshe had never learned to swim.

Someone poured wine on Bysshe. More wine, she guessed, than he had drunk in his lifetime. This, with the oil and salt, caused the flames to glisten and quiver. Heat from the sun and fire grew intense; the air felt tremulous. The flames, the pyre, the body undulating before Mary's eyes made her dizzy.

She raised her eyes to the sea. Byron was swimming hard, the sure, swift strokes taking him farther and farther away from her. Was he distancing himself in spirit as well? Could life ever be the same for any of them?

The flames leapt; the furnace turned white-hot. Mary caught her breath, choking back a scream as the corpse fell open. Mary held a handkerchief to her nose against the putrid odor of burning flesh but stayed as close to the blaze as she could bear. She would remain with him to the end. Before her eyes, Bysshe's dear body was reduced to a skeleton . . . all except . . . his heart. Possibly gorged by blood, Bysshe's heart refused to burn. Through the smoke and flames, Mary saw it lying among the ashes . . . intact.

Trelawny saw it, too. Unsheathing his sword, he plunged its blade into the flames. There was a new smell of scorched skin, singed hair. Trelawny's cuff was smoking as he reached forward, face white, jaw clenched. It was too awful. A collective cry went up from the crowd. Many drew back, horrified, as he skewered the heart and pulled it free from the skeleton. Seemingly oblivious, Trelawny took out his handkerchief. Carefully wrapping the heart, he slipped it into Mary's reticule, whispering, "His last gift to you."

Stunned speechless, Mary could merely stare at him.

When the flames burned low, Trelawny cooled the grate with seawater and swept the ashes into a pile, which he placed in a small wooden box.

They were walking toward Trelawny's carriage when Leigh Hunt called out. The spectators, who had begun to drift away, stopped to watch curiously. Leigh was hurrying toward them, the heavily pregnant Marianne following behind. Mary braced herself. Leigh would want to talk, and all that Mary wanted was to go home to her little Percy, hold the child to her heart, and go to sleep.

But Leigh wanted more than talk. He wanted Bysshe's heart. "My right as a loyal and loving friend is far greater than yours as a failed wife," he told her.

Failed wife. Mary gasped as though she had been struck. "You cannot mean that!" The tears she had struggled to hold back stung her eyes as she grasped the heart from the reticule and held it to her own.

Trelawny pushed forward. "How dare you!" His hand moved to his sword hilt. "The man's ashes have not yet cooled and you are fighting for his heart? One more word and you will have me to contend with!" Trelawny turned back to Mary, gently led her to his carriage, and helped her to climb inside.

"Bysshe—his ashes," Mary said, faltering.

"I will take care of them, I will take care of everything." Trelawny cracked his cane against the door panel, and the carriage sped off across the beach.

FORTY-EIGHT

With Bysshe gone, nothing could have induced Mary to remain at Casa Magni. The morning after the cremation, she began to pack her belongings. Claire and Jane watched desolately; soon they, too, were packing. There was nothing to keep any of them in Lerici.

Mary decided to secure lodgings in Pisa for herself and little Percy. Then what? She didn't know. It was mid-July; Mary had the remainder of Bysshe's allowance from Sir Timothy. It would last through the year. Then what?

Claire and Jane insisted on moving with her to Pisa. "We can pool expenses," they said, making it easier on all of them, but it was Mary who paid the lion's share.

Trelawny continued to be a dear friend, handling the grimmest details. He and Albe presided at Ned's private cremation. They would not let Mary or Jane attend. "A rag retains its form longer than a dead body," Albe told Mary when pressed. "A funeral is a satire on our pride and folly. Don't repeat it with me. Let my carcass rot where it falls."

It was all horrible, too horrible. *How can I bear it?* Mary wondered more than once. Of course, she did bear it, comforting Percy, seeing to his needs, and trying not to think of her own. Claire and Jane, too, were bereft. The women said little to each other. It was difficult to say anything without one of them bursting into tears.

Mary thought often of her old friends Leigh and Marianne. Why had they treated her so badly at the cremation? One afternoon

Mary picked up a book that had survived the wreck. It was dry now, though badly damaged. Looking closely, she saw the name Leigh Hunt written on the flyleaf. Mary imagined that Bysshe had borrowed it. On an impulse, she decided to return the book herself.

Wrapping it carefully in one of Bysshe's handkerchiefs, she set off. It was a long walk to the Palazzo Lanfranchi, where the Hunts still occupied the first floor of Albe's home, but Mary was trying hard to economize.

A servant showed her inside and bid her wait in the elaborate drawing room. Mary fought back tears. The last time she had been there was on the frantic night when she had come in search of Bysshe. Mary seated herself on a velvet-tufted chair and waited.

A moment or two later, Leigh appeared. "Did you want to see Lord Byron? He and the countess are out shopping. Marianne is resting."

"No, I came to see you, Leigh." Mary was puzzled. Leigh was the same man she had known and loved—tousled hair, tattered linen, loose, shuffling walk—but his manner was withdrawn, one might even say cold. Surely she imagined it. Mary removed the package from her reticule, explaining, "I thought you would like to have this back. It was with him when . . ."

"Good of you to bring it." He extended his hand for the package. "I loaned it to him that last night—his last night. We strolled together along the banks of the Arno. It had been storming earlier but cleared, the moon—" Leigh stopped himself abruptly. After a pause, he asked, "Is there anything else?"

Mary started, looking up in surprise. Was he dismissing her? What else could she think? "I had best be on my way," she said, rising to her feet.

"Yes," Leigh agreed. He walked her to the door and closed it firmly behind her. Mary turned and looked back at the palazzo in pained bewilderment. Leigh had been her friend and confidant for years. Why would he desert her now?

Mary took a hired carriage home. She was crying softly when she reached her lodgings and wanted only to be alone, but Claire was sitting in the tiny parlor. Though Mary tried to slip past, Claire spotted her. To Mary's surprise, Claire got up and embraced her. It was so unexpected that Mary cried all the harder.

"It is a dreadful time for all of us," Claire said, patting Mary's shoulder softly, "but surely for you most of all."

That was something coming from Claire. Mary drew back in surprise. "There's something else," she admitted. "I went to visit Leigh. I thought he would be happy to see me, he always has been, but he seemed so . . . so distant. It was as though he were angry with me for something. I cannot imagine what it could be."

"Come sit with me on the couch," Claire suggested. "Perhaps I know what this is about."

They sat down and Mary turned to Claire. What did she know?

"Jane has been saying things about you, unkind things. She's likely to have been talking to Leigh."

Mary's eyes widened. "But Leigh has been a close friend for years; he scarcely knows Jane. Why would he believe her? What kind of things has she been saying?"

"That Bysshe was unhappy with his life and that you did not understand him."

"Really! Is that not what married men always say?"

"It would seem so. Bysshe sometimes said it to me." Claire paused as though lost in thought. "I used to feel that you did not deserve him, but lately I have come to see things differently. I think you are the only one that Bysshe could ever really have loved because you are the only one brilliant enough to challenge him."

"You flatter me."

"Not really; anyway, that bright little brain has also worked against you."

Mary looked at her in bewilderment. "What on earth are you talking about?"

Claire sat back and regarded Mary closely "We all know that Bysshe was brilliant and talented, maybe too much so for his own good. He needed a mother-wife, someone who would live only for him, who could buffer him from the world and temper her needs to his. Harriet might have grown into that kind of woman. Who knows, we were all so awfully young. Anyway, that was not what he wanted. He wanted you."

"Well, he got me and look what happened. Jane is right, he was not happy. I think about it all the time. I blame myself constantly. The guilt is almost as hard to live with as the loss of him." Mary's lips trembled from the effort not to cry. What was Claire trying to say? Where was she going with all this?

"But you were not happy either," Claire reminded her. "You are also brilliant and talented. That is what drew him to you in the first place and kept him with you no matter who he loved for the moment or imagined that he loved. Bysshe was so proud of you— of your success, of that way you have of drawing exciting people close to you. He wanted that, needed it. He wanted the pearl of you, but not the irritating grit that creates the pearl."

"What irritating grit?" Mary sat up, hands on her hips. "What are you talking about?"

"The grit was your grief, your melancholia. He felt shut out because it wasn't about *him*."

Mary rose to her feet, fury flowing through her like waves of molten metal. "I have been pregnant five times and have but one living child," Mary shouted. "Would that not be enough to give any woman melancholia?"

Even as she spoke, sudden, unwanted thoughts stirred in Mary's brain. Was Bysshe not *her* pearl, his idealizations and susceptibility to women the irritating grit around him? Oh, if that were true, the worst had happened. The cruel sea had claimed her pearl forever.

And then another thought: *Could this have been his wish?*

FORTY-NINE

The next afternoon Mary returned home from a stroll to find Claire packing. "There is nothing left for me in Italy," she announced. "I will join my brother in Vienna. Charlie will help me." Claire looked at Mary, dark eyes beseeching. "If I could but borrow enough for coach fare . . . Think of all we have gone through together."

And all that you have taken, Mary thought, but gave her the money.

Jane, too, wished to go, she to London. "I want to take Ned's ashes back to his homeland." She hesitated a moment and then continued tentatively, "Mother is all the family I have left. She disowned me when I eloped with Ned, but if she could see my children . . ." Jane paused, fighting back tears. "It is best for the children that I go back, but I—I—will be so lonely. It has been twenty years since I left England."

Listening to this diffident, downcast woman, Mary chose to ignore Claire's disclosure. What did it really matter now what Jane had or hadn't said?

Mary gave Jane money for her trip and something more. "I, too, have been away from home a long time. I lost contact with most of my friends, but there is one that I still hear from upon occasion. I think you would enjoy one another's company." She quickly jotted down an address and handed it to Jane. "The man's name is Thomas Hogg. You will, I hope, give him my regards."

The next day Byron came to visit. Mary felt a glimmer of pleasure for the first time since Bysshe's drowning. There was not a
person alive whose voice had more power over her than Albe's.
Something in its strange, almost melancholy timbre linked pleasure with a kind of pain. Mary loved to banter with him about
books and philosophy, to listen to his poetry, but on this day the
conversation took a different tone. "The Hunt children are willful
and unruly," he complained. "Truly, Mary, what they can't destroy
with their filth, they will with their fingers. The little blackguards
are driving me mad."

Mary studied Albe from beneath her lashes, missing his usual
debonair manner. He had not been himself since the cremation.
But then, how could he be?

"Teresa wants to move to Genoa," he told her. "I have about
decided to indulge her."

Mary caught her breath. "What of the *Liberal*?"

"The *Liberal* can as well be published in Genoa. We can all go.
I would welcome your articles, and I have other work for you as
well. How would you like to fair copy *Don Juan*?"

Mary was delighted with the project and the money she would
receive, yet hesitated, sensing there was something more. "What
else would be expected of me?" she asked.

"Well, you *could* take in the Hunts. I will keep the *Liberal*
alive for the sake of Bysshe's memory, if nothing else. I will also
continue to pay Leigh for editing and writing, but I will *not* have
that wretched family in my house. The children—six of them with
another on the way—tease my animals unmercifully. Only yesterday I set my bulldog to guarding the rest. The wretches tried to run
the gauntlet, and that damned goat of theirs got an ear chewed off.
You should have heard those brats wailing, their damn fool mother
as well. Mary, you cannot imagine."

Mary could well imagine. She knew the children. A more
important issue was the cruel way they had treated her at Bysshe's

funeral. Then Mary thought of her own mother, her own birth. "Marianne's health has always been poor," she reminded him. "Now she's again pregnant. Her doctor fears she may not survive childbirth."

"Really?" He raised a dark brow. "Would that be such a bad thing?"

———

Mary was surprised to find the Hunts on her doorstep the following day. Despite their hostility toward her, they had come to propose sharing living accommodations. It was a matter of simple economics, Leigh and Marianne explained. Besides, life at Albe's Palazzo Lanfranchi had grown intolerable for them. The couple disapproved of Byron's open living arrangement with Teresa.

Angry as they were with Mary, they were quick to confide in her. "We get up early," Leigh said. "While Marianne sees to the children, I busy myself in the garden, writing and editing. Byron and his woman rise at noon and then parade before us, she with her sleek tresses fresh from the bath. He is flaunting her and their relationship."

Marianne raised a more significant concern, confiding, "I fear Byron does not respect Leigh's work. He is disappointed in the *Liberal*. Those fancy bigwigs he ran with in London don't care for it. They have poisoned his mind. Byron calls the journal an embarrassment. He no longer wants to be identified with it, much less subsidize it."

Despite Albe's previous assurance, Mary feared that without Bysshe to play peacemaker, the *Liberal*'s days were numbered. She could but nod sympathetically.

———

After closing her apartment in Pisa, Mary and three-year-old Percy traveled north to Genoa. Her intent was to find a pleasant home, large enough to afford privacy for both herself and the Hunts, yet well within their means. At first she thought Casa Negroto the answer to everything. Located less than a mile from Casa Saluzzo, the mansion that Albe planned to lease, the house was large, with dozens of rooms to accommodate the Hunt children. It was also surprisingly inexpensive.

For a few weeks Mary, who had traveled ahead of the others, lived there alone with Percy. On occasion the solitude was welcome and she was almost content; but, more often, Mary fought an almost irrepressible urge to walk into the sea. Only the need to care for her little Persino kept her alive.

Mary tried desperately to immerse herself in her child's well-being and to think positively about the future. The house was situated on a hillside with a commanding view of the sea. She envisioned a peaceful, pleasant winter spent copying Byron's manuscript, doing some writing of her own, going for long walks, and helping Marianne with the children. Mary did not think the Hunt brood entirely impossible.

She thought wrong. The clatter of six pairs of children's feet, the angry shouts, and unrestrained boisterousness was beyond belief. Albe achieved sainthood in Mary's eyes for enduring them as long as he had.

But that was not all. As winter set in, Mary realized why Casa Negroto had been let so cheap. It was almost impossible to heat. The winter of 1822–23 was the coldest in many years. Icy gales swept down the mountains into Genoa. Mediterranean storms smashed against the hillside. The house's high-ceilinged rooms were like ice caves.

The winter was dreary in other unexpected ways. Though Sir Timothy had steadfastly refused to acknowledge her, Mary had never doubted that her husband's father would want to assure his grandson's security. Her confidence increased even more when Albe agreed to act as her executor. Nevertheless, the days of waiting for Sir Timothy's response to the news of Bysshe's death were an agony. It seemed to Mary that the entire future of her dearest boy hung in the balance.

Finally, on February 24, Albe arrived with a letter from her father-in-law.

"You aren't going to like this, Mary," he said, handing it to her, "but I urge you to consider the contents carefully."

Mary took the letter and opened it slowly. For an instant the words blurred before her eyes. *Despicable!* Sir Timothy had called her despicable. The woman who had *destroyed* his family was not to receive a penny! Worse than that, Sir Timothy had applied a hideous condition to any aid he might *deem* to grant Percy. Only if the child were placed under the care of a guardian approved by Sir Timothy himself would he then *consider* providing the boy with an adequate though limited maintenance.

Adequate though limited maintenance! Percy farmed out to a stranger! Mary's hands shook with anger as she crumpled the letter and threw it on the floor.

"Don't be too hasty, Mary," Byron warned. "It is always assumed that a child belongs with its father or, in this case, its father's family. A connection with Sir Timothy will ensure Percy a position in society, and eventually, of course, there will be the question of his inheritance."

"A connection!" Mary snapped. "Is that what you gave Allegra? A *connection*? Much good that did her!"

Byron's face went white. His furious gaze fixed on Mary for only a moment. Then, turning on his heel, limp barely visible, he strode from the room and slammed the door behind him.

She froze as waves of anger, fear, and frustration swept over her, leaving at last a deep well of pain. Mary was certain that she would never see Albe again.

FIFTY

Now fierce remorse and unreplying death
Waken a chord within my heart, whose breath,
Thrilling and keen, in accents audible
A tale of unrequited love doth tell.
It was not anger, while thy earthly dress
Encompassed still thy soul's rare loveliness,
All anger was atoned by many a kind
Caress or tear, that spoke the softened mind.
It speaks of cold neglect, averted eyes,
That blindly crushed thy soul's fond sacrifice:
My heart was all thine own—but yet a shell
Closed in its core, which seemed impenetrable,
Till sharp-toothed misery tore the husk in twain,
Which gaping lies, no one may unite again.

Mary put down her quill. Sitting alone at her desk, she sobbed for all that might have been. If only Bysshe were there beside her. She longed to touch his face, to hear his voice, to tell him of her feelings, her deep regrets. If only . . .

Sir Timothy's icy rejection was a second blow; the sudden estrangement from Byron, her longtime friend, the third. How could he possibly imagine that she would give up Percy, the only reason left for her existence?

In the midst of this, Mary received a series of dunning letters from her father. With Bysshe gone and the royalties from *Valperga* beginning to dwindle, William looked to her for financial support. When she had nothing to give, he made no effort to conceal his anger and disappointment. Mary was appalled; she felt their widening rift as yet another loss.

Casa Negroto seemed to be crumbling around Mary. Illness rendered Marianne dull and lethargic, confined to her bed. Leigh closeted himself in the room he claimed for a study, leaving their children to run rampant. They were a household of three adults and seven children but could afford only one servant. Rooms were often thick with dust, the kitchen covered in grease and stacked with pots and unwashed dishes. Mary had never been domestic but did appreciate cleanliness and some degree of order. She was dismayed and often exhausted by the amount of daily scrubbing, cooking, and polishing necessary.

Worst of all, the Hunt children were a mean bunch who teased Percy unmercifully for his Italian-accented English. The house rang with their taunts. "*Persiiiino!* Come play your *bambino* games!"

Finally Mary could stand it no longer. "I have heard enough," she cried, hands on her hips. "Shut your mouths or I will shut them for you."

"Mary!" Marianne, wrapped in a blanket, stood at her bedroom door. "Is that any way to address little children? We are raising free spirits and never raise our voices to them."

"Then it's time you did. They are not free to persecute my child, and if they try it again, they will have me to deal with. I hope everyone understands that."

The ensuing truce was at best uneasy.

Mary's journal was her only confidant, indeed her only refuge. Often her entries took the form of letters to Bysshe. "When spring comes," she lamented, "leaves you never saw will rise from the ground—flowers you never beheld will star it—the grass will be of another growth." There were so many things she longed to say to him. It seemed somehow inconceivable that life was continuing on, almost as though he had never existed.

Just when Mary felt that she could bear her life no longer, Trelawny returned from Rome. He took her to dinner, to the theater and opera. They went on long carriage rides. Mary had always been attracted to Trelawny's swashbuckling ways and rugged good looks, but now his kindness and generosity drew her even more. Trelawny was a witty man, a thoughtful man, and, unlike Bysshe, a man who got things done.

His purpose in going to Rome had been to see to the interment of Bysshe's ashes. "I found a secluded corner in the Protestant Cemetery in which Bysshe might rest," he told Mary the evening of his return. "Perhaps even now he is looking after Willmouse."

Quick tears sprang to Mary's eyes. Trelawny dabbed at them gently with his handkerchief. "I did not tell you this to make you cry. I want only to make you happy. I want to take care of you. Always."

And was that not exactly what Mary wanted, needed? She hesitated. "It is too soon," she said at last. "It would not be fair to you. I am still grieving. Perhaps I will always be grieving."

"I will wait," he said, helping her down from his carriage. "Just allow me to see you. Perhaps one day I will convince you."

What could Mary say to that? She enjoyed Trelawny's company. He was lighthearted, uncomplicated, easy to be with—such a contrast to Bysshe. His attentions were flattering and she enjoyed that flattery, but was it right? Was she being untrue to Bysshe's memory? Perhaps so, but, other than little Percy, Trelawny was the one bright spot in her life. As for the future, time alone could tell.

She linked her arm in his as they entered an outdoor café. The table he found for them had a spectacular view. All of Genoa was spread before them, lights glittering like jewels.

"From this distance, we might be looking at an Italian city of the fourteenth century," Trelawny surprised her by saying. "We could even step into the pages of *Valperga*."

"You've read my novel?"

"Read it and loved it. You brought a distant time to life. Reading it was a vacation into the past. What a gift you have."

A wave of pleasure swept over Mary. How different Trelawny's reaction was to Bysshe's. "I'm so glad you enjoyed it."

"I suspect that in writing about a long-ago uprising, you were mirroring the failure of a more recent revolution. Your Castruccio sounds like a little Napoleon to me."

"You surprise me," Mary said. "I see you as a man of action. I should have thought reading a bit passive for you."

"Then you misjudge me. I read *Frankenstein* as well, many times. 'Beware for I am fearless, and therefore powerful.'"

A delightful shiver ran through Mary's body. "Are you then my creature?"

He took her hand in his. "I should like to be?"

———

As weeks passed, Mary became increasingly aware of how much Trelawny's kindness belied his strong physical presence. He was alert, not only to her needs and problems but to those of others as well. Mary had not seen Byron since her rash outburst, but Trelawny visited him often and talked to her of the changes he had observed. It appeared to be a bad time for her old friend. Byron was drinking more and eating less. He virtually ignored Teresa, had given up his daily horseback rides, and no longer sailed the *Bolivar*.

Mary, who had been sitting beside Trelawny in his carriage as he related this, turned to look at him in concerned surprise. "That doesn't sound at all like the Albe I know. Pray tell, what *is* he interested in?"

"Fighting for Greek independence."

"Do you think him serious?"

"It surprised me as well. I should never have thought he'd desire to don a warrior's plume. A Greek prince—Mavrocordato, I believe is his name—is organizing a brigade to fight the Turks."

Mary flushed at the name, remembering her admirer from the Pisa days and his morning Greek lessons. Alexander had always been a firebrand. From time to time, she'd wondered what had become of him. She was happy to know Alexander was still alive, still fighting for his noble cause. How much longer could the Ottoman oppression of Greece be tolerated?

Looking up at Trelawny, she studied the expression in his clear gray eyes. "I wonder if you do not also desire to don a warrior's plume. It would be a grand adventure. Surely you have thought of it."

"Thought of it, of course," he admitted, "but I prefer to remain near you."

———

Mary's fondness for Trelawny increased with each meeting. He had a ready, easy smile and a confident stride. Mary liked the way he moved, the way his presence filled the room. Trelawny's attentions had eased her through a most difficult time. She admired him immensely, but was that love? And if so, was love what she wanted? Life was moving fast, closing in on her before she was ready.

One day Trelawny drove Mary to a nearby lake, where they stood together feeding the swans. A little path led to a grassy knoll, where a bench had been placed. For a time they sat quietly, admiring the tranquil view. Their friendship had been drifting along oh so pleasantly. She would have liked to continue that way indefinitely, but there was too much left unsaid. Turning to him, she broke the silence. "I feel certain that Byron desires your companionship in Greece."

"Yes," Trelawny admitted, "he wrote to me when I was in Rome. As a matter of fact, I have the letter with me." He reached into his waistcoat pocket and handed a paper to Mary.

In smoothing out the page, she noted that it had been creased more than once. Trelawny had obviously given its contents considerable thought.

Scanning quickly, she read words scrawled in Albe's familiar handwriting. "Pray come, for I am at last determined to go to Greece. They all say I can be of use there. I do not know how, nor do they; but in all events, let us go."

"I should imagine that you, too, desire to take up the cause for freedom against tyranny." Looking up at him, Mary noticed a slight tensing of his jaw.

"I should rather take a trip with you. Let us go to Rome. We can walk together beneath the cypress and laurel trees that I planted around Shelley's grave. He is buried on a slope next to the old Roman wall. It's a quiet spot. Perhaps sometime far in the future we, too, may lie there. But for now, I should like you to see the stone I placed on his grave." He paused a moment before reciting softly,

Nothing of him that doth fade,
But doth suffer a sea-change
Into something rich and strange.

"They are beautiful words," Mary said. "I cannot thank you enough for all that you have done."

"I do not want your thanks. I desire your love." His eyes were on her, searching, intent, so intent.

Mary had to look away. Again she had the sense that life was speeding out of control. She was not ready for decisions, yet the possibility that this dear friend, this man whom she had been strongly drawn to from the day they first met, might be lost to her forever weighed heavily. They sat for a time in silence, she uncertain what to say.

At last Trelawny asked, "Is it not time for us as well to make a sea-change? Our life together could also be rich and strange."

"Perhaps," she conceded. "But each of us has matters that must first be attended to. You belong in Greece with Albe. You were made for grand adventures—your days as a pirate, your duels—if you miss this one, you would regret it forever. You might also come to resent me for being the cause of such regret. Besides, it would appear that Albe needs you at his side . . . I worry about him."

"But what of you?" Trelawny asked, taking her hands in his. "What will be your sea-change?"

Mary's eyes caressed his rakish face, the full lips twisted now in a wry smile.

Her heart ached at the thought that she might never see him again. "I shall go to London."

"London!" He sat back, startled. "You've said nothing about returning home. I thought you loved Italy."

"I do! Even if its sky did not canopy the tombs of all my lost treasures, I would adore Italy, the sun, the trees and flowers, the easy life, and all the habits that I have acquired these past five years, the memories . . . I love Italy in more ways than I can possibly describe, even to you."

"Then why? When did you make this decision?"

Mary smiled ruefully. "Only this morning. Last night, when you took me home from the theater, there was a letter waiting from my father. It contained a most disagreeable clipping from the

Courier in London." Mary took the paper from her reticule and read aloud to him: "Shelley, the writer of some infidel poetry, has been drowned; *now* he knows whether there is a God or no."

Trelawny took her hand in his. "That *is* rough! But I don't see what you can do about it."

"There is a lot that I can do! The publication of Bysshe's poetry will assure his place in history. Only yesterday I was pondering my own future. Where was my place in the world? What was I to do with my life? But when the letter came, when I read the clipping, I knew."

"But can't you do that here—with me?"

Mary shook her head. "Bysshe's poetry was written in English, and it must first be published in English. London is the center of the world of letters. It must be done there. As it is now, few know his poetry beyond a small group of friends—enemies, too, it would seem. I must piece Bysshe's work together and bring it to life. It's my obligation to make certain that the world recognizes and reveres both the man and his talent. Knowing what they are saying about him, I must go back. It is the least I can do for him, and all that remains that I *can* do."

Trelawny cupped her face in his hands. "What about us? Are you saying that we can never be? How long will this crusade of yours take?"

"It is not a crusade; it is an editing job, pure and simple. I have copies of all Bysshe's work. It's really only a matter of organizing his verses and finding a publisher. I am thinking that it will take two years. In a sense we each have a war to fight. You will tend to yours and I to mine."

Trelawny's gray eyes flashed as he regarded her eagerly. "Shall we then come together in London in two years' time? To celebrate our victories?"

"I should like that," Mary said, raising her eyes to his, touching his cheek lightly, "but I make no promises."

FIFTY-ONE

Mary sat at her desk, studying the page before her. Marianne's letter had arrived at her London address only that morning, the familiar handwriting igniting a host of memories. Her last days in Genoa, Casa Negroto's clutter and confusion. The horrific birth of the Hunts' seventh child. Leigh, tears in his eyes, fleeing the room. Mary standing by Marianne's bed, wiping the sweat from her face, offering ice to suck, back rubs, desperate words of encouragement.

"You are my dearest friend," Marianne whispered hoarsely when the ordeal was over. "How could I have forgotten that?"

Leigh, too, was effusive, grateful. "You are a woman of courage and a loyal friend," he told Mary. "I have misjudged you. Those things I said—I was wrong."

Mary was happy at last to leave on pleasant terms.

Now here was Marianne writing from Genoa: "Vincent is six months old, hardly a baby anymore." Scanning the page, Mary thought the tone wistful. Dear God, were seven children not enough for any woman? Or perchance it was Leigh who wanted more . . .

She opened the top drawer of her desk and took out a fresh sheet of paper. Mary wrote with care: "A woman is not a field to be continually employed either in bringing forth or enlarging grain."

Sighing ruefully, Mary sat back. Who was she to give family advice? Mary's relationship with her father had improved little over the years. She had been touched when William reached out to her after Bysshe's death—the first overture since her elopement years before. William had urged her return to London and surprised her by saying, "You will always have a home with me." Mary had taken him at his word.

It began well enough. When her ship docked, her father and Willie welcomed her with open arms. Godwin, who had virtually ignored Willmouse, seemed delighted with little Percy's enthusiastic chatter—a mishmash of Italian and English.

Mary's hopes ran high, but once she was settled into the Godwin home, life was far from perfect. The house the Godwins had moved into following their eviction from Skinner Street was small. There was little space for shelves, thus fewer books—some of Mary's favorites were missing. An antique dining table—so many memories of Bysshe—had been sold. A wing-back chair, once her mother's, was gone. Fortunately the portrait of Mary Wollstonecraft remained. Mary was relieved to see it ensconced in her father's small study.

As ever, tension crackled between Mary and her stepmother. Though she knew the story well, Mum asked endless questions about Claire and Byron, making it painfully clear that she considered Mary responsible for all that had gone wrong. Mum also considered any letter that came to the house public property. This made it awkward for Mary, as Trelawny wrote regularly.

Mary followed the War for Greek Independence avidly in the newspapers and was surprised that Trelawny wrote little of the fierce fighting, the heavy casualties on both sides. His letters were at first arch: "I should not wonder if fate, without our choice, united us; and who can control fate? I blindly follow his decrees, dear Mary."

As weeks passed, he slowly became more ardent. "Time has not quenched the fire of my nature; my feelings and passions burn fierce as ever, and will until they have consumed me. I wear the burnished livery of the sun. I love you with all my heart."

Mary couldn't have Mum poking her nose into that unresolved alliance. She and little Persino needed lodgings of their own. It was also essential that Mary see to her son's future. Once again, she applied to Sir Timothy. The result was a series of protracted and humiliating arguments. The baronet, still stung by the elopement, wanted no family publicity. In the end he granted Mary one hundred pounds a year with the stipulation that if she ever published a biography of her husband, the income would be severed immediately. Mary was forced to abandon the dream she'd had of writing a history of Bysshe embellished with cherished memories of their life together. It was a bitter blow, but, for the sake of Percy's future inheritance, Mary was forced to abandon the project that meant so much to her.

Life at the Godwin house grew ever more trying. In addition to ongoing problems with Mum, Mary faced mounting tension with her father. Sadly it centered around Bysshe. Mary had not been home long before she realized that her father bitterly resented any mention of her husband.

It came to a head one evening at dinner. Mary had just seated herself at the battered oak dining table when her father looked up, thick eyebrows together in a frown, and announced, "Your blessed Bysshe, the man you worship as a saint, was a cold-blooded skinflint."

Mary looked at him amazement. Angry tears stung her eyes. "Bysshe went into debt again and again for you! Who else would be so kind and generous?"

"Never you mind. I have finer friends than he ever was."

Mary was flabbergasted. "Who are you talking about?"

"Caroline Lamb, *Lady* Caroline Lamb, is heading a public subscription on my behalf."

Lady Caroline Lamb. The name rang in Mary's head. It seemed only yesterday that Claire had taken her to tea at Byron's home.

How well she remembered the carriage ride, Claire telling her of Caroline's gift to Byron. Mary barely suppressed a giggle.

Later that night in her small room, Mary shared the gossipy morsel with Claire, who was working now as a governess in Moscow. "The weather is terrible, the children worse," Claire had recently written. Perhaps this bizarre new connection would amuse her. Mary had another tidbit to share as well. Jane Williams had recently moved in with Tom Hogg. They were calling it a marriage. Mary was mildly amused. At least Tom was consistent. He had always admired Bysshe's taste in women.

Mary found the romantic dramas going on about her comical. They reminded her of a poem of Bysshe's.

Lift not the painted veil which those who live
Call Life: though unreal shapes be pictured there,
And it but mimic all we would believe
With colours idly spread,—behind, lurk Fear
And Hope, twin Destinies; who ever weave
Their shadows, o'er the chasm, sightless and drear.

Mary's smile faded as she reached for a list of houses to let, torn from the day's newspaper. In short order she found lodgings at 14 Speldhurst Street, a tree-lined mews off Brunswick Square. The tall brick building had been divided in two. She and Percy would occupy one half. The rooms were small but adequate. Soon Mary had created a space for herself and was busy collecting and collating copies of Bysshe's unpublished poetry, a daunting task in every way.

Percy watched in wonderment as his mother attempted to sort stacks of paper that spilled out from Mary's small study into their parlor. "Is that trash, Mama?" he surprised her by asking.

"No, little Persino, it is treasure." Mary didn't wonder that her son would ask. Bysshe wrote poems on anything available. Much of his work consisted of loose, nearly illegible fragments that had to be pieced together, while other poems competed for space with doodles of boats in notebooks that had been stuffed helter-skelter into cabinets, desks, and trunks. Mary was hard-pressed at times to tell which scrap of the poem was the beginning and which the end, or even if the scraps were from the same poem.

The challenge of making order out of chaos forced Mary to center herself, forging ahead despite the waves of sorrow and regret that often swept over her. She sought desperately to not only reveal her husband's brilliance to the world, but enshrine his reputation. The suddenness of Bysshe's death had initially enabled her to put aside the emotional storms that had marked their life together, but now, confronted by his own written words, she found it increasingly difficult to ignore the discontent evidenced in his poetry.

Most striking was the verse "To Mary," written during the dreadful weeks that followed Willmouse's death. Mary reread the poem and wondered . . . *What was the matter with Bysshe? Did he care so little for Willmouse? How very selfish!*

As if that were not bad enough, other poems revealed her husband's fascination with Claire and his adoration of Emilia Viviani and Jane, while depicting Mary as a cold, emotionally remote wife. She was furious and wanted nothing more than to burn the poems. The conflict raging within her made Mary physically ill, forcing her to retire to her bedchamber. Though aware of Bysshe's attachments, Mary had never fully realized their intensity. What a fool she had been! He had demeaned her to other women only to elevate and flatter them while aggrandizing himself. How could she honor the memory of someone so callously cruel?

Angrily Mary flung off the covers and returned to her study. Bysshe's poems covered the floor. Furious, she grabbed at them, crumpling and tearing the pages into bits. Percy, awakened from his nap, stood at the door, mouth agape. "Mama—the treasure! What are you doing?"

"You were right. It is trash."

Mary called out to Nettie, Percy's nurse, and asked her to dress the boy and take him for a walk. When they were gone, she returned to her bed.

"I cannot deal with this," she raged. Yet somehow she did. Forcing herself to go back to the torn and crumpled papers, she slowly, painfully pieced together each and every fragment. Bysshe was an utter cad, but his work was precious, the poems not only her son's legacy, but the world's. For better or worse, she must be her husband's curator.

Mary was hard at work when an angry note arrived from Trelawny. He had grown so heartily sick of Byron's whims and delays that he had left him in Missolonghi with Prince Mavrocordato's regiment and gone to join the ranks of another Greek freedom fighter.

Trelawny's letter contained a poem that Albe had written just before their breach. Sadly Mary read:

The dead have been awakened—shall I sleep?
The World's at war with tyrants—shall I crouch?
The harvest's ripe—and shall I pause to reap?
I slumber not; the thorn is in my Couch;
Each day a trumpet soundeth in mine ear,
Its echo in my heart.

Byron, the bad and the beautiful. The news of the rift between the two men distressed Mary more than it should have. She supposed it was simply melancholy at the breaking up of what she'd come to think of as the "Pisa Circle." Time had dimmed her memories. Mary thought only of the happy times. She treasured those days. Maybe, too, she regretted Trelawny's desertion of Mavrocordato, the dashing Greek patriot so imbued with patriotism. Whatever the reason, she could not shake a pervasive sense of unease. She worried for Albe without Trelawny's strong presence at his side.

Mary continued her sorting and cataloging until one morning her concentration was broken by a frantic banging at her door. Flinging back the bolt, she confronted Mum, her face red, her hair hanging in disheveled strings.

"He's dead!" Mum screamed. Despite her words, Mary sensed an air of excitement about her, perhaps even of pleasure.

Her breath caught. "Oh, no, not Father!"

"No, not your father, blessed be. Whatever gave you such an idea? William's a tough old bird. He's like to live forever."

"Then who?" Mary's heart thumped heavily. *What now?*

"My daughter's seducer. Your fine-feathered friend the Lord Byron. Everyone's talking, the newspapers are full of it. You'd know, too, if you didn't stay cooped up in this garret. His lordship died of a fever in Greece. Serves him right for running off to fight someone else's war. The doctors did what they could, bled him plenty of times, but that only made him weaker." Mum shrugged her heavy shoulders. "Lords die like anyone else when their time's up."

"But his time was not up! Albe was alive and vital—how could he be dead?"

Mum said nothing. She had turned her attention to the house, wandering here and there, poking into this and that, opening up drawers, glancing at letters.

The shock was like a physical blow to Mary. Her friend had departed for Greece filled with courage and idealism only to be felled not by a sword or gun, but by fever. There was an absurd cruelty to his death that struck Mary to the heart. How could it be that Albe—dear, capricious, fascinating Albe—was dead, lost forever to her and to the world. To think that her last words to him were angry, ungrateful ones. How cruel she had been; he had only been trying to help.

That night Mary sat at the desk in her tiny, cluttered study, the floor still strewn with Bysshe's poetry. It was hot and sultry, every window open wide in hopes of catching a reluctant breeze. Wiping the tears from her eyes, Mary picked up her journal. The blank page stared back at her. What was there to write? After a time the quill began to move almost of its own volition. "Beauty sat on his countenance and power beamed from his eye. His faults being, for the most part, weakness, induced one readily to pardon them."

———————

Two months later, on July 12, 1824, Mary and Jane—Jane Hogg, she now called herself—stood at an upstairs window of Mary's home waiting for Byron's funeral procession. Jane chattered freely about Tom, her children, her mother.

Mary, her heart besieged by memories, heard little. She saw Albe in his magnificent Napoleonic carriage, Albe sailing the moon-tossed lake. She remembered the quirks, the daring, the kindness, and, yes, the cruelty that comprised his sweet, savage nature.

So many memories, but one stood out from all the rest: a long-ago night at Villa Diodati. "We shall each write a ghost story," Albe had proposed, turning to her. "You and I will publish ours together." How could she forget? The dark lord had inspired *Frankenstein*. Indeed, how could she forget anything about Albe? But now he and Bysshe were dead and Claire half a world away.

At twenty-six, Mary felt like an old woman.

The great bells of Westminster Abbey tolled once and then again. Mary looked down and saw the streets clogged by men and women waiting silently. First came the High Constable, clad in deep mourning and leading a riderless horse. Behind them came the hearse, covered with a black pall and surmounted by black plumes. A long line of carriages followed, noble, shiny vehicles belonging to the peers of the realm, yet ridden by their lowly pages. It was thus that England's lords and ladies registered their disdain. They had neither forgotten nor forgiven their fellow peer's fall from grace.

The crowd below remained silent, the only sounds the creak and rattle of carriage wheels on cobblestones. Slowly the procession rolled by on its way along Oxford Street, up Highgate Hill, and on to Newstead Abbey.

Mary and Jane spent much of the day talking and playing quietly with their children. Alone that evening, Mary sat down at her desk and took out the worn journal that had been her closest friend and only confidant for so long. Idly she flipped through the pages, whispering softly, "All my yesterdays."

After a time, Mary picked up a quill and wrote: "What should I have said to a Cassandra who three years ago said that Jane and I—Edward and Bysshe gone—should watch the funeral procession of Lord Byron up Highgate Hill? How young, heedless & happy & poor we were then & now my sleeping boy is all that is left to me of that time—my boy—& a thousand recollections that never sleep."

FIFTY-TWO

Death was a subtle sweetener, Mary realized. Much of the pain and frustration she'd felt toward Bysshe had faded in the past two years. She remembered mostly good things. The painful and laborious task of compiling his work was complete. Regardless of all that had passed between them, Mary and Bysshe were partners in the end. She had brought forth his creation. Mary was satisfied, but also abysmally weary. What if editing was all she could do? "My imagination is dead, my genius lost, my energies asleep," she bitterly confided to her journal.

Mary deplored the loss of Albe as well, describing him as "that resplendent spirit whose departure leaves the dull earth dark as midnight." She missed both men desperately.

Alone with little Percy in their small lodgings, living through a dismal London winter, Mary felt isolated from everything that had once inspired her. She was numb, devoid of passion or excitement. Would this twilight existence last forever?

As one winter day followed another, she bundled Percy up and took him for walks. Surely the blustery weather would rouse her. It did not.

Mary turned to books, read voraciously, craving stimulation from other writers. Thomas De Quincey's *Confessions of an English Opium-Eater* had caused quite a stir. People still debated it. Mary had at first turned the pages eagerly but soon put the book aside. She had been there. Her childhood friend Charles Lamb had recently published a book of essays. She read some of them, smiling at memories of times gone by. All so long ago. Finally she picked up a poem from another old friend, Sam Coleridge.

In Xanadu did Kubla Khan
A stately pleasure-dome decree:
Where Alph, the sacred river, ran
Through caverns measureless to man
Down to a sunless sea.
So twice five miles of fertile ground
With walls and towers were girdled round;
And there were gardens bright with sinuous rills,
Where blossomed many an incense-bearing tree;
And here were forests ancient as the hills,
Enfolding sunny spots of greenery.

Putting the book down, Mary walked to the window and opened it wide. She leaned out and felt gentle sun bathe her face. Below, buds dazzled, blades of grass poked between cobblestones. *Where have I been? Spring has come without my even knowing. Soon it will be summer.* She would plant flowers and sail tiny boats with Percy.

Ideas bubbled forth like fine champagne. Mary's imagination, her own "Kubla Khan," was back in full force. "The eclipse of winter is passing from my mind," she scribbled gleefully in her journal. "As I pour forth my soul upon paper, ideas take wing and rise and I feel again the delight of expressing them."

The grand idea that triggered her inspiration was simple. Sir Timothy might prevent her from writing directly about Bysshe— he stood ready to cut off the small stipend that was her only support—but there was no way he could prevent her from describing what she considered to be his essence. She would bring Bysshe back to life in the pages of a novel.

She must be careful. This must be a wartless Bysshe, with none of the selfish rebelliousness that had shocked the world and mortified his father. She would portray her husband's "Ariel self," the lighthearted, playful part of him that she had loved best—but also the part that inevitably brought her the greatest pain. How pleasant to have the freedom to choose!

Late one evening, Mary was hard at work when her father dropped by unexpectedly. "I came to see how you and Percy are. You haven't visited us for some time. Once again, my creditors are closing in . . ."

She hesitated. Sir Timothy's stipend was not nearly enough if she was to send Percy to Harrow and later to Oxford. Her son would one day be a lord of the realm. He must be ready. Mary scrimped on everything, putting aside all she could. How long since she'd had a new gown? Sighing softly, Mary reached for her purse.

"I have money for you, Papa. I would have brought it to you, but I've been working night and day on a new novel. It holds me in its thrall."

Godwin picked up the banknotes and counted them carefully before pocketing them. "A new novel, is it?" He nodded toward the stack of papers on the desk before her. "May I take a look?"

"I should be pleased to have your opinion," she said, handing him a sheet of paper. "This is a description of Adrian, my primary character." Her father took it and began to read aloud:

The matchless brother of my soul, the sensitive and excellent Adrian, loving all, and beloved by all, yet seemed destined not to find the half of himself, which was to complete his happiness. He had often left us, and wandered by himself in the woods, or sailed in his little skiff, his books his only companions. His slender frame seemed overcharged with the weight of life, and his soul appeared rather to inhabit his body than unite with it.

Godwin cleared his throat noisily and handed her the page. "I assume this to be a word portrait of your late husband. Though well written, it is certainly not the man I knew."

"That is your misfortune, Papa. It is the man I knew and loved." *Some of the time, anyway.* "Writing is wonderful," she told him. "How grand to transform people and circumstance into what they might have been."

When he said nothing, Mary handed him another sheet. "Perhaps you'll find the character of Raymond more to your liking, though I doubt that Mum will agree."

Her father again read aloud:

"I appear to have strength, power, victory; standing as a dome-supporting column stands; and I am—a reed! I have ambition, and that attains its aim; my nightly dreams are realized, my waking hopes fulfilled; a kingdom awaits my acceptance, my enemies are overthrown. But here," and he struck his heart with violence, "here is the rebel, here the stumbling-block; this over-ruling heart, which I may drain of its living blood; but, while one fluttering pulsation remains, I am its slave."

"What do you think, Father?"

"Well done, my girl, that is surely a fine likeness of your friend Byron. A memorial, in fact. I shan't show it to your stepmother, though. Let her wait for the book."

"I've a ways to go yet, and then must find a publisher."

"What is its theme?"

Mary thought a moment, sitting back in her desk chair. "You might say it is another horror story, though this time there's no monster, unless it be man himself. I'm calling it *The Last Man*. It is a novel set in the twenty-first century, when a terrible plague devastates the world. Only one man remains."

"What an extraordinary idea! Are you finding it difficult to write?"

Mary looked up in surprise. "Not at all! Once I had the germ of the story, it took on a life of its own. It is as though my soul dictates the words. I can think of little else. In a sense, I am 'the last man.' Loneliness has been my companion for as long as I can remember."

"Indeed." Abruptly Godwin picked up his hat and cane. "I can see that you are busily engaged. I shall be on my way."

Mary's *The Last Man* was not long in finding a publisher. A French translation of *Frankenstein* had been published with a new English edition planned to coincide with the premiere of a theatrical production.

Suddenly, it seemed, there were invitations to parties, the theater, and the opera. Mary was a celebrity, meeting all kinds of new people, many of them men. Prosper Mérimée, the author of *Carmen*, proposed but was rejected. Washington Irving was her close friend, as was Thomas Moore, an Irish poet and songwriter, whose "Last Rose of Summer" Mary loved. John Howard Payne, an American actor-director, was another admirer. When Mary said no to his proposal of marriage, he wrote the song "Home Sweet Home" and returned to the United States

These proposals were relatively easy decisions, but Mary had not succeeded in driving Trelawny from her thoughts. Two years had passed since their last meeting, and now a letter arrived informing her that he was en route to London. What now?

Mary put down the letter and walked to a large gilded mirror in her bedroom. Would Trelawny find her changed? She scanned her image critically and was reasonably satisfied by her reflection. "You are one of those rare women who actually seems to improve with age," her father had told her only the week before. Mary considered this reassuring, as Papa had never been one for flattery.

She regarded herself thoughtfully. *I have finally found my way,* she realized. *I enjoy reasonable success as a writer—at least I can pay the bills.* But it was more than that. Mary loved concocting strange stories.

She found joy as well in her little Persino, a sturdy, happy boy of six, who showed none of the brilliance or complexity that challenged his parents. He was unlike anyone in Mary's family or Bysshe's. Charles, the son of Bysshe and Harriet, had died recently in a tragic accident. Sir Timothy was seventy-three; surely he wouldn't last much longer. One day her Percy would be heir to the Shelley title and fortune. He would never have to worry about money.

Trelawny, Trelawny; Mary's thoughts returned again to that romantic rogue. What if *he* had changed?

In an eager exchange of letters, they planned their reunion: dinner first and then a play—the premier performance of *Frankenstein*. Mary's novel a play! She was excited but frightened as well. The producer had not conferred with her, had not even allowed her to attend a rehearsal. What might they have done to her creation?

———————

Mary had her gown made to order for the occasion. The style, reminiscent of the clothing worn by Greek goddesses, was beautifully draped and cut low to show off her shoulders and a good deal of cleavage. She had nothing to regret on either score. The fabric of the gown was white silk shot with gold threads. Over this she wore a red velvet pelisse also trimmed in gold.

"You look beautiful, Mama," Percy told her. She had allowed him to stay up to see his old friend.

Trelawny pretended not to know the boy. "This strapping lad can't be little Persino!" he insisted. "But you"—he turned to Mary—"have only grown more lovely. Percy is right; you *are* beautiful, Mary."

"And you are handsome as ever," she said, smiling up at him. "But I fear I see a new scar." She traced a line down the side of his face. "Actually, it makes you look more like a pirate than ever."

"Is that a good thing?"

She smiled up at him, cocking her head slightly. "To me it will always be."

Dinner was an elegant affair at the Green Park in Mayfair. Mary was too excited to eat much but enjoyed her champagne. It was so good to see Trelawny, and now she was about to see *Frankenstein* as well.

The English Opera House was packed, but Trelawny had reserved box seats—rich red velvet ones. Sitting in the reflected glow of an immense crystal chandelier, Mary looked out over the vast hall with its high vaulted ceiling and crimson carpets. It seemed as though everyone was craning to get a better view of her. She prayed that the play would be good. How awful if it were not! The gaslights dimmed and Mary caught her breath, feeling the ripple of excitement around her.

Soon she was totally absorbed, caught up in the elaborate production, the faithful rendition by brilliant performers. Mary shivered deliciously. Those were *her* words, but how beautifully the actors interpreted them. She barely suppressed a gasp as the selfishly ambitious Victor Frankenstein cried, "Devil, do you dare approach me? And do you not fear the fierce vengeance of my arm wreaked on your miserable head? Begone, vile insect! Or rather stay that I may trample you to dust!"

She sighed at her monster's reply: "All men hate the wretched; how, then, must I be hated, who am miserable beyond all living things! Yet you, my creator, detest and spurn me, thy creature, to whom thou art bound by ties only dissoluble by the annihilation of one of us."

Watching spellbound as her story came to life, Mary thought, *I, like the monster, was born only to be abandoned, but out of that anguish has come my creation.* The guilt that had been Mary's life companion was being lifted away, and with it the crushing sense of obligation. In their place was an exhilaration unlike anything she had ever felt. It was the rebirth of a spirit no longer fettered by the example of a brilliant, iconic mother, a celebrated but grasping father, or a flawed genius of a husband. Perhaps the work would take on a life of its own, extending far into the future. At the very least, it would not die on her.

In the coach going home, Trelawny took her hand in his. "I still want you, Mary. I love you now more than ever. Say that you will be my wife."

Mary studied his face, rakish, rugged, and yet so tenderly endearing. Trelawny was a good man, an exciting man. There would never be another like him. She had thought of him for years, months, weeks, days. Never had her heart been certain, but now she knew. Mary didn't want Trelawny or any man, and certainly no more children. Having had enough of love and loss, she was at last free to be her own creation.

"I am afraid, dear friend, that my answer is no. Neither you nor anybody else. Mary Shelley shall be written on my tombstone. And why, I cannot tell you, except that it is a strong name that stands on its own."

AUTHOR'S NOTE

This is a work based on the life and times of Mary Godwin Shelley. Certain dates and incidents have been slightly altered in the interest of telling Mary's story in novel form.

When Mary Shelley bid her "hideous progeny to go forth and prosper," she couldn't possibly have imagined the impact "the grim terrors" of her waking dream would have upon subsequent generations of readers.

In 1816, the "Year Without a Summer," the world was locked in a protracted volcanic winter caused by the eruption of Mount Tambora on the island of Sumbawa in Indonesia. It remains the worst volcanic eruption in recorded history, but at the time Mary and her friends were merely annoyed that the continuing storms kept them indoors.

Mary's response to the enforced inertia was to transform a private vision into a collective nightmare. Her novel was nine months in the birthing. It was published on January 1, 1818. No one then could have imagined that the book would never go out of print, or that it would inspire not only countless theatrical productions and films but seemingly endless literary knockoffs. Most certainly no one realized that Mary had spawned a whole new genre: science fiction.

Mary went on to write scores of paranormal novels, colorful travel books, and articles on a wide variety of subjects. Bysshe had wanted their son to be graduated from Harrow and Oxford. She was determined to make that happen. Mary lived by her pen, *had* to, for Sir Timothy granted her only a tiny yearly stipend, this to be administered by lawyers. He never deigned to meet Mary or Percy. Out of her meager funds, Mary supported her father until the octogenarian's death in 1836. Mary was then thirty-eight.

Though devoid of his antecedents' talent and brilliance, Percy was a loving and dutiful son to Mary all of her life. Upon graduating from Oxford, he moved in with his mother. The two lived and traveled extensively together.

It was a happy time for Mary, made even happier by the demise of Sir Timothy Shelley in 1844. The baronet died at the age of ninety, "falling from the stalk like an overblown flower," as Mary put it. For the first time, she and her son were financially independent. Percy inherited the baronetcy as well, becoming the 3rd Baronet of Castle Goring.

If anything, Mary's contentment increased with Percy's marriage, in 1848, to the former Jane Gibson St. John, a wealthy widow. Jane liked and respected Mary and proved an eager accomplice in the sanitization of Bysshe's life. The two women were determined that the poet's views and actions in life would not stand in the way of the public's acceptance and eventual reverence for his work.

Mary lived with her son and daughter-in-law at Field Place, Sussex, the Shelleys' ancestral home, until her death from a suspected brain tumor in 1851. She was fifty-three.

On the first anniversary of Mary's death, the Shelleys opened her box-desk. Inside, they found locks of her dead children's hair, a notebook that she had shared with Bysshe, and a copy of his poem *Adonais* with one page folded round a silk parcel containing some of his ashes and the remains of his heart.

Claire Clairmont returned to England in 1836 and worked as a music teacher while caring for her mother. Jane Godwin died in 1841 at the age of seventy-five. When Sir Timothy died, Claire was able to inherit twelve thousand pounds that Bysshe had left her in his will. She returned then to Italy, where she surprised everyone by converting to Catholicism, a religion she professed to hate earlier in life. She was to say of Byron that he had given her but a few moments of pleasure, but a lifetime of trouble.

Claire settled eventually in Florence with her niece, Paulina. Traces of Claire may be found in *The Aspern Papers*, Henry James's literary gem in which the narrator-protagonist attempts to steal memorabilia—including steamy love letters of a famous poet—from his aged mistress. Claire died March 19, 1879, at the age of eighty.

Though the "handsome, dashing, and quixotic" Edward Trelawny knew Bysshe but six months, he dined out on the connection for the rest of his long life. Trelawny's friendship with Mary foundered with his desire to write a tell-all biography of Bysshe. Aghast at the idea, Mary sought to keep private matters private and refused to assist him.

To oblige her, Trelawny wrote about himself. The memoir, *Adventures of a Younger Son*, became a bestseller, enabling him to travel freely.

Trelawny's adventures continued. While fighting in Greece, he was shot in the back. The musket ball was removed by a captive doctor held at gunpoint. Upon recovery, Trelawny journeyed to the United States. While visiting Niagara Falls, he decided to swim the rapids. He succeeded in crossing under the falls but nearly drowned on the return swim. On the same trip, he demonstrated his sympathy for the abolitionist movement by purchasing the freedom of a slave.

Trelawny returned to England in 1835, married twice, and was twice divorced. In 1858, he published *Recollections of the Last Days of Shelley and Byron*. The volume was well received and established him as the preeminent Shelley expert. He has since been called one of the "key makers of modern celebrity."

As he grew older, Trelawny remained active, swimming regularly, chopping wood, and digging in his gardens, which he turned
into a bird sanctuary. Evenings were spent in town with a variety of
women. At an advanced age, Trelawny lived with a much younger
woman, Emma Taylor. He referred to her as his "niece."

In August 1881 Trelawny suffered a fall while walking. He died
two weeks later, just shy of his eighty-ninth birthday. Trelawny's
ashes were buried in the Protestant Cemetery in Rome. The plot
had been waiting for him since 1822 when he purchased the
adjoining one for Bysshe.

At Trelawny's request his grave marker bears a quote from
Bysshe's poem, "Epitaph."

These are two friends whose lives were undivided;
So let their memory be, now they have glided
Under the grave: let not their bone be parted
For their two hearts in life were single-hearted.

ACKNOWLEDGMENTS

So many were involved in the creation of this book, beginning with John Wilson, who sat with me on Mary Wollstonecraft's grave, and Vern Appleby, who walked at my side as I followed in Mary Shelley's footsteps. Each in his own way encouraged and inspired me.

But could the book have ever been written without the various members of my writing groups? Very possibly not. Plodding through the nitty-gritty with me were Kevin Arnold, Brent Barker, Genevieve Beltran, Kathy Fellure, Lou Gonzalez, Sally Henry, Sally Kaplan, Pam Mumdale, Monika Rose, Amy Smith, Rob Swigart, Sandy Towle, Jennifer Tristano, and most especially Lucy Sanna.

And could it have reached an audience without my discerning agent, Harvey Klinger? Maybe not. And what about Amazon's wonderful Jodi Warshaw and her fabulous editing team? What's a writer anyway—without an editor.

A huge thanks to all of you.

BIBLIOGRAPHY

Ackroyd, Peter. *The Casebook of Victor Frankenstein*. New York: Doubleday, 2008.

Austen, Jane. *Northanger Abbey*. New York: Modern American Library, 2002.

Austen, Jane. *Pride and Prejudice*. Ann Arbor, MI: J. W. Edwards, 2009.

Bigland, Eileen. *Mary Shelley*. New York: Cassell, 1959.

Byron, George Gordon. *Selected Poems*. New York: Dover Thrift Editions, 1993.

Chernaik, Judith. *The Lyrics of Shelley*. London: Press of Case Western Reserve University, 1972.

Dunn, Jane. *Moon in Eclipse, A Life of Mary Shelley*. London: Weidenfeld and Nicolson, 1978.

Eisler, Benita. *Byron, Child of Passion, Fool of Fame*. New York: Vintage Books, 1999.

Gaull, Marilyn. *English Romanticism*. New York: W. W. Norton, 1988.

Hay, Daisy. *Young Romantics*. New York: Farrar, Straus and Giroux. 2010.

Holmes, Richard. *Shelley: The Pursuit*. New York: New York Review Books, 1974.

——— *The Age of Wonder*. New York: Pantheon Books, 2008.

——— *Footsteps*. New York: Viking, 1985.

Isenberg, Nancy. *Fallen Founder: The Life of Aaron Burr.* New York: Penguin Group, 2007.

Johnson, Barbara. *A Life With Mary Shelley.* Stanford, CA: Stanford University Press, 2014.

Johnson, Diane. *Lesser Lives.* New York: Alfred A. Knopf, 1972.

Jones, Frederick L., ed. *Mary Shelley's Journal.* Norman: University of Oklahoma Press, 1947.

McFarland, Philip. *Sojourners.* New York: Atheneum, 1979.

Marshall, Peter H. W. *William Godwin.* New Haven: Yale University Press, 1984.

Means, Marilyn. *Midnight Fires.* Palo Alto: John Daniel / Perseverance Press, 2010.

Montillo, Roseanne. *The Lady and Her Monsters.* New York: William Morrow, 2013.

Murray, Venetia. *An Elegant Madness: High Society in Regency England.* New York: Penguin Books, 1999.

Nitchie, Elizabeth. *Mary Shelley.* New Brunswick, NJ: Rutgers University Press, 1953.

O'Brien, Edna. *Byron in Love.* New York: W. W. Norton, 2009.

O'Brien, Michael. *Mrs. Adams in Winter: A Journey in the Last Days of Napoleon.* New York: Farrar, Straus and Giroux, 2010.

Poole, Daniel. *What Jane Austen Ate and Charles Dickens Knew.* New York: Touchstone, 1993.

Shelley, Mary. *Frankenstein.* New York: Barnes & Noble, 2012.

────── *The Annotated Frankenstein, with Introduction and Notes by Leonard Wolf.* New York: Clarkson N. Potter, 1977.

Smith, Robert Metcalf. *The Shelley Legend.* New York: Charles Scribner's Sons, 1945.

Shelley, Percy Bysshe. *Ode to the West Wind and Other Poems.* Mineola, NY: Dover Thrift Editions, 1998.

Stallworthy, Jon. *A Book of Love Poetry.* New York: Oxford University Press, 1973.

Stocking, Marion Kingston, ed. *The Journals of Claire Clairmont.* Cambridge, MA: Harvard University Press, 1968.

Whipple, ABC. *The Fatal Gift of Beauty.* New York: Harper & Row, 1964.

Wollstonecraft, Mary. *A Wollstonecraft Anthology.* Bloomington: Indianna University Press, 1977.

Wright, Nancy, *Percy Bysshe Shelley: Selected Poems.* New York: Gramercy Books, 1994.

ABOUT THE AUTHOR

Antoinette May is the author of *Pilate's Wife* and *The Sacred Well* and coauthor of the *New York Times* bestseller *Adventures of a Psychic*. An award-winning travel writer specializing in Mexico, May divides her time between Palo Alto and the Sierra foothills.